Magdalene

Magdalene

a novel by
CAROLYN SLAUGHTER

M. Evans and Company, Inc.

New York

Note: There appears to be no information about Mary Magdalene apart from what is in the Gospels—nor is there any reason to suppose that she was the un-named whore mentioned in St Luke 7.

This then is simply a work of the imagination.

Library of Congress Cataloging in Publication Data

Slaughter, Carolyn.
  Magdalene: a novel.

  1. Mary Magdalene, Saint—Fiction. 2. Jesus Christ—Fiction. I. Title.
PZ4.S63126Mag [PR6069.L37] 823′.9′14 78-27132
ISBN 0-87131-279-4

M. Evans and Company, Inc.
216 East 49 Street
New York, New York 10017

Manufactured in the United States of America

9 8 7 6 5 4 3 2 1

One

Today is my birthday, today I am thirty-seven. And look, here is my face floating in the polished silver mirror. The eyebrows are heavy and pulled straight across; the small mouth droops – it is quiet, it is peaceful. It is not waiting. Once, a fine trickle of pink spread across the cheekbones; and now my mouth has faded too. And my eyes, my eyes that I cast at young men as they stood limpid and cool under the trees – they are coals gone cold. How dully they regard me. Can it be that I am no longer vain? My hair is brushed, but carelessly; the curls run wild without a comb to hold them down. The skin has no lustre; it is like pearls kept in a box, never worn.

It is very late and beginning to grow cold. But I cannot go to bed and must just sit here, thinking, thinking. My thoughts flutter like moths in candlelight. I reach for them; sometimes it seems that I have them. Then my mind goes still and I see that I have captured none of them. But do not think me unhappy. Do not think that. I am looking in a mirror, dreaming. Waiting for no one. I am at peace. I feel it in my heart, my breasts and belly – this small basin of peace.

Now it is morning. The clouds are flung about the sky, this way and that; the swallows bob. I sit in my mother's garden, in the little cottage she kept after her marriage and visited each spring. The fig trees are crippled and past bearing; the orchard has been neglected and chickens no longer peck at the edge of the vegetable patch. But it is still as beautiful and benign as I remember and small red roses clamber up the wall, hiding a crack into which creeper has grown. We will put all these things to rights. And in a little while I will take Elizabeth with me into the woods to collect daisies. They will be growing still in the place my mother used to take me to. The last time I came here I was ten years old; it was the year she died.

I want to start right at the beginning. Once I have told you everything, I will do what is required of me. My head is filled with people – they push and squabble in the small confines of my brain, wanting a birth. And I am heavy with them, having carried them too long.

I was the last child in our family and the only girl. I was called Mary after my grandmother. My oldest brother at the time of my birth was twelve; then came Simeon and Jonathan, the twins, who were nine; and then my favourite brother, Joshua, who was just three years older than I. We lived on the borders of Magdala, very close to the shore. Behind our house was a small wood of carob trees, which nestled close to an orchard. This orchard was modest also, but it had mature and well-cared-for fruit trees that yielded many more pears and plums than we could ever consume. There was also a fig tree, which formed a natural hiding-place, because its trunk bent grandly to the ground and the branches grew at extraordinary angles. It was under this tree that I made my house, dividing it into rooms by the protruding roots. When I was very young, I would spend solitary hours under this tree, dressing and undressing my doll.

It is my mother that I remember most dearly. The first thing I think of is her hair. It rippled about her small face: dark waves getting smaller and finer as they reached her waist. I used to sit on a small stool that my eldest brother, Reuben, had made from dark olive wood. I would bend my feet under this stool and watch my mother having her hair brushed by Zinna. It used to frighten me when my mother threw her head forward: her hair then splashed to the floor and her face was taken from me. I sat stiffly, praying for her face to return. When it did, and she smiled at me, I would relax and sit happily as the maid went on with her endless brushing; listening to the slow wind-sound of the long strokes through her curls.

Then she would go to her bath, dressed in a long white robe. She would reach over the deep tub, crushing flowers, balm and rosemary and sprinkling them on to the water. And I was allowed to throw in two pink roses. She looked so beautiful with her soft dark head and white shoulders floating above the petals. She had a weakness for Eastern spices and ointments and measured very carefully some thick oil from an alabaster pot, which she then stirred gently into the water, her hands moving backwards and forwards. I must have learned from her, very young, a love of adornments and the need to pamper myself. It was her only self-indulgence and I am not sure that my father even knew of it.

My mother. I would run after her as a small girl; she walking with swift, slim strides that hastened into a graceful gallop — along the corridor, through the door, across the room with the long tables; I could not see the tops of the tables, but sometimes I could smell the richness of the food on them. And away she would run into her private room as I followed, desperate to catch her. Terrible to walk into her room and find her gone! It frightened me until I remembered that it was a game we played and that I must find her. I was afraid until I could actually catch and hold her to me by the smooth cloth of her skirts. And again, I would be alarmed and guilty when she'd kneel in front of me, straightening my thick hair; her face turned up

8

like a small white plate; and her saying, 'And have you been good today?' I would feel my face slide and droop as I gathered together all the small sins in my mind – and they filled it. I had no goodness. I wanted it, looked and prayed for it, but it hid from me always, as she did. I loved and wanted her because she and goodness were inseparable; and I could never quite capture either.

O the memories are running away from me. I think about the lovely night we stayed up listening to stories under the trees; and the talk of the adults buzzed in the distance. Joshua found a moth that had flown into the flame of the candle. It lay fluttering weakly in the palm of my hand. We watched the lovely, shimmering purple and green threads of colour in its wings; the silky softness of its body. 'It's too beautiful,' Joshua whispered. 'It will not live.' Then Simeon smashed his hand down and the moth ceased to flutter. Joshua and I looked at him, saying nothing.

And the day that the little girl sat in the dust storm, screaming with pain and terror; old Joseph running to her, gathering her up in his arms and carrying her inside. The smell of the morning when the rains came; the lilies of the field; the poppies that filled my hand. The room with purple drapes, the blood – no, not that, not that. The day he smiled and it shocked my body just to see him smile at me. Shaken, lost, knowing it all, how it would be. I'd kill for that smile again. I must tell you all this. I must. But I will try not to treat my memories too gently.

I address myself to you, only to you. You hear my thoughts. You see me as I sit at the edge of the sea, drawing back my toes from the chasing waves as I hear my nurse call; moving towards her bright figure under the trees, her hands clapping, her face so urgent.

'Come, hurry, your father is going to Nazareth.'

And there I am, running away, over the hill, under the trees, beyond my nurse who walks slowly – and on to the chatter going on outside our house. My two brothers are sitting on their donkeys, and Reuben looks with impatience behind him for father, who is always late, who lingers too long with our mother.

'Let me go, let me go with you,' and father looking down at me, his face vacant, thinking of other things, already in his mind down the road.

'Another time. We are late, the others will leave without us.'

The dust on my face as they ride away. Suddenly I am aware of the sun expanding with heat. The snort of my father's horse; my mother turning quickly from the door, her hand raised in farewell. Tears prick my eyes but vanish as Joshua comes running, angry to have missed their departure. And now he and I are both running back to the shore, to climb in the empty boats and rock there, rolled in the nets with the smell of fish pushed in our faces.

9

I am riding on Reuben's shoulders, so high I can catch the leaves, so high I can see the pivot around which his hair falls in dark clusters. A woman runs through the trees. Her dress is ripped and her hair is in disorder. A horde of people pursue her with branches and ugly shouting. Reuben tells me that she is an evil woman and the people will deal with her. Joshua says to me, 'Don't worry, they will not kill her.' But I cannot forget the terror in her face and the way her eyes were big and black and her mouth moved piteously, like a fish. A long time later, I heard how a similar woman had an earthen bottle thrust up her body until it shattered.

I keep thinking about my grandmother, who ruled us all; whom my mother adored and my father feared. My grandmother lived in a separate part of our house; there was only one door leading from her rooms to ours and there was only one handle to this door – it was on her side. My grandmother had a mass of hair, white and without a shine; but deep and dense with a faint scent of rosemary. She held it together, wound in tight coils, with the aid of one twisted grip. When she brushed her hair it sprang into long wispy strands like a cloud breaking up in wind – so like a cloud that you would expect to see the sun glide from behind it.

She was a tall, elegant woman; the only mar to her dignity was her hands, which were twisted with rheumatism, swollen and discoloured. Her left hand was permanently cramped into a claw and she suffered great pain with her fingers. My mother – little Miriam my grandmother called her – was her greatest love. She was always more gentle with my mother and would drop her rather stiff, formal speech only when speaking to her. They spent a great deal of time in one another's company, though my mother rarely went to my grandmother's part of the house. They were mainly together in my mother's room or in the kitchens. I have the clearest picture of my grandmother sitting on a hard couch, watching my mother in silence as she sat moistening her finger, taking the thread carefully through the muslin. They did not speak a great deal when I was present, but understood each other perfectly.

My grandmother's family, as she told me very often, came originally from Mesopotamia, from aristocratic and cultured circles. This is what she used to say as she bustled about, 'You won't find any darkness, any Egyptian in me' (this was a jibe at my father, who did have a little Egyptian in him!). 'No,' she would continue, 'none of our family have that darkness, that thinness across the eyes, that hook in the nose. You are fortunate, Mary, on your mother's side, to have such good blood. We go back in a straight line, no curves, no embarrassing diversions – in a straight line to Reuben, Jacob's eldest son, the first son of Israel. There's no pollution, no mixtures crept in, no marriages outside the tribe. Be proud of such a lineage.' How could I not be!

She loved to tell me the story of herself and her husband leaving Mesopotamia when she was still a young bride, untroubled by children. They had settled in Galilee and by the time Miriam and her sister were born, my grandfather had started his trade in dried and spiced fish, which were shipped from Caesarea to Rome. My grandmother's greatest failure and shame had been her inability to provide her husband with a son. She told me that she had suffered horribly in childbirth and had lost three daughters due to their weak blood. She understood these losses to be a vindication from God and always quoted moodily, 'I will greatly multiply thy sorrow and thy conception', whenever she spoke of her dead children, finding in those words all the explanation she required.

It was because my grandmother had produced no heir that Miriam, the eldest daughter, had married my father, who was beneath her in blood and culture, but who had at least the advantage of being in the fishing trade. And upon my grandfather's death he had come to control the family business, and very well too by all accounts. My grandmother never interfered with his handling of the business, nor in the education of her grandchildren; in all other matters, however, she felt a special right to criticise and manipulate. She was often very harsh towards her family, and particularly venomous to my eldest brother's wife – whose father was a shepherd, and who, in her nostrils, smelt constantly of sheep dung. I think myself that the girl particularly irritated her because she was a good provider of male children. But of course my grandmother never referred to this, drawing only on the vices of the poor creature: her vanity, her 'cheap laughter in the night', and worst of all, her constant forgetfulness of the fast days.

But I adored my grandmother. I loved to watch her cooking; she always prepared vast, spectacular meals, but she rarely ate herself; her function was to thrust food at everyone else. She loved to cook the innards of animals and fowl, chopping them briskly, singing softly in the kitchen as the dark odours crawled out of her pans, settling on the wood, in the niches of the stone floor and in the private folds of her robe.

'Taste, taste, you must always taste – though it means that you will not be able to eat like the others. No matter, you must taste to get it right. Get those fingers out of my dish, child, you taste later. Only I taste now.'

Once I asked her, 'How do you get the cake fat like that?'

'What a question! I beat it of course, and it protects itself from my spoon by putting on a jacket of air. The more I beat it the more jackets it puts on – then quick into the oven it goes, the heat catches it and holds the air so that it cannot get out. And that's how it gets fat.'

How I smile, thinking of her, her tangy words: 'Giblet soup, that's what I'll give them, with barley, lots of barley to fill it out. Take the kettle off the hob. Here it is then, giblet soup, a good soup. Yes, I know you do not like it; no need to make that face. Too good for anyone under fourteen years. A wedding soup. You'll like it when you know what's good for you. Your father – even he likes giblet soup. Yes, you can put some sherbet in the water if you must. You tell the cook to keep away from those street sellers, you don't know if their hands are clean – they give the sherbet with a scoop do they? Well, do you know if they use the scoop to scratch their back? Keep away from street sellers and dirty turbaned persons. Oi, you look like your mother looked child – sweet, sweet, laughing.'

The peasants loved her; she was kind to them and though she often spoke brusquely, they took no offence. They considered her a healer. The physician lived a little way off at the other end of Magdala, but he had to see money before he saw a patient. My grandmother's remedies were simple and free, and they often worked. She and my mother took me in the early morning to gather herbs before the sun spoiled them; she claimed that nowhere else had such healing herbs as the hills above the lake. My mother sang on these walks, 'The flowers appear on the earth, the time of the singing of birds is come.' Her voice sounded so sad, as though it were looking for something it had lost.

My grandmother wrapped each spray of herbs in small squares of damp linen and put them into the bag that hung from her shoulder. She would spend as much as three hours looking for the most fragrant herbs. I remember the poppies, because their leaves were so big and the flowers so fragile; I wished I could have a dress of exactly that fierce red. But my grandmother was not interested in the flowers; she picked the leaves carefully, and after she had dried them, she would grind them into a fine powder. She said that they made as good a sedative as opium. 'Hurry, stop dreaming,' she would snap at me as I dragged behind her as she darted in and out of the trees. The grass was dewy and I hoped for mushrooms, but I did not like to make her impatient so I always obeyed. She knew exactly when the sun had risen sufficiently to affect the herbs and would stop dramatically and say. 'Now it's too late, we have enough.'

Then my grandmother held my hand on the way back. I was intimidated by her old cramped fingers and the thick blue veins that struggled beneath the transparent skin. I look at my hands and they have always seemed old to me. Not beautiful, certainly not beautiful hands, too square. And the hand that held the pen once, that stroked the child's cheek – it has always been the oldest hand: it is more tired, more worn. And the rashes that afflict my skin always spread on this hand first.

At that time I was tall and straight; dark-eyed with definite cheek-bones and a neat mouth. My mother said that I belonged to the sea because my hair was curly; the maids said that I belonged to the devil because my eyes were so black. My hair was drawn back from my face by two slim braids, the ends of which were fastened at the back of my head by a silver pin shaped like butterfly wings. My mother dressed me always in white and ignored the fact that it was the colour reserved for holy days and feasts. My dresses were gathered above the waist and trimmed with ribbons; my grandmother embroidered small flowers around the neck and sleeves in dainty colours. On days when my mother felt festive for some reason, she would dress me in pale green linen, very light and fine; and I loved this dress best of all. I would run to the top of the hill behind our house and spin round and round; feeling the soft cloth rising and rippling in the wind.

It was my mother who taught me my lessons; she was very strict. She would read to me from the Scriptures and then ask me questions; and we would not progress to a new story until I knew every detail. She also taught me to read, as her mother had taught her; she told me it was the greatest gift she could give me. At the end of the day, she and I would sit quietly in her room and she would explain, simply, for I was only eight, the laws about the purity and preparation of food, and the rituals I must understand to be a good wife and mother. She taught me these things early, as if she knew, even then.

It was only later that I learned, with my brother, what an ample education would be found at the wells. We listened to the traders chatting together and watched gaily-dressed foreigners spill out their strange songs and stories as they watered their animals. At the village gates, the elders gossiped and bickered together, discussing commercial business and the latest results of the law-suits at Magdala. But all this was later; to begin with, my education all came from my mother and from any snippets of conversation that I picked up on the way to the synagogue.

I loved to watch my mother light the Sabbath candles; she lit one extra for each of her children, and covered her eyes with her hand and prayed after lighting each one. She then brought in fresh branches of myrtle and decorated all the rooms with them. She polished the goblets used for the Sabbath benedictions, and washed with her own hands the embroidered cloth that covered the Sabbath loaves. I found it difficult to sit and think quietly with her hour after hour; or pray with the concentration that she did, but I did realise how solemnly she took these things and tried to do my best. She always said, 'Be still and rest, so you will understand the nobility and

13

holiness of the Sabbath.' And I would sit by her side, my dress folded neatly, my face arranged in a suitable expression – trying to cast the frivolous thoughts from my muslin mind, praying always to be as good as she. But how long the day seemed when one was not allowed to stir from the house all day.

Always I used to think: will I be like my mother? Will I walk in the shade and keep my eyes averted? Will I go, as she did, through the kitchens – carefully checking that the cooking things were correctly placed; looking for uncleanness, watching for signs of theft along the neat shelves? Will I lock in the cupboard all the special things: the blue Passover plates with a cross in the centre; the little tied bags of spices and herbs; the heavy bottles of ointment and salve; the cloth bags of salt and the bottle of fiery drink for visitors and sickness.

I wanted to do all things as she did. She would walk to the long pantries, with the keys clanging in her hand, towards the sprays of currants and raisins hanging on the wall; and she would stop and press one between her thumb and finger and pop it into her mouth, looking thoughtful. Then on to the dark pantries, where the purple plums wrinkled and dried; the figs turned brown and their pips darkened. In one corner, the pearly onions and garlic glistened, their stalks flaky as an old man's skin; and in the other, the thick smell of pears oozed from their wrappings, each one stitched into its own linen bag.

And always in my mother's eyes was that singular sadness; that glance backwards to a softer past, a place she never spoke of. I see now how much she and my grandmother must have fortified one another over the years: my grandmother who always felt alien in Galilee, my mother who lacked companionship of a more sensitive kind than her husband could provide. I remember my mother's admonitions: 'As your mother, I command, I beg you to learn, to understand and find the heart of things. Be honest, speak the truth; and if you cannot always love God – then fear him.'

And to brush away the gravity of her words, she would touch my forehead and say, 'And never speak to, or accept sweets from, strangers. Come, we will go and make a cake – a cake full of dates and sultanas.' So we would walk down the cool corridors to the deep room at the end, where the clatter of the slaves would cease at her presence. As the fire roared, she would pummel and pull at the dough, flinging it on to the table, chasing the flies away, her cheeks streaked a pale pink. And I, watching her fingers dance, her long nails come and go, would shuffle and smile – waiting to lick the little she would leave me in the bowl.

My grandmother died that year, the year that I turned eight. She did not die at our house, but at the cottage that I sit in today. I was not there and my mother did not return home for many weeks: and I was sick without her and could not understand why she had deserted me. I was angry with my grandmother for dying, for taking herself from us; for keeping my mother away so long. My mother – melancholic, elusive – had never left me for more than a few hours and I had always known where she could be found. The day they told me that she was coming home, I was violently sick. And the moment she walked through the door, I knew that things would never be the same. She held me to her very tightly for an instant, smiling, and stroked my hair; but when I looked up into her face it was dark and drawn and her eyes were closed against everyone. Looking into them I saw only myself, I could not find her; and then even the looking at myself came to an end. It was as if she had slammed a door shut and her eyes had gone altogether. Each day she withdrew more into herself; our lessons got short and I felt she was thinking of other things. She began to spend longer in her room, praying; and she would not answer the door when I knocked and called. I left the roses there and usually they were still in the same place many hours later. And then being with her became as painful as being without her: she was impatient with me and I knew that she wanted to be alone. My father and his sons continued as usual; but I felt that my life was over.

My father. I hardly think of him. Is it because in the early part of my life I was nearly always in the company of women? I never understood him very well. Still today I find it hard to shape my mind around his character; it is easier to remember how he looked. He was tall and strongly built, with a long face and hair that fell straight and thick. His dark eyes seemed always to be looking at one another; there was a crease like a cut on either side of his mouth and he had a sharp, bent nose. He walked slowly, with a slight limp in his right leg – where a horse had rolled on him; and he carried a stick. The top of this stick was worked into a snake's head, with its mouth open; and the length of the stick was crooked, like the body of a snake. He used to poke with this stick at things that displeased him: like my brothers' feet when they were dusty, or the slaves asleep under the apple trees. When he poked with this stick, his nose would curl contemptuously, and I cannot think of the stick without recalling that cutting Egyptian nose.

'Oi, what a nose,' my grandmother would laugh, holding her finger against her own straight nose.

My father had no time, nor room in his heart, for a daughter. Indeed, the occasion of my birth, I was told later, had been more a matter of consolation than congratulation. Yet he always seemed kind and attentive to my mother, having great respect, and I think that her strength helped him to curb his own rash and somewhat greedy nature. When he had first taken over control of my grandfather's business, he had been unpopular with the Romans. They found him coarse in comparison to my reputedly gracious grandfather, of whom I do not have a single memory. My father must have struggled, and probably resorted to bribery, to get the fisheries back to the successful and prosperous early days of the trade.

Because his lineage was not purely of Hebrew stock, he developed into a most rigorous Jew, observing the smallest requirements of the Law and expecting his sons to do the same. How well I can see us all gathered together in the morning to listen as my father recited the benedictions monotonously. And then each of my brothers would have to recite a psalm. We would lower our heads and pray, but I would often lift my head a little and open my eyes to try and catch sight of the tall man who brought the goat's milk and the women who sang in the street, carrying trays on their heads full of fragrant hot bread covered with cloths, and fresh fruit, cheese and butter. My father's voice would boom, 'My sons, do not forget to pray.'

'And I father?' I would ask.

'As I said, do not forget to pray.'

And I was hurt, as so often, and thought: does he see me?

Has he confused me with someone else? Does he wish I was someone else? Does he hate me?

The only person whom my father seemed to fear was my grandmother. She was suspicious of his sudden bursts of piety, which would affect the whole household, and then, just as swiftly, fizzle into a more normal observance of the Law. Once, when my father was obliged to pick up a dead rat which had been lying in a grain-house, rotting, he went to great lengths to cleanse himself: washing and re-washing himself, his clothes and in particular his hands – using great quantities of water.

'What is the sense in washing off your uncleanness in all that water when a little will do as well?' my grandmother said impatiently and I remember the look he aimed at her. She walked out of the room smiling, but muttering under her breath, 'Hypocrite', just loud enough for him to hear. He never responded to her cracks, but always found an opportunity to get his revenge.

My grandmother had bought some beautiful plates, made of polished metal, from a foreign traveller, a Syrian. She showed them to me, telling me that the pomegranates worked around the lips of the plates were ancient symbols of love and fertility. She promised to keep them for my wedding, but added that in the meantime we would of course use them on special occasions. She brought them to the table on her birthday. When they appeared, to my great astonishment, my father leapt back from the table as if in the presence of something evil.

'I will not allow metal in my house,' he yelled, ordering the slaves to take the plates away and destroy them. My grandmother quietly remarked, though her hands were shaking, that there was no uncleanness in metal, unless it had been defiled, and no mention of it in Leviticus either. She added, 'One of the elders in Magdala has a Passover plate of the same substance, only not so fine as these', and she stroked the polished surface with her finger. In great anger, my father threw the plates, one by one, on to the floor, shouting at her, telling her that for all she knew the metal had come from the earth of a foreign burial-ground. I remember how my grandmother bent and picked up each plate tenderly; and how her cheeks, which always reminded me of the pressed petals of roses, were suddenly tinged with purple.

When I was a little older I was allowed to go to Nazareth. My father had business contacts there and went often, as did my three eldest brothers. Joshua had been a few times, but this was to be my first visit; and we were to stay with my father's brother, a weaver. My uncle had three sons and they had come to stay with us in Galilee once or twice; and had brought with them wonderful rugs made from goat's hair, dyed red and purple. On their last visit I had been very impressed by Benjamin, who was the same age as my twin brothers. He was a thin, nervous boy with a wild smile; and while with us he had run off into the mountains with a band of Zealots and they had caused a lot of trouble for the Roman garrison in Tiberias. Most of the youths had been flogged and executed, but Benjamin had escaped and returned to us; the soldiers had come and searched the area for a few days, but they did not search our house – probably because my father was a well-to-do citizen who never made trouble for the authorities.

While Benjamin was hiding in a small cellar in what had once been my grandmother's house – delicate, romantic dreams had budded in my heart concerning him. These dreams were so fragile that had they left the inner closet of my mind, they would have shattered immediately. But as it happened, Benjamin and his family left very early one morning and returned to Nazareth. He did not even say goodbye to me; but in his absence I imagined – O how many times – something in that fanatical smile of his, something that spoke only to me.

When we went to Nazareth, the almond blossom was falling. Irises, wallflowers and lacy wild flowers had hatched after the rains; the sky was weighed down, sodden as a leather bag and the country was green and tender. Before starting on the steep hill up to Nazareth, we stopped at a well surrounded by strange caravans. There were travellers from India with bound heads and features quite new to me. I noticed the young women who were drawing water for the handsome travellers; and how the girls let their eyes sidle from beneath their hair as they hitched up their skirts to pour the water. An elder spoke roughly to one and she looked ashamed. We followed the women as they carried water on their heads up the road to Nazareth; they walked steadily, moving their hips, one hand going up from time to time to adjust the thick pad of cloth that the pail rested upon. Jonathan sniggered and said, 'Look how her hips wriggle, and see those two big citrons that rub together inside her dress.' My father turned and shouted at him, and I was afraid of the anger that I saw in his face.

Nazareth was humid and the ground greasy where so many feet had trodden in the soft earth. There were more foreigners than I had ever seen and the noise and the smells of the market-place delighted me. We walked down small, cool back alleys with stalls on either side selling, spices and dyes, herbs, figs, olives and a host of exotic fruit and vegetables. I stopped to look at a stall piled high with yellow, red and green powders and then spotted the man who sat in a dark corner, minding the stall. He was the most singular of all: his face was dark yellow and his eyes had been pulled tightly back into slits.

We had a feast that night, and as it so happened, I had brought with me my most beautiful silk dress. My aunt tied my hair in many tight plaits and said that I was like my mother. As I looked down at the little pleats that flared out at the bottom of the dress, I thought of my mother and felt sad. Her face had changed so much that I was afraid to look closely at it. She did not look old, or even ill – she looked as though her heart was sick and there was an emptiness in her that seemed to be spreading all over her body, making it look vacant and lost. I felt wretched and could not stop thinking of her.

But then Benjamin walked in and sat down opposite me and I felt that a bird was fluttering inside me. The food was beautiful – broth, thick and golden; hot bread; spiced lamb; vegetables that we had brought from the plain where they grow best; little meat balls in grape sauce; pastries, honey cake – everything rich and far too much.

Benjamin began pushing politics at his father and mine; they said little but were anxious for him. Simeon agreed with everything Benjamin said and soon the talk grew excitable and my father poured scorn on it, because he would not see the point of revolutionary chatter – to him it was youthful folly and he had quite enough of that at home. Then Simeon seemed to accuse my father of licking Roman boots to keep his business healthy. This was too close to the truth; and the hatred between them knifed its way across the table and disturbed the atmosphere for a while.

All the time the maids came and went in their blue aprons, and my eyes lay dreaming on Benjamin as he talked and smiled his wild smile – and looked at me not once. It got late and I began to wilt in the warmth from the inflamed voices and the wine. My aunt suggested that I go to bed. My lovely silk dress whispered as I rose – and still, he looked at me not once.

I have only been to Nazareth twice in my life. The second time was when I was thirteen; we went to Benjamin's wedding feast, which lasted well over the seven days. Benjamin was captured by the Romans a few years later, and he is dead now – as all first loves must be.

On this visit, a strange boy attended the wedding feast with his parents. I had seen him once before, walking down the street. My cousins had laughed at him and said that he was peculiar. I had noticed him because he was quite unaffected by their laughter and their jibes; it was as though he walked in another place altogether, where only he existed. He must have been about eight years old, at least four years younger than I. When we met, he looked and seemed years older and spoke in a strange way: quiet but precocious. He irritated all of the children; and my cousin Peter tried to make him appear foolish, but did not succeed. The boy had soft brown hair and grey thoughtful eyes; they looked patient, unlike any child's.

I never told you, but that is how I first remember you.

So we went back to Galilee after that first visit, and when I stood at the top looking down at that vast sky of water, I was so happy to be back among familiar things. I began to imagine my mother waiting at the door, her face soft and smiling. But when we got home, only Zinna stood by the door, and when she saw my father she began to cry. My heart was like a stone in my body, a stone beating against my ribs. My mother was ill, they did not have to tell me. She had a fever and it was contagious, so I was not allowed to see her. I sat outside her door each day, with a small knife tucked under my skirt, in case anyone were to try and harm her. I never once heard her voice. And I hated the fat physician when he came, looking bored, wearing a stained leather apron. He never greeted me, only stepped over my feet on his way into her room.

In the hush of the night, I was woken by a sudden harsh cry, repeated over and over until my whole body shook with the raw horror of it. It was my father and his voice was high and deep at the same time, crying, 'Alas, alas my wife', again, again, like the howl of a jackal in the night. In the morning he came to us, with his clothes torn, earth rubbed into his beard and face, ashes on his head and deep cuts upon his body.

'These rites are condemned,' Reuben said gently, but was ignored. My father told my brothers to lie on the floor and he snatched at my hands and put them on my head, 'Make the sign of sorrow,' he howled, 'your mother is dead, dead.' And he ripped at his hair and some came away, tangled among his fingers. He told me to sing a lament which my mother had taught me. I sang: 'The Lord killeth and maketh alive: he bringeth down to the grave and . . .' O God, I am sick, sick, sick to think of it. My eyes tingle, thinking of it, feeling as I felt then; those cruel waves of grief that killed thought, smiles, dancing on the hill, collecting flowers – killed them all as she was borne up on a vast white wave and tossed down, down, till the sand swallowed her eyes.

There was the strangest sensation of spring flowers in the air. I heard a low chanting from the other end of the house; a voice surging and falling, monotonous, dispassionate, as all religious chanting seems to be. I remember how the sun shone through the window on to my face and how the room was filled with a great light – radiant and blinding. My father had left; my brothers were silent. I began to speak in a wild way, high and ecstatic, possessed by the light and the clarity of my thoughts. No one could understand what I was saying and Joshua ran to get my nurse. She looked at me as I stood there – stiff and silent – and led me to my room. She drew the drapes so that all the light from outside was blocked out. Yet light was all around me. I fell to the floor, unable to bear it; and a voice spoke loud in my head, so loud that I felt my head would split open.

Afterwards, I felt sure that I had been told something that I alone could understand: my mother had been removed from me by theft; she had not died but was waiting somewhere for me, hiding herself for a short while: quick there – behind the drapes, under the chest, beyond the archway. Voices swift – among the shadows, in the candlelight – a slight, slim shape running upon the staircase: 'Catch me, catch me – if you can.' I can tell you this and know that you will understand. I can see the sympathy in your eyes, for you are so close, you seem to live inside my heart. Sometimes I hear my voice speaking your words.

The day after my mother died, a close friend of hers, Martha, took me aside and told me that my mother would be buried in the burial-chamber with my grandparents. The place is built out of a rocky cave, in a little wood. It is not far from here. 'Come, embrace your mother,' my father said to my brothers, and began to lead us towards the room where my mother was lying. But Martha whispered, 'Mary is too young, let her be.' I turned my face away, so that they should not see my smile, because I was certain that her body would not be there.

Martha brought mourning bread to our house and explained to me that we would fast for seven days and that no food could be prepared in our house. I looked hard at her, wondering how she imagined she could trick me with these lies and rituals about death. I would not touch her bread. For many weeks, my father kept away from everyone and all we knew of him was the jarring sound of his voice crying out from the book of *Lamentations*: 'Pour out thine heart like water . . . He hath made me drunken with wormwood . . . Behold and see if there is any sorrow like unto my sorrow.' I smiled, thinking him mad. But my heart turned inside me hearing his grief and I wanted my mother desperately. I wanted to touch her, to hold her, then and there, fiercely against me. I did not know when she would return. Sometimes I would run up into the carob trees and call for her and search in all the caves. Once, I thought I saw her, running in the distance. One night she sat at the end of my bed, but when I reached for her, she disappeared. But wherever I went, I was searching for her, and nearly always my searches ended in tears. It was years before I could believe in her death . . . but I do not want to think of that.

Only Joshua understood my desolation about my mother, because he shared it. I did not tell him that I believed my mother had been stolen in the night; I felt that that was a secret I could not share. Thus we protect ourselves. We spoke very little about our mother, the most was something like, 'She would have liked that rose', or, 'If she was here, I would give her that poppy to put between the linen in her flower press.' But he comforted me and took me out of myself and into the countryside again. We used to go down to the fisheries and watch the fishwives gutting and cleaning the fish on the stone slabs; singing and laughing to lighten their work. I liked best to go down to the shore when the boats came in and the nets were emptied. Joshua liked to pick up and hold the squirming, silver bodies, but I was afraid of their eyes and the slide of their skins. And I couldn't look when the knife slipped into their sides; and there was one particular fish that seemed to scream as it died.

'They bleed like us,' I said, turning away.

'All things bleed, even the leaves,' Joshua replied.

I was lucky to have Joshua. When I was with him I was able to wander about quite freely. He took me to the pastures and to watch the tilling of the land. When it was time to harvest, we went down to the fields and the men tied the corn in bundles to make it easier to cut. Then they sat in the shade, sharpening their scythes and laughing together; their brown arms pulsing with muscles and their faces full of good humour. Some of the simple women squatted on their skirts and rocked their babies and the children ran and played as children do; but I was no longer one of them.

The corn was cut with fast easy strokes – how simple it looked from the edge of the field: one arm swinging smoothly back then forward – and the bundles fell. And their faces, the young men's, when they came for their goat's milk sweetened with honey and their lumps of bread, their faces shone with sweat, but no weariness. I envied their strength and wanted to touch them. They drank and went back and back until all the corn had fallen and lay wilting and fragrant on the ground. Then the women would stride in with their forks and rakes and would pitch and toss the bundles on to the little carts. They did it gracefully, quickly, but not carelessly. The little children would scamper between their skirts – for the gleanings were always left for the poor.

Night came very quickly and the gold light dwindled as everyone became aware of a great hunger and a chill in the air. The people talked about the goodness of the harvest and said that there would be fine corn for the Feast of Weeks. I felt one of them at last; the day had been like a tonic and my loneliness was eased. Joshua and I began to walk home, and I looked back at the field with a deep, blue light falling on the soft curves of it and the small white houses clustering in the distance. I can still taste that day between my teeth.

My father always went to Jerusalem for the feasts, as did my brothers. I stayed with Martha and she was very good to me. She gave me a small embroidered cloth with flowers and poplar trees, which she had made, and underneath the flowers were the words from *Daniel*: 'And many of them that sleep in the dust of the earth shall awake.' I loved to go with her and her small children, up the steep road to the Sanctuary for the Passover readings and prayers; and come back and stay close to her as she did the things that my mother had done. They had goblets with strange handles: shaped like open birds' wings; and their Passover plate was much smaller than ours and less beautiful – it only had little paintings of bitter herbs around the border and no little cross. The Exodus story was recited, not read as in our family; but we ate exactly what I had eaten with my mother in Passovers gone by; unleavened bread; bitter herbs picked from the same spot in the valley, the same spices; eggs and roast lamb in ungenerous portions. I felt close to my mother because of these familiar rituals, and also because Martha, unlike my family, used often to speak of my mother, remembering her recipes and sometimes making me my mother's special drink of wine mixed with honey and balm.

When Joshua came back from Jerusalem and turned twelve, he began to prepare for his Bar Mitzvah and this took up most of his time. He used to be drilled each day in the sacred texts and taught how to wear his phylacteries – but it made me laugh to think that he was really supposed to keep his mind on these the whole day long. Sometimes he used to sing me a little from the Prophets in traditional chant and I loved the way his voice bounced up and down, because he always overdid it.

'Expression, that's what it needs,' he would whisper very seriously, winking.

Joshua was tutored each day by a nice, pious young man with no sense of humour. Joshua got him to instruct me for a few hours each day to get rid of him, and this he did, always very sourly. But I loved the mornings spent quietly reading the Scriptures and discussing the difficulties, and the time always went too fast for me. Then Anas went back to Joshua and I was solitary again, though not unhappy. No one seemed to miss me when I wandered about the countryside, so I began to spend more time at the well and listened to conversations avidly. When strangers sat under the trees, away from the crushing heat, there was always someone who could translate their gibberish to the listening crowd, of which I was one.

As I grew up, my father became increasingly brisk with me. He avoided speaking to me unless he had to, and I think that after my mother's death I slipped out of his eyes altogether – and was glad to do so. He dedicated himself to his business. And after the torrential grief for my mother, his piety had slithered into convenience.

Then, I made friends with an old woman, reputed to be a witch. One day, she took me into the mountains and showed me a cave. It was small and deep, with a narrow inlet of light from an opening in the rock ceiling. I stood at the mouth of the cave nervously, but she pulled me in after her, laughing at my fear and insisting that all the demons were out that day. In one corner of the cave, lying in a small tomb, was an image of a man, made from a piece of wood and bits of the real man's clothing and hair. The old woman looked at the image a long time, then began to call up demons against him – at least, that is what I gathered from her incantations. And then the atmosphere of the cave became dense with maledictions. The skin down my spine trembled and my hands were damp.

'If the man is innocent,' she whispered, 'the demons will fly from him.'

From somewhere in the cave, I swear it was not from her mouth, a high scream echoed.

I left then and ran out into the sunshine, fearing that the demons might attach themselves to me. Below me, the green hills shimmered and the air was clear as water.

She joined me later, looking well-pleased in an inauspicious manner. Made brave by the light and her returning laughter, I began to question her.

'What is Satan made of?'

'Of air, naturally.'

'Why not of water?'

'Because water cannot fly, blockhead.'

There was a silence as she clicked her tongue and gathered her black bag together; and as I thought about Satan and seemed to feel his fingers on my neck. I had heard my father say that Satan hid in purses of gold and in the folds of the garments of rich merchants. He seemed to say it bitterly, with envy, so I was not sure that he could be believed. Also, my grandmother had once said that she had seen Satan looking over my father's shoulder.

'How,' I asked then, 'if God is altogether good, how did he make evil?'

'If you are weaving,' she answered gravely, 'there is always the rough wool that you put to one side, but it too has a use.'

'Can God do away with Satan whenever he wants?'

'So they say.'

'Why doesn't he then?'

'Am I God that I know what he wants to do?' she snapped.

Impatiently she led me down the hill and away from the cave, where my silly questions had disturbed the aura of mystery. I spent a lot of time with her, but never learned very much. And I thought often of Satan, wondering whether he had, like God, a plan for me – and which of them I should give myself to...on dark nights my allegiance went always to God; on a bright blue morning I went searching for Satan.

When I went walking today, I remembered the leper boy; and it reminded me of the day you were so angry, above the lake. Your face, when you came, was golden and clear, and your eyes were the same shade – but when you left, your face was dark and bruised. You pushed the boat out and left all the people standing there. They too were angry, particularly the little group of lepers standing on one side, patiently. Later, when I saw you again, you were still angry – 'Mankind is never grateful; I fill their cup with wine and get back vinegar.' On that day I felt such despair – to stand before your face and know I could not win your look.

Later, you would come and tell me your thoughts, just as Joshua had done once. For hours we used to walk along the shore, talking, talking; and unlike the others, I did not just listen, for I was less simple than they. You were not threatened by my intelligence then. But I was afraid of you, afraid of too close a brush against your arm, too long a look in your eyes. My blood rushed upwards in a frenzy and I clutched my arms across my breasts to flatten them – their insistence, their tingling demands. O but you were strong then, noble, proud; not one of your ideas had a leak.

Once I saw you touching the sores of a sick man; the wounds were fetid and crusted; they stank. I recoiled from this, and, for one ghastly moment as your head bent, I thought that you were going to kiss his sores. I was almost sick. You did not, but your hands lightly touched the hurt places in the way healers do, until the man smiled at you, eased.

It was terrible, but I was angry with you for this and suspicious of your motives.

'Would you call that love?' I asked in a surly fashion. You smiled as though such foolishness needed no answer.

'You should be careful what you call love,' I insisted, 'there are those who commit themselves to some great duty, some responsibility, and call it love. But perhaps it is more of a penance.'

Your look was pained. 'You're right of course; you understand all the dark things. But I am a believer in penance. His sores heal me a little.'

You turned from me and for a time after that I dared not question you. I tried also to silence the tongue in my brain, because it did not matter – all my silly doubts – to people you were what you seemed, what you said, most of all what you did. They loved you for that. I knew what you were. And still loved you.

When I heard you speak, I found myself watching the people around you in amazement. A man who had been working with concentration on the edge of the crowd, pulling his needle through leather, would stop as if involuntarily; a face slack with misery, or curled into a jeer would lift to attention. But no one pushed to get nearer; no one spoke. Their hearts were in their eyes and their eyes were on your face. It was almost possible to hear them breathe. I knew then that you had a divinity which dazzled and bewitched – them and you – and let you carry a multitude in the crook of your arm. And I wished it was otherwise.

When you had done something extraordinary, you were often angry afterwards, and said once, 'I hate miracles, hate them. People should believe without them; they should look to God.' I said miracles were more important than God; but you refused to see that God could only be understood through a miracle and was hidden otherwise. I asked lightly who should take credit for the bad miracles: the famines, earthquakes, floods? Then you laughed loudly – knowing how infectious your laughter was. So I dared say it – 'You want them to love and be captivated by you, you alone, separate from the Law and the priests.'

'Yes, yes, why not?' you said gaily, like a child with a golden ball.

'That is vanity,' I said sternly.

You laughed again and pulled my hair, 'No, not at all, because I only lead them to God in the end.'

'You are better then than the angels?' I asked softly, but I smiled because I liked your boldness, though it was full of presumption.

Now they try to pretend that you were never angry, never even ordinary. Why is it that when a great man dies they must creep in with paint-brushes – erasing an ugliness here, a small imperfection there? They slide their hands into your rough curls and smooth them;

re-align the twisted curve of your mouth until it becomes a sweet smile. Are they ashamed of you? Or just making of you what they need, now that you can no longer protest? I remember. I would not rearrange a hair on your head.

The nights are so long and deep and there is no lullaby. I cannot hear the sea from here, but I feel it in my blood, ebbing. I walk up and down this narrow room, which used to be my mother's, back and forth, and back and forth; my body making waves in the still air. And in the corner, those stiff lilies, their savage perfume makes my eyes smart. I wish that cool moon would move from my window. When did the moon first affect me? I cannot remember, but I think she has always watched me with her one cruel eye. My heart beats quietly and my womb is asleep. How long ago. I cannot weep for you to-night, nor for myself being without you. I am glad that the earth cannot kiss you, nor the worm's moist mouth. But this terrible second side of my brain prods at me, knowing no man can escape death and decay; no body fly intact to heaven. O why are you not here to explain these things to me? You made it all so simple. And I cannot, I cannot. I hurt myself with these thoughts and must leave them. Wait, wait with me.

One day up on the hill, I thought that soon I would grow up, soon my skirts would be long and trailing; my veil delicate and flimsy. The folds of my skirt would billow behind me as I walked, and beneath my dress would be layers of petticoat, one upon the other, each with a different flower scent. And when I sat, so elegantly, all my skirts would ray about me like the sun. Someone would watch me and smile, discerning my specialness. And then all that thinking and learning and obeying and praying would be for a reason. But that day, as the flowers tossed in the breeze and the gulls idled, I could hardly wait, and the only thing that kept me from bursting with anticipation was the thought that in a little while I would be going to Jerusalem. To Jerusalem for the Passover. All the world would be there and perhaps this thing would happen to me and I would become what I was destined for. Someone would give me a loop of silk, or a coronet heavy with roses, and I would take them and smile. I would whiten my cheeks with chalk and darken my eyebrows with kohl. But then I grew ashamed of these thoughts; most ashamed when I found myself dreaming of the day when young men would be grovelling at my feet, and I would wrap my hair around them, catch them up and spin them till they were giddy with my curls.

How strange it is – I am not the woman sitting by the garden wall; I am again, in mind and body, a small girl up on the hill. I am not remembering her, the way one is taken back by a scent, a colour in the trees. I am not remembering her. I have become her. I am twelve. It is the new moon, the first day of the month. The torches are lit on the mountain top and there will be a feast.

We were going to Jerusalem and my excitement was so strong that it was like an extra burden to carry. It was not hot, but the wind blew and covered us with sticky dust. The land, after we had left Galilee, became more arid and flat, and then after some days, the first hills appeared, grey against the sky.

And then I saw, far away and gathered around a small blue hill, a nest of white houses. We went up into the open land away from the road and soon found fresh water. Flocks of sheep fed near the stream, moving slowly forward, one after the other. A shepherd sat on the ground banging stones together and a sheep, coughing, reminded me of home.

We awoke early to begin the climb to Jerusalem; the air grew cooler, the land more green. Birds careered in the pale light, the hills grew closer together and vines hurried up them; the wheat gleamed like new gold. The climb to Jerusalem was steep and made more difficult for me because my breath kept getting lost in my great excitement. It took us many hours to reach the outskirts of the city.

Then I looked up and saw Jerusalem – a city towering above the rock, hewn out of it. A place of infinite whiteness, the rock lightly tinted with gold; the palaces, the columns and towers – immense, spectacular. My city: my heart was touched as never before. Olive trees, stark and small, made the only relief against the glimmering whiteness. The sky was emptied of colour; the earth, the stones – the colour of dust. Up and up we went, into the old part of the city and the dirty hubbub; the children jeering and throwing stones, the new smells, the heat, the walls – so high, so high. Alleys with traders, barbers, weavers, jewellers and forecasters. I saw linens and silks more beautiful, more sheer than I had ever seen. And dark-skinned hands pulled always at our clothes, trying to sell us anything: 'My sister, my mother' – and asking always for money, 'Just give me something, a little, it won't hurt you. Your God will reward you.' And father shouting, 'I'll give you a kick in the backside, idle, foreign scavenger.'

We were to stay with my mother's sister and her husband; they lived in the Upper City. My father took us to their house by a short cut running through the little alley-ways behind the theatre. From the mount I could see the fortress, rising high and dark across the valley. My aunt greeted us all warmly and showed us to large rooms, with rich, heavy furnishings, but no flowers. My father was ill at ease, and he kept looking at my simple clothes with embarrassment. I just wanted to sleep. I was glad that my aunt did not resemble my mother.

It was early morning and my eyes and body were tired after a sleepless night in an unfamiliar bed. The sun had just risen, and the streets outside began to bustle with the cries of vendors. A slave came into my room with a jar of water and poured it into the basin – carelessly I thought, and she tossed me a surly look. I wondered where Elizabeth had got to, and missed having a rose floating in my wash bowl, as at home. I could hear the sounds of a waking house, of water pouring, of servants rushing to and fro with clean linen and oiled sandals.

When I had dressed, I went to find my brothers, and when the household had assembled we set off for the Temple. The streets were busy, but not hot. The Scribes were setting up their tables, and a dove-seller spoke softly to a lady at a loom. And then it was as if all the people moved in one direction, soberly, reverently. I looked up and saw the Temple. My heart moved, and I was so proud, so proud to be a Jew, with a Temple so fine and beautiful. We climbed the steps and heard fierce arguments with money-changers, who solved all problems by shrugging their shoulders and then moving on to the next customer. The priests strutted like doves in their immaculate white robes; their faces were a dull, grey colour and their bodies plump, from sacrificial fasting, or so Simeon said.

The Passover in my aunt's house was solemn and beautiful and I found myself more affected by the ritual and the prayers than I had ever been. I sat quietly reading each day and learned to recite most of the story of the Exodus by heart. I was a little calmer and gentler with myself than before, and when Simeon began to mock the High Priest, saying that the man was in league with the Roman governor and the other hypocrites, I became angry and distressed and could not speak to him. I wanted everything to be at peace and he had made a rupture and restored feelings to me that I did not wish to have. I hated him for that. He knew it and it amused him; so cruel and careless he always was.

When the Passover celebrations were over, we did not go home. My father disappeared for most of each day and took Reuben with him. He refused to take Simeon and Jonathan and it angered them, as they felt it was their right to be involved in my father's business transactions. So the two of them remained at home with Joshua, my aunt and myself, tormenting us all in their boredom. My aunt said to me one day, as we sat together sewing, that my father was thinking of taking up residence in Jerusalem. I refused to believe it. My aunt did not contradict me when I insisted that she must be mistaken, she merely looked down again and continued to stitch. I could not bear the silence and began to plague her with questions. She knew nothing more than that my father had decided to base his business in Jerusalem and begin exporting other items to Rome. She added that my uncle thought it would turn out to be lucrative and that he had chosen a good time to expand, because the Romans were being particularly tolerant at that time. I then became alarmed and could say nothing more, because my thoughts were causing such havoc inside me. Finally, I left the room and went in search of Joshua. He knew nothing, nor did the twins.

I lived in fear for two days; and then my father announced his plans to us all at dinner. He had drunk too much wine and his voice skidded at the end of his sentences. Joshua looked at me and gave me a little reassuring smile, but I barely noticed it for my eyes were hooked into my father's face – and I waited. He merely said that we were all going to live in Jerusalem in future.

'Not in such a fine house as this of course,' he said with a sarcastic tilt of his head, 'somewhere less elevated no doubt, but good enough for us simple folk. Well, I've taught my sons my trade, to try and prevent them becoming vagabonds; whether it has worked remains to be seen. Reuben will remain in Galilee with his family and take care of the fisheries, which will continue as usual. Simeon and Jonathan, and their wives, will come here too – and perhaps we will see a little more of them than we did at home.'

My twin brothers winced at this remark, because both their young wives disliked my father. Then my father smiled and said that Joshua would of course stay in Jerusalem and continue his studies with the best tutor that money could buy. 'He will be a credit to me in my old age,' he said sentimentally, ignoring the yawn that came from Simeon's corner.

And again, I was in a turmoil, my stomach heaving and tears filling my eyes and I was forced again to whisper, 'And I, father?' He looked at me then and said vaguely, 'Well, naturally you will be here too. Yes, of course.' It was obviously of so little concern to him that he did not even have to make a decision about me, any more than he would think to consider whether he ought to bring some occasional piece of furniture when he moved house. One day, I vowed, one day I will be noticed, one day they will hang on my words and wait for my smile. I was angry and I determined to speak up for once and cease to be the scared shadow on his wall.

'I would prefer to go home to Galilee,' I said firmly, 'Reuben and Ruth will take care of me.'

He looked irritated for a moment and frowned, then dismissed my remark by a flick of his hand.

Joshua said quietly, 'I think, father, that Mary would be happier in a place she knows, she will be lonely here with no one to . . .'

'No,' my father's voice barked, 'No. Just no.' We all went silent and I locked my jaw and the channels to my eyes and concentrated on biting through my under-lip.

The next day I watched them leave from the roof and then I cried and raged, and when these passions were finally spent, I lay listlessly on the roof-top, looking up at the sky. I stayed on the roof until it got late. The moonlight was luminous and I could have read by it, had I cared to, but I was bitter against my father. I wanted to injure him; I thought I would make spoons from his bones when he was dead.

My aunt thought me very odd: she could not understand how the gentle, pious girl of the Passover had transformed herself into this sullen, speechless creature who spent all her evenings on the roof-top. When I told her that my only wish was to go home, she seemed annoyed and reminded me that I should honour my father and not cause him any more difficulties. She suggested that I study the Psalms. I realised that she resembled my mother in that they both had the same high code and religious faith, but she was a little harsh and intolerant and my mother had always been gentle. I had felt fond of my aunt when we first arrived, now I disliked her and felt unwanted in her house. It was clear she had seen that I was not a good child. No good child thought and behaved as I did. She had seen my bad nature and had directed me to the Psalms. But now I did not feel repulsed by my lack of goodness, as before. I was a little excited by it, as though it set me aside and made me special. My life was not going to follow a dreary course; it would flow and flood and burst out of its confines. I would study, I would work with the concentration and fervour of Joshua. No one would stop me. And being good would be of no consequence when one was wise.

Jerusalem frightened me. The air in the streets was so heavy, so turgid – as if it had never left since descending from heaven – just dragged itself back and forth in the dust, in and out of a million noses. People did not look at one another as they rushed by; their faces were closed and empty; and there were so many beggars without infirmities. The poor were aggressive and hateful, and spitting, always spitting – little, round balls that curled in the sand. Only the Romans were more frightening, they marched murderously, flicking at heads with whips from the safety of the horses – so proud of the clatter of their helmets and shields.

My uncle was one of those men who, like my father, was seldom at home, and my aunt rarely spoke of him. Once, in the evening, he put his arm around me and his hand slipped beneath my arm, appearing again by my ribs, high up, just below the breast. He left it there for an uncomfortable length of time, then moved it higher, quickly. I said nothing; I was unable to move. Later, I felt that I was doomed because of this silence and I thought that now he knew too that I was a wicked child. Late one night, as I was lying in my favourite place in the corner of the roof, watching the stars, he came and sat close to me. His sandals were close to my leg, but again, I was too petrified to move, though critically aware of his touch. He began to tell me about astrology and said that the Romans would not make a move before a consultation; but that to the Jews it was a heathen practice and he had only dabbled in it once, for curiosity. And of course the predictions were false, and he had lost a lot of money.

He was talking very fast and his body moved nervously, but his feet never twitched. And all that day I had felt a cumbersome depression; by the evening, with him, it was as if a stone had begun to grow inside me, gradually getting colder and heavier, so that I was oppressed and afraid. Now, when my uncle bent with a jerky movement and pushed his hand under my skirt, along my thigh, I felt my eyes clench and hot pricks of fear ran under my skin. Yet still I could not move. He got up swiftly and left me on the roof; and the stars looked down, knowing.

When my family came back, I left my aunt. My aunt, who never understood how I hated to wear that thick, rough nightdress; and how I longed for the soft, linen one I had worn and worn in Galilee for so long that the scrubbing on the rocks by the pool had made it thin as a dragonfly's wings.

We went to live in a fairly big house, which was built of that beautiful rose-coloured stone; and the walls had creeper growing on them. There were some big, old poplar trees in the garden and a cage full of fluttering, cooing doves. The house was dusty and unwelcoming inside, and upon further examination, it was obvious that the place was not accustomed to people. Mice scurried to cover when a door opened; birds nested in the timber and the walls had been taken over by mould and fungus. My father began to shout and said that the property vultures had sold him a place fit for swine. Jonathan murmured that perhaps he should have realised that one got little for the money in Jerusalem. My father stamped furiously around the building; while the servants began patiently to work their way through dust, grease and droppings. It became clear that he had been sold the house by a Roman agent and Joshua found this most worrying. He kept insisting that he could not understand why father had decided to do business with people he loathed, especially when it was customary for these things to be arranged by one's own people; and this avoided, as well, the risk of serious cheating. It was at this point that I first understood that there was no consistency in him; he was swayed as easily by a woman's skirt as by the wind or a whiff of wine.

The innovations that he had made in the trade at Galilee – using faster ships and introducing ventilated wooden containers with special linings to store the fish in such a way that they did not dry and deteriorate on the long voyage – caused business to thrive and increase. In Jerusalem, he soon became a wealthy man and we moved to a spacious, white-columned house higher on the mount. My father travelled a great deal around Judaea, but he also returned to Galilee at regular intervals and made trips to Damascus. When he was at home, it was clear that he had grown dependent upon wine, which made him fat and loose-featured. He began to set aside some of his Jewish habits – the ones he was so rigorous in upholding when my mother was alive – and even became forgetful of the Sabbath. Then, for some unaccountable reason, he would be filled with remorse and would fast for many days, weep crapulently in the mornings and offer extravagant sacrifices at the Temple. He would force us all to take part in his excesses. At the same time, it was clear that he was fraternising with the Romans in a way that no respectable Jew would; and nothing Joshua did or said could persuade him to loosen his connections with them. We came to know also that our mother had floated from his mind, for he had taken to seeing women of that sort. I never forgave him this infidelity.

But with Joshua back, I was no longer confined to the house and the needle. Joshua was intrigued by Jerusalem and took me with him when he went exploring. I grew to love the market-places, because although the people and the coarseness had intimidated me at first, I now found that these were wonderful places to become anonymous; no one cared who you were, or what you did – money was all that mattered. The market we frequented most was divided into different sections for fruit, vegetables, spices, pottery and so on; and there was a completely separate part for live animals and birds. The most mysterious corner of the market was around the little booths that housed the sages and soothsayers, and beyond them were a group of astrologers. I spent most of my time at this end of the market because here one saw extraordinary people: Indians and Persians in beautiful flowing colours; more of the secret men with pulled eyes; wealthy sheiks and humid girls. There were few children here, and even fewer of the peasant women in their black, winged robes. Romans soldiers of meagre rank went in for consultations and came out frowning; the higher officials tended to come out looking well-pleased and hopeful. These generally wandered over to the small stall that dispensed potions, charms and probably poisons. Joshua never left me alone in this quarter for long, and insisted that I cover my face and keep to the dark places.

I see as I remember, that I forget the things that I want to forget; the things that you cared about so much. What of the man who crouched on the stone steps, his body covered with thick crusted sores which his nails moved in always? The idiot who hid his round face, blank as a pebble, from the light? He would press into a corner – I can see his dark head – and then his claw would dart out and hook on to a passer-by. His mouth would slice open into a smile as his eyes blinked rapidly, then the tears would come. Yes, I remember, and all the poverty too: how people who had so little had to gaze at so much richness. Their poverty had a desperation that I had not seen in Galilee – in Jerusalem the poor were just too many. It was the little children with their bloated bellies and their big sick eyes that made me want to run and run. I was told that parents had maimed their children in order to make them beggars; I was told this so that I would not be taken in by their cunning. But I found myself imagining how a mother would take the rock and break the bones – and the pity of that is inconsolable. When I think of you, I am made to feel so inferior – sitting here clutching at my past so I can avoid facing the future. But I have been poor too. Do not forget, how poor and how sick, until you came. And now you have gone. Do not rebuke me.

Last night, I looked up at the moon, full and round and wearing your face. What were you whispering? Your lips moved, so, into a round and you smiled your child-smile. Then the leaves of cloud brushed your smile away. What were you whispering? I want to think quietly of you, closing my eyes; I will not run my hand through my hair nor turn in the chair. I will cover my eyes with my hand because ideas try to catch at my eyes. I want to think of you, you. I will think as you taught me to think, becoming the thought. O you, you.

I have you: impatient toss of your head; walking with the stone edging between your fingers; the little language of your chin – tight when you were angry, so tight that the skin sank along the jaw bones. And the rebuke, always the rebuke, as your hands turned inward, your body moved away. You burned me – still I am smarting from those quiet killing glances. Terrible to be found out so quickly, unable to hide anything, like a child with a torn dress; a leper before the dove is released into the heavens. You knew that I was stained, you knew how much. But sometimes I could catch you, sometimes touch you quickly and feel your blood turn; sometimes hold your despair close to me as though it had flesh. Your mouth, all those silent hours when your throat hurt, your mouth basking in the warmth of my thoughts. I wanted to bend and kiss your throat, once, twice. And now, I almost weep, thinking of this. Your sudden laughter – 'All my words, my shouting above their heads – a piss in the ocean.' You were so scornful, so far from us all, and I used to think what a horrid boy you must have been; how people must have longed to give you a good whipping. Sometimes this scorn of yours made my nails bite into the inside of my hands, and I wanted to hurt you.

O but the day you chased me under the pine trees, and I never knew that you could run so fast – because always you paced out your steps carefully and steadily, not to be tired by the heat, to keep on walking as long as possible. And when you caught me, you whirled me round, till I fell and held on to the tree trunk as my head seemed to spin round and round it. Do you remember how the grasses danced in the breeze as we climbed to the top of the hill? and you lifted your arms high in the air and yelled at the wind, 'I SHALL NEVER DIE.'

Elizabeth has come and is slowly brushing my hair. So calmly the straight strokes run down my back. I look up at her face, her face like a still river, observing all around it without a ripple.

'I didn't know I had screamed, Elizabeth.'

'You are tired, that's all. Lie down and take deep breaths. I will stay with you until you sleep.'

Elizabeth is singing in a clear low voice, her lullaby; something she sang when she first came to us and was so far from home. I listen to the sad lilt of it, and it occurs to me that she must always have sung it more for her comfort than mine – 'Where the little green hills dance down to the sea...' She was not much more than a child when my father bought her and she had already been bought and sold twice before. I look at her face again and observe how well she hides everything. Once, long ago, when I was so sick and sad, she sat beside me, and that face like a statue watched over me until the madness had gone. Only once, I saw her face flicker for a second as a tear ran down it – as if it had risen in spite of her, and flowed unchecked also in spite of her.

I reach over and take her hand and wait for her small smile; I feel certain that she knows what I have just remembered. Her body is so tall and ungainly, but her hands are small and fine – all these years she has washed and cared for me with those hands. Even if I freed her, as I have often tried to do, she would not go, nor give a reason for staying. And now her hands hold the brush as it moves in a quiet rhythm, as my thoughts do.

34

TWO

They come to see me, they come to sit in my garden and touch the flowers lightly and drink my wine. They tell me of the events in Jerusalem – the squabbles between your brother and Peter. They tell me, too, of a man called Paul. They call him a babbler whose words get muddled in the heaviness of his beard. They tell me that this man is persecuting little nests of your followers, who now begin to re-emerge. Your brother, it appears, is frightened by this. Perhaps he understands how willingly we Jews have always moved towards martyrdom. And all the while, they pluck at the flowers and their faces are uncomposed. I have nothing to say. Soon these spring flowers will be dead; the rains lost in the soil and the garden littered with husks and the skulls of baby birds. There is a time to lie fallow. This is my time.

They have gone. The sun is breaking through the shell of the sky; it will not rain today. And I am happy suddenly. I understand your words now; it is clear. Words mean nothing until you can hear them and say in your head and heart – yes, that is true.

You told me in Capernaum, near Peter's house, that when you were small, about seven years old, you used to ask your mother about your birth. She would tell you nothing, except, 'You are God's child.' You grew up and the feeling of your strangeness grew in you. You asked more questions but none of the answers satisfied you. One day, you had a dream as clear as a vision, which told you that Joseph was not your father. When you awoke you knew that it was ridiculous for your father to be Joseph – humble and hardworking, but who could barely read and spoke only of building. You said that Mary, your mother, was like a simple child: her face was round and soft; her mouth was always slightly open, in a half-smile. If she was working and you tried to talk to her, she had to stop in order to speak because she said she could not do both things at the same time.

That day, I did not feel afraid of you. I hardly knew you then and I found you conceited – but that day you spoke to me easily, as though I were a man. I liked that, and I wanted you to know that I was not ignorant. When you told me that your mother had once said that Joseph was not your father, I said that in Greek myths that I had read, very often mortal women claimed that they had got with child by a lustful God and that this was a common ruse to avoid responsibility for bad conduct. You looked at me sharply then as if I were questioning your birth. Then you added thoughtfully that there were times when your mother said things that were untrue, because often the truth was too difficult for her. When I met your mother she was exactly as you had described her. But she became so frightened as things progressed. I felt such sadness for her because she seemed to think she could protect you, and you were often impatient of her care.

I remember your face; your mouth; small teeth in a long mouth; your eyes like a sea of waves. I never thought that your face was composed of clay.

I often wonder why Peter allowed you no smiles. Remember when we sat around the fire late that night and you were happy because the people that day had loved you and many had come to listen? We were all singing softly and I was mending your coat. You began to sing with us, but Peter, like an old hen, told you to preserve your voice. Your voice: so euphonic in the morning and so rasping by the end of the day. You smiled at him softly, and said that you had always sung out of tune anyway – it had made your brothers laugh.

But I was cross with Peter, because he was always trying to separate you, to set you apart on a pedestal; I think he almost felt that he had discovered you. I was jealous of him, because there was so much time when he was beside you – and I could not be. I can still see how you looked at the plain blue hills and your eyes caressed them; and it was as if they had waited for you, as objects wait for eyes to find them before they can come to life. And people responded to you in the same way, waiting for your eyes. I can hear your voice saying those beautiful words; once you asked, 'Who put them in my mouth?' as if you did not know where they had come from.

How quiet it is. Quiet as the days when you disappeared up into the hills. When you came back you would speak to no one until something had recovered, settled in you. Words, smiles, touches – how false they can be. Only thought is pure, is endless. When someone enters the room I am no longer myself; I do not think – I listen, I pretend. In isolation all my being is true; all my recollection, however painful, is not warped by the presence of another. I would do without speech, without people. I have grown; my mind has stretched so far that it can fill all voids. In solitude I recover, I grow sweet. Sweet even as the memory of myself.

I was thirteen; how clear my skin was – ripe as a new plum. I was beginning to grow used to Jerusalem. The biggest event of that year was the arrival of Mattathias, Joshua's new tutor. He instructed one or two of the clever young men who lived on Mount Zion. When he first arrived it was clear that he did not care for our father; but he and Joshua liked each other immediately. I can still hear their chatter bobbing up and down the corridor and Joshua's laugh rising like a lark.

It was Mattathias who told Joshua, a little later, that our father was considered most unrespectable by Jerusalem society. Joshua had mentioned this, hoping our father might be embarrassed and perhaps become more temperate. But father had barked, 'And what's so new about that? When have I ever been respectable? How could I be so with this face and this name? You will just have to put up with my unrespectability – or go and live somewhere else as your brothers have done. This tutor – he's a damn Pharisee is he? They're all the same. It's impossible to live as they demand, they don't themselves – stinking piety.'

Joshua said reassuringly, 'Don't get excited, he isn't one of those, he believes extreme views defeat their object, making it impossible for people to offer their lives to God.'

My father's ill-humour evaporated as speedily as ever, and he decided that he had made a good choice after all. Joshua said, 'I am learning about the Stoics now, father', and was surprised when father said wearily, 'Yes, well, you carry on, it always seemed nonsense to me that a man could be indifferent to both pleasure and pain.'

Joshua then slipped in quickly, 'Father, it will be all right if Mary has a little instruction too, won't it? Just for an hour or two when I am reading.'

Father said, yawning, 'It is as foolish for a girl to be wise as it is for a cow to walk on two legs.' But Joshua made light of it and finally got father's agreement because he would never refuse Joshua anything. Then, we only had the problem of presenting the idea to Mattathias.

Mattathias was tall and hard with something a little hirsute about him – a slight roughness which contradicted the smooth polish of his oval face, with its serious, firm mouth and very straight eyebrows. He did not laugh very often, but smiled when he was thinking; and when I watched him write it seemed that his hands could not have been made for any other purpose.

When Joshua began studying philosophy, he became so entranced by the old Greeks that he would sit and talk to me for hours and I was able to absorb something of what he was learning. I was desperate to study myself. And so I started to sit quietly in one corner of the study-room while Joshua was being instructed. I am not at all sure that my presence was appreciated by Mattathias, but I was so silent – never daring to cough or creak my stool. Joshua would say glibly, 'You don't object to my sister, do you? She won't disturb us.'

Mattathias said nothing. But, as the days passed, a curiosity grew in him and he would begin to wander in my direction, surreptitiously sending a long glance across the book or paper in front of me. Once he asked roughly, 'Who taught you to read and write?' After I had replied, he walked on, back and forth, his hands clenched behind his back as he forgot me again. I began to take notes of what he was saying, and later asked Joshua to explain anything that I could not understand. And then, one morning, Mattathias picked up the paper in front of me and looked hard at my notes.

'I will teach you Greek,' he said.

It didn't take me too long to learn Greek – how fast I learned things once – and then my brother and I began to read Homer, Sophocles and Euripides together. Mattathias never allowed us too much of these pagan works and knew that his primary task was to instruct Joshua in Jewish thought; he said, as a justification, that one should not understand one's own culture in isolation and that the Greeks must be read for the sake of beauty. I loved *Medea*, sympathising with her; and I wept for *Oedipus*, which Mattathias considered the finest of the tragedies. I understood Antigone's words, 'I never knew how great the loss could be, even of sadness' – how many times those words have come to my mind since then. I told them to you once, do you remember? And you quoted, 'To be wise is to suffer.' I was amazed, knowing you had not read Sophocles, and you laughed and said, 'Don't be so foolish, you told me those words. I have a good memory!'

Mattathias never spoke to me of himself, or of his personal hopes and dreams, but he told Joshua that when he was fifteen he had looked carefully into all the sects, and after taking three difficult courses of instruction he had decided to live his life by the doctrines of the Pharisees – a sect he felt had something in common with the Stoic school.

Yet, across the bare table, with only a few books and pens, in the room where he instructed me in the mornings, Mattathias and I explored each other in silence: intuitive, tremulous silences that conveyed with the subtlety of dreams. Sitting side by side, hearing my breath, tasting my breath, he would explain, interpret, wait for my answers. Sometimes we would argue because I could not accept doctrines that he no longer questioned. It never seemed right to me that Adam, by his disobedience, had poisoned the world for all time.

'We cannot escape the evil of our bodies,' he would insist quietly, 'the world is corrupt and we can only live good lives by observing the Law.'

'No,' I would argue, sometimes surprised myself by my own vehemence. 'We must get close to God in our own way, it's no use to be good merely by obeying the Law.'

He would begin again, explaining his arguments patiently and deeply. Occasionally, his voice would become flat and he would admit that the Law did not eliminate, or even diminish the ugliness and brutality of the world.

'Then, it is not enough,' I would say triumphantly.

'No,' he would agree, suddenly looking much older than his twenty-four years, 'our world has become weak and flabby. All things have lost their fatness. There is madness, but even the madness is dull. There are no men, no good men to lead us. Only poverty and corruption abound. No one expounds any more, there are no prophets, no seekers of truth. We have become feeble.'

I looked at him and he seemed so sad. He lived on another plane where I could not follow. At times, I could see him looking across at me, as if from a far distance. But I yearned to catch up, to fill myself with the knowledge that he had. I read, I studied. And then, all too quickly, I was fourteen.

Fourteen – and I felt so old. So much happened that year, so much too quickly gone. It was a year like a season.

My father called me into his room one day and showed me to a stranger. The man was not much younger than my father; he was dressed in the best linen, with a purple cloak made of heavy wool across his arm. Though his face and figure were heavy with fat, his deep curly hair, fatherly beard and the warmth of his black eyes made him quite appealing. He was the kind of man who would make beautiful children. He looked hard at me, walked up closer and spoke to me a little. I answered him conventionally, wondering what could be the point of this interview. There was a silence, and then my father said I could leave. A few days later, he called me to him again and informed me that I was to be married. To the stranger I had met. He told me formally that the man's name was Moses, which I knew to be an Egyptian name, and that he was a wealthy merchant whom my father was entering into partnership with. Then he said that I could go. I was so stunned that I did go, without a word – something I raged with myself for, later.

Then, ugly scenes began to take place in our house. Joshua was appalled that my father was actually going to sell me off, as he aptly put it. He had found out that the wealthy merchant was much older than he looked and had a very crooked reputation. Yet, I was betrothed and my father was discussing the most favourable terms. Jewels and lengths of expensive silks arrived as presents for me, and my father refused to return them; he too received rich gifts. I became desperate and my desperation made me bold. I refused to marry the man. My father laughed in my face. Sometimes, while I sat at my books with Mattathias, we could hear my father's voice pleading, then roaring, at Joshua. Mattathias never referred to the problem, but he was very aware of it. My own unhappiness he understood after a swift glance at my eyes at the start of each lesson; but he never alluded to it.

After months of tears, tantrums and rages, I sat at the table beside Mattathias, subdued and feeling hopeless in my heart. I kept lifting and dropping the edges of the paper in front of me.

'I am to be married,' I whispered, 'our lessons will have to cease.' My voice was low and detached, I was vanquished by all the un-pleasantness.

He looked at me for a long time I remember. Then his eyes fell affectionately upon his well-fingered Septuagint and he shrugged his shoulders lightly, 'I think, in that case, we ought to leave tonight.' I jumped up and spun round and round, hugging myself. And I knew that I would go with him, for he had suddenly great authority over me, because I wished it, he wished it; together it was a wish.

I did not finish my lesson that morning, but went to my room and called Elizabeth. Her eyes grew large and bright when I told her; she did not smile, but began to walk around the room, nervously taking out clothes and replacing them. I held her around the waist and made her spin with me. When she had recovered her balance, she smiled a little smile at me and shrugged.

It was late in the afternoon; Mattathias's time for taking his leave of my father. He did so as usual. And exactly three hours later, as we had planned, I walked out on to the white street. Elizabeth gripped my hand hard and gave me the small bag, then disappeared. I walked into the flowing evening and he came towards me. And all the world was sucked into oblivion, save only him. His face was long and melancholy, until he turned to me and smiled. Then I grew dizzy, and the streets rushed past and the flowers and trees gave us their scent. Our feet drummed together on the caked earth as our pace quickened, until, like guilty children, we began to run. I looked at him and laughed. I was beautiful again: my black hair was long, untouched; my cheeks were polished with smiles. The door of my life blew open and I leapt through it, carrying my golden dreams.

You have brushed these memories from me like so many cobwebs. You have filled my mind again with your words and I must let it be so. I must let all else fade – for you are the king of my memories. I keep thinking, 'Such things must be forgotten, if life is to be endured.' Endured – how much has been endured? and some things cannot be forgotten. But what interest are my thoughts, my memories to you? But of course I do not think for you; I do it for myself and I could not stop if I tried. All these things have survived in my mind, without the edges being torn or frayed, intact they lie, waiting to be brought to life again – for me, for me. Now I exist through them. The world cannot, you cannot, take these memories from me. You do not wish to – I was frightened. Forgive me.

And so, gently, I ask you to remember the night we were all to go to Jacob's house, and he had asked me to cook the evening meal. I was so pleased to be able to cook for you that I spent the whole day preparing it, though I should have been working with the women. Later, everyone came. I wore the dress that you liked, pale pink with tiny white stripes. Then you came and everything fell into order. The idleness and loose talk trickled out; everything was brought to a connection. The men grew tall and industrious, the women began to move and bustle – there was a purpose in our activity.

You were standing across the room talking to Peter. And I moved forward like a moth to a flame, desiring a brighter place. I hid my hands beneath my apron, for although you would have considered it praiseworthy for my hands to be ruined by working for the poor, still I was ashamed, because of my awful vanity. I waited for your smile, drinking your words because I was so thirsty; you turned to me and your mouth lifted pinkly and I was surrounded by radiance, floating on it. Before you came I was nothing, we were all nothing, just poor destitutes without a country, a future. When you came everything changed. And you knew it. Walking into a room you would stop as if to say, 'I am here, it is all right.' And yet you wanted, needed our eyes; could not exist if we did not turn our heads. So we changed; and I changed most of all, dropping my eyes at your feet. But then it was only your limbs that I wanted, your face to turn backward and find mine.

We were all happy. Do you remember? You had not mentioned that you would be going away, alone, for days. The flames in the grate heaved and tumbled, and the iron bars to protect Jacob's children from the fire cast a pattern on the floor; slim streaks of shadow like the strings of a lyre. Your head was thrown forward, your hair fell red-gold about your face. The light from the fire fell on it in ripples, making it seem to breathe. I wanted to touch the tender place at the back of your neck that the sun never sees. I want, I ache to touch it now.

I began to place all my lovely dishes on the table, for you, only for you. Golden fish, trembling in oil and lemon juice, white ribbons of boiled fowl sprinkled with herbs; lentils like small coins in a blue bowl. Rice and hot loaves and fresh green salads.

I knew by the way you looked at me that it was a night that I could glow. My features were composed in my face; my hair behaved, falling smooth and shiny, and my skin did not have that darkness, that heaviness that surfaces sometimes below my eyes. That night I knew I could knit our friends together as I did in my weaving, making each strand connect with the others neatly. I smiled over the chicken at Peter and he stopped scowling; Judah, when I spoke to him about his sick mother, ceased trying to steer the conversation round to revolutionary talk; and poor clumsy Matthew, when I passed him more wine, did not fuss so with his fish bones and even gave up looking so lost. I could do these things because that night I was full of peace, made strong by your proximity. And surely a woman can always be strong, for she holds the spoons and passes meat on to empty plates. She can fill and fill so much emptiness with her pans and her spoons, her hands and her eyes. There is a power in being able to give. You taught me that, in other ways; and it is true.

Sometimes you would look over the candle and its small flickering light somehow seemed to draw us closer together; you would take my face and caress it with your eyes. Outside the full moon made the sky light and blue, and the trees were painted with dark, thin strokes. Peter kept getting up and walking to the door; he would stare out into the darkness and listen. Watching him, your head fell sadly into your hand. Your mother began to weep silently, using the end of her apron to dab at her eyes. You looked at her sternly; she stopped weeping but her face was crumpled.

I see the full plate of fruit and the grapes spilling over the lip, shiny as wet stones, round as moons. The pears, the plums and pomegranates – I have polished them all for you. You take a pomegranate; anyone else would have spoiled the carefully arranged fruit: the domes, the curves and crests; but not you. You hold the pomegranate – see your hand, brown, small fingered, with a white scar where you once cut yourself deep into the thumb while carving wood. You cut into the tough shell and with your teeth peel back the skin, your teeth wincing at the chalky flavour. You open it out with your hands – a bowl of rubies. You shake and spill them into one hand and pass some to Andrew. And how they love you. All their pettiness, and even Peter's anxiety, vanishes as you say, 'Can any of us make a thing as perfect or as beautiful as one of these seeds?' And you turn the tiny square of brilliant red in the light, as though intoxicated by it – your mouth made exuberant and so lovely suddenly.

Sometimes I think that you are not dead, but have escaped to another country to continue your dream. For that is all life was to you: a dream, a dream of heaven. But there is too much filth and disease for it to blossom here. Are you waiting somewhere? O no, not for me, for the dream. Let no one take it from you. I would gladly kill for your dream.

The rain comes thick and fast, the thunder is without anger. Elizabeth will not be asleep; she will be standing by the window, waiting for the lightning. She tells me that I do not take care of my face properly anymore. Every day she bullies me with this, pointing to the unused pots of oil. Yes, I know that if I do grow old more quickly than I ought, it is my fault for allowing it. There is no one to glow for in this isolated cottage that hides at the end of an overgrown grass track and is too far from the sea; but that too is acceptable. Life changes, but not memory. There was a day when you told me not to take the pebble from the lake, 'You won't want it once it has dried. How do we know how the stones feel?' O, I know how the stones feel – cold, cold. And you, you, did you know how I felt? How I feel now?

I will think no more of you. As I lie here with my arms straight and my hands flat I wonder about Mattathias again. He would be forty-seven now; perhaps his hair is grey and his skin will have slipped under his chin? Perhaps he has forgotten me and that night he took me to his parents' house in a little village some distance from Ephraim?

We were tired and bedraggled and it was very late when he knocked at the door. There had been no time to warn his parents, but Mattathias's mother prepared food for us while her son explained things to her, her husband and his younger brother, Ben. I felt strange and shy in their house and so I said very little. His mother became very distressed when she realised that we had run away against my father's wishes, and her first thought was that I should return the next day. Mattathias then told her the whole story, and when he had finished he said firmly that the most important thing was for the two of us to be married as quickly as possible.

Mattathias's father, still rubbing his bearded face to keep himself alert, said, very sensibly, 'Won't he come after you to get his daughter back?' I then discovered that Mattathias had arranged things with Joshua so that he would tell my father that Mattathias had been asked not to come for a few days, to enable Joshua to help look for me. It sounded plausible; there was no reason for my father to suspect Mattathias.

We spent what remained of the night discussing the arrangements that had to be made. Mattathias's father obviously approved of his son's impulsiveness, but he grew weary of the details and began to doze off, only waking when his wife's voice rose and she prodded him impatiently in the side. She was concerned that the wedding might not be legal unless money was given to my father for the marriage contract. Her husband said, 'Since when has money made a marriage legal?'

She scoffed and replied crossly, 'Since always money makes every-thing legal – you're so dreamy that you don't know these things. If you ran the farm as I do you'd know better.'

Mattathias agreed to send my father an appropriate sum to com-pensate for the loss of money which would result from the broken engagement. He would, at the same time, tell my father that we had

43

been formally married – but at that point we would have to leave at great speed. I had no doubt that my father would feel entitled to some kind of retribution, but Mattathias said I should not worry as he had already thought of a place where we could go. And, it was agreed, finally, that we would be married in two days' time.

Elizabeth arrived and I greeted her with relief. She had left Jerusalem before dawn and had brought some more of my possessions and a great deal of the gossip, which was by then circulating in my father's house. It seemed that he was absolutely furious, but baffled, and had sent servants off in the direction of Galilee. In the confusion Elizabeth had managed to slip away unnoticed.

Mattathias's mother had decided to ask only a few close relations and friends to the wedding; and the servants and the dressmaker were sworn to secrecy, which is always a pointless exercise. I barely had time to think in those two hectic days. I was sewing frantically, a few more petticoats and nightdresses, though Elizabeth was doing most of the work. Mattathias's mother was hot and irritated a great deal of the time and I think she blamed me for not allowing her to enjoy her son's wedding in style and comfort; but as her sweet husband kept pointing out, it would have been the same panic and fuss even if they'd had a year to prepare. She was not unkind to me, though, and after she discovered that I had no mother she softened considerably and kept appearing with lengths of cloth and pretty trimmings. She gave me her own wedding veil, which was made of exquisite white silk embroidered with silver flowers and tiny amethysts. In each corner was stitched a little fish for fertility, picked out with tiny pearls. The house was overflowing with flowers; the cooking went on all the time and the smells of baking and spiced meat crept into all the corners. And Mattathias and I were so happy, like children before a birthday party, saying, this is how it is going to be and we shall have this, and that, and everything. The future was painted in bright colours with no clouds.

Mattathias spent hours talking to his father, but I felt that those discussions did not centre on our marriage. Soon after we arrived, when it had dawned on me that Mattathias could not return to Jerusalem and therefore his work would be over, I asked him how much this troubled him.

To my surprise he said, 'Not at all. For a long time now I have grown away from my teaching. I don't feel I can instruct with my own views so uncertain. Jerusalem sickens me, the greed, the hypocrisy. And the rich young men I am supposed to teach aren't interested. I'm glad to be out of it.'

'But what will become of us now?' I asked.

'We will go and live far from here until things have cooled down with your father. We will continue to study and read, and I will try to decide what to do about my professional future.' He seemed so certain that I believed him. It took me so long to realise how unsure and confused he really was.

But it was the month of flowers; the irises and lilies were thick on the grass and the ground was soft and only faintly dusty; we were to be married and I thought it must be the most beautiful thing in the world. Mattathias and I had decided that the ceremony should take place at night under the stars.

The moon was almost full as the guests came walking over the moonlit fields, trailing flowers, and singing. The young men gathered together around Mattathias, playing flutes and tambourines. They came to the door and knocked, and I went out. My gown had come right in the end; the silk clung to my arms and breasts and fell loosely below my waist. Elizabeth had brushed my hair a hundred times and plaited it into seventeen slim braids, leaving a few loose curls at my forehead and tying some of the braids about my head in loose coils. The rest fell freely to my shoulders and each one had a small silver coin attached to its end. The veil was placed carefully over my hair and face, and a small circle of lilies rested on my head. Mattathias stood there smiling gravely, arrayed in a white robe with a silver band around his waist and a purple robe flung over his shoulder. He looked so beautiful and calm with his smooth face and the ringlets down each side of his cheeks very long and tightly curled.

I was led to a small canopy under the trees. It was silent and the candles flickered on serious faces. Mattathias's mother stood very upright in her pale blue gown and his father looked dreamy and a little sad. I allowed myself only small peeks through the shroud of the heavy veil and tried to walk gracefully, without dropping the flowers that clung to my waist and the hem of my robe. I stopped under the canopy. Then Mattathias walked and stood beside me. I was taken and placed on his right side. We both turned our faces in the direction of Jerusalem and bowed. We sipped from the same goblet and Mattathias said, 'She is my wife and I am her husband, from this day for ever.' The words went round and round my head as we went into the garlanded room and danced and sang; as everyone got merry with wine and ceased to chafe and itch in their best clothing. There were soups, great plates of grilled fish with the best olives, chicken with sorrel, savoury ground lamb in vine leaves, roast beef, honey cakes and biscuits, sugared almonds, fruit, cheeses. And everything was cooked to perfection.

The hours sprinted by and the men began to stamp their feet and roar out all the old songs; children, with crushed clothing, fell asleep in corners, and young girls sat coyly with little beads of perspiration on their foreheads.

Then Mattathias and I left to be alone. Before the wedding, he had given me a book of instruction on the proper observance of my role as a wife – his mother had insisted. Inside he had written, 'Behold thou art fair my love, thou hast doves' eyes.' Now he gave me a silver bracelet and a pomegranate. Lastly, he gave me the wedding contract, for it was mine to keep.

We lay together in that room with polished wood on the floors, and soft couches with damask-weave cushions; and I thought as it happened – this is not as I expected. There are odours around me, falling on me; earth smells, clay and bread smells, the scent of a dead flower, of an animal in the bushes. There is a well in my body I had no knowledge of. There is fear and heat – pain. I am rippling, flowing; but my head is still. I hesitate, I stop and watch. How beautiful, how white our bodies, quivering, spilling. My head is struck off, the walls tumble, the linen darkens. And I shall rock him, rock, as the waves do the sand. His head sleeps on my belly; the moon slips over his shoulder. And now I am broken, no longer whole. I shall be broken many times. And there is a wound in me, a wound deep against the lid of my womb, making a smarting, a lingering of salt – sharp, unbearable.

We slept, and how strange to lie beside another body, to feel the warmth stealing across the sheets. I did not sleep much, but lay watching his face as the moonlight lit up his fluttering eyelids. He barely moved in his sleep, but sometimes made small, soft noises as though something in his dream had startled him. Very often and gently I leaned over to kiss his mouth.

In the morning they looked at me – but I looked back. A little later we prepared to leave and Mattathias's mother began to cry. She looked tired. She was talking to her son as he collected his books into a small pile, 'I had wanted you to live with us after your marriage,' she said sadly. 'I know this is usually offered by the bride's parents, but in the circumstances . . . We could provide for you and you could continue your studies. You will ruin your life going off this way.'

Mattathias said patiently, 'Mother, don't be foolish, we cannot stay here. Mary's father is not known for his good humour and her twin brothers have acquired a reputation as rogues and vagabonds. It is not safe.'

'Such a family to have married into,' she sighed. 'If only you would stay close to us. You are going so far away.'

'I must,' he said briskly, 'and it's what I want. I am over twenty and assume responsibility by tradition. So enough of this gloomy talk.'

His mother sat down dejectedly in a chair and said, 'You have disappointed me, Mattathias. Things have not gone as I expected of you, or for you. You have taken this girl from her family, against her father's wishes, married her hastily, and now you would sneak out of our house like a thief.'

46

'I have, at least, not discredited her.'

'Perhaps not.'

'Not perhaps.'

'Very well, but what of us?'

'What did you want? I did what was right by her and have broken no law. Nor have I brought shame on you.'

'It is not what I expected, I thought you would be near me. Things do not bode well.'

'Don't,' Mattathias said brusquely, 'I have things to do.' Then he added more gently, 'It will be all right.' But she went out of the room very upset, and when we left a little later, she could not bear to say goodbye. I was guilty for taking her son from her and felt that I did not deserve him.

You said to me once that I deserved a great love and that it would heal me. You made it clear that you were not the one. But I would not believe you.

All the way to our first home, Mattathias was telling me how the house looked and he seemed happy and relaxed to be away from everyone, embarking on a new life. We felt like adventurers, brave, witty, full of optimism. We rode at a comfortable speed, taking with us Elizabeth, of course, three male slaves and an old freedman, Jonah. We travelled west in the direction of the coast and found the village we were looking for surrounded by great long orchards of pear and apple trees fluffy with white and pink blossom. The house belonged to Mattathias's uncle, who was a physician who preferred to be known as the beekeeper. This uncle was away in Alexandria for a year, looking into a new species of bee, and we were therefore able to take advantage of his empty house.

The house – I loved it from the start. It was small, flat-looking and surrounded by willow trees and one stately old cedar. The walls of the house were peeling a little and were yellowish in colour because they had not been white-washed that year. A purple creeper had taken over one side of the house and its star-shaped leaves went up the walls in dense layers. We went round to the back of the house, where plump red chickens fussed and squawked in the mud and a cat balanced sleepily on a wall. The back garden was rectangular, with low clay walls that supported the branches of a young pear tree; and at the end of this was a neat vegetable patch. In one corner of the garden, a little way off, was a primitive-looking hut, from whence emerged a scruffy man with puffed up eyes and a most unwelcoming expression. He would not be convinced of our identity until Mattathias had passed over a generous supply of wine. His name was Abraham and he looked after the bees and chickens. He showed us around the property. There was an unused dairy, with an old wooden churn that had turned quite white with use. Broken forks littered the corners and old nets and bee-masks hung on the walls. On the other side of the house lived the chickens, in a large, dilapidated old barn with dark beams and a disgusting floor made treacherous by chicken dung. From time to time, a chicken would swoop down from a high beam and alight on one of our heads.

We were told that our nearest neighbour was a farmer – who cared so little for the opinions of others that he had married a Syrian. Just outside the dreary little village which we had passed through on our way lived a physician who actually practised the profession. Perhaps there had not been enough sickness for two doctors, and he had pushed Mattathias's uncle out? But the area was not sparsely populated, and there were extensive cornfields and orchards as far as the eye could see. We were then taken to the bees, but only at a distance. They ruled over a well-kept plot of land with high walls covered with flat climbing roses which had a delicious scent. Through a locked gate we observed swarms of bees in frantic activity. They lived in beautiful hives made of polished cedar wood and decorated with carved flowers; and in the centre was a stone bowl of water on a tall pedestal. Abraham told us that we were on no account to go into the bees, as they were all at that time in a highly tense, excitable state of mind.

Elizabeth set to work on the inside of the house and a cook was sent for from the village. She only remained with us for one day, however, as she was surly and refused to use the dairy. She was replaced by a scrupulous young cook who had worked for Mattathias's uncle before and understood our orthodox ways to the finest detail. I was very happy to be the lady of the house at last and began planning meals and cleaning operations for the slaves.

In the mornings when I woke, Mattathias was always gone. I knew that he sat in the garden with his hand curled under his cheek and a small smile at his mouth. Yet I felt often at this hour an intangible unquiet that seemed caught like the wind in trees. It caused me to pull at the soft cloth of my nightdress, sensing pain somewhere. Why must he be gone when I woke? When the wind blew benignly through the window and filled my eyes with sunlight? But I pushed these brief nameless fears behind me, leaping out of bed and throwing my light dress over my head, waiting for Elizabeth to brush my hair and oil my face, hands and feet with the fragrant olive oil I had brought from Jerusalem. I filled every room with flowers; I made sure that everything was spotless and gleaming; that sprays of rosemary hung in the linen cupboards and that the pantries were filled with freshly-ground flour and new cheese and butter.

'Have you become such a housewife that you've lost interest in your studies?' Mattathias asked one day as we walked arm in arm

48

through the orchards under the dripping blossom. I hadn't. Now that my house was in order I was eager to get back to work.

I loved the weeks that followed in the little house set back against the willows. Mattathias read and prayed in the morning and later walked back and forth at the top of the garden where the orchards began. I worked quietly under an apple tree, where he had set up a table for me. Every day I wrote him a letter in Greek. I was supposed to put down my thoughts about points of religion and morality, things we had discussed together. But, as the days passed, I wrote and the morning filled the paper: the birds' hubbub in the bushes, the maid hurrying with the bucket full of steaming peelings to the trough, where they would release a wet mist and a damp odour. The song of the raven, so urgent, the notes shrill and final. The dark smell of meat on the spit; the gentle smell of fruit splitting and softening in pans. And in the kitchen, the maid singing her sad Egyptian lament, a song from the Exile.

I can still see the light on the curved grain of the table; the sharp purple of the creeper rising up the white wall. And he, walking in the sunshine towards me, his face serious and thoughtful. I look at his slightly toppled cheekbone on the right side of his face which, when he frowns, gives him an enquiring look. I jump up and kiss him all over his face, his eyes, the dark mat of his wild hair. He holds me back, laughing, saying, 'Enough of this, we are supposed to be working . . .' but still laughing – until he begins to read my letter and his face goes quiet. When he has finished, he looks at me with admiration – and how it pleases me – I who am so afraid of frowns. He says, 'You have a way with words, they respond to you.' And, neatly in the margin he writes the corrections for me to copy.

'Come with me into the orchard,' I breathed, tugging at his arm, longing to lie with him on the earth. And the lessons were forgotten as we discovered each other, as I felt the same need to consume his body as I had to consume his mind. We lived so completely off our passion that all else seemed to pall, but at the same time all things had for me a new vitality, a beauty I needed to express. The next day I would settle down to my Greek writing again and try to keep to serious subjects, but always I would find myself sliding back into the real, pulsing world around me.

Having found such a gentle, clever husband, I began to find more favour with myself. He helped me to trust my beauty, for he always touched my fingers and my ears as though they were precious; and he made me feel wise when he admired my phrases. Sometimes, in the deep lull of the night, I would wake and see him looking out of the window. I would get out of bed and stand beside him, saying nothing, but feeling most clearly a restlessness in him.

'Are you becoming bored with our little existence?' I would finally have to ask, because I could not bear to think a thing and not have it answered.

'No, it is not that, don't think that,' he would say gruffly, pulling my head against his arm. What was it? He never said; I never knew, because always he would sense my hurt and take me back to bed and comfort me.

Then he began to write more each day. He said that he was trying to sift out some convictions by putting down all his views on paper. I spent more time alone, happy, walking by the cornfields away from our land, gathering thistles with edges as sharp as spears and white wild flowers with flopping heads and great blue eyes. When it grew cold, I would draw the green cloak about me, listening to the twigs cracking under my feet, and go home to fill more bowls with my flowers.

Sometimes, when he looked up and saw me coming back from my walk, he would gasp and his face would look suddenly humble. 'How lovely you are,' he would whisper almost sadly. My neck was long and white, without one line. It curved languidly into my throat, falling its long distance without haste; not propping, but lifting my face. For what is a head, or an intelligent face, if it is brought low by a lazy neck?

Today, I cannot remember my face; the colour of my eyes. I need to be told. Long ago, something pounced on my opinion of myself and flattened it. O long before you, you would not have been so cruel, but you told the truth always and that can be very cruel.

In those days, as a young bride, Mattathias was all that I needed. I was constantly excited, as though each day would bring a surprise, each flower produce a pearl. I had found a warm side of myself through him and I wanted nothing more than to fall asleep each night hearing his breath.

One day, he watched me pack shiny black olives into jars – closely as my mother had taught me, shaking them down into the small pockets of space, but not bruising them with a fingernail; then flooding the little spaces between the olives with a light olive oil. He helped me to bind on the covers and then said, in his slow sedulous way, 'If I act, if I give my life to action, ordinary everyday actions, there will be no possibility to explore, to probe, to reach profound depths of understanding.' I did not understand what he was struggling to tell me, because I was dreaming of our children: my daughter, beautiful with her sewing; my son ploughing new fields – because all things must continue as they always have. And seeing my thought was not with his, he would stop. Because he did not need the smiles of others to bring him to life; he was complete in solitude.

He said, lying on the grass with his chin tilted and his eyes squinting up at the sun, 'Think of the peasants all around us, each day organised, each day full of busyness; following the seasons, paying homage to them, and working, working. No time for thought.'

I said what was in my mind – how odd it sounded on that bright afternoon – 'You are the winter.'

He looked at me, strangely, deeply, and perhaps he was a little afraid. He said nervously, 'Your sentences, sometimes they are so odd, sometimes the thoughts you mix together, they jar.' He laughed, 'It's nothing, very often the effect is beautiful.' He lay back on the grass with his eyes closed. I could not get into his head and at the real thoughts that lay behind his words. He was remote, cool and quiet. And I, I felt a burning, a full passion that was almost a fury. I took his hand and bit his finger so that he cried out. I held his hand softly and began to lick down the sides of his long fingers. He shuddered, and in his eyes he looked trapped.

Then, later, in the mornings he ceased writing. He spent hours seated in the shade with his Septuagint in front of him; but often he did not look at it for hours. The brief spring was over; summer came in, blown on a hot wind; the slaves began to grumble and were slow in their work; the sun shone more harshly each day. Mattathias took to reading inside in the early mornings, and when I rested at midday he did not lie down with me as he had done before. He went into his uncle's study and there I found him often, praying or meditating. He no longer read any Greek with me and our lessons were confined to the Scriptures. I did not question any of this; I only wanted to please. He seemed very quiet; but to me he was even more gentle, more careful than he had ever been.

On most days, I walked along the edge of the olive groves when the sun had lost its sting. The grass was parched and beginning to turn grey; the fruit trees drooped under their load and in the village they were already reckoning how many fruit pickers would be needed for the fruit gathering. I looked for the biggest, most radiant poppy, and when I had found it I placed it carefully in my mother's press between her old muslin. It is still there: I have never pressed another flower since then. I remember how flowers bored you – it upset me.

It had been a sultry day, with more flies and gnats than usual. I was tired; I felt unhappy and could not say why. I went to say goodnight to Mattathias, who was at the other end of the house, in the study. He was calm and seemed less preoccupied that night. I looked at him for a long time from the door, then went back and kissed him twice on each side of his throat and under his chin. He held my face and smiled, 'Are you all right?' I nodded, feeling miserable. He looked down again at his paper and I was struck by the way he lifted his hand to write – a perfect movement.

No air stirred in the bedroom; the wallflower petals had fallen to the floor; my hair clung damply to my forehead. I let it down, brushed it slowly and then scraped it tightly up to the top of my head in a knot. My thoughts were dishevelled and I grew weary of them. I got into bed and slept immediately.

My hand, just now, circled the loose head of a rose. I squeezed and pressed it until my palm was tinged a faint red. I am afraid. You must help me. These petals are malignant, as are my thoughts; and I don't want to, don't want to think anymore. Only to forget, forget. Torn petals are all about me. I have pulled each one apart, slowly, painfully, into fragments turning purple. There is a wet, bruised smell. When you saw me like this, with this wild look in my face – I know without looking it is there – your fingers would press into my arm. I can almost feel them now, pressing, hurting. The effect is the same – slowly I grow calmer. Stay with me, stay.

No cry woke me; no animal in the bushes; not even the owl's wings sweeping aside the hot air. I heard feet stumbling through the darkness, dragging across the floor. In the small light, I saw Matthias leaning against the door. He moved forward, his feet sounding not his own. A sick fear rose in me. I sat up. 'What is it?' He did not answer, just shuffled slowly towards me. I reached for the candle and groped at the wick which had sunk into the wax.

Mattathias stood by me; I looked at his face in the candlelight: it was white, horrified; his teeth clenched together, his jaw shuddering. 'For God's sake, what is it?' I cried again.

He rocked slowly and began to recite darkly, 'An eye for an eye.' Then, 'I have killed a man for a wound, a child for a bruise.' I wanted to scream at the dreamy ghostliness of his face. He slumped to the floor and I began to shake him wildly, asking, asking.

His voice spilled, 'Your brothers were here, those two.' And then dreamily, 'They came to avenge you.' Thick red drops falling slowly, heavily. 'They quoted the Scriptures at me.' He moved away from me, managed to get to his feet and staggered to the bed, falling backwards on to it. There was about him that red-raw smell – blood in the hills. I watched his stomach as it rose, stopped, then fell in regular patterns. I could feel the pain in each breath. I was stuck in my panic but a voice screamed in my stomach, somewhere deep down a mouth opened and howled. His eyes did not stir and the waves of breath rose and fell, rose and fell, while below him the blood slowly seeped, covering his thighs. I knew then – and screamed; beating my hands against my face, running from the room, into the passageway. Elizabeth shaking me, the words garbled, hysterical. She went running to the door for the doctor, her hair flying behind her. I went back to the bed and his hand touched me. Sorrow shook me with both hands; my mind split like a nut. I buried my face in his neck and wailed. His hand rose and touched my hair lightly; then his fingers stiffened, pushing into my skull with excruciating shudders.

My hands are cold now and I want to weep, for him, for you; for such pain as you both have known. And I have only watched. His face that I had forgotten, it is crying to come back. That night, when the air was clammy, I could only bend and kiss his lips, keeping them warm, feeling the breath still coming weakly. The doctor, panting, pushed me away, putting his hands on the stained linen. No, don't touch him, no, please. I spun my face around; I fainted.

He lay so quietly in that white bed, for days not a word, his face formless as sand, his hands hidden beneath the sheet. Saffron rays of sun fell on the bed, and his face was grey. I knelt beside him all the time, waiting, forgetting even to brush my hair or change my clothes. Day after day nothing altered; my head would flop on to the sheets, Elizabeth would tug at me; the doctor would come and reply to my question in the same way, 'Who can say, we must wait and pray. So much blood.' And that phrase pawed at my brain hour after hour – 'so much blood, so much blood, so much blood.'

He opened his eyes one morning very early; the dawn blue was like moonlight as he moved a fraction on the pillow, then went still. Two days later he woke with a great scream. And I began to moan and whimper and my hands would not stop shaking nor my teeth stop chattering. His eyes looked at me flatly for a long while.

'Do you remember?' finally I forced myself to ask.

'I remember,' he said, and the tears leaked from his eyes, making tracks down his cheeks. I pushed my head into his shoulder; but there was no relief in his being alive because of the great grief in us. I learned, for the first time, what grief really was; and this time I could not delude myself. I had tasted grief and I knew that it was endless: a taste, bitter as aloes, that would never leave my mouth.

As the days melted limply into one another, each noon more cumbrous than the last, his face gradually took up a little colour. I watched him as I would study the cup of a flower unfold, waiting for the golden centre. But the bud never unfolded, the growth was arrested and something old and forlorn clung to him. He hardly spoke to me, but lay beneath a blue cover like a mad, moody beast, his face turned away from the light. Sometimes we spoke quickly of other things, ashamed of the unspeakable. But once when I was leaving the room, he whispered hotly to me, 'Each day I wait, thinking my voice will rise high and shrill from my throat.' And I ran back to him, flinging myself across him, grinding my nails into my hand; wanting to mutilate all the world for his mutilation, wanting to rip at myself in my agony.

Days passed breathlessly; I watched the swallows turn in the sky; and from the field in the distance the scent of the harvest wafted – the sticky golden odour of wheat. The colours of the flowers were violent:

the red flames of the poinsettia, the scarlet-tipped hibiscus, and every-where those bright flowering shrubs smothered with blooms.

In the midst of the harvest season, I noticed a change in Mattathias. He seemed to grow cool in the wilting heat, his face softened and his eyes did not stare with that blighted frown. Then he had a visitor. It was at the time of day when the flies are exhausted by their frenzied activity and take to the walls. When the glare seems to rise and settle on the rooftops with real hostility. The visitor would not allow his feet to be washed and insisted on being taken directly to Mattathias. I tried to keep him a moment, to explain; but he told me curtly that he knew everything – Mattathias had written to him. I could feel how he disliked me; his small cold eyes scrutinised me with blame. His hatred wounded me, as did the fact that I had no idea that Mattathias had written to him. I took him to Mattathias and left to get refreshments. When I returned with the maid, who began pouring the drinks, they were deep in conversation. Their hunched backs seemed to say that my presence was not wanted.

The visitor, Saul, stayed the night but he exchanged few words with me and took his meals in Mattathias's room. Normally I did, but although Mattathias asked me to stay, I declined. Saul stayed one more night and the interminable discussions continued. It seemed like a conspiracy: all I heard was a deep buzz behind a closed door. The next morning, Saul left at dawn, not taking his leave of me. His face stayed in my mind, with its heavy eyebrows and the little puckered lines on each side of his mouth, as you see on old people. When he had gone, Mattathias said, 'Forgive me for being preoccupied with him, I know you didn't like him.'

'There is something vicious about him,' I said angrily.

'Yes, I think you're right. But I have known him a long time. I met him first in Jerusalem. He has lived a reclusive life for the past four years, with a community by the Dead Sea.'

'O I'm not surprised – one of those lot.'

'You say it scornfully,' he remarked, 'why is that?'

'Well, they think themselves the chosen ones, don't they? The only ones who really understand and live by the Law.'

'They believe that our society, and the priesthood, is corrupt, certainly. But so do I.'

'But what do they do about it? It's just sterile to hide away in those caves praying and washing. What will come of that?'

'Action is an offence,' he said quietly. 'We are a people who hardly ever act. For centuries we have accepted foreign domination without fighting it.'

'That's not so – what of the Maccabees? And all the risings in Galilee?'

'There are always exceptions, but in our case not many. We cannot take on Rome, it would be ridiculous to try; but too many of our holy men have turned their coats altogether and actually plot to help oppress the people for their own gain. So there's no way to fight the priesthood, because to fight them is again to take on Rome.'

'Ah, but you are a Pharisee and the Pharisees have everyone's confidence. You could do something . . .'

'I have been a Pharisee,' he said dejectedly. 'That too is over.'

We were silent for a while as the room filled slowly with the morning light and I heard the maids busy with buckets in the kitchen. I got up and sat close to Mattathias, grateful to have him to myself again. He took up my hand and began tracing the lines on my palm with his finger.

'I have made a decision,' he said breathlessly. When he had said it I realised that I had known something was to happen, something horribly to alter. He got up and went to stand by the window. His back seemed flexed; his neck looked very stiff.

'I am going away.' He did not turn to look.

'I am going to join Saul's community.' I waited; my stomach rose; all thought ceased, only his words roared in my brain. I waited, but he said nothing more. Cool went my heart; I told my voice to speak softly, 'Then you are going for ever?'

'What is for ever? where is it?' his voice quivered but his back was strong as a wall. I turned and sat on a low couch, rubbing my hands.

'Why?' I asked, counting my breaths.

'Why? – you ask me that?' His voice was thick with a sudden wrath, 'I am not a man, not a husband, not . . .'

I interrupted him, my voice shrill, 'I don't care. It was my fault, I am to blame. Without me it wouldn't have happened.'

'I care, I care,' he shouted. 'Don't you see how I care?' His voice sunk, 'The dream is ended, all dreams are ended.'

I pleaded, 'Don't go, don't leave. You are the only one who ever saw me . . .'

At last his back slumped. His head lifted slowly and his voice was dreamy, 'How many hours have gone by since it happened? And each one was filled with the same thought: things happen for a reason, you cannot fight the consequences. I don't even want to. This is what I want. I want it soon, soon – before my skin softens, my voice . . .' And then his fist flew into the wall with the sound of a whip; he gave a small soft groan. I ran to him; he turned away, clutching his fist; his shoulders bent.

I touched his shoulder and he spun round, his hands biting into my arms, and mercifully I could think of the pain of only that for a moment.

'Listen, listen carefully,' he said. 'There is no way back. A little time with you, a little time to think and love. It is over. I will go to

55

the Salt Sea and live a life of prayer and study. I wanted that, even before I did want that. When I could, had the chance to act, it was not enough. Now I want to live in my mind, to find the truth of things. And you, you must have someone to take care of you, to make you smile, give you children.'

'And where do I find such a person?' dully I asked. I began to cry, tears tickling my cheeks hotly.

'Do you think I will just leave you here and go?' he demanded.

'What will you do with me?'

His arms came around me and he rocked me, rubbing his face in my hair. 'O I am sorry, so sorry. You talk so coldly, and your face, your face – you are so beautiful. I cannot . . .' He released me gently and walked away. He stood by the door a few moments with his back to me. Very quietly, very deliberately and without turning, he said, 'In ten days I must be gone.'

Ten days. I remember each one. I can see myself sitting on that couch watching him go. Then I ran to the window and watched him leave the house and walk past the chickens, up the garden and into the orchard. Sometimes he would stop and almost turn. Then he disappeared into the trees and the sheen of the day stole him from me. He did not return for many hours. When I next saw him I was stiff and tight-lipped. I did not want to be near him and went for a long walk, though the heat was unbearable and all things that afternoon looked dry, dusty and without pity. I kicked at the dust and felt very angry and humiliated. I would not show him my pain; if he was going to desert me then let him do it soon. Later, I walked slowly home.

He was sitting in the study, his face half in shadow.

'When do you go then?' I asked coldly. His face came round to look at me, slowly, 'I told you, in ten days.'

'Perhaps you would rather go sooner?' He did not reply.

'We must talk about these things,' I said purposefully, 'there are lots of things to discuss. What are your exact plans?'

He walked up to me quickly and sat down, making me sit beside him. 'Do not be this way,' he said simply.

'I'll be whatever way I choose.'

'Very well. What do you want to talk about?'

'My future, for a start.'

'What do you feel you would like to do?' he asked humbly.

'O, so *I* am to be considered now, am I?'

'I had to make my decision on my own,' he said, 'you couldn't help me, you might even have persuaded me to do the wrong thing.'

'The wrong thing? So it's the right thing, is it, to desert a wife for a bunch of cranks?'

'Don't speak like that. I've never seen you angry and it doesn't become you.'

'What does become me then? What plans do you have for me?'

'Perhaps we should talk about it another time. You are hurt and angry. I understand. You can hit me if it will make you feel any better.' He was calm, he was remote, he was infuriating. And I was so young, so bruised; and worst of all – so innocent of his feelings.

I ran off and hid in the laundry room where I battered my head against the wall and bit the insides of my lips until they bled. Then I began to think of our short life together. Every memory seemed perfect: each meal I had prepared and cooked for him; our long conversations at night, when he told me about his life before we'd met. Each kiss seemed softer suddenly, each caress more tender. And I realised that I'd been living in a state of shock since that night – that night when my brothers came with knives and carved into him. For her sake, they said – cutting – a tooth for a tooth, dishonour for dishonour. O the sickness of it, the pity of it.

We had never spoken of it, not once. I had never even allowed myself to imagine it. I began to do so now. All I could think of was the pain, the knives, the blood, our tears, our silence. I could not think of the reality, the detail – my mind drew a bolt at that. He would never tell me anything about what had happened and I would never ask him. And since that time, I had waited and watched, my dreams reserved, but nothing had changed for me. And he, he had been chewing on the shreds of his life, trying to force a decision out of emptiness. He had faced up to the violence and its aftermath; I had never even allowed myself to think of the nature of his injury – when that surfaced, I hid – in pain, guilt, anger; in pity, for him, for me – but always, always, the reality was held at bay.

That night, we had dinner in silence and immediately afterwards he went to the study. I walked up and down in my room, tried to sew, put down the cloth and paced the room again. I wanted to speak to him; my mind was brimming with the things I wanted to say. I prepared a speech, went through it once, twice: Mattathias, I know how you feel (how could I?). And again, I wanted to say: I do not care. It does not matter. Stay here, study here. We can manage. You need not teach. I will take care of you. Just wait a little, see what happens. Ten days, ten days and one is nearly over. Stay, wait. I will give anything, anything. I would go to him and say these things – when it was a bit darker, when the house was still – then I would go. The house grew silent, the sky outside inky. Still I did not go. I gave myself more time – when I had tidied my hair, finished the seam on the cloth. I did none of these things; and I did not go.

When he came to bed I was sitting with my back to the door and my arms knotted about my ribs. It was very late and I had been crying for three hours and he had not come. My face felt huge and gross; my eyes smarting slits. He walked round so that he could see me.

'What are you doing?' His voice was puzzled.

I began to rock myself, gently back and forth. Then I cried out, 'Why didn't you come? Why didn't you come? I have waited for hours.'

'I thought you would not want to see me. I felt your hatred and kept away.'

'But I needed you. Why didn't you come?' my voice stretched to tearing.

'I didn't know. You were so cold, so angry. How could I know?' He sounded crushed, confused.

'But it's *you* who have decided to go,' I shrieked. He sat down, his head flopped forward.

'When I first told you, it was a relief. After the hell, the doubts, the questions and the hopelessness – it was a relief. And now there is a void growing.' He shook me suddenly, 'God, what could I do? What choice did I have? I am forced away from you.'

'You said you were already moving in that direction,' I reminded him dumbly.

'Don't read things into what I say. I merely said that I was moving towards a non-secular life before this happened, but I could have had that, and you.'

'You still can.'

'No.'

'If you don't want it.'

'It's not possible.'

'Why not?'

'All right, if you insist. I will go through it,' he said, but I saw the pain in his face, the dread, and I said, 'No, leave it, it will only hurt you.'

'Perhaps I must.' He walked away from me. 'I have become un-natural, like a freak flower, a woman without breasts. You do not want to think of me this way. You will not think of me as I am so I must make you. I have nothing to offer you. If I remained, my life would be spent selfishly, in isolation.'

'But still you would be here,' I put in quickly.

'It would be meaningless; we would only become bitter. I would grow hideous to you.' I turned my face away from the brutal images he forced on me.

'But I love you,' he said quietly.

My body began to melt and flow again. I felt for the first time the cramps in my crossed legs, the ache where my arms had hugged my ribs so fiercely. My face seemed to soften from its bloated ugliness; my mouth felt warm and real again.

'Then it's all right,' I whispered, moving to him and taking his head in my arms. He began to weep, and for an hour he did not stop shaking and the tears fell like hot wax down my body. But now it was simple for me. I accepted it: I knew that he would go and that there was nothing else he could do.

And I wanted something more beautiful, more tender for us than we had known with our bodies. I wanted each day to pass serenely, each hour to trickle by with a softness and a purity that would remain with us always. And it is so, for I can see each of those remaining days as though they were views from a high hill on a clear morning.

I woke the next day and kissed his face a hundred times. I brought him pears and melon, and washed his face with scented towels. I put on a beautiful dress and Elizabeth covered my head with curls bound with silk ribbons. We walked up to the orchard and lay under the trees. All things were suspended. The day was sacred. We spoke as though we had just met and knew nothing of one another. He read *Oedipus*, but I stopped him. I wanted to stay so close, so tight with him – so that in the dry days ahead I could drink the memories. But, under that great apple tree, my body ached for him. And I would have broken but for the desperate determination that all things must be perfect, lucent for him. So I lay there holding his hand, telling him stories about Joshua and me as children. When I stopped speaking, a pain would begin to creep from my stomach to my eyes and tears would diffuse the leaves shimmering in sunlight; the flashes of silver; the sky like flax-flowers sprinkled with milk. He lay his head on my belly and fell asleep; the noises in the grass subsided; a wind blew his hair back from his eyes, and I did not dare move my cramped hand for fear of disturbing his sleep.

The next day he woke earlier than I. It was a magnificent day; the sky had put on a performance just for us. The sun made slow entrances from between plump white clouds; the poplar trees gleamed, washed clean by last night's rains. Mattathias went and bathed, and from that day onwards he bathed every morning and every evening, as did the sect that he was to join. He also began to wear only white and he ate very little and drank no wine.

That day, I began to stitch a new pair of slippers for him. I did not think what floors his feet would tread in them; I only thought that he needed a new pair of slippers and that they must be the most beautiful pair he had ever owned. The cook had acquired for me two strips of leather. I oiled and buffed them until they were soft as silk and then stitched them to the thick cloth that formed the upper part of the slippers. This cloth I had embroidered with golden bees, which I had been observing closely so that no mistakes should be made.

When they were finished they were very beautiful, and he looked sad taking them from me. And now I know that where he went he was required always to walk bare-footed.

When he was praying or reading, I would write feverish little notes of love to him; filled with a thought that had flitted through my mind, or some sight that pleased me in the garden. Often the paper was crowded with memories – of Jerusalem, our first lessons in Greek, quotations from books, our wedding, the warm nights – but when I got to those I stopped abruptly, as though I had bitten my tongue. I would sprinkle fine ash on the ink and blow it off, watching the blue whoosh of it in the air. These notes were placed always just outside the closed door of the room he happened to be in. He never replied to them. After all this time, still that hurts me. I am unable to dispense with old injuries.

Then, from my writing table I would go to the kitchen and pound almonds until they were as fine as sand; breaking eggs and beating them into the corn-flour until beads of moisture formed on my fore-head, and my dress was spattered with little stains. Elizabeth remonstrated about all the extra washing and managed to tie back my curls with a yellow scarf before they dripped into the cooking. She would watch me pouring the honey from a great height into a bowl and smile indulgently as I sucked at the apricot stones. Mattathias ate very little of the cakes I baked for him, and often I felt that he only did it to avoid hurting me. Each day was filled with a flurry of activity: extravagant plans which I threw myself into with febrile enthusiasm – always thrusting myself on to the next and the next, to try to avoid the cold catchings of my heart. I think of myself; small, slim, there I stand biting my finger, horribly frightened; always spinning myself in circles one way or the other – poor little thing.

I would find him often in the garden looking over the gate at the bees pirouetting in the sunlight. His face, daily, took on a more lean, chiselled look. He did not speak a great deal, but smiled often, softly. On some days, however, usually late at night when he seemed afraid to go to bed, he would talk about purity and ritual; the complications of the laws and how the Sadducees twisted them for their own con-venience. These conversations became so convoluted that they left me baffled – it all seemed to come down to interpretation. Listening to him, I felt that he was too lofty, too fine for me; I could see it in the tranquil expression of his eyes. Once, when I confessed that I was lagging behind his theory, he smiled so engagingly that it seemed as though nothing had happened, and he said, 'Nonsense, you under-stand very well and cut through things better than I can.' Later, when he was walking with me, he said also, 'One day you will under-stand that I am happy just to wait for the Teacher, the Messiah.'

Looking at him sadly, a little in mockery I said, 'But the end of the world is so long to wait; there is always someone to say it will be tomorrow, but it never is.'

'We have been promised, we can only wait,' was his reply.

'O,' I said crossly, not wishing to be cross, wanting him always to remember me without my quick irritations, but being irritated all the same, 'some say that he has been already – Teachers, Messiahs – they are always with us and when they die their followers always claim that they are raised from the dead.' (It chills me to think of my words.) Then I saw his face; he looked disappointed, and I could not bear to let him down, because this was his dream. So I moved closer to him, to quell my sudden terror of the shrinking hours.

And I began to see how, once his decision had been made, there must have been a great distance between us in his mind. He smiled sweetly at my gifts and the care that I lavished hourly on him, but he had gone a little; he watched me rather than participated. He was so strong, or so he seemed to be.

'Have you left me already?' my voice was almost inaudible.

'No, I am full of you, heavy with you.' His voice shattered and slid into his chest.

Can you see me? Walking in the garden, stirring in the kitchen, a permanent smile on my lips; full of Mattathias, his needs; running to sit beside him with my sewing as he reads. How well I played my game. Only brief moments of panic or sadness crept in when I was foolish enough to forget what I was playing. There came a time when he ended the game by saying, 'Come, now we must sit together quietly and talk about what you should do when I have gone.'

'No, not now,' I said quickly, listening intently to the flop of the ripe pear hitting the ground.

'Now, we must do it now,' he insisted.

'Yes, you are right, then we can forget about it.'

He frowned and said, 'I will discuss these plans with Jonah as well. He is about to take a letter for me and I want to be here when he returns with a reply.'

'Yes,' I said meekly, 'what am I to do?' He looked closely at me and his brow furrowed, then he began to detail carefully for me what I should do; I had to force myself to listen.

'When I have gone,' he began.

'O do stop saying that,' I interrupted.

'Very well, but this is what you should do when the time comes.' How remote he looked; already he had prepared himself for a solitary journey, a bleak destination. 'Everything will be arranged and settled. If all goes according to plan, you must leave here with Elizabeth and Jonah and go up the road towards Gaba to a place on the outskirts of Galilee.' When he said Galilee, my heart perked up and I smiled at him, thinking he had chosen Galilee because I loved

61

it so. And just to think of the name – Galilee – it seemed so soft that I could almost rest my cheek on it. And now and for ever Galilee will have your name added to it, and I cannot think of one without the other.

'Not actually in Galilee – very close,' he continued. 'There is a family there that I know well, at least, I know the sons well. The eldest, who is somewhat older than I, is a widower with two young children. The other son, about my age, is the one I am closest to. We studied together in Jerusalem, but he went back to the country and is a wood sculptor now. I have not seen him for some time, but I saw Simon, the elder brother, only a few months ago when he asked me if I would consider instructing his young son. I was heavily committed at the time, and the boy in any case was too young. Now, what I have done is this: I have suggested that you go and live with the family and be taken on as a teacher for the boy. I have said that this would be a temporary arrangement; that you wanted to leave Jerusalem to avoid being pressured into a bad marriage.'

I was silent, watching the moving curves of his forehead and the straight line of his nose. His words disturbed my reverie. 'Now,' he said urgently, 'it is vital that they do not know that you are married.'

I woke from my dream. 'Why not?' I asked sharply.

'Because a married woman would arouse great suspicion, as would a widow, which was the alternative that I considered. A young woman, however, just coming for a short spell, is perfectly acceptable. It also means that you would be paid something, not much, but something, for teaching the boy, and would not be a dependent.'

'It seems strange,' I began gloomily.

'No, not really,' he insisted, 'there is no reason why you should not teach; women do in Jerusalem, occasionally.'

'But do they teach boys?'

'I don't know, but it does not matter. I have told them that you are well educated. When the boy is older, he will obviously need a man to instruct him. You could give the little girl lessons too – remember they have no mother.' He began to plead, 'Look, they will not be suspicious, unless you make them.'

'No,' I said, finding myself barely able even to follow his words, 'I will not make them suspicious.'

'I'll be quite truthful with you,' Mattathias mumbled, with a tinge of shame in his voice, 'I would hope that you would remain there a long time.' I turned to the window where it was growing dark among the trees. 'I would hope that you might marry Simon. I have great respect for him and . . .'

I jumped up at that and said that it was out of the question, and anyway, I was married already, had he gone mad? Very quietly he said, 'Mary, I am going to divorce you.' He looked at my stunned face, took my hand and whispered, 'I must. It's only a legal formality. Grounds for divorce are not necessary – I have known men to divorce a wife if she is just a slovenly cook.' The words sped off his tongue, as though he was so familiar with them that they contained no barbs. 'Unfortunately, as a woman, you may not divorce me. It does not work in reverse.'

I was speechless and sat down, staring at him, wringing my hands together; all my bones growing cold and rigid. He came and sat beside me, taking my hands and forcing them apart, 'Mary, you must re-marry and live a good, full life. Of course I must divorce you, you see that, don't you? You must be free. But they should not know that you are a divorced woman; in a small village like the one you are going to, you would be a target for acrimony and jealousy. You are too beautiful not to arouse envy.'

He had decided everything – how capable he seemed; I watched him, wondering. There was no point in saying anything; there was, in any case, no alternative. I had no home, no family, no one I could turn to.

'I must tell you also,' he said, and his voice was very humble and sad, 'that I will tell Samuel the truth. He's the younger brother. I trust him utterly and if he were not married, as he must be by now – he was betrothed two Passovers ago – I would entrust you to him rather than Simon. He will help you in any event. And it's important for someone to know the truth, so that there will be someone you can talk to about what has happened here. Mary,' he pleaded, 'you say nothing, you sit there stiffly, rubbing your fingers. I have tried to do the best I can. I know it is meagre, shabby, you deserve far more. But it is all I can do. I can't be responsible for you myself, so I must entrust you to someone else. It is just as painful for me.'

I was angry and hurt at the same time. I did not trust my mouth to say the right things, so I sat there looking down, feeling my head fill with blood and my eyes with tears. Then I got up and went and sat quite still in my room for some hours. I began reciting Psalm 4 to myself, repeating, time and time again, 'Commune with your own heart and be still.' And be still, and be still. I went to sleep; and in the morning, while he bathed, I continued to sew his slippers.

It was nearing the last days of the month of harvest. The messenger came running to announce that the moon was full; there was to be a feast in the village that night.

Mattathias and I walked down the hill to the village square in the cool of the day; I held his arm like a wife and lifted the hem of my long creamy dress that Elizabeth had just finished. All the villagers were gathered about, busily setting up tables. Horses and little carts came in from the outside farms; children danced in circles, singing loudly; and a blind man, with filthy clothes and running sores, was chased away by a priest. The young men were throwing down dry manure and splashing it with water. Then they stamped it with their feet to make a circular floor, hard and dust-free, for the dancing girls. Mothers fussed at their children and began piling the tables high with roast meats; bread and honey cakes; cheeses and the best fruit and vegetables.

We were shy, Mattathias and I, but they were kind to us; and our neighbour, without his wife, brought over a flask of wine and stood with us under an oak tree. The young girls, dressed in flowing white robes, came slowly down the hill, singing; while the young men moved into little groups and began to talk boisterously. The girls walked on to the prepared floor and waited for the music. Then they danced, looking like graceful reeds swept this way and that by a river; and I wanted to be there, right in the centre – curving my body into those sweet notes, stretching my arms as they did – blossoms falling from my hair. But instead I sat quietly watching them, beside Mattathias, asking him whether he were not tired – was there something I could bring him?

It grew dark suddenly and torches were lit. The young girls sat demurely at their mothers' sides, sipping wine and looking coyly out of the corners of their eyes at the staring young men. Voices got loud and faces pinked; the women cooled themselves with straw fans and exchanged confidences with people from the outlying farms. They talked of their children; their dreams and hardships; the preparations that must begin soon for the Ingathering, and the never-ending work of it all. I listened, envying them their stability; the confident way that they swung their little children on to their hips and settled them to sleep with the smoothing of a hand.

But Mattathias was becoming restless, so we slipped away. The moon was full and proud in the sky, chasing the clouds away with a majestic glare. The notes of a lyre playing softly made us walk slowly, as though reluctant to move into the silence ahead of us. And then a rough voice began to sing a harvest song, and all the voices took it up until the night trembled with the melody. Mattathias stood quite still, like an animal listening in the woods; then we walked on.

By the time we reached home, I was drowsy. I sat on my stool, undid my comb and felt my hair tumble down to my knees. Mattathias stood behind me and took the brush from my hand. He began to brush my hair, as he had done so often before. With a harsh movement he stopped, throwing down the brush; and, turning to look at him, I saw a terrible expression on his face: twisted, sour.

It was the eighth day. A letter had come back that morning with Jonah. Mattathias was sitting inside with me; the curtains were drawn because the glare upset him. He looked up from the paper – he was preparing a list of readings for me to go through with the child –

and said briskly, 'Everything is settled. They are expecting you.' I nodded and went on with my reading: 'He that hath clean hands and a pure heart.' Mattathias got up a moment later and left the room. Was there a note of impatience in his footsteps? But the day passed smoothly, like the others; sometimes the atmosphere was moody, more often, tranquil. My mind was in shadow, wanting only cool things. He would stroke my cheek lightly and walk out into the evening to bring me great untidy bunches of wallflowers; and their scent was numbing to the senses. He allowed me always his proximity: to take his hand, to snuggle beside him as he read; and if there was pity in his kindness I did not look for it.

That night he became dreamy and sad; I felt estranged from him and kept trying to make him smile. I see now that he was frightened, that he was blocking me out to fortify himself as he approached that cold moment, so close now. But then I did not understand it, did not want it. Then, I wanted to say to him: look, I am carrying myself, all of myself, to give you. My gift landed in his lap, unnoticed, like a flower fallen in deep grass.

The night and his silence became swollen and I began to panic: 'Don't you love me, do you wish you were gone?' My voice was hot and agitated. He looked up, O so slowly, and frowned; it was as if he had made a little X against me, neatly in the margin. And as always, when I knew I had displeased him, I became very still, sat very straight and waited – knowing that he knew too. He came to me and laid his head in my lap and I stroked his rough curls, hour after hour. He was a long way beyond tears.

On the ninth morning, I woke terrified: in my dream they had been taking him away from me, and hard as I ran I could not catch up with the little band of men dressed in white, carrying knives. But no, there he was, dark hair mussed on the pillow, a little smile on his mouth as though he were reading as he slept. I could not bear to wake him. I ran out into the garden and filled my skirt with daisies and wallflowers and the little red wild flowers from the orchard. Then I sat beside him and waited for him to wake, having strewn the flowers all around his face and down the empty side of the bed. The damp, morning smells woke him and his eyes opened quickly. He sat up, rubbing his forehead, disturbing the pattern of the flowers. 'How sweet you are, how sweet,' he said; his bottom lip quivering slightly. I laughed like a child, grabbing him to me, rocking him. We sat there a little while, touching the flowers; then I ran downstairs to pile a tray with milk, honey and fruit. Elizabeth looked at me from below her lashes, but I brushed her protectiveness away. I would not leave him, all day I would stay beside him. When he bathed I would be just the other side of the door, because now he did not like me to see him bath. (And once, when I had run into the room naked, he had turned away in confusion. It had frightened me so and I had never done it again.) But the morning was banging at the curtains and I opened them because he liked the soft, glossy, early light.

We studied together and in the early afternoon he lay quietly beside me on the bed. I rested my head against his chest and felt the profoundest contentment. I thought, this is how it must be to die – a feeling of escape, of release from all but one feeling, that of peace; at last the ending of thought. He sat up slowly and said, 'There is a man whom I must see now, Mary, you need not concern yourself with this. Stay here in the cool. I will return.' My mood exploded, a feeling of gloom came over me as he carefully arranged his hair and put on his sandals.

'Where are you going?' I asked fearfully.

'I'll be back, wait for me – please.' He smiled so bleakly.

He was gone a little while but I could bear it no longer. I ran down to the study. Mattathias sat at the table with an elderly man who had a thick grey beard and a big nose. Mattathias was bending over, writing on some thick paper.

'What is it? What does it say?' I demanded shrilly, feeling demented.

The man stood up guiltily; Mattathias came quickly to me and held me by the shoulders with both his hands; they hurt me, his hands hurt me. 'It only says, as I have told you, so that you may re-marry . . .'

'What does it say?' I screamed, and the stranger took two steps backward, looking embarrassed.

'It says,' he whispered hoarsely, 'it says simply: She is no longer my wife and I am no longer her husband.'

I do not know how I got back to our room; I remember a strong, tangy smell in the air when my eyes opened and Mattathias's face, white and stiff. He took my hand, 'Mary, Mary, I told you, it had to be. It is so painful, so painful.' His head slumped forward.

I touched him lightly and put on my perpetual smile, 'Can you get me some water please?' I asked; and he jumped up and ran to the table, spilling it in his haste to help, to comfort. And I loved him with a passion that shattered my insides; wounded my body, and left me, smiling, smiling.

We were walking to the fields, talking of the moon which was shrinking a little more each night, 'Let's stay up all night and not sleep at all,' I said.

'Yes, we can do that.' He took my hand and wrapped it around his back and so we walked. The stubble in the fields was turning brown and ugly, soon to be burned; but that night the fields glowed a soft yellow, like spilled cream, and the trees stood perfectly still as a fox called in the distance. Suddenly, I ran ahead of him into a clearing and I began to dance. I was a leaf in the wind, swirling, turning, rippling; lifted by an eddy in the air, spiralling up, floating as though on water, then falling, falling. I knew I could dance for ever. I was extraordinarily beautiful, glowing like the moon, cool, ghostly, untouchable. I danced, not seeing him until his hand held me and he said, 'Please, stop, come away.' His touch shocked me, waking me to his presence. We walked back, our steps in time, but as his thoughts fell I could not catch them. Instead, I looked up at the moon, the aching, ghastly moon and smiled.

'What will we do all night?' he asked and all the panic had gone from his voice, as though he felt safe again away from the outside elements. He opened the curtains and let the moonlight dribble on to the floor. Nine days had passed; tomorrow he would be gone. I knew these things vaguely, as one is aware of people coming and going when one is ill. This was the last night, tomorrow the tenth day – then nothing.

'I will sing to you,' I said, and I sang a lullaby that my mother had taught me long ago; but I was tired suddenly and lay on the bed with my fingers pressing against my temples, where, it seemed, a pain was beginning. He lay next to me and he was so still that I thought he was sleeping. I got up quickly and lit candles, more candles, more – until the room throbbed with a soft pink glow.

Mattathias sat up, began arranging the cushions for me, 'Come, sit by me, I shall tell you a story,' he said, his voice almost patient. I sat down on the cushions happily. He closed his eyes. 'Once, when I was very young, we went to Jericho. Jericho is a place on a small hill, with palm trees and lush, exotic fruits and damp nights. It is said that Herod had to sell his plantations there to Cleopatra, and it grieved him more than anything, for he loved the place. I hated the place. It made me feel sticky, and the only things that pleased me were the trees with their soft blue buds: they looked like moon-flowers lying on that red earth. My father then took us on to the Dead Sea; I had heard of it of course, but never seen it. The heat became salty as we reached the mountains around the sea; they glared fiercely down at us – granite with deep folds, and the earth all around was dry as the hide of a camel. In the distance were the Mountains of Moab; and there, shimmering like a sapphire, was the Dead Sea – beautiful, cool, so inviting.

'We came nearer, and as we did so I became aware of a stench of death, a foul, putrid emanation that seemed to have driven away all birds, ants and living creatures and left only their carcasses in the strange shapes of the salt pillars. Nothing moved, nothing breathed.' He stopped. 'Yes?' I asked, waiting for the story. 'That is all,' he said, smiling, 'except that I loved the place. I felt that I had been there before and would come again. And that all life was like that sea, sequinned, beautiful, but lifeless. (You and he, the same in this – hating the world, fearing it . . . I could make a religion of Life.) 'And now,' he

67

said, almost gaily, 'I will bring you some wine because you are looking serious and I know that in a moment you'll start arguing with me.'

I only thought – no, not tonight; tonight I will say nothing, tonight I will be your slave, do whatever you wish. But I said, 'Don't tell me such gloomy things, I am not in such a hurry to die.'

'Nor I,' he said seriously, 'but if I were to die tonight, I think I would have missed nothing.'

The wine made me dizzy. The wax dripped and the scent of it was delicious. Mattathias fell asleep in the early hours of the morning, lying on his side with his hand curled around his head. I decided not to wake him, just to wait with him until it was light.

When I woke, yellow darts of sunlight pierced my eyes. I sat up too quickly and my head swam. The house was very still and the room was empty. I sat quite stiff in the bed, rocking my body from side to side. My eyes dropped to the floor, where a crumpled cushion lay. I got out of bed and felt faint; fine threads were spinning my head round and round, little flowers were growing under my nails, ants crawled in my ears and a vine took root in my stomach. I screamed. Elizabeth ran in, looking once around the room, then back to me. She walked to me with her arms held out, as though pleading. I opened my mouth to scream again, but stopped. I stared at her as my body began to sink. And I decided, It is enough, I am closing, I will stop.

I was in my bed, the sheet was strapped tightly about me; the doctor's face hung by the thread of a spider's web. Vinegar was pressed to my nose; I retched. Someone was singing in the garden and the bees had come closer. Just outside my window they were swarming with deep, undulating voices. The bees spoke to me, the doctor spoke – there were things that they wanted to know. But I smiled because my voice and ears had crept inside my body. All things had ceased. Only my eyes watched, my eyes said, I fade, I grow thin, I disappear.

Later, I saw Elizabeth and I remember her hands, because they were always kind, never an offence. She was patient as a tree, growing in her place, quiet, caring; bringing the bowls; touching my lips with a spoon, and if I stiffened, withdrawing. When I screamed – that day when the light began ripping at my eyes and the noise whined in my head – she ran to the window and tore the curtains together. Then she sat, she sat and waited for the screaming to end. She had kindness. Not like those others, later, who tied up my hands, who lashed my poor body to the bed. She had kindness; she spread it all around me like a blanket keeping out the cold. I love her for that. One day, she brought me a little honey cake in a veil of rose petals; I ate it, and all the petals, and we laughed, we laughed.

Then something happened. What was it? Something happened

which shut out the noise again, bringing a cold silence. It was when I entered that room and saw, by the inside stone of the fire, a fragment, a burnt cinder with some words on a patch of white – words I had written to Mattathias; it was dated the sixth day. There were other words – all burnt. I did not go in that room again. When we left, Elizabeth collected my books and papers together. The door was closed like an angry mouth when I walked past it.

There were some days – I have put these aside in my mind tidily, like things one finds in drawers: scraps of lace, a pressed flower, a painted shell, scented papers – things we keep to look at again and smile. There were slow walks Elizabeth and I took in the garden; the rains had come and taken the heat away; the days were fragrant. Sweet-smelling jonquil and cyclamen turned their heads in the grass, and it was green again. Chicks had hatched and crouched like saffron balls at the foot of the pear tree. The nights were cooler. The bees were quiet, sleeping with their gold.

At night, I would sit at my sewing, frowning a little, trying to make the stitches very small so that the cloths for the dairy would not tear with all the washing. Often Elizabeth would come and look at me, as though I lacked something. I would smile, liking her protection now because it was light, not assertive, as is a man's. I would show her the moon, or a colour in the trees. She would stay with me a little, and when I looked at her directly she would leave, knowing I wanted it. Some days, I felt that God hovered about me, in His white flowing robes, looking for a foothold, a way into my heart. I would have liked to let Him in, if He could bring a little warmth, but His smile was frosty, aloof. I bent to my sewing and He rose and flapped into the dark.

There were days when I sat quite still, trying to remember, but unable to. My mind alighted a moment on a face, an expression, a sprinkle of words, then it fluttered off again with as little purpose as the ants seem to have climbing up and down a tree trunk, round and round, imbecilic in their agitation.

Elizabeth told me it was time to go. Jonah was impatient; we had waited too long, the heavy rains might come and make travelling difficult. I was neat, I was ready, waiting.

I wore a light cloak and dark veil, and I sat in a corner, not looking about me, waiting for the animals to be loaded. Elizabeth, frightened but determined, handed me a little roll of paper. I looked at her, at it, then back to her. She thrust it at me, 'I must give it to you,' she said miserably and, picking up a bundle, she went outside. The light leapt in at my corner, then retreated as the door shut. I looked at the paper. I recognised the neat hand. There was a step outside the door; almost I thought – It is him. I read: 'This is all I have to leave you: words. Nothing is more precious. I will not forget. I will keep you locked inside me. I will draw you out in thought and in dreams and let your instinct guide me, as it always has. You will sleep beside my ribs as before. Do not grieve for lost things. Be happy. I shall not forget.'

I sat quite still. I saw his face smiling; his hand lifting in that beautiful gesture as he wrote. I knew he had gone for ever, like the ripple on the pond as the pebble sinks, like the mist in the morning. I knew he had gone. And the silence was furry and moist and full of claws. I began to weep, in an animal way, full of convulsions and ugly noise that rose from the base of my stomach and forced itself achingly through my heart. And once I had begun, I felt that I would be crying, crying, endlessly.

I have taken the ring off my finger. It lies small and gold on the table. I took it off because my fingers are red, raw from the rash on my hands. I look at it in its simplicity, and now I understand. I understand that Mattathias had to become that bitter monastery; those days of washing and fasting and eating rules. He had to become that dry wilderness, that cave on the mountain – because all that remained for him was extremity. Extremity – I understand that too now.

When my mind slackens, as it does now, I find myself always drawn back to you. As though all other thoughts that I have are just attempts to hide from you.

Words – there is nothing more precious. If so, these are my gifts. Do you want them? Did you ever want them? It doesn't matter. The day has a purpose; it is altered by the blue weaving of my thoughts. It is not meaningless, because of you. These are little releasings of grief. I never grieved for you. When the shock passed, I, like the others, became intoxicated by your death. What else could we be? Now, slowly I am circling you, cautiously trying to find you. I do not doubt you. But now there is only the reality of your absence. Just as God was absent at your death and you screamed up at Him, forsaken, shattered – that is how I feel. Who were you? That you had the power to make us all love you, battered, broken as we were? That you had the gift of making people forget their meanness and open their baskets and give? Where are you? Yes, I can say it. Do not fear for me, do not pucker up your eyes so. I know. You are dead. Dead. I have shouted it aloud. I KNOW.

But you have made me love this moment with my mind poised, full of thoughts caught in a mesh, waiting to be untangled, to fly out into the grey blue air. This is all there is. I do not fear it. There will be no more lying together; no more bearing of children; no more looking for the most silver fish to put on your plate. I am living in the narrow folds of my heart; but how wide the world is in my memory! Look at this white square of room. All things around me I love: the candle-light makes a leaf on the wall; your head is tilted towards me, your eyes are full of magic like a child's. Only you could look at a dirty old man and see his vanished sweetness.

And yet, you made me feel, or maybe I just felt it, that I had no right to your hand. That day, when the woman threw the rock at you and it grazed your head. Your fingers touched the blood in wonder. The woman shrieked and disappeared. You did not understand that it was her fear, because her son walked with you, that lifted her arm. I reached for your hand, taking it nervously, like a young girl. I wiped the blood on my skirt and held your hand – the flesh, the small bones, the scars. We were alone then, you and I. Peter had run after the woman, with John following. I held your hand, it shook and suddenly you cried out, 'Mary, Mary', closing your eyes.

But now it is quiet, it is ended. My life is narrow as this room, this bed. No voice calls in the distance; no child turns in his sleep and cries. (O some days, I would give anything for that cry again in the night, again, again; breaking dreams like cups.) My hands rub against each other as though gaining comfort from their closeness. I have withdrawn into a small place, and when my thoughts swarm, as they do now, it is like bees caught in a small space, with no escape. 'Mary, Mary', closing your eyes. Then you brushed my hand away lightly, 'It is nothing,' and walked to the water, where you dipped your fingers into the lake and put the water to your forehead. I felt it, my mouth gasped with yours at the sudden cold.

You have left me. The world is a long grey sheet, winding and unwinding, and the wind blows it this way and that, never ending.

But when I found you – yes, it was I who found you, not the other way around – then I was looking for something unbroken, something to join the severed edges together. There was no calmness in this, for as I think it, it seems a calm searching. It was not. It was a black and violent search, rising out of the depths of my desperation and lone-liness. The touch of one person, the sitting beside one person, once it would have been enough. But when I found you, I had lost that. I no longer understood it. For I was broken and could find no comfort in the white moon or the fold of a flower. All I could cling to was my high, false laugh, my running full of madness and the scream that echoed always in my brain.

You touched me and made me a child again. And Magdala came back to me, fresh and clean as if I still sat there, young and pink by the nets. Your mouth forgave me. But I went with you because your eyes wished it. That is why. I understand eyes. I followed you only for that.

I stop. My hand goes to my head and I hear my breath coming

jerkily. And I can hear your silence. Sometimes you were silent for so many hours. Often it was taken as a rebuke: we were all so conscious of how far behind we fell. But you had no thought of this; you simply understood the frailty of words. I do not. I cling to them as to a log in a swollen stream. I cling to them and they comfort me. See how my mouth moves, touching, licking, loving each word that runs down from my mind. But I understand the frailty of my mind, and that I cannot let it wander in and around you for too long. I must sleep. My hair falls like grass over my face and I am so tired.

Morning – did I sleep? Your face, you, how you haunt my recollection. All night long you came and went, bringing me smiles, flowers; one kiss.

You come back again. I see you under the trees, resting. The others have gone on ahead. I do not follow them, but stay by the stream, out of sight. Do you know I am there? You fall asleep under a pine tree with your coat rolled up under your head; one arm covers your eyes. I move closer and watch your hands as they sleep. Good hands, hands that can make things, fix chairs, carve a bird smoothly; healing hands, that take pain, guilt, away with a touch. The left hand has puckered skin down one side: white jagged scars like arrows in the brown skin.

When you wake I give you water and we begin to walk by the stream up into the forest. It is hot and your eyes look tired; but you are happy and tell me silly stories and we laugh. I take off my shoes and walk along the bottom of the stream, looking at the smooth grey pebbles and the water-grasses. You walk on the bank and, after a while, sit, scooping the water up with your hands to wash your face. It drips off your curling beard and you rub it roughly with the back of your hand. I splash water on my face too and it runs icily down my neck; my cry breaks the silence. Then a cuckoo calls and is answered among the branches.

The end of my skirt is wet, so I sit down on the opposite side of the bank and spread my skirt out, flapping it with my hands to get it dry. 'Will you take off your clothes?' mildly, how mildly you ask it. I look at you, surprised, pleased – but your face is like still water, unhurried by currents. I lift the wet cloth up over my head and bend slightly to place it on the ground. You watch me carefully as I rise, slowly your eyes move down my nakedness. 'I have never seen a woman before' – whispering, marvelling, so I must believe it. Suddenly your face dapples, as though in shadow. You look at my body again, this time hurriedly, nervously, as though it pained you. I snatch up my dress and put it on with quick, awkward movements; wet layers of cloth sticking together, making my fingers fumble. Your back is towards me.

We walk on, even our breathing is muted. And I love you, I love you so, for looking and not taking. But somewhere, also, I hate you for it.

Such a deep night, by the lake. Your hair scatters on the sand like dry ferns; your eyes close. Bending, my hair falls into yours – quick, my lips touch yours and move away. Your eyes whip open, your lips part, your head raises itself and repeats my gesture. I smile, 'You kiss like a young boy.' Small mouth knowing only a mother's kiss, body white as the snow on the hills, unmarked by a print. No flaw in you. How quickly you move! – like a slap. O you have cut me with that movement; my hair wilts. I move ponderously like a wounded animal. And you, turning your eyes, you groan, and I cannot bear it. I walk off into the night, holding my stomach where I ache, ache – knowing that in the days ahead you will make a distance.

O go – leave me – for God's sake let me be. There is pain for which no words, no thoughts are, or ever will be, enough.

Three

Elizabeth standing by the door startles me. She begins to dress my hair.

'No, do it plainly, pull it back, so.' I sit, feeling her fingers lightly smoothing and coiling. Suddenly I smile, 'Elizabeth?' I want to ask her if she remembers the day we arrived at the house where Mattathias had arranged for me to go; but seeing her long, flat eyes turn up at the edges; her head tilt, listening – I cannot ask.

'Do we have enough stores?'

'We need more grain and perhaps some fresh fish.'

'Send someone, will you?'

She nods and I reach for the money-box and thank Joshua in my heart for the money he always sends me, without which I would be destitute. Joshua: a fine professor now, with eight children. I have not seen him for years; he did not approve of my life, nor of you.

I do not remember the journey, the getting-there. I only remember arriving: a little village presented itself at the end of a winding road. The wind was blowing to the west; the clouds lolloped along in a grey sky as the evening murmured drowsily. Children played with marbles on the road and old men with blank eyes sat and drank sweet wine, sat and drank, occasionally tossing out a piece of advice to the dusty children, which was ignored. I had no place there. And I thought: What is it that sets me apart from these people inhabiting this piece of scraped ground, this earth rolled back to accommodate white houses huddled gloomily together, with patches of vegetables and hedges of flat, furling roses? The shepherds returning with their black goats looked remote; and I felt the same as I watched a woman flinging water from her pail on to the stone steps, then scrubbing, then rising to fling another pailful. It cascaded down the steps, lighting up the dull texture of the stone. With a sharp sigh, she disappeared. Elizabeth tugged my arm. I moved reluctantly from watching the water making runnels in the yellow ground.

Dark women, shawling their babies, rocked their thoughts as they watched coldly my progress up the street, past the straggling thorn trees, the bored gaze of the dusty stones. A band of little children began to follow us, whispering, pointing. I turned to look at them,

74

smileless, and they retreated in a block of grins. Doors opened and faces stared out; sometimes there was a quiet greeting, but suspicion shone like little green jewels in their eyes, and distrust in their careless leaning against brooms.

At the low end of the village, near the well, Jonah led us to one of the white houses. Chickens scattered as we approached and a voice called out from inside. The walls of the house were peeling and the door needed attention. A big woman opened the door and stood there. She had the face of a chameleon: her mouth was long, thin and snapping; her skin sallow with dark blotches on the cheeks. She stared at me so viciously that I felt that she was trying to scrape off my skin with her eyes. She did not utter the formal greeting of welcome, but, summoning a smile from somewhere cold, stood back, ushering me in. Inside, it was dark and there was the smell of meat cooking. I stood awkwardly for a moment, and then a long thin man appeared and boomed. 'Welcome to our home.' He took my cloak, and, followed by the woman of the house, showed me to a room at the end of a long corridor. I was able to see into other rooms through open doors and they seemed shapeless – the walls were dull and faded; objects were placed without thought, and everywhere there was an ugliness, a bareness. My room had a low couch, a bare wooden table with a basin on it and on the floor was a rug with a dark stain in one corner.

'You will come and meet the family when you are ready?' the man asked and I forced a smile and a nod. His wife pressed her lips together; and when they had gone, I listened to their feet tapping down the corridor. I sat down, then lay on the couch and closed my eyes and stayed like that for some time. I made no attempt to alter the grim appearance of my room. I let myself believe it was all I wanted, because it was all there was.

Later, Elizabeth came and washed my feet and hands and tried to say cheerful things. Then I went down to meet them. I stopped outside a door which had voices behind it and a panic turned my flesh hot. I wanted to run away; I had a sudden hatred for Mattathias. When I entered the kitchen, a man's back was stooped over a bucket and he was ducking his face and neck into it. He groped around blindly for a towel and something in me moved towards him, then checked itself. I wondered which of the sons he might be, and, at that instant, he turned about, holding a towel and rubbing his wet, bare arms with its rough cloth. His mother said, 'This is Mary, whom we have been expecting, and this' (she said it proudly) 'is my son, Samuel, the younger.' I smiled politely, but he gave me in return a sweet, shy smile, full of nostalgia. His face was plain, pale, with a heavy moustache; his eyes were flat and grey.

'Forgive my appearance,' he said, rolling down his sleeves and running a hand through heavy fair hair, 'I was covered, as usual, with wood shavings. They seem to settle everywhere. Won't you sit down?' He pointed to a most beautiful chair; carved, polished oak, with heavy claws at the ends of the arms and feet. It was the only such chair in the room, the rest were stick-like and rough.

'It is the chair he made,' his mother explained. I sat, letting my fingers caress the smooth talons, then held them tightly.

Presently, a slightly older man entered the room and after greeting me, he too washed his hands. Then he turned to me and said, 'We have heard about you from Mattathias – he is a good friend; you're welcome here.' A hand knotted in my stomach, I took a little breath and forced his name back, thinking – They will not be suspicious, no, not of me. I will behave perfectly. They will know nothing. Two children appeared from nowhere and stood in front of me, wriggling their feet.

'This is Jacob, and this, Hannah,' Simon said, pointing to two brown heads. Their grandmother pushed them towards the bucket, where their faces and hands were washed hurriedly. Then she took a brush from among the onions and pulled it through their hair. Immediately they looked sleek and gleaming. They watched me: the little girl's eyes took in every detail of my dark travelling dress and she looked curiously at my hair. The boy ignored me and demanded his dinner.

We sat down at a long table with a heavy grain in the wood. Crude bowls and dark bread were placed on it; but beside the bread there was a knife with a delicate olive-wood handle – my eyes fastened on it with relief. I wanted to touch, to feel the curved slopes of it. Mother – as everyone called her, except the children – placed a big tureen of soup on the table.

'Marrow soup,' she said sharply, flicking her hand at Jacob's elbow. I looked into the bowl while a rude soup, brown, with little greasy pools of yellow, was ladled into the bowls. When I drank it, it left a layer of fat on the roof of my mouth. The soup was followed by carp, cooked to a tough dryness; and then fruit. After dinner, everyone disappeared. I approached Mother and asked if I could help her, but she dismissed me almost rudely. I went to my room and slept, not allowing myself reflections of any kind.

In the morning, the commotion of people rising and washing woke me; but I could have slept for ever. No part of my body wanted to rise from that unfamiliar bed to face an unfamiliar day. It was Elizabeth, again, who got the morning started. Everyone had eaten breakfast and disappeared by the time I got downstairs, so I did not have any. I decided that it was time to give my first lesson. I found Jacob outside, crouching in the sand, watching some ants climbing up and down the slopes of a rotting pear. I suggested that we might have our lesson; he looked up at me as listlessly as I felt, and rose lazily, shaking the dust off him. We walked inside together and I could see Mother watching us by the door, her mouth set in some attitude that she had formed.

'Where shall I instruct the boy?' I asked. She showed me silently to a room at the back where the only books were holy ones. I fetched pens and paper, determined to teach the sullen boy something that day.

Jacob knew how to read, but he read without comprehension or interest, merely sounding out the words. He was quiet and whenever I corrected him he would fix his eyes on me very coolly before continuing.

'Who taught you to read?' I asked, 'your mother?'

Again he diminished me by his calculating stare. 'No, my father of course.'

I tried a little – 'My mother taught me to read.'

'But you're a girl,' he said disdainfully. Then he almost shouted, 'It is not right that a woman should teach me – a girl.'

'Don't be so foolish. I'm only teaching you to read properly. When you can, you will be instructed in the Torah by your father. He is too busy to do this and you must get your grounding with me. Comprehension of these things is not quite beyond a woman, you know. Where did you get such an idea?'

'I don't know.'

'O well,' I smiled, 'if you study hard, you can go to an Academy and become a real scholar – that's best of all. There is a good Academy in Galilee. Would you like that?'

'Who knows what I would like?'

'Don't you?'

'Who knows?'

I could see that it was going to be difficult for him to accept me, and, for my part, I was not prepared to impress him with my learning. Every day, he made strong attempts to persuade me that I was not needed by him, treating me with coldness and indifference. But, at the end of each lesson when I had said, 'You may go now, Jacob,' I would find him always just at the door, reluctant to leave the room. I never turned to look at him, but bent over my papers, writing. I could feel his eyes boring into me, and then, when next I twisted my eyes – he would vanish.

In the late afternoons I would go for long walks. The donkeys at this time were returning, strung together and loaded with baskets carrying rocks back from the quarry. A smell of cheese and raw meat rose nauseatingly in the air, so I did not breathe through my nose until I reached the baker's door and then I let the lovely smell of yeast fill my nostrils. It was also the time when the old widows went walking in their proud black – their lives gone out, their eyes sharp and cutting as birds'.

Some days, Jacob would take his lessons at the hottest time of day, so that he could help his father in the fields from early in the morning. On these occasions I would take my walks in the morning. A monotony of spirit filled me always on these walks. I allowed my heart no activity. Quiet, trailing my thoughts, I watched the women washing their clothes against the rocks in the pool. They looked up slowly as I passed, and looked down again, slapping, slapping; the suds rushing back into the water. And when I walked along the fields where the men were harvesting, the young ones pricked up their eyes for a moment and then, too vehemently, began to work again.

Their glances lowered my spirit; their curiosity was an unkind thing. I would hurry past and relax only when I reached the high ledge where the village ended. It overlooked lines and lines of olive trees and long fields of balsam. I would stare down at the regular patterns, wondering how they could plant so straight. When I was certain that I was quite alone, I would tell myself – I see everything, I notice all things, but none affect me. I sleep, I dream as I walk. Colours were heightened; odour and noise seemed to reach out cruelly and force themselves on me. Once, only once, I thought: This place stinks, rots with humanity. I too will rot here, breaking up into grains of boredom that the wind will blow away. But such thoughts were painful, so I drifted instead into a languid state where all passion was silenced.

Your passion – you buried it – in those deep, dark depressions when you would tolerate no one. You knew how it felt to be so emptied – as if the head and the heart had been ripped open and shaken out.

When the air hung limp in the curtains, my hand would move slowly to my hair, settling there uncertainly. Then it would drop and pick off a fleck on a black shawl, or fall dreamily into my lap. Sometimes I would unplait the neat coils that Elizabeth had bound that morning; my fingers untwining, feeling the hair slip, lifting up strands and musing about nothing but the slow gust of wind in the curtains; the butterfly lighting on the daisy. I would lie on the bed and watch the ceiling – see the crack in the plaster, the dust on the beam, a dark patch where rain came in. One day, I could not contain it; pains rose, snatching at my heart and my tears fell, fell. I pushed my face into the covers and tore at them with my teeth to stop myself screaming. I knew if I began, there would be no end to it.

So, the days passed. Mother would allow me to touch nothing in her kitchen; it was her domain and no little task was lowly enough for me. I kept away from the room because she made me feel a burden. In the beginning, when I frequently asked to assist, she would say, 'No, keep your hands for holding books, my hands are for work, real, women's work.' I would look at her red, raw hands, like hunks of meat, and it seemed that her roughness of mind and manner was distilled into the ugly movements she made with her fingers, the coarse food she prepared with them, amid sighs and complaints. In my mind she sat heavily, legs crossed, arms drooping. She seemed like a beacon of life to come. Could I be like that? And how could I, at fifteen, not find her repulsive? She was in all ways ugly: her face clumsy and fat, as though the bones were missing; her voice like a chopper: a dull, repetitive thump, thump – making all words unlovely. Her eyes never saw the little buds fill and burst; the swallow's wings dip and dance in the blue air. She had never looked into Homer and gasped – never smiled up at the trees and felt fortunate. Or had she? No, she had not. Everything in her told me so. She had known nothing but the circles of birth and work, sickness and dirt. All things were flattened for her, colourless, dingy. She could not understand how desperately I clung to my books and to the last shreds of feeling that surfaced when I looked at the wind-flowers and stroked their petals.

I observed her, her family and the two children dispassionately, as I did all humanity. She was right to hate me for that.

Whenever I could, I escaped from the house, finding new ways to flee the village without being observed. There was a walk up bare hills to a mountain that no one went near. I approached it through fields which were too rocky for ploughing, past women moving like bright shadows through vines, their voices a happy hum in the distance. Then I would climb and climb, feeling all my muscles straining as my body came to life. When I reached the top of the sharp mountain, I began to feel benign, cool again. I lay on my back under a sycamore tree, breathing in the dampness of the earth, my head resting on my bent arms. After lying like that for a while, I would stretch each of my limbs as far as I could and then let my body go slack. I would sleep – loose-limbed, uncoiled. No other sleep has ever been like that sleeping on the mountain; it was as though my body, exhausted, had floated away.

As I descended the hill, I could see the sprawling little village spread out before me and people carrying baskets laden with wood. And I felt taller somehow. I was very upright, very proud; no one could touch me. The mountain dwelt in me; its shadow sheltered me.

I cared nothing for people, with their little sneers, their conspiracies of spite that caught at my hair and my clothing as I passed. Looking back at the mountain, it seemed to bow its head and changed from brown to gold.

In my sleep there were no dark turnings. The nights were long and silent. Sometimes, at dawn, a hen flew off her perch, flapped her wings and settled again; and I took the sound of that into my arms, sleeping better for it. In the mornings, the little girl, Hannah, woke me by placing her cool hands over my eyelids. I would lie quite still, not playing the game, until her suspense got the better of her and she would lift her hands to see if I were awake. She watched me as I got dressed, entertained by my femininity, missing her mother as she saw the linen flop over my head, my hands arranging the folds of my bodice and tying them in place with a purple or green sash. Her eyes roved my hair as Elizabeth brushed it and bound it quickly, expertly; her smile was tinged with sadness and with a loss she could not comprehend.

'Come,' I said brightly, not wishing to be implicated, 'breakfast, then I can teach you a bit before you go out to play with Sarah.' The spell was broken, her face rounded and dimpled again.

Jacob was squatting on his haunches under a tree. I walked up behind him and noticed the outline of his top lip – sharp and beak-like. I looked down and saw that he was stabbing at a dragonfly with a thin, pointed knife.

'Stop it, stop it,' I yelled, pulling him by the shoulders, so that he fell into a sitting position, looking up at me moodily.

'Why?' he demanded, 'it's a fly – nothing.'

'It's beautiful,' I cried, aching, as something hidden, forgotten, rose in me. He picked up the knife, which had fallen from his hand and, very deliberately, plunged it into his palm. I looked at his round brown eyes and then at the blood that had begun to ooze slowly each side of the knife. He pulled it out of his flesh unflinchingly. We looked at one another as he closed his hand and cupped it in the other to catch the blood.

'What did you do that for?' I whispered angrily. He shrugged, looking above my head, using a trick I knew well: casting out emotion by concentrating on a patch of blue in the sky or a leaf falling.

'How old are you, Jacob?' I had never asked before, guessing him to be about ten years old, but not caring. He did not answer.

'Are you ten?' I asked carefully.

Suddenly, his head jerked forward and tears sprang out of his eyes, 'I'm nine, damn you, I'm just nine,' he yelled, and as my hand impulsively reached for him he pushed past me and ran up into the meadows – fast, slender as a wild hare. His figure disappeared and so did any feeling I had had for him.

Jacob was like you. When I think of him, I am reminded of the story you told me about yourself, when you were about his age. A Pharisee once told you – he is still alive, I saw him once in Capernaum, by the synagogue. He is a giant of a man, with hair like white-hot ashes and a broken nose. He told you a fable about each generation having to bring forth a martyr: men who would suffer or die simply to make life better for the rest. You were small, you hurt so much for other people – their indignities, their suffering. You had once seen a man put up to his arm-pits in dung; towels were wrapped around his neck. Then his mouth was forced open with tongs, a wick was kindled and thrown into his mouth and the dung was set alight. You trembled violently watching him, not with fear – with awe. When you told the Pharisee about this, and asked him why his own people could treat him with such cruelty, he did not answer – just let his eyes sink into your face. You began to drown in them, deeper and deeper sinking into a dream of your own martyrdom. And after that, to be ready for it, you sometimes stuck needles deep into your flesh or buried your face in water till your body seemed about to burst. One day, you put your hand into the fire; you took it out, looked at it, then slowly you put it back where the flames rose the highest. You kept it there. You said you felt no pain; that only your mind burned.

It was only later, much later, that the pain began – when your mother screamed and Joseph began to bandage the red, oozing wound, crying out in bewilderment as you remained silent and would not explain. But his sadness threw cold water over your mind and made it feel again, and all night long you had to force yourself to stop screaming. At that time I could not, could not hurt myself. We were so different, you and I. We were so different that in the end we seemed exactly alike.

Why did you choose to go to Jerusalem when you did? You said you did not seek a death. It is lies. You went just before the Passover, with the city full of political disturbance; with Pilate terrified and the prisons full of rebels and Zealots. And they call you a pacifist now! You – who committed so many breaches of public order and went for the priests. How could you expect to survive? You did not intend to. They say you cared nothing for politics – you! What are they making of you? Have they forgotten the knives they hid in their cloaks? Your rages in the night when no one could stop you? O you were gentle too – such gentleness as I have never known; but you knew it was not enough. You knew that day, when I threw my head into your arms and I was wet with fear and the greatest fear was your willing acceptance. But my fear did not touch you; sometimes nothing, no one could touch you, or save you.

Now, I am bereaved of smiles – all those soft hours – gone, gone. All I have left is the memory of your eyes: two pools of sea water in clouded hollows. My grief would be a grand thing – infinite, inconsolable. But I have no grief. I have kissed the moon; slept on the clouds. I have no grief. I am Mary, I lie fallow, peaceful as the furrowed brown earth, dry and drugged with sleep.

But I have been other Marys. Once, a cold girl, burning, I remember her. There was a lull in me then, as in the village, before the land was

81

ploughed over and enriched. The animals rested; the children played with less intensity; the old men talked less, but drank more. Then the rains came and spoiled the last of the wheat which had been set aside for the poor. They came begging to the doors and picked up a few ears of corn. The harvest had not been good; people were cautious after the previous year's drought. While we ate, Mother kept reminding everyone to be grateful: there were those who only ate once in every two days; there were those who picked and fried the flowers from the trees to satisfy a corner of their hunger. But she sent the poor away empty-handed.

As the corn shifted and creaked in the tall barns, I made a silence around me for many months. Even Mother's tongue, darting out like a fork full of poison, would leave me unscathed. In her house I felt tiny like the little brown insects that crept around the back door. I thought that if I opened my mouth to speak I would stammer or lie, so I curled tighter inside myself. Sometimes, I thought of myself as I had been – a young girl and slender, and the years ahead like trees full of blossom. Then I had so many kisses to give; days and days to fill with laughter, and nights that would rock like the sea. Now I had grown old somewhere with the same speed as the seasons.

I put my heart into my sewing. My embroideries became small and delicate, woven on the lightest gauze, in the gentlest colours; quite unlike the intricate designs of Galilee, with birds and plants and lots of dark blue. I would hold a piece of cloth a long time in my hands, and then, very carefully, choose the silks: cream, pale blue, lilac or a soft green. Without tracing on a design, taking tiny stitches, my fingers would create a pattern which was hardly a pattern at all – just threads of colour and little coils reaching a smaller and darker centre. I would make little coverlets, or neck scarves, which I knew I would never wear. Once, in the middle of a square of fine cloth, I stitched a tiny anemone in a dove-coloured silk. It pleased me more than anything I had done before. The work became lighter than flowers, little gossamer trophies that I folded with care and placed in boxes scented with rosemary and took out sometimes to hold against my cheek.

Sometimes, Hannah would come and watch me sew. I would sit outside under a tree, and often I would keep a flower upon my knee and try to copy it. Hannah was a quiet, thoughtful child. Her curiosity, like her brother's, was immense, but his was crueller – but, perhaps that is just the way boys are. She would sit and watch and then say, 'Let me try.' Often, I was barely aware of her presence and any request was an intrusion. But there was about her dark, very straight eyebrows and pale eyes a lostness, a misery that I could not quite shake off. I taught her to sew – simple stitches in straight lines, hemming and making borders. And because she persevered, biting her lips and unpicking, I also taught her how to embroider little flowers and animals; and I could see that it made her happy.

It was a sleepy afternoon; the sky overcast and the trees quivering in the wind. Hannah knelt by my side on a rug. She moistened her finger, squinting her eyes and aiming the thread at the eye of the needle, until she managed to draw it through with a soft sigh. Mother came along the path around the duck pond and reached our private corner under the pine tree.

'O, sewing? Well, that at least is useful,' she said, taking Hannah's cloth carelessly, so that the silk slipped out of the eye. I felt the child stiffen and sensed a loathing in her of the kind I myself felt in the presence of Mother.

'May I see what you are doing?' she asked me with strained politeness. Reluctantly I passed her my square of gauze, feeling my fingers shiver as her rough hands opened it and her brow wrinkled and her nose rose.

'What is it?' she demanded rudely.

The child and I breathed in the same slow way, waiting, a suspended stillness in us both.

Mother shrugged, 'I've never seen anything so silly – what's the good of such cloth? Wash it once and it falls to pieces. The stitches so small you'd hurt your eyes to see them.' I held out my hand for it, and she dropped it.

She told Hannah to come inside to help with the vegetables. The child sat still and then said, 'I will come in a moment.'

'Come now,' she snapped, walking away. Hannah sat looking after her with that melancholic gaze of hers.

'You'd better go, we'll do more tomorrow,' I said, re-folding my cloth.

'She doesn't like me to be with you,' Hannah said quietly, putting away her work.

'No.'

Mother's voice cut the air, 'Hannah, come this minute. Now. I tell you for the last time.' Hannah rose and walked very slowly into the house.

I sat and felt an anger rise in me. A stiffness grew behind my knees and rose up through my thighs, filling all my body with wood. I picked up the small flowers in my lap and began pulling off each petal, each stamen, ripping at them until their pain joined my own. Then I crushed them in one hand and rubbed them between my palms, until all that remained was a pale stain and a thin segment of darkening pulp. That was how I began to kill flowers. And on all the days ahead when my anger or pain could find no victim, I attacked the flowers – maiming or killing them and their suffering served as mine. It was only years later that killing flowers was not enough, when the pain had to come closer – into my own flesh. O I see you now with the red roses that bloomed at your wrists, your feet, your beautiful soft forehead; the red roses that dripped down into your eyes and I could not wipe them away.

I will light a candle for you, for you my love, love. I can see the shadow of myself in your eyes. I am there, still. A little smile tugs at the corners of your mouth like a pink wisp of cloud in a clear sky. Why could I not court you? I should have, O I should have – sweetly, lightly as the young girls do. All those days I used to think – If he would touch me – just once – I would be so beautiful I would disappear.

Come close, I want to sleep, I must sleep now, I will do what I do when I am very tired. I will lie quite still a moment and think until your face fills out behind my eyes. Sometimes, I am made afraid because your eyes move closer and closer until they look lurid and lunatic, with purple candles burning in the centre. I blink and you are gone. I begin again, until the face that my head paints is soft with clear, golden eyes and creamy skin – but your skin was not creamy, it was dark, lapped by the sea and the wind; rugged to touch. I will hold still, to keep you; and bend the cushion into the empty hollows of my body. If I could but sleep. I would like to sleep for ever.

Remember, I went with you up into the hills to see the sick child? We had to go quickly and you had not eaten all day and that worried me, but my fretting made you impatient. How cold it was. When we got to the place, it was very dark and the mother ran out, crying, clinging to you: 'Do something. O please, they say you can do anything.' How pale and glassy the child's skin looked in the light of one flickering candle. The woman would not give you any peace, so I asked her if she would leave the room to let you pray in silence. But she kept babbling: 'She never cries, never, she was so happy always. She sat with me as I kneaded the bread, watching and passing the flour – always happy. Keep her, save this one I beg you. The winter took my little boy, years ago.'

All night the child lay still and feverish; but her skin was white and clear. You touched her forehead, expecting it to be cold, but it was hot and damp. Hourly, I saw your despair as you knelt by her and prayed and pleaded and the mother kept coming and looking and crying at you, as if you were withholding something from her. The last time she came in, she looked at the child and her tears stopped. She began to sway her body back and forth, holding her arms to her stomach. You lifted your eyes to the child's face and groaned loud and deep. I wanted to cry, and ran to the mother. But she did not feel my arm about her.

She said stiffly, 'You must stay here the night, it is too cold to leave.' She scooped up her fragile, stilled girl and carried her from the room, as though rebuking you. Your head dropped on to your open hands and you cried, 'Why won't He hear me? What have I done?' I whispered, 'Be still, you expect too much.'

'No,' you replied bitterly, 'it is them, they expect too much.' You wanted to leave the house, but I would not let you; the rain was falling and you were stooped by fatigue. All night I stayed beside you, holding your hand as you lay, confused and tired, hovering on the edge of one of your attacks. But it did not happen. You managed to fall asleep and that saved you. It was only when you were exhausted and had not eaten for days that you said and did things that no one understood.

In the mellow light of dawn, you woke and turned to me, with great boulders for eyes. 'Mary,' you whispered, 'I did not know how lonely I have been; how lonely I am. Only when I waver, I see how great my needs are. I did not know my heart could be so touched, not by all people, but by one. I cry for things I need and have never known.' Your head came down on my shoulder and I caressed it with my brow. Your hand rubbed my hair, your fingers felt for my eyes and mouth – and grief was an unknown thing, Death vanished in a breath; all life met in your fingertips.

Walking back down those bitter hills, you said, sadly, 'They skip like children under my small miracles. Words fly into my mouth and my hands have powers I do not understand. Then there is nothing; then He fails me. And I have to go away for many days before I can make a sign.' And I asked you, 'What do you do when you are alone?' 'I do nothing. I give myself up utterly. I cease to be. My body trances; I am at one with heaven and God sleeps in my brain. Then, when He has come back to me, I can do anything, anything. The poor will love me again and the sad mothers.'

O my dear, you did not understand that their bodies were hungrier than their souls, and that they believed you would fill their mouths.

I wish, today, that I could be that cold girl in the village again. Which is better, tell me, to be dead, or to be as I am now – like an eye scraped clean, peeled and then put to the flame?

'Who do you say I am?' you asked me. And I was silent because I could not answer, I did not know, really did not know. You smiled grimly, and said, 'You think I'm a madman, don't you? You think me possessed and *you* surely would recognise it.'

I screwed up my nose at you and said, 'Yes, you're a madman, but what madness, what lovely madness. Yours will hurt no one.'

Your look suddenly was wild; your mouth twisted sharply, 'O yes, my madness will injure and injure – for ever.' There were days like that, when you felt your effect was enormous, your power illimitable. I did not understand it. I had felt such powers myself, for brief moments when I was mad – but you did not seem mad. If you were possessed, it was only by light, by warmth and goodness. There was no evil in you and madness is evil, destructive and awful.

How much I must have hurt Hannah in my cold, clear madness. But she crept closer to me in spite of my efforts to keep her at bay. She must have felt as I so often felt with you. When I walked off across the meadows she would ask, 'May I come with you?' and sharply I would turn and say, 'No, I will go too far for you.' I did not soften my words with a smile. When I returned, she would be sitting just where I had left her, turning strands of grass in her hands, patient as an animal. Her face would turn up, an oval of oatmeal with two sad eyes.

'I was just waiting,' she would explain. I would sit beside her silently, unwilling to talk and unable to care. One day she said, 'My mother had such long hair, it went down her back to her knees in a long plait. I learned to walk holding it.' She picked up the hem of my skirt, 'Your clothes are different,' she said. 'When you walk there's a rushing sound.'

'And your mother's?' I asked, 'how were her skirts?'

She turned gloomy, 'I only remember her hair.'

Why didn't my feelings rise in me then, as I feel them do now? Why did I sit so rigid, with Hannah's hands clinging to my skirt as the closest contact I would allow? There was a small stone rolled up against my heart; it would not shift for anyone.

One Sabbath, after the singing at the table, Hannah rose from her normal seat, carried it around and placed it by my side. She sat down firmly. Mother, from the door, where she was carrying in a dish containing a malodorous substance, ordered her to resume her usual place. Hannah said nothing, but began twisting her fingers together on her lap.

Her father said, 'Do as your grandmother says, Hannah.'

She bowed her head. 'I do not want to sit next to Jacob anymore.'

'Why not?' her father asked, 'have you been fighting?'

There was silence from both children and then Jacob blurted out savagely, 'Hannah has forgotten our mother.'

Hannah ran from the room; everyone else went on eating as though nothing had happened.

For the first time, I looked around the table and wondered how they all spent their days. I studied Simon and his face did not flicker. He was a mystery to me. Mother sometimes said to Jacob, 'Your father has gone to check whether the caravans from Nazareth have arrived,' or, 'Your father will be back in a few days from Tiberias . . .' And there was Samuel, who was hardly at home except for the evening meal, who was polite to me, but remote. There were strange comments that his mother made about a certain Ruth – odd, spiky remarks that made everyone's eyes roll over to Samuel, but he appeared not to notice. I found myself staring at him. Then his eyes rose from his plate and fixed very directly on mine. Suddenly, it came back to me that he knew about my past and in confusion I dropped my knife and began to grope for it under the table. He stooped to recover it and, at the same time, both our hands reached out for it and touched; mine retreated, his very calmly encircled the knife. He rose and handed it across the table to me with a small, sympathetic smile, which curled behind his eyes and was gone.

Jacob persisted, interrupting my thoughts, 'Hannah will not come with me now to take flowers to the burial place.' A commotion arose from Mother, who said that the child was disobedient and lazy and only wanted to sit around sewing and idly looking at words.

Simon said quietly, 'She is to be instructed in these things, Mother.'

'But it goes on all day long. She will not help me in the kitchen, she has been turned against me. I know all about it – I'm not to be fooled by clever looks,' she said, turning her red gaze on me.

'We must not be impolite to strangers in our house,' Father said mildly, 'especially not on the Sabbath.'

But Mother was not to be stopped, 'This house is not the same. The children are unsettled. I have extra work to do; people spend their time reading and walking and sewing useless things. We are not accustomed to these goings on.'

Simon began to say that he was satisfied with the arrangements and that both children were being taught as he wished. Mother, waving a spoon in the air, so that little drops of soup sprinkled on to the table, shouted, 'I am the one who has to put up with it all day long. You all go off to your work, you don't have the trouble, the worry . . .'

Father rose like a poplar; crossing his arms across his chest he boomed out 'Peace' in a splendid roar. Silence fell; Mother pursed her lips as tight as a prune, sniffed and removed the plates noisily. I felt myself shake, and finally, terrified by what words might leap out of my mouth, I left the room.

I was sitting by the window in my room, wearing my prayer shawl and trying very hard to concentrate on the Sabbath Psalm: 'O Lord, how great are Thy works and Thy thoughts are very deep'; but the next verse kept giving me evil thoughts – 'A brutish man knoweth not; neither doth a fool understand this.' There was a knock at the door. I went to open it and Samuel stood there, 'My brother had to go to Hannah, but he asked me to apologise to you for my mother's rudeness.' I shrugged. He went on, 'I too am sorry for it. Please feel appreciated by us for what you are doing for the children. They have suffered without their mother, as you can see.' He nodded briefly and was gone.

Jacob, at our next lesson, would not look at me. He answered, in a surly fashion, my questions. Then he said rudely, 'I'm tired of reading *Genesis*. I know it all – why can't we read about the wars?'

'The wars?'

'Yes, in *Joshua*.'

'But we have not studied *Exodus* – surely you want to read about Jacob in Egypt?'

'No, I know all that.'

'Very well,' I said carefully, 'you may turn to *Joshua*.' Looking at him, I wondered if he felt he was dominating me, so to redress the balance I said, 'But I will question you about *Exodus* later.' We understood one another.

Then I began to notice that Jacob, like his sister, was trying to nudge against my indifference. Once, when I was beginning the long walk up to my mountain – just a little to my left, but well within sight, a small figure was running, steadily, rhythmically, but at great speed. I recognised the red jacket that Jacob always wore, which his mother had made for him. The darting figure took no notice of me, but I was certain that he was aware of me, and that, had I not been going that way, he would not have been there at all. I walked on at my own pace, seeing the red and grey figure diminishing in the distance as he sprinted towards the craggy slopes of the mountain. Then my eyes and my interest lost him. It was beginning to grow hot; the earth was turning again to a powdery yellow and blowing away; the trees were darkly leaved and the wheat in the fields was tall enough to sway with the wind. I climbed the mountain and reached a little place surrounded by large boulders, where lots of daisies and rough red flowers grew.

I lay on the ground drinking in the solitude, full of that particular serenity one feels on a high, deserted hill. I drifted off into a half-sleep and must have lain there for some time, because when I woke my throat and eyes felt dry almost to soreness. I sat up and saw, in front of me, but right on the peak of a tall boulder – Jacob – hands on hips, just staring down like a warrior. It was like waking to find a lizard perched upon your hand. I leapt to my feet in a rage and yelled at him to come down, but he turned and disappeared. My anger was not so much that he had been watching me without my being aware of it, but much more that he had broken my relationship with the mountain; and that all around me now I felt his presence – his eyes on something which I felt was mine personally. The golden mountain seemed tarnished suddenly and the daisies dripping over the rocks looked sullied. I watched them with a fascinated horror as their delicate white petals seemed to stretch out for me: I rose quickly, afraid to touch them. I was aware then how some of the colour had gone from my anger; and I wondered why.

When I next saw Jacob, I pressed my voice quite flat and said, 'Jacob, why were you spying on me today?' It was dark, he had leapt up from the table after dinner and made for the garden, but my fingers had stopped him at the outer door. 'I often go there.' He made his voice bored.

'O, so you've followed me before, have you?'

'Lots of times.'

'Why?'

'Just wanted to know what you get up to on your own all the time.'

'I see.'

'Grandmother says you're distracted.'

It hurt, that. He began kicking at a rock obstinately, but each kick had more power behind it, so that after a few such blows I was forced to say, 'Stop it, Jacob, stop it.' He let his foot fly once more into the rock and then sat down on the ground as though overcome suddenly by pain. I knelt and reached to take off his shoe, but he pushed me away and removed it himself. Looking at the broken skin and the rapid bleeding, I was horrified and said, 'Why do you hurt yourself like this?'

'Who cares?' he snapped, 'who cares?' and his fierce face creased and ran with tears, which he tried to hide by turning away to shake out his shoe. But I cared – surprised, alarmed – I was hurt by his tears, by the shaking of his shoulders. I did not know what to do, how to react to my sudden concern. I reached into my bodice and said, 'Here, take this,' passing him a handkerchief.

'I'm not crying,' the little, biting voice insisted.

'I know, it's for your foot, wrap it around the first two toes.'

He did so and his hair falling forward, the darkness, the untidy thickness of it, brought a spasm to my throat and my hand went its own way and touched his head. He suffered it. It was enough for us both; and we parted in silence.

For the first time since my arrival I now began to ask questions. One morning, very early, when Jacob was waiting for his father who was strapping on his shoes in the kitchen, I saw that they had nets and pails.

'Where are you going to fish?' I asked, kneading the dough, which was now the one task that Mother allowed me, as long as I did the baking before she entered the kitchen herself.

'We go to a big water hole on the west side of the village; some of the fish were brought down from Galilee and there are regulations so that we do not over-fish the waters,' Simon said. 'There are good carp, but Jacob prefers the little silver fish because he can take as many as he likes of those; they breed like flies and none have to be thrown back.'

'I used to live in Galilee,' I said quietly, surprised to hear myself say it.

'Did you?' Simon asked. 'We have family the other side of Nazareth; you will meet them soon. They stay with us for a few days before we travel together for the Passover.'

I gave them a flask of milk and some bread wrapped in a cloth which Simon stuffed inside his leather bag and drew the thongs together. I thought of a hand, lifting in a perfect gesture to write. Then they went out into a clear, rosy morning and Jacob nodded to me before turning away.

I was happy at that hour; happy to be doing something useful with my hands. I loved the stickiness of the dough and its springy softness and ripe smell. I used to wake at the hour when the first cock warbled in the dim light, before even the maids were about. I simply tied my hair back with a ribbon and drank a little water before setting to work. Mother had given me strict instructions for making the bread, but since she was not present, I milled the coarse flour again and discarded some of the husk that she left in to avoid waste, but which had a bitter toughness. The kitchen almost seemed my own at that cool hour, but had it been mine I would not have had it so rough, so devoid of colour. I kneaded the dough thoroughly, then found the smooth-sided knife and cut the dough into six even blocks, which I re-kneaded separately. One of these loaves I always gave a good punch in the face, saying, 'That's for you, Mother,' and, smiling to myself, I would find that my energy was increased to continue with the heavy kneading.

As the loaves swelled under damp cloths near the oven, the maids trooped in, yawning: the bread went in just before the maids' skirts began to billow across the wet, scrubbed floors and I could hear Mother's footfall at the other end of the hallway. Elizabeth then filled a jug with water and we waited until we could hear Mother waking the children before going back to my room. I knew that when Mother tasted the bread she would say, 'Why is it that you can never make it taste like mine?' Hannah would retort with blazing cheeks, 'I like the bread,' and be scowled upon for her ignorance. Father would ask for a slice more with careful indifference; and I thought at these times that he could be mistaken for a gruff man were it not for the small but sublime smile that tweaked at his whiskers.

Elizabeth and I sometimes had long conversations in my room, waiting for the bread to cook. I used to sit by the window watching the sky changing colour and the clouds fluffing out their feathers, as she confided in me about the swanherd, whom she had taken a liking to.

There was something dark and unfathomable about her own eyes which reminded me of a swan's. She laughed loudly when I told her so; and it was almost shocking that she should laugh like that, because she was a woman who hardly even smiled. I began to question her avidly about the swanherd, but she would tell me very little. In the end I forced her to take me down to the pool where the swans were kept. She would not allow him to know that we were there, so we hid among the bushes like children, watching him. And he was very beautiful. He was young and gracefully tall, with a dreamy, sensitive face and brown hair that fell loosely over one eye. We watched him in silence as he lifted a young swan from the pool: holding it by the neck and very expertly getting one arm around its body before folding first one wing and then the other neatly against his side. He stroked her neck and spoke softly to her before examining one foot, which appeared to be damaged. But it turned out sadly, for the swanherd loved only his swans and found them more beautiful than any human. They say that swans die of love, but I am not sure, I think they die probably of frustration. Soon, I did not ask Elizabeth about him any more and her laughter did not surface again. She did not like to talk to me for long in the mornings, saying she had work to do. It was as if any conversation reminded her of something she was trying to accept.

Once, when I went to the pool but stood back among the trees – yes, I went to look at him: he was so beautiful that you wanted to wash him all over, hold his flesh against you and feel it smooth and warm as a child's – I saw her, Elizabeth, just watching him as I was. I waited until she left and then caught up with her as she walked; I did not tell her that I had seen her, but I could see that she had been crying.

As soon as I had begun to relax my heart, I found that Hannah started to please me. She was a child you could speak to about anything and she always had the ability to see things and people in a sharp, original manner. She was especially percipient about Samuel, who was very fond of her and had made her small toys from sandalwood, which she dressed and coddled and never tired of.

'He is sad, you see,' she would tell me gravely. 'He was to be married, but not now.'

'What happened?' And there it was – she was able to provoke my old curiosity.

'They wouldn't tell me,' she said. 'Nor will he, though sometimes I say, "Where is Ruth?" and he looks angry.'

'Is that the Ruth your grandmother makes remarks about?'

'Yes, she's the same.'

It was spring and there had been no rain since early autumn, and those rains had been meagre. Everyone in the village was worried. Father went off to the meetings about how to preserve water for the dry months ahead. Every night at the table he would push back the blue cloth he wore on his head, revealing a white strip of forehead, and say, 'It will be a bad summer again and we will lose more sheep and goats.'

'Perhaps we should buy camels,' Jacob said, but no one seemed to laugh at these things any more. Soon, each household was allowed only one pail of water a day and one extra each second day for washing the children. This water was then given to the animals to drink. It felt too hot for spring-time; the wind blew, making matters worse, and there was no enthusiasm in anyone; only an anxious apathy. Father went each day as usual to see that the fields were being taken care of, but the wheat was stunted and the barley had grown spindly and colourless. The labourers lost interest in the weeds, which thrived in spite of the drought. There seemed to be countless cockroaches, almost like a plague, and instead of getting used to their presence people grew frightened and intimidated by them as if they were an evil omen. I began to think that if all the world perished, the cockroaches only would grow and flourish.

But my own problems were more urgent. It was almost the Passover and I could not avoid making the journey to Jerusalem with the rest of the family. I could not sleep wondering what would happen were I to see my father or brothers in Jerusalem. I did not know what to say to Mother, who would expect to meet my father and would expect me to stay at his house. All night long these thoughts festered in my brain and no solution presented itself.

Mother's brothers and their families arrived from Nazareth and filled the house with noise and preparation for the journey. With all those extra people, the house seemed to be splitting its seams. Rugs and rough mattresses were put on the floor and Hannah was delighted to find herself sleeping at the foot of my bed as there was no one else who could possibly share my room and all available space was needed. In normal circumstances we lived too close together: at night I could usually hear Father's cough and Mother's voice droning on endlessly until it sent me to sleep. Often, I was even able to hear Jacob's energetic tossing in his room, which was some way from mine. Now the small, thin house was unbearable. People often had to walk sideways in the corridors, pressing up against the walls; and although there was friendliness and a lot of laughter, these things only served to increase the tension in me. Mother also was constantly bad-tempered. I did notice that Samuel did not sleep at the house and I wondered about that.

The day before we were all due to set off I began to feel feverish. I said nothing about it and Jacob and I spent a few solemn hours together reading the Passover story. In the late afternoon I took a walk up into the woods and felt as though the heat were pressing down into my head. All around me the lack of rain was pitifully evident. It looked like late summer. There was a white dryness in the woods; the roots of the trees were creaking for water; no new leaf was born and the clouds turned to junket in the sky. Somewhere in the distance I could hear the sound of wood being chopped. That sound, and the feeling that I had of the colours around me being stretched, made me frightened, and feeling damp and hot I went home.

That evening I could barely support myself during the long prayers; the joints of my thighs had turned to milk and then my whole body melted. When I came round, Father was holding a wet cloth to my head; a moving mass of dark heads and eyes swayed above me; Hannah was crying and Mother was saying roundly, 'And this is what comes of a girl never having to work in the fields.'

Simon felt my wrists and said, 'Well, she cannot make the journey tomorrow, her fever is high.'

Mother said, 'It is nothing, she must travel for the Passover. It would be a sin not to.'

'It could be infectious,' Father said, 'the land is unhealthy in a dry season, so are the animals.'

'No excuse is good enough for missing the Passover,' Mother insisted, folding her arms and looking at me furiously.

'Don't I remember,' Father put in lightly, 'that your old mother never made the trip to the Temple?'

'That was different,' Mother snapped. 'She was lame in one leg and didn't want to burden us.'

'A virtuous woman would surely have hopped,' Father teased and she mouthed an insult at him. He shrugged his shoulders and, turning to his sister-in-law, Susanna, who was very sweet-tempered, he said fondly, 'Who else but me would have put up with such a woman all these years?'

Susanna had a narrow but deep forehead with great blue eyes above cheeks which swelled very round and pink. Her face tapered down to a delicate chin with a tiny dimple embedded in it. Her mouth trembled with laughter at Father's remark and she whispered, 'We could never put up with her for long; that's why everyone was so glad when you turned up.'

'She's a good woman,' Father said loudly, 'a worker, but,' he added quietly, 'she has little time for kindness.'

It seemed that at least five women escorted me to my room, but in fact there were just two of Mother's sisters and Hannah. I was put to bed and told that I would be bled later. I was brought some bread and soup but could not take it. I slept very little during the night and woke very flushed and weak. Elizabeth came early to say that everyone had left, and that Father had decided at dawn that I should not be woken. She said that Hannah had vomited in the night and been feverish and she had stayed behind also. I went to see Hannah, who had been put in another room as soon as I had developed the fever. I found her in the kitchen with the maids, looking quite healthy and well.

'I thought you were ill,' I said, surprised. She gave me a wise, womanly smile.

'You mean you weren't really ill, just pretending?' I demanded.

'O, I was sick,' she said, giving me such a knowing smile that I did not dare reprimand her at all. My fever had left me entirely by the time the leeches arrived.

Hannah and I spent the Passover quietly and peacefully together. I sang to her from the *Song of Songs* and we repeated the prayer for dew many times each day. We spent the first evening of the Passover with Father's infirm mother and her two brothers and ate with them, while Hannah, as the youngest, asked the questions after the meal and had them laboriously answered by the two old gentlemen, who quoted great lengths of *Exodus* and *Deuteronomy* with real pride and pleasure. By the time grace was said, Hannah was very tired and a little drugged by her generous gulps of the strong wine and I took her home.

I was happy to be with Hannah and almost imagined her to be my own daughter. I brushed and arranged her hair and watched her try on my clothes and put my oils on her face. Something of the great freedom expressed by the festival entered me, and I was optimistic, almost joyful. I found that I missed Jacob and I thought sometimes of his father. Recently, I had noticed that if Jacob came to ask me something, or Hannah took my hand, I would see something in Simon's eye that troubled me: a little, tugging look, a smile shaped like a question mark. I found myself caring also that Father might lose his livestock and hoped and prayed that it would rain before the summer settled in. But then, even the drought did not seem such a harsh thing: there was beauty in the colours of the fields though they were the wrong colours; the white woods took on a muted softness in the evening that caused me to remember other spring-times, other lives.

In the quiet house, very late, while Hannah slept on a little couch and never stirred in her dream, I took off all my clothes and stood looking down at my body as I had done as a young girl. It was still white and tender, but a slight darkening, like the first tint of a bruise, seemed to have altered the smooth flesh in its curves and hollows. Running my hands down the sides, the skin seemed defenceless, sad. But if I sighed, it was not from sadness or sensuality, but something deeper, quieter and more reserved. I lay in bed feeling melancholy, and wondered where the sudden drought could have come from.

While the images around me hover and dissolve, merge and alter, you alone remain unchanged. You sit quietly in one corner of my being, silent, pensive; sometimes jolting me painfully into recollection by a slow turn of your head or by a sudden fling of your words – which brings chaos into this room so peaceful, so undisrupted in its calm routine.

Elizabeth has set me to work stitching a new green shawl. But I love the old shawl. The one I once wrapped around Mattathias's eyes in the garden and then whirled him until he fell and I caught him in my arms. The shawl is so old, so frayed. I wore it that day . . . It has an oval stain where my little son's finger was wrapped when he cut it on the tough grass. He did not cry, but looked with curiosity at the blood. I wanted to cry; it was the first blood of his that I had seen.

Now Elizabeth hands me a bowl of hedge plums and I take one and rub it against my skirt so that the white fur vanishes and the redness blazes. I wish I could give it to you.

How much time I have. Outside, under the tree, a dead chicken hangs, blood flowing through its beak. Someone will cook it. Someone also will store the apples tidily so that their skins do not touch. But I do none of these things. All those years, when people pulled pieces off me – wanting this, that, here, now; a child snatching at my hair to pull my face round. Now there is only time. He was right, Mattathias, to say action cancels out thought, or at least makes the struggle for thought unbearable.

How much, how much you wanted: give everything, you cannot give a little, give it all, forget everyone save me. 'Nothing will hurt you,' you said, 'nothing can touch you – you are clean, you are free, nothing will hurt you again.' O and I believed you. And every day it was true. I slept each night as though I had drunk wine, but had tasted none. I woke in the morning smiling, having given everything to the poor, even my vanity. I was rich because I was happy, happy. And you, you were altogether lovely. Your hands took all the things that tumbled me; that caused my hands to rip and slash, my mind to burn one moment, the next – turn to ice. And is there still a crackle that sometimes I hear when the fire is dead?

There were things, once, that I forgot, as though they had never been. I was defeated utterly when they said later – you did this, you tore her clothing, you bit into the branch of a tree. Once they even told me that I had washed and dried your feet, using my hair as an apron. Is it so? I cannot tell. No, it was not me. I think they were talking of some harlot; and whatever I have been, I have never been that. There are things now that I will not remember, because I dare not be overcome by them again.

'Nothing will hurt you ever again.' But I could not find you. I called, called and you did not answer. 'A spring shut up, a fountain sealed.' Nothing will hurt you – but it did, it does. You lied, you lied to us all with your impossible love. The love I offered you, the only possible love, you scorned it. You wanted to vault me to heaven. I wanted to marry you.

Do I know what is happening in this solitude? Two years of quiet, of nothing but this endless, aching thought. Do I understand what is happening? That it is part of a process, a moving-towards – what? A greater silence? Or towards a cry? A shriek that will rive these cool blue walls of thought rising and rising and shatter my very foundations. I must make this pass. Back, back. Pick out of the net one memory that will not hurt, pick it out and nurture it.

They all returned from Jerusalem. There was yeast in the new bread and I was lighter. I was glad to see Jacob. He hovered about me, rubbing his ankle with one foot until he yanked out a lump of words – like something he had hidden in his pocket,

'I wondered how you were, I hoped you would be better.'

Little tug at my mouth as I feigned a casualness I no longer felt, 'O I was soon better.' After our lesson, I said, 'While you were gone I thought about my brother in Jerusalem, Joshua. I wished I had given you a letter for him.'

'Well, my father goes to Jerusalem; he could take it for you.' Then he frowned, 'I didn't know you had a brother.'

'Yes, I have a brother. He's three years older than I and very clever. Was it nice in Jerusalem?'

'It was like it always is. We stay with grandmother's relations and they are boring and she always complains about the poor people who sleep and eat in the outer courts of the Temple. She says they have no right to be there, but of course they do for how else could they come? It's stupid.'

When Jacob had left the room, I began a letter to Joshua. I told him as much as I could bear to look at on paper and asked for news of home. When the letter was written I felt much easier. I went outside.

The afternoon was overcast and we all watched the sky; the beaks of birds pointed upwards; the children panted under the trees, watching the clouds. Mother repeated that the lack of rain was a chastening from the Almighty and wondered what could account for it, while her darting looks made it clear that she had no doubt where to lay the blame.

I was awakened at dawn by a sound like the crack of a whip; I ran to the window. The sun was nudging a red face above the cover of the trees; the sky was torn into grey strands. Then the lightning was followed by thunder and the rain came down very straight, as the sky turned dark and dramatic. And there was Hannah – running into the rain, catching the raindrops on her tongue. 'I knew it would work, I knew God had ears after all.' She danced wildly as the rain fell, lifting her arms to the sky, clapping her hands. Jacob ran out and took her by the hands and the two of them in their flimsy nightclothes were leaping and laughing at the heavens. The drops came down harder and harder and the doors opened, as women and children – barely covering their nakedness – ran out into the street and sang and danced together. The men loitered in the doorways, rubbing their noses with sleep and embarrassment. I did not go out, I pulled my shawl tighter about my shoulders, but in my heart I danced with them. I turned and saw Samuel standing just behind me, his face creased from sleep, his thin lips smiling; and I was suddenly glad that he was there.

Hannah ran to me, a child running through bubbles; her hair hung in pretty tails around her face; her body was drenched. She pressed herself to me and I gasped at the cold. I took her off to dry her. We passed Mother, who, after a quick cluck of her tongue, managed a smile. Later, we had a huge breakfast, after a long and heartfelt prayer of thanks for the blessing of rain.

It rained for many days. Trees that were blind now made a million green eyes; the grass took on flesh. It was beautiful to walk, which I still did alone, unless Hannah could positively not be dissuaded from joining me. Primroses and violets grew thick on the ground and the birds' singing was like laughter.

One evening when the house was empty, Elizabeth filled me a bath in the tub in the kitchen. She poured in buckets of steaming water until her face shone from the heat and into the water she trickled a pot of oil which she had acquired for me from a travelling salesman in exchange for some silk. I climbed into the tub and lay back reverently in the deep water as Elizabeth smeared on an oatmeal and lavender face mask to lighten the sallowness of my skin. I lay there a long time, with my hair hanging down the back of the wooden tub. My pores opened and relaxed their tension; my skin grew meek and there was no stiffness in my limbs.

The door opened and Samuel walked in. He looked calmly at me, apologised and then beat a retreat through the door again. Elizabeth and I laughed and I got out reluctantly and began to rub myself dry. I went to my room as Elizabeth tried to find Hannah, so that the water should not be wasted. In my room, I folded my arms about me and stood quite still and relaxed for some time; then I chose a soft dress to wear. As the folds of muslin crept towards my warmth and the sweet smell of lavender filtered through the material, all my senses were drowsed and smothered. I was still young, so young – I loved the dreams and the dresses, but the kisses frightened me.

Not many years ago I ached for a kiss, a clean, child-like kiss. Was it too late for innocence after the soiled kisses, the mouths defiled? But mine was pink still and it loved you greatly. O you kissed my mouth, but it was a kindness only. Once when you were tortured; when your hands did not stop shaking – then you kissed me roughly; but with the rope of your mouth gone, I could see that even your thoughts had been absent from the kiss.

'Am I the One, am I He?' you demanded, knotting your fingers into mine. I did not answer. You lay back and murmured, 'I was born before the sky was discharged by the sea. Before I was, there was only water.' What was that? Madness? I don't know. Being inflamed by madness or by righteousness – in the end they are the same thing: they both appear to lack reason and destroy the order of life. Where is the reason in giving everything to the poor – it's lunacy. Or so they said.

It was near the end and your face was refined by suffering into something exquisitely beautiful and fragile. I wanted to touch it very carefully, like the most delicate wind-flower, knowing it had such a little time to be touched. But between those dark clefts in the skull's rocks, how you soared – scattering love, promises, hope, like a rich man's coins. And if you rose higher and sunk deeper than the rest of us – how vast also was your fear: 'Do not turn your face from me, Mary, do you understand what I am saying?' I was desperate, not knowing how to contain you, not knowing where next your actions would drive us. We all sat huddled in that dark room, afraid that the guards might come. Peter scowled across the room and his eyes rolled each time there was a sound outside. I was so tense and my fingers were so stiff that they ached for days afterwards and I kept thinking – I am a woman so small. I cannot keep up with this running. Why must he provoke people? Why can't we live in peace? I asked you why you insisted on enraging the priests and you looked at me as though I were a fool. 'There must be a time when there are no priests and no rituals – no pomp and ceremony, no long robes and special privileges. These are trappings and tinsel. The way to God is within each man and he must find it privately, or not at all.'

'But the priests help us to understand God,' I said stubbornly.

You smiled patiently and touched my nose with your finger, 'Dear Mary, you have always looked favourably on foolishness. If you want to know, you have to be what you know. It cannot be found in the Torah or told by a priest. Wisdom cannot be read or guessed.'

'They will kill you' – the words tumbled uglily into my lap.

You shrugged. 'We are the creators of our own heaven and hell. I do what I must.' You knew exactly what you were doing.

Later, we left Capernaum and went into the hills to a small farmhouse. We all slept in the barn and I watched you sleeping. You slept always with your eyes open – enough to see the grey-blue ripple of them, glazed and still. It was at times like that, while the others were unaware of you, that I knew that there was something a little repellent about you. Perhaps it was because I had so much respect and admiration for you; perhaps it was your conceit? Maybe I just hated you for falling asleep beside me.

It was the way you were going that frightened me, your direction – even though I believe that some people are not meant to live; their birth is an error. They live on the earth as misfits and cannot wait to be gone. You would have been happier on the moon; I, in water. But unlike you, I have no belief that something grander hovers in the wings. I expect nothing and it seems a craziness to long for nothing, yet I do. I am melancholy as King Saul crying into David's hair. How easily my mind shifts and buckles. Last night I woke and my cheeks were cold and wet. I was dreaming of my son. His eyes were dark-deep blue, smiling at me. Then I saw the moon setting in his hair above his little milky face, which faded, faded.

There has never been another spring like that one after the drought. I could see petals without stains, no mud in the water, no blood on the stars.

I was walking slowly through the woods when I suddenly decided to take a new path. Before, I had followed the same track monotonously, sometimes going further than on previous excursions, but always too listless to experiment. The track I followed now took me into a part of the woods where mainly pine trees grew and the ground was often rocky and difficult to walk on. Yet someone had obviously found the most sensible way around the boulders and over-hanging trees and the path followed a well-trodden course. I began to hear a sound that I had often heard in the woods, but paid no attention to. I approached the sound cautiously and after a while I could see through the trees into a clearing. There was a little hut made from stout pine logs one upon the other, and outside the hut was a man sawing wood. There he stood – tall, animal-like in his isolation, bristling with health as his arm moved back and forth as he cleaved. I watched him, moving no nearer. I could not see his face, only his heaving back and the slopes of his arms. Then he straightened himself and turned. It was Samuel. I was about to walk away when I realised that he had seen me. He stood looking in my direction, one hand pushing back his hair. He seemed perfectly at his ease; but I was not. I felt like a trespasser on his privacy. He walked towards me, but I made no move.

'I thought it was you,' he said, smiling, noting my agitation.

'I followed a different track, I didn't realise.'

'Has Hannah never brought you here?'

'No.'

'She knows the way. Sometimes I bring her here – she keeps a secret better than I thought.'

I looked confused, so he explained that the hut was where he did his woodwork, but not many people knew about it. His mother imagined he spent most of his time in the workshops in the village. I was curious by now, but distressed whenever I remembered that he knew all about me. He was trying hard to make me feel relaxed. 'I will show you a few things if you like.' I hesitated and he said quickly, 'Only if you would like to.'

'Yes, I would like to,' I said, wanting to very much.

Inside the hut it was lighter than I had anticipated: long, slim streaks of light entered through vents along three of the wooden walls. There was a sturdy table, with a few tools neatly stacked at one end and on the shelves along the unlit wall was a collection of objects which Samuel was moving towards. He took down a deeply-curved bowl made of sandalwood, with delicate carvings nestling at the bottom. When I looked closer, I could see that they were sparrows clustered around grain; but the work was so fine and light that you could have missed the decoration altogether. The bowl made me smile and I put my hand inside it, 'Is it all right if I touch?'

'It's meant to be touched, I hope one day to be used.'

I felt the little sparrows with my forefinger and then looked up at Samuel, who was reaching for something else on the shelf. He had a high forehead, calm eyes, and hair the colour of olive wood before it has mellowed. His expression was absolutely candid. I gave him back the bowl. He stood looking up at the shelf a little while before handing me a slim plate of dark wood; etched into the centre of this was a fish with a long flowing tail. It was quite beautiful, and as I looked at it I realised that I really wanted to possess it. I held it a long time. I told him it was extraordinary, and if he was pleased by the praise he did not show it.

'There's a small brook near here, if you are thirsty,' he said. 'Here, take this cup.'

I went only because I wanted to study the brown beaker by myself, in the hope that it might give me some clue to his nature. But he led me to the stream himself and I could only look at the cup for odd moments.

When I stood up after filling the cup, I looked quickly at his face, which was as flat and smooth as a stone which has been lapped a long time by flowing water. As I was drinking he said, abruptly, so that I almost choked, 'We are even now.'

'What do you mean?'

'Well, I came upon you bathing and now you have found me out.'

'I hope you don't mind,' I said, feeling that he did.

'No,' he said vaguely, 'I should have brought you here one day.'

This seemed such a strange remark for him to make, because our conversation really only crossed politely over the table at dinner.

'I think I am ahead of you,' he laughed – and his eyes, blue, then golden, escaped from his face and ran lightly over my body. But there was no offence in it; I moved back towards the path to the hut, but not in alarm. Walking back through the woods with the wind tugging my skirt like a child, I felt threatened by a premonition of approaching pain. It was as if Samuel was not only privy to my past, but, in some way, to my future also. But, that I was able to feel pain, even its first dart, there seemed some hope in that.

For three weeks after that, Samuel barely noticed me. And then for some nights he did not appear at all. At last I had to ask, and Father said that he had gone to Upper Galilee to fetch some cedar wood, as the supplies were getting low. When Samuel returned, he seemed more quiet than usual and his face looked very remote. I thought that he must be a man who collected his thoughts carefully – as one collects herbs – and only brought them out to examine when he was alone. His eyes could be so fierce, tearing sometimes at an object, like my shawl, and devouring it with intensity, but then coming to rest on people with indifference. It was this remoteness that I found touching; but when I thought of the word that I had applied to my emotion – touch – it embarrassed me and I tried to put him from my thoughts.

Jacob and I became friends. We had begun to examine *Isaiah* and *Daniel* because Simon had put off his plan to instruct Jacob in the first five books until such time as the boy was older and more receptive. Jacob was a strange, very intelligent boy, with lingering bouts of aggression, and needs that I could not really understand. Once, I came upon him rubbing and snuffling his face into my blouse; I pretended not to notice. He knew that I had, but neither of us referred to it, and this became our way. There were some days he would look up longingly into my face as if it were an altar he begged something of. Being afraid to offer gentleness, knowing he would have to rebuff it, I would say quietly instead, 'So, when do you think you will get the stallion, and where will you put it?' And then he would rush into a detailed and carefully worked out plan for this horse that his father had promised him and which he wanted more than anything else. Whenever he seemed vulnerable or too deep within his own head, I would conjure up the stallion and let him talk about it. Every detail of the horse's life was being worked out in his imagination and I knew that if ever I let anyone else know of this, our relationship, so precarious always, might be damaged beyond repair.

Jacob seldom played with Hannah, who was less solitary and had her own friends. I noticed, though, that when they did play together it was only variations on the same game. Once, when I was sewing in the shade, watching them, I heard Hannah say, 'Jacob, you be the child and I shall be the mother.' She lay down on the ground and pretended to be dead, but Jacob interrupted and said, 'No, I'll be the mother and you the child.' Then he lay down dead and Hannah came and knelt by him, wailing and putting mud on her face. Jacob, as though possessed by something other than the game, sat up and started thrashing at her with his hands. She moved fast, as if expecting it, and said patiently, 'O Jacob, you always spoil it. If you're dead you can't start hitting your child.' And he lay down meekly again. The game puzzled me. I often wondered what the reason could be for his behaviour, which was so often fraught with violence.

Once Hannah and I were walking in the garden; it was dark and cool and the sky was sprigged with stars like roses spun on silk. I began cautiously to question her. 'Hannah? You know this Ruth who was going to marry your uncle once – what happened to her?'

'O she's not dead,' she replied, 'she lives on a farm outside the village; her family only come when there is a feast or something like that. She never comes anymore.'

'What did she look like?'

'Well, pale really, with huge sunken eyes like a well; blue they were, very dark blue, but her hair was brown.'

I decided to confide in her a little. 'I found Samuel's secret place in the woods.'

'Did you?' She was clearly impressed. 'Did he mind, was he angry?'

'O no.'

'I go there sometimes.'

'Yes, he told me. We could go together then . . .' I suggested coolly.

'Yes, I think that would be all right. I'll come with you tomorrow if you like.' She smiled a sweet smile, then said thoughtfully, 'I thought you might marry my father, but he's not like Samuel of course.'

It was my first adventure in such a long time. I was careful to have Elizabeth arrange my hair neatly that morning, and because my hands were growing rough I rubbed oil into each finger until they looked white and smooth. But their shape still irritated me. Hannah and I stopped on the way to rest, for it was a fair distance, and she picked me a little bunch of violets which I put in my bodice.

'What's that stick you're holding?' she demanded, pointing to a piece of wood I had brought with me and tried to hide from her.

'O this? It's just a piece of wood I found a few days ago. It looks like a fish. Do you see how it curves and fans out into a tail and the head has this piece that looks like an eye bubble.' She appreciated it immediately and even discovered a line like a fin on one side.

'What will you do with it?' she asked.

'I'm going to give it to Samuel. He'll like it I think. Anyway, it's a good piece of pine.'

When we reached Samuel's clearing, he was rubbing down the edges of a circular piece of wood. He seemed pleased to see us but went on buffing with a coarse stone, blowing off the shavings and feeling the sides often with his palms. Hannah made her way to the hut and asked, 'Samuel, can I show Mary the doll you are making me?' He nodded and she took me inside the hut which smelt that day of resin and thick oils. The doll was wrapped up in a strip of old linen and Hannah unfolded it carefully. The head of the doll, in very pale, almost white, wood, was perfectly oval with heavy eyebrows and big round eyes; her nose was straight and she had a small, pointed mouth. She was beautifully carved. Samuel had fixed to her head a mass of black wool which curled and tumbled around her face – which had a frail expression upon the mouth, but the eyes, if you looked at them in isolation, seemed languid. Her body was not finished, but her arms and legs moved and Hannah said that she wanted to start sewing a dress for the doll to wear.

'And what shall you call her?' I asked, feeling the polished slopes of the doll's cheeks.

'O, I shall call her Sarah. She looks like a Sarah.'

We went out into the sun and Samuel sent Hannah to the stream to bring him a pitcher of water. She did not return for some time and there were things that I wanted to ask him, but did not dare. Finally, my voice asserted itself and I listened to it in alarm. 'I was told that you would be married . . .' I hesitated and then added stupidly, 'but you are not.'

'No,' he said, 'it would seem not.'

I pursed my lips at this curtness; and then he looked very directly at me so that I began to rummage with my fingers.

'And you are curious?' he asked flatly. I did not reply.

'It's too long a story and I have forgotten the details.' Then, unaccountably, he snapped out, 'It happened that she took to offering herself to all the young men.'

'But why?' I asked in a hushed voice.

'They say in the village that she was one of Satan's wives – my mother is convinced of it,' he smiled sideways, wryly. 'She was just a sad girl. I knew her when she was very young and I suppose she was always odd. I should have known better.'

'Are you saying she's mad?' I demanded in a shocked voice.

He said quietly, 'now she spends most of her days locked up, but can sometimes be seen running around naked in the woods.'

'But she cannot have always been that way – for you to . . .' my voice dribbled into nothing.

'I think she was always that way, but it was buried and only came out when something was required of her.'

'And what was that?'

'O – to be a wife, to settle down, to stop dancing in the woods perhaps.' He smiled limply and I persevered.

'Did you mind her dancing in the woods?'

'No, not if she danced for me.' He sat down and put down his stone as if he had determined something, 'We were lovers very young,' he stated it simply as if he knew that I would accept and not be shocked by it. 'But, I don't think that was the reason she became a slut. I think she understood lust and used it, but had no conception of love. She feared it and tried to escape it and me by throwing her body about. She did not want to be a wife. She would have been a terrible mother.'

'But you loved her?' I quickly asked as I saw the edge of Hannah's brown skirt appearing through the pines.

'O I loved her, but perhaps it was more her flesh that I craved. And in that I am guilty. I don't think of these things much. They seem an age ago. Yes, there was pain, but it is over now.'

Hannah splashed the pail of water down beside the work-bench and plonked herself on the grass beside me, carefully avoiding the wood-shavings on the ground. 'There is such lovely moss by the water,' she said to me, 'on the stones; and ferns like those you sometimes embroider – the ones that are hairy.'

'Yes,' Samuel said brightly, 'I have heard my mother complain about your form of needlework.'

I felt melancholy and stood up, brushing down my skirt. 'I sew what pleases me,' I said defensively, 'but I have also sewn dusters and rough cloths, and I will again, I'm sure. Come, Hannah, your grandmother will wonder where you are.' He looked at me again with that nostalgic tug to his mouth – not as if I reminded him of someone he used to know, I suddenly realised, but as if I reminded him of himself. We began to walk away, after Hannah had kissed Samuel on the top of his head as he again bent to work. We were nearly out of the clearing when I heard his voice calling my name and I turned. He walked towards me holding the fish-shaped log that I had left in the grass.

'Did you forget it?'

'No, it's for you.' He looked at it and turned it slowly in his hands. 'I shall leave it just the way it is – it couldn't be improved upon. Thank you.'

My face was a little glum, but I attempted a smile.

'You will come again?' he asked, 'by yourself?'

I turned to join Hannah, but his voice behind me insisted, 'You will come, won't you?'

'Maybe,' I said, to end it; but a pain gnawed at wounds which seemed hardly healed. And I did not want it, did not want it at all.

I did not go back, but his words and face expanded in my mind; and the panic was abating. A few weeks later – after we had only smiled at one another across the noisy bowls and said no further word

– I was walking in the garden, looking at the moon. He came and stood beside me. I smiled brightly at him and said, 'Have you seen the moon? It's so bright that it makes shadows as sharp as the sun's.'

He nodded and said gently, 'I saw you standing by the meadow. I was watching at the same time, but you didn't see me.' Then he added, 'Now we can really talk, you and I. Now it is time. Before you weren't ready, you were locked inside your brain. Now you are ready.' And because he was so certain, I knew that he was right.

I went walking by the lake today: I had to get out of this little house where the walls sometimes seem to move inwards. The sea made me feel heady and full of happiness. It was brisk blue, flecked with white. I thought of Joshua as a boy, rubbing the pink scales off the fish, and of Father, shouting at the fishermen not to dump their catch so far from the women's slabs. I thought of you kicking at the water with your head down, and then you would shout with the lid off your voice – 'Mary' and I would run down to the water's edge to see what you had found. You would only say, 'I'm starving, when will those fish be done?' and send me back to the fire. But I knew that you called not for that, but because you missed me and felt isolated just for that moment.

When I returned home from my walk they were there: your brother, James, and two strangers. James took me aside in the garden; he was nervous, his forehead sweated. He asked me whether you had written anything down; were there any papers? I told him there was nothing. Why should I tell him? What is it to them? There is so little anyway, and it is mine.

The years are so shocking and we are all in such disarray. Now he tells me that there are sorcerers claiming to be gods in your name, and that some would like to take your ideas to the Gentiles. I do not know what to make of all this. When they use your words, they are altered by whoever speaks them. You said once, 'The wisdom of the Scribes is empty and the elders have lost even the respect of children.' But now, James says it is important to keep in with the Scribes and Saducees. O keep me as the apple of your eye, hide me under the shadow of your wings. Why will they not understand? There was only one of you. Nothing they can say or do will ever be you.

Elizabeth brought me a fish, but I could not eat it. In my mind I kept seeing you as a fish, with a hook in your side, and your eye, weeping – wept blood. She took the fish away and I saw that her face has grown old and her long eyes are dusted with shadow. She worries when I do not eat. I would have liked to have eaten the fish for her sake, but I could not put it into my mouth.

How can he ask me for your papers? He feels perhaps that I have no right and that all things belong to that little community that he is trying to generate? Well, I do not forget that he cared nothing for you until you were dead – none of them did. So I will keep what is yours, what is mine. They shall have nothing that belongs to us. I have not looked in the little wooden box with the carved oak leaves and I could not, not yet. Sometimes I fondle the box because you made it, because your fingers worked the leaves. Some day I shall be able to look at the Hebrew characters again and read that sad, beautiful poetry. For now, I remember well enough.

I went back to the hut in the pines many times and Samuel and I talked, but mainly I listened. I found myself asking him questions, which always he answered honestly and fully, but the answers injured me and drove me from him into a cool inner place. I did not want to know about Ruth; about how he had known her; but I plied him for information and let his replies fly back against me. Sometimes he would spill some words, quite unaware that they took root and grew inside my mind until they filled it. I retreated then into my own thoughts – how the land had looked on my walk the day before; how the sun made shadows on the creamy-brown earth and the ploughed land rippled into waves as I walked. I would stare fixedly at the delicate ridge of pines with rounded branches huddled close to the sky. I loved that ridge better than the other pines in the forest, which were so close together that their individual formations were lost in a blaze of green.

Samuel was like a pine tree himself: tall, lean and self-sufficient, moving in his own rhythm. I had known nothing about him in all the months I'd lived in Mother's house, nothing at all until I came upon him working in the forest. At that moment I knew him well, and yet I also felt that I would never truly understand him; never get any closer to his essential being than I could to that of a tree. He swayed towards me with a confidence I did not understand, and if it was based on experience, I did not want to consider that.

Once, in the sunlight, he let his hand fall lightly on to the crown of my head. I felt my muscles contract and he took his hand away, with no haste. He was, I see now, testing my strength, wondering what I could endure, and at that time it was pitifully little. After closing like a flower, any flare of emotion reduced me to quivering. To a person deprived of warmth for too long, a heavy blanket is unbearable. And so, for me, any tenderness offered was too close to pain.

Soon Samuel learned how to protect me from the snares I set for myself. He would seem to find my questions boring, or answer them briefly, and then try to turn the conversation to lighter topics. Because he had begun to understand so well, he even had the ability to make all his past seem quite unimportant and he had the blessed gift of knowing just how to reassure me any time he felt that a word had cut too deep. Only once he asked me about Mattathias, but I found myself trembling so violently that I was obliged to leave.

That night, looking down at my body, I touched it sadly, knowing it lacked something – seeing the thighs no longer shone and the breasts were chilled like pale lilies. I shivered, not for the cold, but for the pleasure of having myself all to myself. I thought, If I were kissed I might die. I smiled down at my chastity as swans arch their necks at their own reflections. But slowly my smiles grew stiff, and I ached suddenly for the crumpled hours, for the fierce terror of those nights I had learned to live without, learned so well that now I feared another heat might consume me.

But time passed and in the predictability of my days and Samuel's growing patience, I began to feel safe. Sitting quietly beside him in his hut, sheltering from a sudden burst of rain, I felt quite at peace, easy in his company as he split wood into neat lengths and piled them in one corner. He walked past me to look out of the door, and then stopped and looked down at me as I sat stitching a cloak for Hannah's doll. His voice was quite composed. 'Will you marry me?'

My heart began leaping, but I said, 'I've been married already.'

'I know, but it does not alter the question.'

I began to stitch quicker – afraid, really afraid – seeing the drop ahead but running too fast to change direction. He stroked my hair, 'We will go at your pace, I don't want to frighten you.' I was so grateful that I snatched his hand and kissed it before turning my face away. And we did not speak of it again, but both understood the commitment and were waiting.

Simon returned from Jerusalem one evening and brought out of his bag a letter from Joshua. Thus I learnt that my father was very ill and not expected to live to the next feast day: his stomach was rotted by strong drink and he had a lump the size of an apple above his groin. Joshua was obviously saddened by this, but I could only respond vaguely, as though he wrote about a person I knew only slightly. The tougher side of my nature felt relieved that, should he die, I need not fear making the trip to Jerusalem again. Joshua also reported that my other brothers had left Jerusalem and settled near Hebron, but little was heard of them – and, now that he knew, he would not speak to them again. The letter distressed me because I could see how much these things tortured Joshua. The last thing he wrote, characteristically, was about himself: he was to be married in the autumn and hoped that I would come. I never did go. But often after that, a messenger came with letters and money. And one day the news came that my father was dead. I sat and told myself I ought to cry, but no tear came. Later, in the woods when I told Samuel, he was not shocked that my voice was so calm in telling of a death; he merely said, 'If you can care nothing at his death he must have deserved it.' His understanding, as so often, mitigated the guilt that tried always to wind itself into my thoughts.

If I was beginning to feel reassured, it was very slowly. Often when I felt happy and useful in my life, looks, words and insinuations crushed me. But the children helped: Hannah was learning to read, though her mind always attached itself to things that moved, and because words lay still they could not hold her for long. Jacob now treated me with respect and even some consideration, but there were many days when I felt that they both expected too much of me; that in their hunger for affection and care they threatened to devour me. Mother's unkindness to me had shifted to an impatience which would sometimes ignite into petty spitefulness. Still my only task was the bread-making. Samuel advised, 'You must ignore her as I do, as we have all learnt to do.' But to me, ignoring her was giving in to her tyranny; allowing her to misuse; and as the days passed I found it increasingly difficult not to be roused to anger by her. I did not altogether approve of Samuel's handling of his mother: he took no notice of all her jibes against him and Ruth – in a way I couldn't have done. I felt that he should assert himself and put her in her place, but he insisted on treating her in his own way – with indifference. The cool waters of his contemplations seemed to sink the minor upsets which caused me to flounder horribly.

One morning I woke happy – as though all my dreams had been gentle. I hugged Elizabeth when she brought in my water and laid out my linen. 'Why do you always look after me so well?' I asked her. She was surprised by this unexpected burst of gratitude and busied herself untangling the hair from my brush and rolling it into dark balls like wool. I gave her some money, too much, and told her to buy herself a new length of material in the village.

'But for whom should I wear it?' she asked simply.

Her words caught at my memory, pulling a cord painfully, and I said, 'For me, wear it for me.' Then I added, 'And don't buy anything too sombre.' Just as her hand reached for the door latch I said, breathless but unafraid, 'I am going to be married.'

When I had said it, I knew that it would happen. I ran off into the woods as soon as Jacob had finished his lesson – even he had detected my excitement, for he'd said, 'Why are you so jolly? You didn't even frown when I got the psalm all wrong.' I did not enlighten him. When I got to the hut, Samuel was not there and I had to wait a little while until he came back from the village. The expectation heightened my happiness. I waited for him, looking at all the familiar things in his work-shed. There was a pale olive-wood bowl with an edging of daisies that he had given me and a little clay goblet that I drank water from. I looked at the bowl with the carved sparrows and thought of his words: 'It's meant to be touched, I hope one day to be used.' O how I wanted to use it, to fill it with lentils or beans. I wanted a house full of things that he had made; and I wanted the clothes that he put on his body to be sewn by my hands and to embroider the linen for a table he would preside at. I was glad again to be a woman and able to do these things – to comfort myself as only women can – by administering, by filling out the necessity of living with softness – feathering the hard nest.

I watched him as his body broke off from the fringe of pines and entered the clearing; he walked slowly towards the cage of doves and threw them some grain. Then he looked up and saw me, and smiled – O but it was not enough, not enough, and I was disappointed. I had yearned for him in his absence; my fingers had picked up and caressed his leather apron as I had watched his progress towards the hut. Now he just stood, patiently, kindly; but something in me was deflated. I turned away to hide my sadness: why could he not have known?

'Have you been here long?' he asked.

'No, I just came.'

'Good, I don't like to think you might have been alone too long.'

'What were you doing?'

'I was taking some of the resin to the workshops.'

'O, yes.' I was polite, but remote and a little angry with him for nothing he had done.

We sat together on the bench and he looked hard at me, but I averted my eyes. Then he began busily to scribble with a pen on a piece of cloth. I moved over to look. The linen unfolded to reveal diagram after diagram of a little wooden house on rock foundations. Each diagram was a careful layout of one angle of the house and each had neat measurements and notes beside it.

'What is it?' I asked.

'It is a house that I'm going to build.'

'For whom?'

'For myself, and for the wife I'm waiting for.' And he took my fingers lightly, looking up from the busy cloth. 'Must I wait for ever?'

I bent down and kissed him fiercely and in return he kissed me softly and I could not prevent myself saying, 'And have you no passion for me?' He laughed and said, 'Passion is too strong for those who have not drunk awhile.' Now it was I who waited impatiently for him to catch up; now I was in full bloom, but the flowering was too sudden for him. He, who had only known me cold, was still nervous of frightening me. And I hurt because we were out of time.

The afternoon passed quietly as we sat at the battered work-bench which dipped in the centre and he explained to me how soon he would clear a little more of the forest higher up the hill and start to build the house. I had to ask, 'When did you first decide to build a house?'

'I've been designing houses in my head for years, but this is the first time that I have actually wanted to build one.' The answer almost satisfied me. 'I want to build it for you – for us to live in,' he said seriously, and I was comforted as though his hand had stroked me.

'Yes,' I said, almost certain, 'I would like to live here among the pines; I would like to be your wife.' The look he gave me was a little puzzled.

'Are you sure? You must be sure. I won't hurry you and we will tell no one yet.'

We were happy in the months ahead. It was a good summer and there was plenty of rain in the soil: the wheat flowed and the beasts were all strong and fat. I was aware of these things, but all my attention was drawn to the times when I would go up into the woods and be with Samuel. I went usually when the afternoon lull set in; when the sun's rays lengthened and the wind came up, shaking the leaves and grasses. I had learned to love the pines. Looking up their tall, noble trunks to the blue rag of sky I was reminded of how I had once craned my eyes up the Temple walls as a little girl. The spicy smell released by the pine needles and the sun splattering on the saplings with their golden or red trunks – these things made me happy. Yet of all the trees, I was drawn most lastingly to the old ones, seeing in them, as I had in the sea, a certain wisdom.

I began to tell Samuel about the house that Mattathias and I had lived in for that short time and how happy I had been there. My past did not seem to bother him; he accepted it as part of the fibre of my nature and his questions, unlike mine, were not barbs. He seemed wise for his twenty years and had inherited his father's sensitivities. His coolness began to arouse my passion. His hair always smelled of wood-smoke and I wanted to touch it; I wanted to ruffle his composed features, to bedevil his capable hands as they planed and smoothed wood. One day, when the temptation was too strong, I leaned against his back as he sat astride a bench, and rested my cheek on his hair. 'What are you doing?' he asked, straightening. As his face came round to me, my heart splashed at his feet like spilt water.

'I think I love you,' I said – but moving, turning away. His hand cut into my wrist,

'Then don't turn away, come to me.' Nervously moving round to stand in front of him, feeling wretched in my exposure, I wished the sun would retreat behind a cloud or some commotion in the trees save me from his certainty, his quiet orientation.

He pulled me down on to his knees, and, feeling the stiffness in my body, he rocked me, rubbing his cheek against my shoulder. 'I shall be good to you and not desert you. I shall love you as you deserve, if you will allow it.' I wanted to stay like that for ever, as if I were a child again, woken by a dream – crying without end into the pounding darkness, and then hearing a familiar step, waiting for a hand to smooth the hot cheeks.

But I know now that there is no tenderness, no love, that can ever eradicate the terrors of childhood nights. Passion disperses them only for a small flutter. Still I lie wrestling with my childhood. For an hour I have lain straight on my bed, hearing the cries of an animal in the hedges. In the little silence before its agonised wail is repeated, I hear the sound of its persecutor's whoop as the claw sinks again – frenzied, pitiless. And I become the hunted one; each cry awakes an unforgotten howl in my halted throat, while fragments of memory slump against the sides of my brain: it was too close, I should not have come so close; the sobbing, your gaunt body buckling – No, no, please no more the nocturnal killing. The animal out there and I, we draw our fear together, we crouch beneath the night's arched back, awaiting only the last sad sigh of acceptance . . .

And yet – how beautiful it is now to awake to a morning without malice: stretching, creaking my back, tasting the sunshine on my mouth. To hear the birds splashing in the stone basin; to see the footprints in the dew leading to the door, where the milk waits, still warm from the udder. I will not look in the hedge for what I know lies there; I will not seek after severed, lost things. The water will come rocking in the blue basin and I will duck my head and shake the drops into the white towel. I can only do this because I am thirty-seven. When I was fifteen I would have bent and peered and been torn by the clotting blood, the flared eyes. Then, I had to see. Now I know.

Poor Mary in the pines, so frightened, saying, Take me if you must and I will allow it and pretend it is not happening. Not saying it out aloud, loud enough for only the body to hear and the brain to remain deaf. But he knew it, he sensed it in the cramped body locked against his side and he only waited. If my body then felt itself to be passionate, how pathetic it later seemed against Samuel's great passion: when I was warm and aching I only began to approach his fierce heat. All this he knew before it even happened – but I understood nothing.

I was gathering dried needles for him near the stream and he came and said, 'I've come to help you. I need so many of those for the roof.' He then explained to me how it would be done: dense layers of pine needles gummed down to bark and supported by timbers – to make a cool, sloping roof. It was a mild afternoon, growing quite late, but the earlier heat had brought out a heavy scent among the trees and the pine forest murmured with the sound of the tide pulsing in a sea-shell.

We worked until I got tired and then I went to get water for us both from the stream. When I returned, Samuel was resting his back against an old pine and rubbing earth into his fingers where some glue had stuck. My back ached from bending, so after handing him the cup I lay down flat upon the ground and pushed my spine into the hard earth, closing my eyes. He came and knelt beside me, pushing back my hair. I took his hand and covered my eyes with it. Then his mouth bit into mine and my eyes clenched, then opened, opened, closed again.

I lay as inert as the pine needles; shadows fell saving my face: I must cover it. His hands lifting, touching, learning – and I, watching. What is that bird doing in the branches? See how the light quivers – how large my eyes grow. It is not the same. I would have been comforted by the familiar – but this is darker. His mysterious quietness frightens me. And it is so bright. Will no one cover my eyes? I am lost, unclean. I hear a whimper in the bushes. The lilies are trampled. The sun's melted me but I am cold and dry, feeling more alone and indifferent with each touch. The pain in my heart is physical: like the rough thong of a sandal on raw flesh. I long to weep, but cannot.

He, pulling his hands from my eyes, asked, 'Are you ashamed?' And all the sweetness of his nature surfaced in his grey, ordinary eyes.

'No,' I said, turning my face a little and wondering then if I should be ashamed. It was a feeling of loss, and I wanted to say, 'Leave me, cover and leave me, cover all of me with leaves.' He lay by my side and then his hand reached and took mine. How many times – many, many – when my mind was absent, or my body, his hand always moved to mine. I could have loved him just for that.

Afterwards they came – the little pins of doubt: he has used my body as he did hers. I am compromised, sullied and he is not beholden to me. I kept away from the woods the next day, feeling his confusion and hurt from my distance; but too afraid to go back in case his mouth, sated, had turned cold.

Why wouldn't you remember what we did under the fig trees – is it possible that we ever lay nose to nose?

I spent the afternoon with Hannah by the fields, where the men were about to begin the first harvesting. We saw Father striding up to the field, with Jacob following, carrying a loose leather sack. Hannah explained that before any grain was cut, Father always went into every man's fields and carefully selected the best seed for the next year's sowing. Jacob was accompanying him for the first time to see how it was done. The boy was deeply impressed by the gravity of the task. Father had been chosen years ago for this solemn business and no other man in the village was given the privilege. We watched them walking into the waving field and I smiled as I saw Father's white beard bend towards the boy as he explained and pointed, and then, only after most diligent searching, the first grain found its way into the sack. The labourers nodded in approbation, lifted their scythes and began to work. I thought to myself how much Jacob had softened, having learnt to comfort himself by finding harmony in his work.

I waited anxiously for Samuel to come back in the evening – dreading the moment, but wanting it. He returned earlier than usual, and after washing found me sewing in the courtyard.

'I was worried, thinking you might be ill,' he said, touching my hair.

'No.'

He just said – 'O' – and his voice sounded a little disconcerted although his face did not show it.

'You are not angry?' he persisted.

'No,' stitching madly, my foot rubbing at the earth floor in agitation.

'I wish you had come. I thought so much last night and I wanted to tell you.'

'What were you thinking?'

'Well, firstly, that I want to tell Father that we are to be married. And when he knows we can inform Mother.'

'Well, she'll be delighted,' I said sarcastically.

'Don't worry about her. I'll arrange with Father so that the betrothal is not an endless affair like Simon's. Do you still want to be married?'

'If you do.'

'Of course I do.' He pulled the cloth from my hands and tilted up my chin. 'Don't look so sad, it's only a wedding.'

'I worry, about Mother, she hates me so.'

'She will probably change now that you are to be family.'

I doubted it and mulled on my anxieties so much that there was little room for relief. Samuel was so excited. 'I will speak to Father tonight, after dinner. Wait for me by the fig trees, and try to get rid of Hannah.'

I sat under a tree playing cat's cradle with Hannah. Samuel did not come. One of Hannah's untidy friends came bounding down the path and, disentangling the wool from my fingers, she rushed Hannah off in the opposite direction with the promise of a honey cake. I gathered my thoughts together and waited for Samuel. It was owl-light; the garden which looked so dusty and uncared for in the day took on a bleak beauty under the waning moon. I was scratching my fingers, brimming with premonitions when Samuel walked slowly towards me. When he was close enough, I could see that his face was serious. I was expecting the worst when he smiled and called out, 'I've told him.'

'What did he say?'

'He was pleased.'

'Are you sure?'

'Yes of course. But Mother, with her nose for things, came in just as we were discussing what she should be told. So I told her straight out.'

'What did she say?'

'Well, she sniffed and said, "Of course I suspected as much" and refused to say another word.'

'And then what?'

'Father announced firmly that we had agreed a brief betrothal – at that, her eyes looked suspiciously at mine – and that when the terms had been agreed with your brother, we should be married in the spring. Then she assumed a pose of great suffering and patience and said. "If that is what my son wants, who am I to make remarks?" Father said, "Good, it's all settled then and we must have a feast soon."' Samuel smiled and said, 'If he says it's settled, then it is.' He pulled me to him and rocked me and laughed in my hair. He was as excited as a child.

'Why?' I asked.

'I have always wanted a wife.'

Later, walking back with Samuel's arm about my waist and my head bumping happily against his shoulder, I felt safe again as though he had found me in an alien place and taken me home. I knew little about him – nothing, I sometimes felt – but of one thing I was certain: there was no cruelty in him.

Was it a cruelty that made you say, 'Some day I will not be here. What will you do without my hand to hold up your head?' I made you promise and you did – 'I will never leave you. I will be with you always.' I believed you because I used to think, what would you do without my lap to groan into? My hands to stroke your dark-brown hair? You were the goodest one; I could not accept that you wanted to escape. Because I had suffered so, I needed to believe that you could change the world, or at least my small portion of it. One day, my eyes would open and all would be different as in your dreams. I thought you could make it happen; sometimes I believed it so strongly that I thought love must be the most powerful invention Man would ever know. You said, 'All you need is faith.' O I had that, though I had forgotten how to pray – my fingers when I tried to press them together always missed, would not fold together like yours and the angels'. I gave myself up to you utterly, relying on your dependence. Do not think that I am disillusioned that you let us all down. I think of you; sometimes I seem to see you rubbing your side – you must be so lonely. And I would love to kiss you; you had such a mouth: heroic, tender. When I was close to you, I watched as your mouth swelled with words until my eyes fell into it. When they came back to me they saw everything the way you did. When you were angry you reduced your mouth to a pale line like a serpent and the tails of it whipped. Often I longed to bite your mouth; when I did, that time, it gave me the same pleasure as a stolen apple gives a child.

That breathless noon, when the men sat so still, drugged by the torpid air in the curtained room in Stephen's house. The women, waiting for the last guests to arrive, dragged in and out with heavy plates and jugs of wine, which they banged resentfully on the table – wanting only to sleep. Between them, you sailed up and down on the white wings of your imagination – seeing no one, hearing nothing, talking in slow fascination to yourself – until finally you announced, 'Moses never spoke to God.' In the limp silence, you moved to the centre of the room and explained in great detail how Moses had needed to trick the people for their own good. I could feel an anger rising with the hot air in the room, but no one broke into your speech. Watching you, stunned, I knew I would remember always how glossily your face shone, reflected in the beauty of your eloquence. And how strange it was, when we all mopped our brows and felt soaked in our linen, that you sweated not at all, but stood cool, uncreased. But then you spun round on some wretched woman who stood brooding in one corner and thundered, 'That woman is maddened by her memories; they afflict her with headaches that never cease. But I can make her forget every bad memory of her life.' The woman looked at you, began to back away and then fled in tears. You shrugged and began to talk again, very quietly.

Stephen never asked you to his house again because his wife did not remember the incident kindly; she thought she detected Satan's vibrations in her kitchen, and resented that while everyone ate and enjoyed her lavish food, you fell asleep in a corner, having not touched a mouthful.

My life is so light, so light that it soars far above me, and occasionally I reach out my arm and pull down a memory, for the memories are far closer, and I stretch them to their full length to give my life something to do. Yet whenever you spoke of the past, I could see that it meant nothing to you – you wanted none of it back. But I, I wish I could tug at the memories and pull and pull – for I would have all of it back. Samuel; me, that odd girl; trees, violets – youth, youth.

When Samuel and I were betrothed, I felt less isolated from the village. I thought that now I had the right to walk down the street as though it belonged, a little, to me also; and to shoo the chickens from my path instead of walking around them. The villagers, although they would never accept me as one of their own, softened fractionally. The women no longer felt the threat of an unattached woman in their midst and the men slowly relaxed their penetrating stares. I was flung more into the company of the village women now that I had a household to prepare for and a million things that I would need.

I began to sense that the villagers had a barely concealed distrust of Samuel. He had made the distance from them himself, being a man apart in his life and his thoughts and separate from them because of his Jerusalem education. They could not understand why he had decided to carve wood when he could have been a lawyer or doctor in the city. Nor could they penetrate his granite face. When he laughed with them, as he did often, they seemed to feel that he was laughing at not quite the same thing. I understood their caution because I found him a little unreachable myself. Though he was always kind and loving and liked the touch of a hand, the space was made by his gravity, his solitary character and his dedication to his work. I noticed, though, that if there was one thing that clamped down the tongues it was his great skill. He was recognised by the entire community and the neighbouring areas as a fine craftsman, producing delicate, painstaking work that could not be equalled. It was said by some that if you listened outside when he was working, you would not hear a sound, not even of breathing – which they put down to genius, or something more strange, being only familiar with the commotion of village workshops.

You used to say that wood should be used to make charcoal and useful sturdy implements for daily life: they should be made properly and simply, above all simply, because there was too much time wasted whittling the necessities of life into things of beauty. Beauty, you always felt, was only in the soul. For that reason you wore old clothes in dull serviceable colours – until the end, when you began to wear those rough white robes that needed so much washing. Samuel believed the opposite: everything made by his hands was thought out with the greatest care: how the cups should fit the fingers that would hold them, the plates be broad and balanced for the food they must contain, the handle to the jug comfortable to pour from. And when all those details had been perfected, the object itself was polished and given bare but beautiful decoration. Everything that he made I wanted to hold in my hands and use. But if I put a single object on its own in a quiet place and just looked, the thing had a presence and a beauty that was not separate from its purpose.

We were married when due time had passed after the Passover. My days had been spent in preparation, which various women in the village organised and helped; but just before the ceremony itself,

Mother began to take command. She had been surly and uninterested throughout the betrothal period, and impatient of Samuel and Hannah's enthusiasm. In the final week she sat me down and told me the things that she felt I ought to know: how many times and when in the month it was permissible to make love (by her calculations this was only five days); which positions and acts were not acceptable for a decent woman. How much should be spent on food and servants; how often the house should be cleaned; the preparation of food and so on. I was polite, thinking that if there was one household routine that mine would not follow, it was hers.

Samuel and I fasted before the wedding, and the morning before I was to be dressed for my wedding Mother insisted that I drink a sticky draught of some strange syrup which muddled my thoughts and made me sleepy. She then took me to the baths in the village, where I was to be cleansed before being presented to my husband. I went with her meekly into a deep room with a pool of water. Two elderly men were watching in one corner; and then a third came forward to disrobe me and plunge me into the icy water, which rushed out from an underground stream. My nails were then cut, and while I sat shivering in a corner the man who had pushed my head under the water lifted the dripping weight of my hair and hacked it off with chopping strokes at the nape of my neck. A cry came from my throat which echoed bleakly in the little chamber; my hands felt desperately for the rough ends of my hair, which had gone, which had never been cut in my life before. I began to weep and vaguely saw Mother conferring with the man; he argued with her a little and I heard her voice rise, saying something to the effect that I was full of vanity and would be a trouble to her son. The man frowned, then nodded reluctantly. He came and stood beside me a moment, then tilted up my face, smiling, whispering I should not worry – things grew again. His hand lifted and I felt the cool stroke of a razor across one eyebrow. It was over. I just stared and stared, not daring to touch. Then I straightened my face, dressed, and covered my head with my veil and went home to be married.

Elizabeth wrung her hands when she saw me; I asked her to leave me alone. It took me a long time to lift the little silver disc that would reflect my new face. When I did, I dropped it again and covered with my hand the empty place where a dark eyebrow once had been. I cried until Elizabeth came back and put her arms about me and slowly opened one of her hands to reveal a soft flint of charcoal, which very carefully she traced above my eye and said, 'There, it is perfect; no one will know except that cruel bitch.'

The wedding had the quality of a nightmare for me. The syrup was still effective and all that I could see with any clarity was the floating vastness of Mother in her rose gown; and always it seemed that in her hand dangled, gleaming, a thin-bladed knife.

Only much later, when Samuel and I were closeted together in our bridal room, which he had filled with flowers, did I remove the veil which I had pulled down low over my forehead. Then he noticed the shaved eyebrow. I explained to him what had happened, keeping my face bent, feeling more humiliated and injured now that my ugliness was revealed to him. He sat quite still a moment and then flew from the room. I could hear his voice, and Mother's cringing tones, wrestling together in the garden, but every now and then a burst of music or the clapping of hands obliterated what they were saying. Having by now fully recovered my senses, I moved to another upper room so that I could hear more clearly.

I could not see them because they were almost immediately beneath the room I had chosen. Mother began to weep under the lashings of Samuel's anger. I could tell that she was astounded and did not know what other course to follow. Hearing him revile her, after all the occasions when I had found him tractable, even cowardly, I was immeasurably comforted. I felt a glow of gratitude for him that he should protect me from her bullying.

When Samuel returned he was still shaking with anger and I was too harrowed to try to comfort him with my kisses. I could not lift my face to his scrutiny, so finally, with one hand holding up my head, his other hand gently wiped off the charcoal and he kissed and kissed the naked place.

I wept more that night than I care to remember. I seemed suddenly burdened by pain, my past, and so full of fear for the future that nothing could ease it. I remember how lovely his body was – such eyes as my memory has – long limbs with slim curves at his waist; the straight, true lines of his limbs and the flatness of his stomach seemed to have been delicately chiselled to give the appearance of both strength and languor. His hands, when he lay or sat, always rested one upon the other in a particular pose, and when he had finished drinking from a cup he balanced it upon his knee without appearing to be conscious of its precarious position.

The moon looked through the window and a breeze nestled into the drapes. We did not sleep. His rebuke to his mother had given me a feeling of security and I was cool, waiting. Before, I had known that soft burning in the outer rim of my body; but this was deeper, at the lips of the womb – flames lapping, swelling, tightening: I am a flower torn, flooding open, then melting, in the place where the child shudders to life: the root of sorrow. I lay thinking, I have melted, become fluid. I smile and I smile as his hand strokes my head. We lay surrounded by silence; the guests had all gone home and the tambourines were barely a memory.

I began to grow hot and full of panic, but continued to lie quite still beside him. He did not sense that everything had altered, that my mind was spinning and crashing into insoluble objects. Then I was weeping again and had to bury my face into the pillow.

'What is it?' he rolled over, turning me by the shoulders, and I could only gasp, 'The linen, I will have no linen.' But he did not understand and I had to explain that a wife must keep her linen to prove, if anyone should question it, that she was a virgin. Mother would expect to see the linen and would cause trouble if I refused to show it. Samuel did not say anything; he rose instead from the bed and quietly left the room; I heard the doors closing softly behind him and recognised the rusty creak of the kitchen door.

It was much later when he returned, almost dawn. He held in his arms a bundle of white linen which he handed to me. I took it and opened it timorously, and saw, spread across the centre, a long stain of blood. 'What is it?' I asked, dropping the sheet. He looked at me and said, 'I killed one of the white doves.' And how I loved him. I rubbed my head into his tussocky hair and stroked his cheeks and I noticed with wonder how closely he had touched my heart. When the sun rose, we fell asleep exhausted, drowned by one another and full of a peace that was deeper than sleep.

Later I was to ask him – too many times – 'Do you love me? Do you love me best of all?' And even later – 'Did you love her body as you do mine? And those others, those passing girls, was your passion as strong then?' And he answered, 'My passion for you is no less than for the others; my blood flows as it always has. Passion is always and only passion.' He never saw how that injured me; how it made my flesh want to remain cool and chaste, away from his. It was the saying of it that hurt – the loud words that tapped away inside my heart. I thought how there had been one whom I had loved once, hotly, fiercely, and even his remembered face caused tears to peck at my eyes. But I would not have told him this. He would sense my withdrawal and it hurt him, so he said, 'Love is not the same as passion. It is quite different. So is marriage, and I have married only you. My past is over, it's nothing.' But it was my past that was inconsolable.

He never understood that I had to scrape off the surface of everything, to enter it, not by knowledge necessarily, or even to say afterwards – it is this or that – just simply to know, by instinct to know. He did not want to go into things, or into the deeper recesses of our minds; he wanted all things to go by quietly: to touch them, to feel them, but not to slice into them. He knew, yes he always knew, but he had to be forced to tell.

We still lived under Mother's roof and I found it more and more unbearable. She hated me now with a more carefully concealed intensity and made a point of always being polite to me when Samuel was present. He was rarely present and my life continued in the same way. I liked to keep up the children's lessons and it gave me something to do. Mother would never agree to my cooking a meal or preparing anything for Samuel – it was her kitchen, her son. As each day passed, I loathed her more, until I could not stay in a room that contained her sullen countenance, her gross body and red hands. I felt that if I touched her flesh I would recoil. Things reached such a point that everything about her became despicable. This caused gulfs between Samuel and me, because, although he understood the desperation I felt, he was powerless to say anything more than, 'I can't do anything more, I am building the house as fast as I can.' So I waited, but all the time I knew that even when we had gone to live in the woods we would never be rid of Mother, she would always be present to torment me. I suppose I resented that Samuel could not feel the same hatred for her that I did: it was something we could not share. She was his mother and he could only sympathise with what seemed often a strained patience. And that was not enough. If I walked into a room and found them talking happily together, I felt sick, it was a betrayal, and I disliked him for it.

I used to go to the forest and sit watching Samuel as he worked. As I sat there I was conscious of only seeing his back, and that seemed to symbolise his immersion in his work and his separation from me. Although he said, 'But I am with you, and I am building for you and working out everything so that it shall please you . . .', still I felt alone. I began to creep back into the consolation of books, re-reading all that Mattathias had left me. I would sit in the shade and read while he worked, and it pleased him because he felt that though we did separate things, we were still together. But I was jealous of his thoughts and imagined that they had nothing to do with me. Sometimes, I would try to write, as I had once in another garden, but the words had left me and the pen would drop from my fingers as I would find myself staring at Samuel, wondering if he thought about the girl Ruth, wondering if he resented me for hating his mother.

What did you do with the poems I wrote you? There was a time when you carried them with you wherever you went . . .

In the nights Samuel was able to comfort me, but I longed for something more lastingly present than his physical love. If I tried to explain it, he said, 'But I always think of you, whatever I am doing, wherever I am.' I felt though that I never possessed him. Always, while with him, talking to him, lying bound to his body, I was aware of movement; of his little withdrawals into himself as his thoughts slipped out of me, as his eyes shut like windows. Only while he slept he was defenceless, child-like, mine – but of course not mine at all because then he roamed in dreams and a silence that I could never penetrate. Yet I felt I had him then, because he made no movement away from me – he was still, quiet, containable. It was out of this sorrow that my love grew, without it my feelings dwindled. I would lie beside him as he slept and my love would fill my body until it had to flow out through my eyes. If he woke and spoke to me, his words, however sweet, would disappoint me. My inner voids made all things insufficient.

When the house was almost finished, he decided I should come with him to Galilee, and my listlessness vanished. To be out of Mother's house for days, for days! To go home! We were very happy then. I looked down on Galilee with older eyes; I wanted to gather it all up into my arms and hold it tight. So beautiful – a cradle of quiet hills rocking the water; cooling me, calming me.

While Samuel spent the days with timber merchants, I stayed by the water and talked to some of the people I had known as a child and they seemed exactly the same, while I felt that my childhood had all happened in another century, perhaps even to someone else. We went in the evening to see Reuben and Ruth and spent one night with them, but I was awkward with my family and afraid of questions. We went to Upper Galilee, into the big forests, and saw lovely cedar trees. And in an inn where woodmen gathered I finally gave myself up to him utterly, trustingly, not holding my heart back. I felt so happy that I told him I wished we could do what it said in *Deuteronomy*: that when a man has taken a wife, he should not be charged with any business, but should be free at home for a year to cheer up his wife.

Out of this quiet time, I seemed to make a pact with my body – I gave it away: my breasts, my thighs, hair, every nook and corner of flesh. And he gathered it up as a precious gift, giving in return bliss; stunning, consuming bliss. If we walked in the woods, we would turn and look at one another and simply stop and lie on the earth. His body was like pears and cream, his mouth like berries. I was glutted on pleasure; my conflicts sank into a warm black earth where no worms lived and love grew into a thing without fear.

Only once you said, 'I am too happy.' O why couldn't you trust it? The ugliest thing you ever said was to me. You tried to deny loving me (shall I remind you how your nails cut into my neck? And to think that I would reach and touch it with pleasure, with pride – proof, proof). You dismissed it: 'I'm like a drunk who can't remember where he left his boots.' 'You bastard,' I snapped, and I seemed to see you shrink to a boy of eight; forlorn, fatherless, creating for yourself that sublime father of air.

When we got home, I began counting the days until we would be able to leave Mother's house. In the weeks before we packed and left she began creating wedges between Samuel and me. When he came home she would rush out to greet him, making a suspiciously big fuss of him –

pouring hot water, bringing him towels. I would stand watching this, made unnecessary, until finally I would leave the room. She made a special effort in her cooking; she prepared things that he liked and then made maudlin remarks about how soon her son was to be taken from her. She began to monopolise him in the evenings when he sat outside working out some detail of carpentry. And if he did not pay much attention to her he did not rebuff her either. I had pushed Mother from my thinking; we did not speak to one another. So my pain and frustration began to descend on Samuel, whom I felt was making my life more difficult by allowing her wilfully to do things that caused friction between us. He tried to avoid situations where she could use her position as his mother to take his attention from me, but her will was more alert, and she always found ways of positioning herself physically by his side so that I was excluded.

Sometimes I would hear her gossiping to the neighbours about me, about my peculiar ways: my odd tendency to read and take long solitary walks. She would not let up the turmoil of her tongue even if I happened to be passing, and when I was just within earshot she would mutter, 'And that's what happens when a man marries from outside his village. Oi, the arrogance of that girl.' Because Samuel did not appear to support me, because he would not actively take my side against her and preferred to remain indifferent or neutral, I looked at him despairingly and grew sad. Sometimes my anger would splutter so horribly inside me that I felt I must explode. I knew that there was no way I could release my rage on Mother; I had to be totally cold to her or she would be winning, so my fury festered against Samuel. He would not be a palliative and soon even his sympathy became meaningless. When we argued about these things he became angry with me instead and tried to imply that my unhappiness stemmed from other sources. And always, if he shouted at me, I was aware of her listening, smiling. In the morning she would mention to one of the women in the street that we were not happy and that we spent our nights shouting at one another.

A rumour was started in the village that our marriage had not been consummated, and as I walked down the streets titters and clucks and sighs of mock-sympathy would follow me. Eventually, the rumours reached Samuel as well; the men in the workshops had begun making remarks, and once when Samuel asked if anyone could come up to the house in the woods to help him, a thick-faced man slapped his thigh and said, 'Perhaps you'd rather we helped you out with your wife? What's she got to show for the marriage?' I did not know what Samuel had said, but I imagined that he might well have treated the man with complete disdain, and been regarded by everyone with the same sentiment because of it. I would have preferred him to have struck the man in the face.

Both Samuel and I began to shun the villagers. Sometimes I was obliged to walk down the street and once came upon an old woman with a dark face, surrounded by white doves. She was about to throw some grain for them when I turned the corner and they all flew off in a wild flurry – like feathers blown by the wind. She turned her decrepit face upon me and shouted, 'You have frightened the white birds, the devil is in you.'

How sad the lines around your mouth, which once laughed so loud that the chickens scattered in alarm.

We went to live in the wood. Mother said she would come and help arrange things and my body stiffened like a rod. Samuel refused and she was defeated and hated me.

When I arrived, Samuel had made a big fire and water was bubbling in a kettle. I had become so impatient of the slow progress of the building that I had not gone into the house for some time. Samuel took me by the hand, proudly, and we walked together into the kitchen, where he had placed plates and bowls and mugs which he had made long ago and kept always, so he said, for me – knowing one day I should come. The floor was clean grey stone, both in the kitchen and the pantry. The dairy had an earth floor, because it was not finished. The room next to the pantry was Elizabeth's and it was homely with a rough stone floor that still looked powdery.

The two upper rooms were small, with timber that fitted together with no cracks, and joints that would prevail in the heaviest wind. The scent of pine filled the room and the dark beams made me feel as though I were deep in a forest. It was such a peaceful little house and so silent: the first night I found myself whispering. It was odd to get ready for bed without hearing Father's cough, or the solitary tread of Simon moving across to the shutters, which he always opened wide before he slept. I began to think with pleasure that Father had given Samuel and me as a wedding present two fields for wheat, and Simon had given labourers to help with the work – so it seemed that we were self-sufficient and lucky.

That first day in our house, I loved Samuel properly again because he had rescued me. He could have done anything to me, and I wanted him to, to make up for all the ugly words and tears and frustrations that our marriage had known. Now that I no longer felt the swish of Mother's skirts in my face, her menace evaporated and I wanted all our future days to be peaceful.

He lay staring up at his beautiful roof which had taken up so much time and effort and there it was: solid, deep, with broad timbers and only the wind to rustle its curved slopes. 'It's a beautiful house,' I whispered. 'Everything is perfect and the kitchen is all mine. Tomor-

row I will bake a plaited loaf because now we are really married.'
And we loved each other. I, not just giving, but wanting and taking
and finding that my body moved in time with my head. He, sensing
that I no longer looked askance at him, tried to devour me and found
that I was just as hungry. The wind cradled the house; my body was
one long soft sigh, releasing steam; his fingers caressed all the ripples of
my flesh and never lost their heat.

Often, in the daytime, he would put down what he was doing and
come into the kitchen where I was cooking or sewing. His hands
would move questioningly all over my body as though I were something that he was about to mould. His face, snuffling into the tendril-
ling ends of my hair, would emerge smiling at the fragrance of bread
and honey cakes and his teeth would sink deliciously into my neck,
making my toes curl. Everything came to a halt as we rushed upstairs
and then flung ourselves into a passion that I had only glimpsed
before during our time in Galilee – and then lost. And all night long
our plangent happiness would shake the new timbers and frighten
away the owls.

But in the village new rumours gained momentum – Mother having changed the tide of talk to remove any slight on her son's virility.
She now felt it her duty to come with a pack of ripening and chil-
drened women to give me potions and waxes to rub into my skin and
water to drink from an ancient well which had brought joy to many
sterile women. I listened to them silently as the children stamped on
my flowers and got into the pantry and spilled the new flour. But after
they had gone my mouth began to quiver. I wanted a child desperately
and these women with their big bodies and full breasts had sat and
sneered at my sad flatness as if it were of my creating: as if my selfishness or
my reading had prevented conception. Samuel said, 'Be patient, don't
be so tense, and I will give you a child as straight and perfect as a tree.'

We never had a home, you and I, but there was a time when you could
almost have wished it: we grew so attached to that orphan boy – he
almost seemed our child. But he broke his leg and you made me leave him
behind . . .

One day I knew that I was pregnant and sat quietly for weeks
preparing my eyes for the child. My belly grew round and hard and
my skin sparkled. In the third month it just trickled away and there
was nothing to show that a life had fluttered there, except for the
circles of blood and the astonishing grief.

Samuel buried his own sadness in his work. He was working very
hard to carve six candlesticks for the synagogue at Nazareth; it was a
great honour and all his time went into seeking out the best oak for
the task. I was desperate when he left me for a few days; racked by

loneliness and anxiety. Lurking in the corner of my mind was the suspicion that he might seek out Ruth. I dismissed it as absurd, but the thought became obsessional and it frightened me because I saw that it could become a cancerous thing between us. I did not tell him, but harboured it, and in my boredom – as he went on more journeys to find the seasoned oak he needed – I found that more and more of my time was spent jealously considering what he might be doing. He would return in real pleasure to be home again and my eyes would slit with resentment and fear. Only his presence around me almost constantly for some days could reassure me. But as soon as I had become accustomed to him, he would go off on another trip. Knowing my insufficiency, he would try to make these journeys as brief as possible, but something in him begrudged me that; for he was solitary and infatuated with his work and I felt sometimes like a weight pulling him down, keeping him from the things he was happy doing. But his absences diminished me, little by little I faded.

O if only you too had understood that. So many days would pass and you would not touch my hand, scarcely dip your eyes in my direction, and I felt as though I were bleeding to death through the vents your silence made in my body. The fatigue of waiting made all things colourless, endless.

You disappeared into the mountains without telling me where you had gone. I looked for you for days, in Capernaum, by the lake. I kept returning to the fishermen and they looked at me with those eyes: glazed, stony with uninterest. I began to will, to pray, that you would reappear. Then I thought that they might have killed or captured you. I could not eat or sleep, just walked endlessly through the night, crying, O where are you? Where? Sometimes I forgot where I was, and once, when I awoke cramped and chilled, I found that I was miles away, off the road, lying in the sand. I picked up handfuls of it and rubbed it into my skin and on my mouth and eyes, thinking: If I suffer he will return. I slept again and at dawn I woke, knowing that when my eyes opened you would be standing there. But there were only the little sand lizards with their flickering tongues and mocking eyes.

Today, the wind scourges the trees. My mind is brittle as a sun-dried twig tossed on this endless wind. Did something just fall from the ceiling? I have looked; there is nothing. What was it that moved so quick, small and dark? There is nothing. A shape in the forest, some awful sad thing among the leaves . . .

I was standing by the stove; it was early evening and quite cold. Elizabeth had gutted the fish and tossed the crawling things into the bucket. The ugly scraping of the fish distressed me. I had become pregnant again and recoiled from such things. So I got my shawl and walked into the pines, pleased by the way one pine, with a mass of branches on one side and an utter lack on the other, managed to keep its balance so gracefully. The other trees stretched themselves up and up, looking away into eternity; then they shuddered in a sudden wind and I began to walk quicker for the cold.

It was not a sharp pain, but it was right in the centre of my stomach; it went quickly, but I turned to walk home. Then it came again and I gasped with the intensity and felt my back clench. I walked slowly now – afraid, waiting, knowing. Nothing happened. Then something inside me burst with a searing pain, my stomach knotted, unknotted, then contracted again as my legs gave way and slumped on to the ground. I knew what it was that slithered down my thighs; and the earth swallowed it without compassion – leaving only a red, bald shape, curled tight on its own silence.

A few days later, Samuel returned. I was sitting in bed; all my heart had spilt in the forest, leaving me with remote eyes that I could barely lift at his approach. He had to be told – how frigidly my mouth said the words – because it had been my secret. I had decided to tell no one: it would be unlucky, the bud would break or wither if its existence was revealed. He sat down unhappily and reached for my hand; his own grief mingling sharply with my own; but I resented that he did not, could not, suffer as I was suffering. I knew that he was shocked by my appearance: my eyes were inflamed, but not by tears; my hair, which I had not allowed Elizabeth to brush, fell into them; my mouth and all my muscles drooped. He tried to hold me, but I did not move. I saw something in his eyes: a despair. He was silent. I knew what he was thinking: my mad one, my moon woman, let me hold you in my arms, let me comfort you. But my eyes looked back dully at him, thinking: I am sinking, my blood flows thickly, my skin changes colour. All the warm moments in that bed were erased; all the fierce passion that made me dread death – all gone in a coldness that tipped even memory with frost. Keep me safe, keep me safe. But he could not. He sat in the silence until he realised that I had become the silence and would lead him to the same petrification. He left and the door to the kitchen closed quietly behind him.

I stayed in bed, barely moving, and did not even go to the synagogue. And then one morning, a woman from the village came to see me. She had heard that I was not well and had brought a cake pricked with cloves and some fruit from her garden. We sat in my room and she insisted on telling me the latest scandal from the village. I sat very quietly while she began to tell me about a barren woman who had apparently stolen from its cot the new-born child of the flour-grader's wife. The woman had then panicked, knowing she could not hide the baby for long, and when, in desperation, she saw that a small band of formidable matrons were beginning to search the houses, she pushed the crying infant into a vat of boiling water and held the lid down as the women went through a vigorous search of all the houses approaching hers. When she answered her door, they were good-natured and explained their purpose; but her face had swollen and turned green and she began to back into a corner, mumbling to herself in terror. They found the dead baby. And, as a fitting punishment for her crime, they made her cut the baby into pieces and eat it. When they had gone she stuck a knife in her throat ... I listened to the end, but then, with my hands gripped over my mouth, I ran from the room, down the stairs and vomited violently under the cage of white doves. She walked past me and looked at me as though I were crazed. And I was, I was – it was weeks before I could dispel those images from my mind. It was months before my body returned: I had left it in the forest, hating it, and I felt that my head had grown so large that it had swallowed my body.

Slowly, painfully, Samuel and I came back to one another, but the magic of our first feverish happiness in the house was gone. He could not understand my experience or my grief, and my disappointment caused me to retreat into my own loneliness. He moved away from me as a protection from pain – and so a distance was made. It was overcome on days when the sun poured through the pines and filled me with tenderness for the quiet, lonely figure working with his wood – creating objects of beauty which never failed to amaze me. His love for me was a constant, often noble, thing – patient, gentle and passionate. But it was not enough to assuage the pain that seemed to be hovering always on the edge of things, waiting to rip at my mouth when it was curling with laughter.

Samuel's candlesticks for the synagogue were exquisite; the priests were delighted and he was asked to carve some Torah ornaments. Before long, he was being commissioned to make candlesticks and incense holders for other synagogues. He came home late and tired; he was far away a lot of the time on long journeys; and our life was not as I had anticipated. He left me too much alone. I did not cry. Once I thought I would cry when I unwrapped the small coat from its linen and found that the moths had eaten holes in it. I could not cry then because I knew that if I had, it would have made no difference.

Four years of months saddened by blood, but otherwise tranquil, went by, leaving me calmer, more forbearing and perhaps a little wiser. Then one spring I again found myself pregnant. I was amazed and walked around with my hands beneath my belly to reassure myself by the little kicks from that unseen presence that grew, each day, a little more tightly around my heart. Samuel was happy and he made a carving in olive wood – very small, just the height of his hand – of me with a floating belly with my arms crossed over it. One corner of our room was filled with a little rocking cradle made of soft pine and decorated with birds and fishes. My hands became busy with a proper purpose: Elizabeth sewed the sheets and swaddling clothes and I decorated them with ducks and flowers and chickens. We were very happy again, thinking a birth could bind us together as once our flesh had done. As each day passed without disaster, I began to drift into a serene world where the only matters of significance were that I bore myself carefully, drank all my milk and got all the clothes ready in time. My single anxiety was whether Samuel would be at home for the birth. He made a journey to Tyre well before the birth was expected so that he would have no commitments. And so I waited.

We have babies because we are so lonely, but they grow away, they die – and still, so lonely, lonely. O he was a lovely child. All memories are lies, you said – lying. His face was round like his father's, but without its stony quality. And he loved me with a pure, sweet passion; a clenching of hands around my neck; nose rubbing into my throat; wetness of his eyes – eyes that the sea slept in. His mouth so sticky, his hands like plump mushrooms.

It was raining so hard outside and it was the wrong time for rain; the crows in the village would say it was an evil omen. The pines were hissing as I lay and thought – only about the rain, not about the birth that was almost upon me. I was calm, breathing in the thunder, comforted by the slap of water on the roof and the sound of Samuel's hammer driving in stakes. I felt that everything was secure: we had more servants; a small granary; a stable with one work-horse and a mule; a shed for the milking cow, shelter for the goats and a run for the chickens. I felt that because these things, and the land and the trees, belonged to us, no one could harm us.

A door began to bang and Elizabeth stopped rubbing my back and went to close it. I looked at the amulet that Mother had given me outside the synagogue; it had the name of the demon Lilith inscribed on it and was supposed to keep evil away. I put it on the floor, out of sight. The midwife came. She was from the village, but was treated with respect and remained aloof from the gossip and pettiness. She asked if I wanted to give birth on her knees, but I wanted to lie down. We waited; Samuel came and went; he seemed calm but I suspected that he was nervous.

I do not remember pain. I told myself, I must not scream, I must not frighten Samuel who waits downstairs, warming little clothes by the fire. I felt once that the child did not want to leave my womb; I hated to push him out. Then the midwife gave one strong pull and I saw in her hands a red boy, a boy, a son. When they gave him to me he was covered with a white, waxy stuff; he breathed quickly and then gave a mighty yell. His face was pink, unmarked. I loved him.

I could hear Samuel running and he came in and held my hands as they shook and grew cold; as the midwife washed the baby and rubbed salt into him to make him strong, before wrapping him in swaddling clothes and placing him at my breast where he fell asleep. 'We will call him Benjamin,' Samuel said, and he was so tender that it brought tears to my eyes. 'It was my grandfather's name; it means son of the right hand — he will work with me and learn to carve wood.' I was proud then and so full of gladness. And all day long I smiled, and smiled, because of him.

I did not mind when Mother came trundling in puffing from the fast walk that had brought her too late. Then Hannah came and she loved him; Jacob was a little overawed, but Father was delighted and said so in his big voice, waving his arms with joy and pouring wine. Only Simon was a little silent, feeling a lack.

In the first days after the birth, I was calm and content. The baby was so good all day; all night he slept — his breath breathless, his skin like petals. I never felt tired; my milk began to flow, my breasts big and hard and beautiful. Samuel and I watched him in wonder as his hands curled and uncurled and his mouth seemed to be remembering another place. On the third day I developed a fever, but did not know it. It was humid again after the rain and steam rose from the earth as from a kettle. I pushed back the covers and felt easier, but then had spells of a great chill. That night Benjamin cried every few hours and I could not comfort him. I felt very ill and fatigued to a point of screaming. Once, at dawn, when he woke me again, I found myself shaking the little body and I was so frightened by this that I wept and wept all over him. I did not sleep for many days after that; if I dozed I came round in a clammy sweat.

Samuel, because he was working hard and needed all his strength, had taken to sleeping down in the kitchen so that he would not be disturbed. He came to see me each morning and then went off to his work; his immersion in the table that he was carving was so complete that I felt he no longer saw me; that he had no comprehension of the sickness and the weariness that seemed to be drawing me towards a dark net. I compared him to the animals; to the aggression of a male swan protecting his wife and offspring, and he was negligent.

On the seventh day I washed Benjamin in salted water and dressed him in a silk shirt, an embroidered over-garment and an ornate hat decorated with pearls. Samuel took him from me for his circumcision, but with my mind and through the fear in my stomach I lived through the quick, sharp cut, the suctioning of blood, the drop of wine on the penis and the wipe of the linen dipped in olive oil. 'And the mother be glad with the fruit of her body.' How glad I was, how glad, but fearful and full of illness. It was a day of festivity. I barely remember it.

When the midwife came again, I had grown very thin in her absence. My eyes were dark and sick through all the nights of sleeplessness and the bouts of nausea and vomiting; my mind churned endlessly, wondering what had happened to Samuel. In the mornings I felt that if I rose I would collapse; if I picked up the child he would drop and shatter like a cracked egg. Only my milk kept spilling over, unhampered by the fact that I could keep no food down. One morning, defeated, frenzied and feverish, I felt I was dying; and that Samuel would still come in, kiss me quickly and disappear into a world of his own. I began weeping and pulling at my hair; Elizabeth could not comfort me, it was Samuel I needed. When he came and bent to kiss me goodbye, my eyes could not focus on him, and as he turned to walk to the door – I hated him.

It was the midwife who saved me; I think it is nearly always women who save each other. She realised the extent of my affliction at once. She gave me potions to help me sleep; sour medicine for the pains in my head and a white, tasteless febrifuge. And I slept at last; slowly the fever left me. But I was like a rag in the rain; limp, lonely, feeling quite neglected and I wondered if I could recover my feeling for Samuel. My anger crushed him; he wept seeing my hard mouth, knowing something had been lost – but still he did not understand how afraid I had been when he had left each day. Some dull light in his eyes had made me doubt him – it was as if he sat always on an edge, wanting to be somewhere else.

Afterwards, when the fever had gone and my body was no longer thin and fat, my face ugly and beautiful, afterwards I loved him less. I still loved him, but a little less – because my safety had gone. Once when I walked outside I found that a whole meadow of white flowers had sprung up from the ground like foam on the lips of the sea. I wanted to be as beautiful as they, as artless, as easy in their loveliness. I wanted to become one of them and could not; but they consoled me and I did not hurt them. I saw then how much the cradle had changed me – I was soft as clay; I had lost my indifference. In the village, violence and misery were all around, but now I recoiled from these things as though they were diseases. Any harsh thing brought tears to my eyes – and yet – how strange to know that if anyone had entered my room and walked too close to the cradle; if they had lifted a hand to my sleeping son, I should have torn them limb from limb, gouged out their eyes. There was a watchful, animal violence in me which had turned me from all other violence.

Mother was heard to remark that at last I had turned placid. And with a grandson to lay claim to, she came more often, but now I found her easier to ignore. She delivered lectures on the amount of wood wasted on the cooking, and my over-indulgence in matters relating to the servants – and these she questioned behind my back. She said these things in a clipped voice, starting each assault with the phrase, 'my dear daughter', and as those words struggled for life in the air I would observe her mouth quietly quivering with loathing. After she had told me exactly how to take care of my child, she would leave, always declining any refreshment and grumbling about the long walk. And the air lost its lingering of grease and exhaled the scent of the pines once more.

Jacob came one day with a little wooden horse he had made for Benjamin. He was a man almost – tall and slightly wooden-faced, but little stars of tenderness shone in his eyes. He was going to the Academy in Galilee and had come to say goodbye. He thanked me for being like a mother to him, and as he said the words his hand rubbed uneasily at his neck – 'And thank you for the books you lent me and the conversations. I hope one day to be clever too.' And having thrown all his jewels at my feet, he bolted like the hare-boy he still was beneath his assumed maturity.

Hannah had reached a sullen age; she would come and spend time with me and watch the baby learning to sit. She carried him about for hours, propping him on her small hip with the ease of a matron. But she was difficult to speak to; she found herself ugly and her body, which was taking shape fast, alarmed her. She wore clothes that made her look flat-chested and she had taken to stooping. I tried to help her through this awkward time, telling her stories to distract her, Greek myths, little tales of my girlhood, but always, when my voice stopped, her head slumped. Sometimes she would say, 'It's easy for you, the hard time of your life is over. I wish I could skip to where you are.' And I would smile, unable to tell her.

I wanted to tell Samuel about the sadness I so often felt because I was unable to forgive him for what I took to be neglect after the birth of our son. I tried, I struggled to put into words the thoughts that distracted me all day, but he never responded with any comment – feeling attacked he withdrew into a silence which I found even more difficult to manage. Frightened by my anger, my resentment, he despaired of me and grew cold.

One evening, while we sat outside watching the sparrows hover and peck at the bread I threw them, I felt suffocated by the silent war between us; the old, swollen quarrel that he avoided by being kind to me and I avoided by avoiding him. Much of me belonged to the moon then; cool, aloof, saved from love by my white ice face that lacerated him daily. I clutched my sleeping boy to me, knowing that I had made him, slowly woven him inside my body like a cloak to keep me warm. And as I looked down into his face,

Samuel began quietly to say, 'I know I cannot protect you. You hide from me, hurt and remote, and I can only watch you suffer, but I do not want to. I can't watch you suffer, unable to help you. What do you want of me?' There were no words. My eyes were dull and I could feel each current of blood ticking under my skin, making me tingle and smart. He could not see that the point in the river that I had reached was hostile and the ground made up of sharp stones and falling rocks. I could not resist the river; I had no strength to. I allowed myself to be carried under and further away from him. And yet, I know now that he wanted to keep me safe, and could not reach me; I could not approach him, could not move for my great bag of pain.

I put Benjamin in his cot and left the house by the back door. I fled up into the farthest edge of the pines and wept with all my body. For what else could I think but – I have married the man and nourished at last from my womb a child, a single, perfect son. I have done my duty – no, more – I have also taken to protecting Hannah and consoling Jacob, who are none of mine. I feed the chickens and take the goats to the hill. I cook the meats and scrub the tables and make a pleasant place to live in. And each night I lie beside my husband in sheets scented by my care. I hold his hand – once I used to kiss his eyes – and I love him with a harassed pain. And yet – O what is it? What do I expect? What do I miss? Why, on warm days when the flour falls to the floor, do I wring my hands and weep as my heart gnashes, gnashes? All around me they are expecting, waiting – and I give, I give. But it is never enough. Because it is myself. How much I expect of myself and always I disappoint. I hold on by the tips of my nails, gritting my teeth, I hang, awaiting the drop, the opening chasm. I will not fall. I will hold, hold – though the screams hover in each tranquil cake that reaches the table perfected. Who blighted me with this woeful need for perfection? Who loved me so little that I have to shine all day and all night – and yet remain to myself always tarnished?

There is a thing so big it possesses my mind. There is no space left for light to creep in. And there is something I am avoiding; a road I cannot yet take, so I trundle and trundle down all the other lanes of my past. When peace returns, later, it seems that a blackness came, a shining blackness that filled out every crease of my mind. It leaves nothing of myself. Do you understand? You who always sat and rubbed your chin while I spoke. O I miss you. Just one more day. Please give me tears, one tear, or something will break.

Nothing is as it was. It is magnified now as when a certain glass catches the sun and makes objects fill and grow. So it is in my head. I am troubled and unable to express these things, and no one to tell them to but you. Words, thoughts, are all too small to explain it.

Your ideas were so immense as to throw into shadow any of mine. In your silence I am struggling to tell you things I am sure you know and understand. Once, in the morning when I came to you, you told me what I had dreamed. I knew that you had not slept the whole night and begged you to stay and rest – one day only, to rest. But you would not. You walked all day as though tranced; often you would turn on one of us and say, 'Mary is tired . . . he is thinking about his mother . . . James is missing his wife . . . Peter's stomach aches . . .' and so on – you were never wrong.

I am not frightened now. When I grow calm again, as I do now, I know that it is a privilege to be solitary, to have overcome the suffering that leads to it. Do the hermits in the hillsides sit and fret over old recollections? Or do they live in present sensations only: water to be fetched, food to be hunted? But how do they nourish and sustain their hearts in the cold caves? Can the heart fall asleep as the sex does? Does the intellect wear itself thin on its own grinder? O I cannot release the dream. But I will learn to sit still. I will try to mould my life the way a single flower will bloom on a deserted wall, untended, unseen, drinking only an inner nourishment.

Sweet child, Benjamin – making water-noises as he learned to stagger through the house; ferny hair at the back of his neck, hands pink with no tremor. A quiet boy with an inner serenity, who wailed on days when I was unhappy, looking anxiously into my eyes for a smile. We loved him, both of us, with a love so strong that sometimes I felt that it had made us love each other less. When he could walk, he used to come with me into the forest and play with the pine needles. On hot days I took his clothes off and let him splash at the shallow end of the stream, and I could see that the water was his element: he was a fish-boy. For hours he would play and float in the water, turning complete circles with his body so that his face plunged into the water. He had no fear; his balance was instinctive and sure: it was my fear that kept me always at the edge of the pool, my hands ready to reach. When he ducked his head under the water, he would come up bubbling with laughter and when he did it again and again it seemed as though he was trying to show me that there was no need for my fear.

As the distance between Samuel and me increased, I poured my love more passionately into my son, because the child-love was an easier thing. I used to watch Samuel's shoulders and his back as they lay turned from me in the night and I wanted to touch the soft skin, but could not. My eyes would stare until they closed with sleep; often if he turned and saw me watching him, he would gather me into his arms, but I lay coldly, trying to fathom the reason for his gesture instead of responding to it. I used to think that my heart, feeling neglected, had grown bitter and that the bitterness leaked stealthily on to everything around me. But as I began to feel Samuel's love waning, as he crept into a solitary, unreachable haven of his own, I needed desperately to re-kindle that old fervour. When he went off in the mornings to his hut – which I did not go near now – or, if he went to see to the fields, I knew that in reality, no longer just in my imagination, I had gone from his thoughts.

So, from the trees, out of sight, I would watch him at work, knowing that he existed only in the immediacy of his actions; his mind had grown around comforting things: wood, shapes, colours – and my abrasions had cut me out of his life. The child in me panicked. When the fright had subsided, I would walk slowly towards him and sit, watching him work. Then I would stand beside him and touch his hand. In the evenings I would bring him cinnamon drinks and little cakes and linger anxiously for his smiles. And always he did smile; that was his great beauty – his gentleness, his ability to forget. And by trying to make him love me again, I ended up loving him – not with the old despair, but with a quiet sweetness that slowly grew more constant.

He had gathered some poppy seeds and planted them for me beside the kitchen door, and after that any plants or seeds that he thought I might like, he would dig up and plant them also. As time passed, they grew and spread into a mass of red and gold with great blue waves of cornflowers. I would show Benjamin how to rub his nose into the flowers and sniff their scent and he was a child with pollen on his face. I loved Samuel for understanding how the flowers comforted me, and the roses most of all – they were so frail, they opened so utterly and waited to be blown.

Sometimes I can go for days without thinking of anything more than whether I am hot or cold, hungry or tired. Watching the flies or the evening lizards; the scorpions shooting in and out of cracks in the wall – nothing more. Then, suddenly, I realise that I am shrinking, becoming tiny, darting and mindless as the scurrying creatures on my floor. And I discover, with a shock, how much I miss the whiff of the cornflowers and the bundles of herbs thrusting their scents through cupboard doors. I remember and long for the saddest moments of my life more even than the happy . . .

It was so hot that noon that the birds flew into the walls and the ants were too listless to crawl into their bodies. You were dozing by a dark screen while a few others slept in a corner and a woman rocked in a hammock, humming and fanning herself with her apron. I had tidied the remnants of a meal that no one had eaten with any appetite. Looking at you, with your head slumped, you were so ordinary, so simple. Later, walking by the lake, I saw you yet another way. I was illuminated by the knowledge that though we ate and drank and slept within your breath, we knew you not at all. Even so, you always remained a man that I, that everyone, yearned to take to one side, just to talk privately with you, to listen to your voice and catch the radiance of your smile. But sitting close beside you, doing those things, your eyes swept me into different reflections, for I could see, among the pale ashes of your eyes, how much you wept in secret.

I wish I could understand you. Some things I do see now: that you had no patience with day-to-day problems – food, where to sleep – these things were of no consequence. Nor could you trouble yourself with the rule of Rome, believing as you did that its end was imminent. Most things become trivial if one believes the apocalypse is about to take place: in weeks, days even. Nor do I blame you for being a little early in your calculations, you were often wrong: you were only human.

I used to think that you must have solved the problems of your body in your imagination. You liked to say it would be a relief to be without a body because a body was so demanding; it grew cold, or hot, sick, and always it had to be fed and watered. It was a nuisance; a weight to carry about which you would be glad to be rid of. I did not believe this talk. I used to think quietly that you wanted it removed because it had desires and needs that your mind could not always sublimate. You lived in a world without flesh, a world of shadows and whispered fears and bellowed promises. But all around you the sunlight fell on dark hair and wild lashes; wine opened pink lips and dancing tongues; we sang and frolicked when we were happy; we swam naked in the streams and you did not always remember to turn your head away.

I remember how stricken your eyes were when I bent over you as you lay among the trees by the lake. And I kissed you, daring everything for the sake of your mouth which ached in my blood, and which I cried for – always to see it slide away. When I think of you, I see you as beautiful; but you were not. Your eyebrows clashed in the middle, often in anger; you were small-limbed with a stooped back. Your nose and face were long, not comely. That is the truth of it. That day, you did not move; your eyes closed in despair and above your head the birds made ready for the night and the first star threw off her veil. I was not going to seduce you, to give you the excuse. I waited, catching the turmoil of your thoughts in the stillness of that place which you had chosen to escape to. I had followed you, but I knew, as always, that you knew it, condoned it. What you didn't know was that I had been in your position many times. I had to move towards you because you were incapable of it – as I had been so many times. So you lay there with closed eyes and allowed me to kiss you. I began to laugh softly; then lifted your head and held it against my breast and rocked you as the boats rocked in the empty sea and the nets were folded away. My hands, stroking your skin – darkened, unloved – waited for your hands to move; for your brain to unknot; for the madness of your cold passion to flicker into life. My pity came rushing to you with my love and I stroked your eyes with my kisses. You were locked so tight within your skull: the fears pounded, dashed against me and then, finally, you pulled yourself straight, dug your fingers into my arms and smiled with bitterness, 'Never before' and added 'nor will again.' But it was your body that trapped me, your kisses the bars of the cage. O you caught me just to mock me, to break my little neck.

You woke with a shudder, pulling yourself from me – your face wrathful, hard. The clear pool of my cheek muddies. What is this bird snatching at my insides? Your weight was such a peaceful thing, like a gift, and now there is nothing to anchor me. I am alone, floating, as your curved back slips into the far trees. My sight has gone; the tree blurs, the grass withers – but my heart grows as loud as the cries of the insects. The moon rises slowly. I hate her, hate her.

After that you fasted. All day, all night, you sat with Peter, talking endlessly, and he with his mouth open like an empty cup to catch your words. No matter that he understood nothing of what you said. Still he makes me fume. In his stupidity, he would swagger a little because you had singled him out to hear your exposition. People with big heads are always stupid. He treated you like a sick child, trying to tempt you to eat, feeding you with a little spoon that you turned from. He had to force a cup of water to your lips to make you drink.

By then, I was full of fury: I could have bitten you on the neck in my rage. Peter went to take fish to his family and I had a chance to approach you. My blood boomed in my head: 'I wish you would get off your cloud for a moment,' I snapped, 'you who love the whole stinking world, but treat a single woman with cruelty.' How you looked up! From so far away. It was hopeless; like running after the moon. Your face ethereal, gaunt and grey; your eyes lambent, not of this world. You looked at me sadly, then reached and touched my hand, saying, 'You are so angry, so full of hurt. Why don't you, can't you, understand?' I had to turn my face away to stop myself shouting, 'And you, what of you?' I went away and when I looked back, your dark head was lowered, your finger traced circles within circles in the sand. You had forgotten. O I cannot bear it. When next I saw Peter, I said he should force you to take more water and try to slip a little honey into it or your body would fill with poisons. And he did, until your fast ended, after twenty-one days ... You see, it is my nature which is at fault. In the end, I would reduce anyone to my own violence and torment. There were days when Samuel was afraid of me, and that is the beginning of the end. There were days when my withdrawals or my angers made him want to strike me and it was at this point that I began to try. There have been a few times in my life when I have tried – to be lovable, to be as we are at the beginning of things, on our best behaviour – hiding the frowns and the fears that vitiate everything in the end. I wanted harmony, peace, solitude, water to spill on my passions, but I could not find them alone, and I was losing the little I still possessed of a husband. I put all my will into reclaiming him.

I sought Samuel out at odd times of the day; I took him things for his comfort. He would work quietly in his faded blue shift, which the leather apron bunched up at the back. He, like the house with the logs filled in with moss and clay, was as much a part of the forest as the trees. Only I grew apart, separate, and my pain soared, billowed, when I saw that his eyes, looking at me, had grown tame.

One morning, wanting to be near him, I ran down to the field where the harvesting was in full swing. The thorn trees split under a coating of dust; the red lilies scalded and the air throbbed with a heavy odour like incense. There they lay – Samuel and two labourers – under a sycamore tree; their sashes loosened and their faces dissolving with sweat. Samuel looked up as I came and walked towards me, taking the covered basket with the loaves and the milk. When we reached the trees by the field, I gave him a loaf to give to the servants, and, breaking the bread, I dipped it in a jar of honey and poured the cool milk. While we were eating, he showed me a blade of wheat and I saw, without knowing what to look for, that it was good grain. He made me look at it in detail as he rubbed it between his hands and I tried to find the same enthusiasm as he did, because the looking and my interest were important. Then, relaxed and cooler, he lay back on the rough grass with one arm over his eyes. That gesture . . . I felt no longer needed, so I gathered the bits of bread together and put everything into the basket. He looked up and thanked me as I rose to go, and I dropped a smile in his direction, but it was desolate.

The sun was beating me on the back of my head as I walked slowly through the cleared ground and on towards the forest. I shrank into its cover with relief and found a log to sit on as my head and my heart drooped. I sat there, pushing my knees together and rocking myself back and forth as the hot wind carried the smell of wild thyme and the forlorn bark of a distant dog. The morning that had started with happiness was slipping into disarray. I wanted to go back to Samuel and somehow pull the separate threads of our lives together again, but I knew if I did and my purpose was not understood, it would crush me. I stayed where I was, brooding.

I heard a footstep and looked up to see Samuel walking towards me. He sat down on the log, putting an arm about me, and his look, when it lighted on me, was certain again. He bit my lips softly and pulled me on to his knees. I let my head fall into his shoulder, so glad that he had come; melting into his calmness and the smoothing of his hands. And I wanted to make up for the loneliness, the pain, so I drew him into me, kissing his mouth which I had forgotten; his skin which had grown sad. He was a lover of wisdom and understanding and he had exquisite ways. My loneliness flew away, and that which had begun quietly later made me want to roll on my back and howl like a cat. How sweet the resin of the trees; the dark dirt of the forest as it mingled in our hair and bodies and cleansed us as only the earth and the flesh sometimes can.

Lying in that unexpected place, at peace with one another, he began to speak to me again as a husband: fretting about the money he was owed and owing; how much he would need to buy oil and wine, and whether the yields of corn and wheat would be sufficient to last us to the next gathering. I felt a need to retrace, to talk about what had happened to make us lose hold of one another, but I knew that he would not allow it. He wanted to push the flatness back and forget by moving forward together – that was his way. So I forced myself to try for once not to look back down into the pit, but up at the sky.

From that time on, Samuel would walk with me as I carried Benjamin on my hip up to the mountain where the goats grazed. We would wait for the little shepherd boy to come with his herd before leaving our goats in his care until nightfall. Once, I took Samuel to my private mountain and he said nothing until we got there, but then told me he had been there before – many times – and we laughed to think we were probably the only two in the village who had bothered with it. We collected herbs together in the woods – thyme, sage and basil, and he took me to where the wild sorrel was most luxurious and knew all the names of the flowers. He was not working so much in wood at that time; he had exhausted the needs of the local synagogues and work from our village was scarce. He had taken to working more in clay, and filled my kitchen with pots and plates, and when there was nothing more that I required he started to do wonderful sculptures: an oak tree with a great trunk and dense layers of beautifully detailed leaves and acorns; under the tree, sheep and chickens clustered. He made larger trees in clay: poplars, cedars, pines and extraordinary olive trees with crippled trunks and serpentine branches. Always the detail was meticulous and the trees were never in isolation: they formed a group, with animals, or a single child swinging from a branch. Thinking about them makes me long to touch them again. Benjamin would stand and look at them, sometimes carefully lifting a finger to stroke a line or a bump on a tree trunk.

While Benjamin dunked and wallowed in the stream, we would

take our clothes off and swim with him, drying ourselves afterwards in the sun, lying on a purple rug that Elizabeth had made. While our son anointed himself with sand, Samuel and I discovered the most unlikely hours and places to fill our need of one another; and our cries would shake the ferns at the stream's edge and flatten the little fields of violets.

Gradually, we became a single person, growing into the simplicity of the woods, where relations did not come; where days passed easily – and in the evenings we sat at the back door, staring into one another's eyes over the roof of our son's head. Elizabeth would bring us wine and olives and disappear into the kitchen, where she would quietly prepare dinner. She was always so still – she never broke or spilt anything, she never raised her voice, but spoke only when asked to, and then as briefly as possible. The skin around her eyes was turning a pale green and it seemed as though they slanted more dramatically upwards as she grew more withdrawn.

Once, when I was salting the meat on a cool afternoon, Mother shocked me by striding in, demanding why we had been absent from synagogue on the previous Sabbath. Samuel clicked his tongue with mild impatience and said that the boy had been ill. I smiled to think that we had been too content to pray. But her displeasure had deeper roots than that one act of negligence. She repeated her complaints about our oddness and unnatural ways and our cursory attendance at feasts and festivities in the village. She managed to poke in a nasty remark about the kind of distracted woman who reads books – but was scowled at by Samuel. She had a mountain of rebuke against me, but feared to utter it. We let her go unsatisfied, but somewhere in my guts I feared her still – not for things past, but for those to come. And I hated her presence in my house. At the door, she turned and said sagely, 'There was a woman in the village, you remember her, Samuel – the widow of the weaver; she would not mix with the rest of us. Two days ago, she was found dead in her bed. She had died of starvation. That's what comes of being superior.'

Father came sometimes and spoke to Samuel while he was working; sitting afterwards at my table, eating a wedge of cake in hands thick but still tender. He had grown old in a hurry, with hair in his nose and a voice that no longer boomed over a woman's incessant grumble. He had lost some of his teeth and his skin had sunk and slipped out of position on his big bones. He never stayed with us long, and as he was leaving he had the look of a man who feels a little guilty; who would go home and say nothing.

Then there was the threshing and the putting away of seed. A quiet time when weddings could take place again because the work of the fields was finished and only the wine harvest still to come – and that was no trouble because the heat was more bearable and the new wine and dark figs kept everyone happy. We knew of these things, but they happened at a distance, as though the village on the edge of the forest was a vast way off. Sometimes I would take Benjamin to watch the women among the vines, with mouths all red and stained fingers – or the men tying up the bags of grain and comparing the weights. Some days we would walk with Samuel down the village street, to buy what we needed, and I would clutch my son's hand hard because there was always a little menace oozing from the old women who sat at their front doors knitting, or the boys who tossed their dice so carelessly, but whispered just a little too loud. Our only misfortune, though, was our mule, who seemed to lose his wits one day – tore himself from the tether and plunged down a cliff at the far edge of the village. Those who saw his fall read the signs.

How much I used to walk then; alone, or beside my son's slow amble. Now, when I walk outside, only in the evenings as the old women do, and a cool breeze blows, I bunch up from a cold that seems to slip through the thinning skeins of my skin so easily. I walk as an old widow walks, with hunched back and slow shuffles – and I hurry home, unable to bear anything very much.

So where is that God of yours? That sweet father riding the rain-clouds, smoothing his long white curls and his holy beard? Isn't he just a voice that cries inside me, or you, or anyone – for justice, for peace and humanity, food for the poor? A voice that groans and demands these things even as the spear is raised? Isn't he also that small voice in me that whispers, Be calm, wait, struggle a little longer, when my heart seems most sick and hungry? Where is the new age of God on earth? And if you believed in it, why aren't you here? But where is the end of the old, corrupt age? Am I deriding you as that old fool did in Bethany, the one who asked if you were trying to make yourself divine by stealing comparisons from the Scriptures? You did not become angry; I was surprised. You looked at him coldly and said, 'I did not say I was God. How could I be God if I pray to Him?' When people make unkind remarks to me I only think of a retort when it is too late. Not you – you were always so quick, and yet still managed to say what you had to say with charm. The poems that you told, so simply, so rhythmically, knowing that they could be remembered and repeated always – like the psalms they slid from mouth to mouth. Sometimes they were so lovely I wrote them down. When you spoke, all tongues stopped – how could they compete? Your voice was slender as a girl's, but with such fire beneath. If someone mocked you, you shuddered and retorted impatiently, 'My life has been foretold in Isaiah and Enoch, before them, I was.' And then you had spoiled it, spoiled it all, because they had a handle to beat you with. I asked you about these claims but your eyes turned wistful as though dreaming, and you said, 'It is like a memory I had before I was born.' We would have to leave quickly the bleating sea, the voices raised in commotion, and make for the hills. You were, I am – perhaps we all are – the people who dance under persecution, who sing in the fire.

How you loved them when they said the things you needed to hear. Then you would promise anything. But if we doubted you, your love vanished – hate and fear sprinkled like tears in your eyes. When the authorities and priests made mock, when they tried to tangle you in your words, or simply dismissed you as another lunatic from Galilee, your anger was a frightening, consuming thing. You seemed to want to destroy them and yourself to prove something which was unprovable. You ranted, swearing that they would see the truth, be forced to swallow it whole. Sometimes you sickened me in the madness of your pride; in the cruel things you said. They were your enemies, but you did not love them. It's a nonsense, that. Later, you were so quiet again, so full of humility, knowing your failures, wanting only to try harder, asking us all to love, to forgive – to live with such charity that I knew it was your impossible dream that drove you to such awful extremes. Great or violent obsessions can linger after death, and perhaps yours will. Even though your dying was most obscene, most horrible, and would seem to have blotted out the beauty of your obsession.

I had to watch as your nature darkened. I had to cheat and steal moments to be with you, to get you alone and comfort you. They all wanted you to campaign in their own directions, for their piffling purposes. As you resisted, you grew weary, sad – and I do not want to think of you that way: sitting in the dust with blue-ringed eyes, picking at the roasted sunflower seeds that I had brought you, not eating anything. Thinking of you that way makes me melancholy, drives me to destinations I would not reach. I do not want to . . .

Look, I can see him, playing at the back of the garden near the vegetables with one of the servant's children. He clapped his hands and sang silly songs and when he was bored he would go off to his father's workshed and build with blocks of wood until I came. And when he was sick no one would say his name. O Benjamin.

I was wiser then, but though I had experienced some things, I still lacked the ability to use the experience to my advantage. I had become intoxicated with dark things and had lost my childhood habit of pretending they did not exist. I found myself creeping back into the memory of things that had hurt me; things that had happened even before I had known Samuel. But as the days turned silkily, as the poppies opened out of their cocoons of red and green, as Samuel brought me joy and kept close at hand, the shadows became less menacing. I made myself put my thoughts into the good things around me: our lands filling with water to swell the seed beneath, my favourite chicken with her ten fluffy chicks, the donkey to replace the mad mule. Storehouses stacked with oil and grain and lots of rich wine to tumble down our throats. And best of all: a house of peace where people cared for one another and Elizabeth was never far away.

Hannah was betrothed and pretty again. She came and went with all her news during those fallow months, but she did not weigh heavily on me as once she had. Her life had taken its own course and it promised to be an easy one. The happy times of one's life go in the twinkling of an eye – it's an old saying but true enough.

I was twenty-two and my son nearly four. In my memory the years were easy; the harvests good – but things cannot have been so peaceful because I did not grow fat as the other mothers did, and my eyes were often the dark wells that they are today. My turmoil has been an endless thing; it did not happen as suddenly as it seemed.

O I do not want to go back there. I am reluctant to do this to him, even in my mind. I turn and turn from it, but always I return to that strange day when the sun was like a white hot stone searing the sky.

We had had no rain and the men in the village were too fatigued to go on with the lopping of the olive trees and the pruning of the vines. They sat around the well complaining, while the women dragged about their work and shouted at the children. So it went for days. Having made the journey to the village, I kept away, because when the villagers were ill-humoured they seemed to hate me. Samuel was tired; he had been sawing wood that day and the dust was in his hair and throat. We did not eat at noon, only tried to sleep, but the house seemed alive with little insects stirred up by the humidity. The animals slumped on the earth, panting, and the birds were very quiet.

In the early evening, Elizabeth cooked some roast lamb with rosemary, and the smell of it filled the air and made us all hungry. I went to fetch Samuel and waited while he quickly tried to saw through a few more logs so that the men would have no excuse not to start work on the new barn the following morning. His face looked faintly grey from the exertion and I persuaded him to leave it and come and eat. He did so, unwillingly, being loth to leave anything unfinished.

We walked together to the house and when Samuel had washed he felt better. We all sat down to eat and it seemed a little cooler, though the room was stifling and no draught penetrated the open door and windows. Afterwards I wished I hadn't eaten so much lamb because I felt slightly sick. When Benjamin had gone to bed, Samuel and I walked over to his workshed again, because there was something he wanted to show me. He seemed very hot and sat down on a stool, trying to catch his breath. He was sweating profusely and his cheeks were inflamed. He asked me if I would get him a glass of cold water from the stream and I went as quickly as I could. When I returned, he looked less heated; he drank the icy water very quickly, and as I turned to find him something more comfortable to sit on, I heard the cup clatter to the floor. Samuel was doubled up in pain and then he fell to the ground with a deep groan. His face had turned blue and his limbs were rigid. He could not speak and lay knotted on the ground for some time. I crouched beside him, but did not do anything more than put my arm across his back until he managed to straighten himself a little. We stayed very quietly, then he leaned against my side and tried to get up. His whole body keeled over, his head jerked wildly and he began to vomit. The thick heat of the evening no longer touched my flesh; now it had a vibrating surface that only assimilated terror. The vomiting continued and Samuel's skin was green and sticky and released a smell of fungus. I was terrified to leave him, but knew I must get Elizabeth to run to the village and get the doctor. All these things flew through my mind as thoughts will fly faster when one is in peril; yet there is always time in one frightened moment to consider countless possibilities. I snatched up my skirts and hurled down the hill, calling to Elizabeth as I reached the house. She came running out, rubbing her hands on her apron. I told her and she ran with the extraordinary swiftness she could always muster in times of crises. I turned and ran back up the hill again.

When I entered the hut, the stench hit me. Samuel crouched on the floor, curled tight into himself – and he became suddenly in my eyes the sad shape in the woods that had erupted from my body. I picked up some linen and went to him, to wipe his face and care for him. My arms encircled his back again and I pulled him into a straighter position, talking quietly to him. I had to use all my strength, but I was strong now, calm, in control. Suddenly, like a felled tree he toppled; his weight rushed against me and pushed me down and we lay flat together on the earth. He was dead.

Stop, please stop now. But I cannot. I could not then, I cannot now. My hands, horrified, sickened, began to pull him from the mess that we had collapsed into. I dragged him to the corner where it was dark, and thought only: I must clean him, must make him clean, clean, clean. I ran to the stream, collected the water in the pail and went back to him. I knelt by his side and washed his face and throat and pulled away the fouled cloth from his body. I washed and washed him. No one came. The hut was dark and dreamy. I was not afraid. I knew what I must do. Gathering all my strength I put my arms under his and began slowly and painfully to drag him out into the open. It was some time before I had pulled his body across the clearing and into the forest. Here the scent was balmy and the sky almost black. I wiped his body once more and took off the remainder of his clothes. And he was naked, clean and beautiful, noble as a tree. I gathered thyme, sweet basil and wild rosemary blossom and placed it beneath his head and arranged lilies in his hair. I offered him to the trees.

It was a long time before they found me. Elizabeth emerged first through the trees with the doctor and his assistant − a young, red-haired boy. They all stopped in a strange, mystified way when they saw me kneeling beside the naked body. The doctor bent and touched him quickly, reaching for his heart.

'He's dead,' he snapped angrily. I nodded. 'What happened?' he demanded. I did not like the way he looked at me; he and the boy moved their heads together − I was afraid of their whispering.

I heard Elizabeth, the silent one, repeating what I had called to her earlier. They went back to the hut and then returned.

'It was a seizure from the heat, or perhaps he was poisoned,' the doctor muttered, examining the body more carefully now.

I hated him for touching the body that had become my own. My hands began to claw at my thighs, I turned my head away. He beckoned to his assistant to lift Samuels's legs so that they could take him down to the village − then my hands and voice rose in agony and I wailed, 'No, leave him where he is, please. Don't touch him.'

Elizabeth came to me and said quietly to them, 'In the morning we will get the men to carry him down. It is very late, do not concern yourselves with it.' The doctor shrugged and turned to go, casting a long frown at me as I resumed my position on the ground.

Elizabeth brought blankets and all night I stayed with him. I watched the moon, almost full, as she rose and rose. I felt her cold hard face dissolve into mine, freezing me over, stopping tears, thoughts. I had her sickness; by the time dawn came I was moon-struck; my head ached with a cold numbness, my tongue was heavy as a stone and my heart had melted to milk. When the first tip of the sun's skull rose in the distance, I was certain: the moon is my mother. I am nothing to the sun. I could not look at it. I hated the pinkness it spread on the sky, I shuddered at its touch. I ran down the hill and into the house, shaking violently.

I was afraid to look at my son; his face a miniature of his father's. I walked round and round our bedroom instead, picking up things as though I had never seen them before; hearing sounds so painfully loud that they seemed to split my ears: a door closing in the distance, a pail of water emptying into a trough outside my window. I drew the curtains tightly because the streaks of light penetrated my skin like knives and always my hands trembled and my face was stretched and dry.

My eyes would not desert the place where he sat, the shadow where his elbow rested; the crease in the cushion where his head lay. My body began to throb with a physical need which was a pain. I wanted more than anything in the world to have his weight on me, his flesh in mine. The pain became so acute that I began thrashing my hands at the wall, cutting my flesh on the rough bark until there was blood on both.

They brought his body down from the forest and laid it out on the floor. Benjamin was taken out of the house by Elizabeth; I did not see him all day. I lifted the sheet from Samuel's face and looked at it: round, smooth, with the thick, pale hair roughened by the water I had splashed on it. How it surprised me, being the same. I had thought that by now his skin would have grown dark and rough and he would have begun to turn back into a tree.

I was not safe. I knew it the moment the door jerked open and Mother walked in. She would not look at me, but threw herself on her son's body and roared with anguish. Father walked behind her; his face running with tears.

Mother turned on me and shouted, 'You have done this, you – you have killed him. Don't think we are deceived. The doctor said he was poisoned.'

Father grabbed her arm with unexpected violence and said, 'I forbid one more word of that, do you hear? He didn't know the cause, it was too late. The heat and over-eating could have stopped the heart. Keep your mouth still. Haven't we enough pain?' He walked across the room and spoke to me in sympathy. I could not say a word for his kindness was making rocks in my throat. His grief, too, was snarling up his words and I wanted to comfort him, but remained silent.

Mother began to anoint the body with spices and then wrapped it in a linen shroud. Simon came, and Hannah, but I could no longer stay in the room as the prayers and chanting and weeping was forcing my brain apart. I thought only of the trees, of the forest, the moon and the process of nature. I could have nothing to do with their grief, it was an alien thing. As was the burial in the rock place, where there were no trees or flowers, only bare yellow sand and gaunt rocks.

It was late when they left; I looked out of the door as they walked off with lowered heads; Simon supporting his father, who turned once in my direction. Mother shouted at him angrily, telling him to hurry. He went, in her time not his, and his legs walking away were shaky. It was dusk. I was not tired, except by their presence. And then I saw a group of villagers standing at the bottom of our little hill, looking up. I shut the door hastily.

All night I walked back and forth. I could hear Benjamin crying in the low soft way he had. I did not trust myself to go to him. At dawn he awoke with a piercing cry and I ran to him. His arms stretched out for me and I held and rocked him, kissing his thick hair and soft neck until he slept. It was then that I was smitten with grief, and it was a monstrous, ugly thing, full of anger, bitterness, remorse. Like a wild beast, I wanted to tear at flesh, my own, ripping out great bloody hunks of it and forcing it down my throat. Later, the tears came; the loss, the loneliness – the painfully accumulated sorrow. Then, there was only the madness that veered from dreams of my own death: violent, grotesque; or hours when I would walk, smiling, holding my son's hand and picking flowers, saying it was all a dream that would soon pass away.

I am afraid to get so close to it. One death leads to another – to you – and back beyond to my mother, waiting somewhere for me, until the day I realised that she had gone. I knew this when I saw them bringing the sick child past our house in Magdala and the servants whispered and said she would be dead before nightfall and would have to be buried before her father returned from his journey for the heat was bad. I looked at them, and ran up to the trees where my tears were so hot, and so big, and kept falling for I knew that she was no longer waiting. Even now, all these deaths later, I am aware how I have never lost my need for a mother.

O sweet Samuel, if you were still here you could make a big fire, pour wine – let these things bring warmth to me as the wind screams outside, calling me. Fill my arms with flowers, deep, fleshy flowers, big and red. Take away these broken branches, withered petals, touch me, touch. If there were birds in the pines still, if we lay and loved as the owl swooped and the rain beat like waves on your roof still. If you were here, as you were. If I were still I, and you still you.

No one came to see me when I was mourning. After that, every day, in the late afternoon, villagers would swarm at the bottom of the hill. They grew bolder, sometimes coming a little way up the slope and shouting insults. Once, a man threw a stone and yelled, 'Witch'. Every day they came a little nearer, like rats made brave by hunger. One woman shouted that I had tried to hide my husband's body in the woods; another that I mourned on those days when it was not lawful to mourn. Still the rains did not come; people had nothing to do but find a reason for it. They would come and sit on my doorstep now and mutter among themselves: that the wheat had died in the ground; that the new barley had run to seed.

A fat old rabbi said, 'And does it not say in *Jeremiah* – "Your wrongdoing has upset nature's order and your sins have kept from you her kindly gifts."'

Each evening I had to go up to the pasture to collect the goats. I was intimidated by the thought of leaving the house. Coming back with the string of goats, two women rushed at me and began ripping my veil, shouting that I had turned against their customs and led a sinful life.

They tore at my veil as though it were my face, and one hissed. 'There, that is what you wanted.' The head-covering fluttered to the ground in shreds and they stamped on it, spitting. There was a humming in my head and my blood seethed, but I walked to the shed and put the goats away; my hands shaking, my tongue clenched between my teeth.

All the servants left. Elizabeth and I struggled to keep things going as best we could. Most of the day we hid in the house, only leaving very early to take the animals out to get what benefit they could from the scruffy meadows. In the evenings, if either of us ventured out, we were greeted with jeers or stones. Benjamin was terrified and began to call for his father in a high scream; he clung all day to my skirts and was so tormented by dreams that he slept in my bed at night. It was the only comfort: to have his downy body beside me on those still nights and to rest my head on his shoulder as his hands clung to me in his sleep.

One morning – after I had left the goats with the simple boy, who seemed unaware of who I was or he surely would have refused to look after my animals – I could not bear the thought of returning to the house. The villagers did not come for their vicious entertainment until later in the day, so I knew that my sleeping boy would be safe in Elizabeth's care. I walked up into the woods and tried to force myself to devise some plan. I did not think I could continue to live much longer where the women grew daily more inimical and Benjamin was turning into a child tormented even by the sound of a footstep. I decided it would be best to try to speak to Father and ask his help in selling my land and animals; and then I could go to Galilee, or even to Joshua in Jerusalem.

I walked slowly back home, feeling easier. As I approached the end of the forest, in the absolute still of the morning, a noise took hold of my heart. I came closer to the clearing at the back of the house and a great roaring and crackling sound filled my ears, but it was not until the first wafts of wood-smoke swirled into my face that I realised what it was. I ran wildly through the trees and stumbled into the clearing where the smoke caught at my eyes and throat and spun me round, making me cough almost to retching. Our little house, the pine house, was merely blackening logs in a high river of fire. I began choking, running into the billows of smoke and the screeching flames until my screams were silenced by gags of fumes and I was forced to swallow my son's name.

Away from the flames I saw Elizabeth: is there something in her arms? Is there, is there? She began running towards me, but the smoke kept obliterating her darting figure. She reached me and dragged me backwards as I fought her to try to return to the house:

her arms were empty. But she said, 'Come quickly, he is safe, up in the woods, come away.' I stopped, exhausted, unable to move. Then from the front and side of the house a small band of women, shading their faces with their hands, came running towards me. I ran with all my strength, trying to follow Elizabeth, but I tripped and fell and as I got up I saw the women flying towards me, black robes slapping in the fierce wind; voices a high-low shriek like a bat. O I am so tired and their feet grow loud; the smoke drags across my eyes, the stones raise their heads to impede my way. She pulls my head back, her hands threading into my veil, my hair. They surround me with hisses; beating my body and face with their fists; lifting stones – one crushes my cheek: O kill me, I do not care, just let it end. I sank to the ground, giving myself utterly up to death, waiting, my breath already half-departed from my body.

There was a stillness; no stone fell. I waited, then lifted my head from the dust, feeling the blood run into my mouth. I turned my face, unable to rise, and saw a tall rabbi standing at my side, his face melancholy, darkened by smoke. He bent to help me, and for a moment I was angry with him for saving my life, for making it all go on.

'You must leave here instantly,' he said gruffly, 'go on to the next village, take a northerly route through the forest. Find my brother. He is a doctor and will take care of you. They have stolen your animals, but I managed to catch the horse as it bolted and have tied it to a tree. I'll bring it to you. Go quickly up into the trees and wait till I come.'

I ran. I found Elizabeth in the trees, holding Benjamin in her arms. He is so still, so still. I take him. His head curls so soft, so silently into my shoulder; his mouth moist on my skin. Does he breathe? He is so light suddenly and I hear no breath. O make him breathe. His face small, grey; so still this tumbling boy.

Elizabeth's voice comes from a frightened place. 'The house, it caught so quickly, from the back, they started it at the back. It caught like dead leaves. I ran to Benjamin. He was sleeping, but a log had fallen on him, only a small log. He was drugged by the fumes – the log or fear – I don't know. I ran with him out of the front, up into the trees, waiting for you. I should have stayed in his room, I should have slept with him.' She was sick with fear. I took her hand and we looked at one another in silence.

The rabbi returned with the horse, who was tugging at the rein and rearing; his eyes like shelled eggs. 'Here, go quickly, they are still there, taking the chickens, sacking the woodshed.' He was full of fury and yet he would not look me in the eye. 'My name is Judah, tell my brother I will come later. It is the first house in the village, with an old fig tree in the centre of the garden.'

Elizabeth rode in front, with me behind holding Benjamin tightly to me. Each jerk of the horse's body tore into my nerves as it shook the little body in my arms. Once the horse stumbled and I cried out. The child let out a tiny cry, a bleat. It seemed to come from his eyes, his smoked hair; his soft, damp palms. And it echoed in me so that I found my eyes splashing and the salt filling my throat also as the tears trickled down on to his face. I tried to relax my stiffened body to make a soft place for him to lie; I tried to respond to the horse's rhythm so that he would not be jarred. But the effort of concentration was making me more fraught, so I sat holding him, unable to think, only to weep.

We reached the village. Elizabeth slipped off the horse, then, looking at me swiftly, she tore a strip off her petticoat and placed it over my head. I was stunned that, at such a time, she could remember niceties. A woman came running in a loose gown – 'We have heard, come inside, you are welcome.'

My tears fell and fell as her husband came out and took Benjamin from me and into the house, where he laid him tenderly on a low table; he looked at him carefully, then said, 'The child is very ill, I'll see to him.' He took Benjamin from the room and I ran after him, terrified that I would not see him again.

'No, it is all right,' his wife said, sitting me down firmly, 'he will be put into one of our children's old cots in a quiet place and given medicine. Don't worry, come with me, I must take care of that gash in your cheek.'

A servant came and took Elizabeth with her, but I was so frenzied that they had to reassure me many times that she would return quickly. I was given a room, water, and towels, and after the doctor's wife had cleansed my wound, she left me to wash. I sat a long time just looking at the water, turning circles in it with my finger; when I thought, I cried.

The doctor came and sat beside me; he did not speak for some time and I could not ask. Then he said quietly, 'He is still unconscious, and the fumes may have damaged his lungs, but he is a strong boy. Don't worry. We must trust in the Lord.' He looked at the wound on my cheek and covered it with a dressing; then he held my hands firmly and said, 'Now you must try to become calm, relax your body, your mind – sleep if you can. I do not understand these people, but they are simple and easily provoked. Fear makes brutality. And please, do not concern yourself about your future. You may stay here as long as you wish. I knew your husband, a fine craftsman – a recluse of course, but that has never been a sin.' He smiled wryly. 'These things pass. Be calm for your son's sake.'

I took the water and washed my eyes and hands and then I looked for the woman and asked to be taken to Benjamin. He was lying on a low cot and he looked so small. I spoke his name quietly, but he did not stir. His cheeks were stained a deep crimson; there was a white circle around his mouth and his eyelids seemed covered with chalk. On his cheek was a small black streak and I wiped it gently away. I stayed at his side, never taking my eyes off his face. Often I would bend and kiss his white mouth, again and again, hoping it would revive him – but also to reassure myself that there was breath in him still. Elizabeth sat in the corner, not moving, not speaking. Sometimes I would look at her and see that her hands, which normally lay flat and small on her knees, were pressed together on her lap as if in supplication. I knew her thoughts; the repeated laceration that whispered: why did I not, if I had only ... The colour faded slowly in Benjamin's cheeks, so that his whole face became like marble. I stroked his face endlessly, it was warm and soft. Once he moved and his hand flew above his head as though warding off a danger and his mouth opened noiselessly for a brief moment, then closed; I pressed my lips against his, agonised.

The rabbi, Judah, returned and he came to see me. His face was still dense with anger and I wondered why. 'There is nothing left now,' was all he said to me. I shrugged. He looked at Benjamin, then his eyes alighted on me with pity – and I didn't want that look. I hated him for it, for making the terror surface in me again. His brother came in and looked at Benjamin again, feeling his face, his wrist; if only he would say something, even his hands look blank. Suddenly, Judah demanded roughly, 'Why did they hate you? What did you do to them?'

The doctor frowned at him slightly and said simply, 'She was a stranger in the village.'

All night I sat and watched as the candle flickered and burnt low; as the wind coming through the window seemed to carry wood-smoke and the stars were like sparks of fire. I had been told not to move him; but my heart was in my arms and I had to hold him. I lifted him from the cot and held him and all night long he lay so still, his head curled into my shoulder. I kissed his mouth – dry, closed against me. I touched his cheeks. Does he breathe? Does he breathe?

In the morning they tried to take him from me, but I would not part with him; he was peaceful in my arms, his weight so gentle – let him be, do not disturb him. They looked at me sorrowfully and went away. Elizabeth came and said, 'Let me take him, you are so tired', but her eyes were quivering pools of grief. I shook my head fiercely and drew my child to me; he grows lighter every moment, his skin is liquid, his hair floats on my arm. Is it his hand that pulls at my skirt so faintly? Let him be, he is so small – so quiet this tumbling boy. Their eyes flared as they watched me clinging to him, their heads moved together in consternation.

The doctor said, 'Give me the child', and his eyes pleaded so desperately. But I held the boy tighter, pressing my cheek against his to keep it warm. They left me for some hours and I rocked and rocked; and when they came back the doctor reached out his arms and still I shook my head and buried my face in the small body. Finally he said – O I know he had to say it, I know it had to be brutal – but my body died, part of it died when he said, 'The child is dead. You must let me take him.' He pulled Benjamin from me and I howled as he thrust my hand on the heart and said, 'Feel, it is silent. He is dead.'

It is the wail that has little to do with a mouth; the scream comes from all the organs of the body and the body writhes in a pain that splits each hair, each muscle – without bleeding. But we need the blood – to look at, to say, Here is the evidence of my anguish. No blood. Only that wail that no one can hear without flinching, without turning away. And the wail returns again to the body having nowhere to go and finds it empty.

O you can see that I am weeping at the memory, but softly, for it was a death without horror – small, infinitely pitiful. I can hold it to me, I can look at it. O Benjamin, Benjamin, they would not say your name. They did not know that part of my body had died – that I had lost my arms; I had no one to hold. And there is pain when the limbs are gone, there is an ache in the empty space. See how he splashes in the stream and bites my wet shoulder. He pulls himself up on my hair and catches a word – bouncing it up and down as I clap. He flies through the air, laughing; a hurtling boy, tough, tousled. Boy with a mouth full of flowers and pockets full of frogs. A child so tender; mine.

Four

I dreamt that I was holding a baby, rocking it in my arms and crooning. Then I turned back the covers: its face was one round grey stone with a single eye. It was your child. The moon gives children and takes them back, like God. Were you a child to replace another? It is too late; the moon like a slice of glass – awful, sick. The roses are all ill and I love you, love you. And I am weary of beauty. How perfect the cheeks of these petals – I look and I love them, but what do they give in return? A cool stare, a beautiful, indifferent shrug.

I see the ants dithering on the floor, making circles, colliding – one climbing my skirt – and I become a rash of itches that will give me no peace until I remove myself to a place where their frenzy will not touch me. I want to be quiet, so quiet that all things, all creatures will forget me, and I alone can remember: that village, that gentlest of women – the doctor's wife; those still, silent days.

I found a mother when I needed one most, having lost a child, and she, grown older, her children gone away, found her hours empty. She took me from the room where the wail still echoed, put me to bed in a quiet room and tied the sheets tightly around me. She sat and stroked my hair until I slept. When I awoke, numb, stricken with silence, she fed me broth and cut up my bread very small. For many nights she slept in my room and hushed me whenever the flames rose too high or the dream-women raised their fists.

For a week I did not speak at all, and then I began to speak to her more than I had ever spoken to anyone in my life. One word gave birth to a sentence that grew into a long stream of memories, and as my thoughts slowly took shape, the sounds of the words became similar; the rhythms matched in a mysterious way – so that in the end my speech was more like a chant, like religious intonation – and it seemed to have no end. If the light was dying outside, or if it was windy or raining, I felt at peace and my memories surged. But if the door should suddenly open, or if my adoptive mother broke my meditation by dropping her sewing, my song became a lament that trembled, diminished and faded into sobbing. My nightmares, the endless outpourings of my day-dreams, never troubled her; her brow never creased in mockery. For she understood childhood and the beginning of things – when existence is on another plane and nothing is mad or frightening; it is merely a journey that leads usually only to a more mundane place. For her, as for me, the other plane was more real, more lovely than the daily scurry. The magic world had dragons and strange vanishing animals and flowers; water you could dive through for ever and never reach the bottom, nor lose breath; fish you could ride on to find peaches in sea-shells and jewels in the mouths of frogs.

There were times then, and now, when through the mirror of a lost child I could return to that magic place of three years old: before anyone had said – this is how it must be done, this is right, this wrong, this dream, this true. To the time when mud was good to eat and worms to fondle; water was for lying on and stones for conversation, and pain was only physical. Somewhere that enchanted place still exists in me. You found it, you gave it back to me at little times and now it is always there to dig up like a buried jewel.

All through the day we two were alone, and sometimes I think Elizabeth was angry with me for excluding her. I did not notice that then; perhaps I blamed her a little and therefore my exclusion was more cruel. But my mother and I had a communion that made other people a burden. The doctor came back in the evening and took his dinner with us; but often he would have to go out afterwards and sometimes he did not return until very late. At night I was a different person: more frightened, more needful, not of a listener, but of a hand that would stroke my hair and bring me warm milk and biscuits. And she cared for this other demanding child in me too, without comment or rebuke.

Once a week her husband used to take to the poor a bundle of old clothes that she had collected in the village and a big batch of bread that she had made. It was not unusual for sick or poor people to turn up at her kitchen door. She always took care of them in her slow, careful way, and was something of a doctor herself with her neat bandaging and home-made salves. I was jealous of all these intruders and sulked. She would wait until I was ready to smile and then hand me a little cake or a rug for my knees. Later, I began to help her with this work: rolling the bandages, stirring the ointments and putting them into little pots which I labelled very neatly. Our days were filled with industry, and if ever she looked weary or her smiles lagged I grew alarmed and she was quick to reassure me by touching my cheek or by suggesting a walk. She let me know, daily, by the tenderness in her eyes, that she loved me in return.

We went for long walks together and I would go out into the fields and collect her great bunches of wild flowers and watch as her face lit up with surprise as she said, 'I'd never think to pick field-daisies, but how nice they will look in the brown jug.' One night, when the doctor had been away for some days, awake and dreaming I walked to her room and stood beside her bed, waiting for her to awake to my presence. When she opened her eyes, she did not start or speak, but simply moved over in the bed and lifted the covers so that I could sleep beside her. All night I lay on her shoulder with her lips on my hair. In the morning she woke very early, as was her way, and brought me a cup of milk and a bowl of grapes, each one peeled and pipped.

After some months, when I was ready to see people again, she took me to meet her friends in the village, and they treated me carefully, like someone who had long been ill. I began to see how much she was loved; but this no longer threatened me because I was sure now of her devotion: everything she said to me was designed to give me strength and confidence. Soon I was ready, grown again, and I did not have the same need of her. She seemed to understand that too, but it hurt her. I decided that I must leave, but I hated to think of going. I could see that a hole would open in her heart too; that she would sit and stitch and be kind and charitable, but lonely and empty again – another child gone and a hearth more silent. She had found, as few women do, something to comfort her, a work of her own, separate from husband and children – but it was not enough. Almost with guilt I asked the doctor to arrange for a letter to be taken to Joshua, so that I could ask him for money. It offended me to have to do it, but I determined that it would be for the last time.

Once, as I sat winding wool, Father came with Simon. They were sheepish, ashamed, and I was cool. They suggested that I return and marry Simon and they reminded me of the Law. I could not bear to see them, and Father distressed me, so burdened by age and sorrow. I would not consider marrying Simon just to propagate their name, and so they left, feeling that they had done their duty. After their visit I felt strong, proud again. I spoke to the doctor and asked him if he knew anyone who would help me find a post as a teacher. He screwed up his nose and said he would think about it.

Several days later, having made sure his wife was not likely to interrupt us, he said that he knew an elderly lady who ran a school for girls, but he did not know that I should even consider it as the place she lived and worked in was Tiberias: 'The woman herself is all right. She is a widow too – but of course you know that all the Jews in Tiberias have ceased to be Jews and I myself would never set foot in the place.' As a girl I had heard stories about the city built on a Jewish burial-ground, and of the unfaithful who lived with the Romans there. I knew even as I was making shocked noises to appease him that I would go there, and he knew it too, though he did not like it. We both understood that I had no choice.

When I told mother that I was going away, she said nothing, but her stitches began to rip through the cloth viciously and beneath her bent head there were tears. I then changed my mind – because I had decided to go straight away – and I told her that I would go with them first to Jerusalem for the Passover. And it was only when the country was green as a sour apple and the blossom thick on the branches that I left her. I left with her the child in me, but not my own child – he hung like a stone about my heart, precious, secret. With his death, I lost the sweetest, gentlest part of my own nature, and it was another woman who walked away.

I used to think that there was only one way that the many different women of my being could not rise in me; only one remedy for the encroachment of these sinister sisters – and that of course was death. Now, I am able to love all the girls, all the women I have been – after all those years of hating them. But I am only able to love them now that they are gone. And perhaps I also miss them.

All my life I have thought, there must be more than this: there must be some emotion that lives up to my expectation. I know now that there is no such thing. What there is, is this: a compulsion to fill out the need for it by making it exist: by creating in the mind one perfect love. (This is only what you did.) There is a pressed poppy on my table. I pick it up and look through the petals. It is exquisitely, perfectly beautiful: a pale orange/mauve with fine lines as on skin; a yellow heart and seeds suspended on black silk. But the poppy is dead. Is that also the only way a man or woman can be perfected in the eyes of others? Is that what they will do to you? Is it what I am doing? You said, 'I will be one of the very few who die exactly when they should, at the right moment.'

Why did you have to threaten like that? How often you dis-spirited me by the weightiness of all your thoughts and endeavours. You had the soul of the deepest ocean; never rocked by the little frothy waves, only by titanic storms. Your heart was without suppleness. When I think of your fixity, sometimes I wonder why I squandered so much love, lavished so much care on you. Because always you had to be retarded, you had at some soft point to say, wringing me – 'It is nothing, all this is meaningless. Happiness, or unhappiness, it is nothing.'

So I went to Tiberias carrying my expectations on the back of a hired mule. As I went I told myself, again and again, as in a litany: 'I need marry no one, no one. There is no need. I can do, I can be.' It was this that made me feel secure, this and the belief that I could protect myself through work, by trying to find what I lacked through my brain and not the hair-shirt of my emotions. I had a strength then greater than ever before: a hard veneer that I believed in. But I was less flexible because of it. I was afraid of the strength failing me; the spontaneity of my emotions at moments of crisis now disturbed me, I did not know how much more I could bear. Suddenly, I really wanted to teach, to study hard, and I persuaded myself that Tiberias must be the ideal place, since it had been Herod Antipas's dream to build it as a city for the promotion of Graeco-Roman culture combined with the spiritual values of our own.

I felt almost happy jogging along under a cloudy sky. I looked at Elizabeth as we rode and thought how stringy her arms looked pulling listlessly at the reins; sometimes she would turn and look at me and her eyes had sunk. For months she had worn the same black dress: she washed it overnight and wore it each morning, nothing would persuade her to wear anything else. Her hair was tied severely back which made her forehead look unnaturally high above the long eyes. Her hands shook a little. None of her grief had been released, it was all strapped tight inside the black dress; and she resented my composure. She did not know how determined I was to show how brave, how wonderful I could be.

In the afternoon, we looked down on Tiberias gleaming white and gold with a backcloth of blue. We began the descent and saw the burning silver of the lake at each curve in the road. This pleasure city was filled with the poor and the scum who could not resist the attractions at the end of the broad steep road that we travelled. Now we went to join them. One final wrench in the road and we found ourselves on the outer skirts of the city. I saw the high houses, the beaten gold of the cupola on the palace. The streets were all very straight and neat and the houses and buildings quite different from those at Jerusalem. As we drew near to the waterfront, I could hear music playing; there were fountains, statues of naked goddesses, and beautifully dressed women strolling among pillars of basalt and granite. As if in mockery of this splendour there was the amethyst lake, and children leaping off the wall into the water with buckled knees, competing for the loudest splash.

Having washed our faces in the lake at a quiet spot between the palm trees, we made our way back to the main street. We were intimidated by the opulence of this quarter and hurried on to less busy streets which were lined with stalls selling lurid articles at exorbitant prices. Farther on, the faces of the people we passed were obviously of a purer breeding than those we had seen in the centre of the city and I began to feel more at home. Little girls played hopscotch in the road and their clothes were plain and neat. At this point we asked directions.

In a well-laid-out quarter with large houses and lush gardens we found the house we were looking for. The buildings here were more traditional, with plain pillars and a welcome lack of statues. The young men returning from their studies had curled side-locks and their lugubrious expressions seemed to indicate immersion in the Torah. I relaxed and knocked at the door. It was answered by a tall slave whose nose seemed to lift at the sight of our simple clothing. I was shown into a small waiting room, from which I could see into a much larger reception room with plush red furnishings and delicately carved couches. On the walls were paintings of young girls in white dresses with long flowing hair and flowers at their throats. The door connecting the two rooms was shut curtly by the slave, who then departed with my letter of introduction. I waited with damp hands until the door opened again and a small, grey-haired woman walked in; she walked with the mannered movements of the Romans, but I could see that this was something that she had acquired. She welcomed me graciously, if slightly patronisingly, and sat down next to me, having ordered cordials.

Carefully scrutinising my face she said, 'You are looking for a post I believe?' I nodded, trying to calm the fluttering of my throat: didn't she know she held my future in her palm? She puckered her forehead and said, 'I hope the good doctor has not misled you.' The words took their effect and then she continued, 'I do run a school, but it is not the kind he probably imagined.' She adjusted the blue silk of her skirt and I was amazed to see that her nails were coloured with some crimson stuff; I had to force my eyes off them. She talked in a slow way as though she were not used to spontaneous conversation; she seemed to be keeping an eye on each word that she uttered and everything about her appeared deliberate and a little false.

'Tiberias is a strange place, very new and still finding its feet. The girls who come to me are the daughters of Jewish families who are attempting to rise in the social world – people on the brink of becoming courtiers who want their daughters to learn the refinements they will need to make good marriages. They are taught by my staff what to wear and what to say at palace gatherings; how to walk and conduct themselves with elegance and a breeding that they all too often lack. The more intelligent ones learn Greek and Latin – that is where you could come in, but I am not sure I really need anyone in this capacity – however, we will see. I understand and sympathise with your dilemma.' But she did not; it was a politeness only. Then she asked me briskly, 'What do you know?'

When I had rattled off my accomplishments she merely said, 'What? No Latin?' I shook my head, beginning to wish I had not come, feeling stupid in the presence of this grand house and pert old lady. She softened and rested her hand on mine, but moved it quickly as if to indicate that she was too fastidious for touch, then said,

'Come, don't be disheartened, you could learn Latin if necessary, couldn't you?'

'Yes, I learn fast,' I replied, not wanting to learn Latin at all. I was surprised when she said that I could stay at her house while she considered things, and that if there was a place for me I could continue to live there, as long as I kept no more than one servant. It was a great relief and I warmed to her rapidly.

We walked through a carved door and I stopped with a cold shock to see that there were olive trees worked in lines along its length. I touched one quickly and she seemed to snap, 'What is it?'

I was shaking and could do no more than toss my head and walk on to the cool verandah overlooking a deep pool. In the days ahead I used to rest my head against that door and caress the trees, thinking of his name, his hands, the sawdust in the little creases of his neck.

We walked to the far end of the courtyard, up a small flight of stairs to a corridor. She showed me into a small room with a bed, a stool, a chest of drawers and table. There was a window with glass panes in it overlooking the courtyard. When I thanked her for her kindness she said we would talk at noon when she had slept on the question, and that if I was bored in the morning I should investigate her library, which was fairly modest but had some books of interest; she pointed it out from the window.

Lying on the bed staring vacantly at the lavender walls and the white ceiling, my body was stiff and it still vibrated with the movements of the mule. I blew out the candle and watched the light from the courtyard making patterns on the window. Far away the soft cry of a child ... I felt that my head was shrinking to the size of a plum, my eyes swam and my knees curled up to my breasts. O if you knew the loss – still – small cheek melting into mine; rolling among the pine needles as his wet mouth splashes my neck; smell as clean as a pansy. The secret life of a child; all we see are the tears, the smiles. What did I know of him? Only how frightened he became as all day he clung to my knees – but once no stone, no rushing water would have made him tremble. The violence that maims, that kills. I cried for him for Samuel and for myself – because they would never again turn the corner and be there ...

When I think of these things, when the knives rise out of the past, they kill me. I am laid open by recalling what I now lack. I sit here cosseting myself in my spinster ways: another rug for my knees; what shall be done about the roof? How my back begins to ache at night. I am knitting a shroud of intelligence, observation and chastity – but then it is revealed in all its paltriness by the sudden soar of my heart when I think of the soft blows of your kisses. I must not think it, because it is unbearable. O love, my love, just one more day of your face. How my thighs ache, remembering. How much I would give you now, having lived without you . . .

When I was in Tiberias, I never once returned to this house or the shores where I grew up – it was a part of my life behind curtains. Tiberias – all those long days as the young women sat stitching in cool rooms; or learning how to wear the most transparent robes without revealing more than was acceptable. They sat before gilded mirrors, letting down and lifting their hair into ringlets and waves, made by hot tongs that released a foul smell. There was a woman who taught the art of make-up and she transformed those glowing complexions into the texture of dull wool, and enlarged their mouths with scarlet dyes which could not be licked. I was required to wear a long, flowing dress with sleeves of the latest fashion; my hair was decked with silver combs and my lips bruised with purple. The girls' gossip was as flimsy as a spider's web and as endless – weaving in and out of the possibilities of success with this or that young man, or the horror of poor Rachel's complexion, and how frightful that all those handsome Jewish youths had gone off to have the operation so that they should not feel embarrassed doing gymnastics naked with the Romans. And would they be all right afterwards?

They did not like me, feeling my scorn of the life they, or perhaps their mothers, had determined for them; and they resented me for telling them nothing of my own life. There were one or two who were staggeringly beautiful and I envied their high breasts and unravished faces. There were a few also whom I did care for: girls who would have been happier spinning in some quiet corner, or reading Hebrew poetry in a garden with their mothers close by. Not surprisingly, three of these were intelligent and thoughtful, and while I taught them Greek, one taught me a little Latin, but at first I had a reluctance towards the tongue. My duties were of a humble nature: reading to the nubile horrors as they dribbled over their embroidery; teaching them some of the Odes of Horace, which first they responded to with sniggers, but finally the gracefulness touched even their muffled minds and I was asked to recite more and more. Some of the lines still hover: 'he sleeps the sleep which men never recover from.' Having remembered that, I went to the shelf and picked up an old copy I found in Jerusalem with both translations and found, 'To live wisely shun the deep sea.' In the library I found a feast of books and read each one very slowly to eke out the pleasure. I found that I had become more scrupulous in my opinions: now I felt odd moments of criticism reading Plato and entertained the heretical thought that the Greeks could not possibly write bad plays having such powerful themes handed down to them.

My benefactress, Martha, turned out to be a most intelligent woman. She spoke often to me about literature and made me impatient to catch up with her learning. She entertained on a lavish scale. I did not attend these functions and lived a muted existence, sometimes slipping to my window to watch the flamboyant women talking in the courtyard before going into the dining room. Why do they all aim so high? I used to wonder, watching the women turn their necks to be kissed, smiling at the men with mouths popping with redness and eyes ringed with blue and purple – endeavouring so hard to be witty and pleasing that the effort always seemed to show. Only once I attended a dinner, because Martha's guests had requested it, saying it might be amusing to see the lady tutors; and so one or two of the more presentable of this pitiful species were put on display. They were obviously surprised to see that I was not ugly or aggressive merely because I worked and had no husband.

That night I could find myself almost noble, almost clever in such a company. When they ate they ceased to have any link with humanity, merely became raw caverns opening and closing on hunks of meat, on little fishes dripping with butter. Their conversation was ribald and there was a round gentleman whose language was so foul as to make even those experienced women blush. I spoke only when spoken to and felt very superior because of it. One man only interested me: he was growing old, he had a sad bearing and hollow eyes. He was treated with enormous respect and looked so spruce and well-kept that I felt he had come straight from the baths. He said very little. Did he feel himself too important to utter? Even as I was thinking this, his voice darted across the table and flipped my thoughts aside. In a cool, bored voice he asked, 'How long do you intend to stay in this place?' and his rudeness was covered by a sudden spurt in the conversation.

Later, talking to Martha, she asked me to tell her what I thought of her guests. I enquired after the man who had questioned me and she replied sharply, 'His name is Boaz. He's an eccentric, disgustingly rich.' She added when pressed that he was a fallen Jew, and a businessman whose pursuits no one dared question. She seemed to suggest that there might be something corrupt in his activities and his life. I was a little intrigued. I respected Martha, yet I could not really respond to her. She often seemed to me admirable and wise; at other times she seemed shorn of all sentiments except expediency and there was a ruthlessness in her that kept me from making a closer friendship. But I was always grateful to her for taking me in and giving me a place to study.

In the early mornings, Elizabeth and I would walk down the quiet streets. She refused to relinquish her black; it was a new dress by this time, but very severe, as if the asperity was worn as a reminder, a penance. I could not bring myself to speak to her about it; instead I presented her with a dove-grey dress and said, 'Go on, wear it.' Her flat, dun face trembled and she began to weep, hiding her face in her arms. I sat her down on a stool and held her hands until it was over, and then she looked awkward and walked quickly from the room.

Elizabeth and I would walk again through the streets before it grew too dark, and slowly we came to explore all the edges of Tiberias. There was a street where the harlots walked, and it frightened and attracted me. Such women intrigued you also – there's no question about it though you denied it. I heard one giggle and say to another, 'Don't entertain any fancy for him – he's God's.' But you weren't, you were mine – I had you then. If only, only . . .

Age began to alarm me. I once thought, Will I become like that one, that old one with the hopeless smile? She waits outside the public urinal, under the tree so that the light will not pick out her wrinkles and the ugly scar on her cheek. A poor child passes, sticking out her tongue and then spitting. Children: so clever, they know who they can misuse. She skulks back deeper. I see her hands rub at her sides, she straightens her coarse hair and begins bravely to look about. But she is without hope: her breasts droop with indignities; her body is uglied by poverty and abuse; her garments reek. I look at her feet and see the deep cracks where the dust is caking. Her face in sunlight would be a little like that. And I told myself firmly, No, I can never be like her. Today I woke up and there was nothing to frighten me. There was bread and milk for breakfast; the linen was clean; nothing to injure me. The boys in the street hitch up their robes and kick stones; their legs shine, their laughter ripples . . .

Yes, I could have been like her. I know that to be a widow is to be a whore. Always in the corners of gardens, of parks – men ogling. Had I been poor – what alternative?

I was drawn more to the dark quarters of the city, where the poor people made me feel less alien, for their simple ways were the ones I had grown up with. They lived in low shacks with no gardens or fountains; but there was a beauty there in the early mornings as we passed through on our way to the lake. There was a soft light on the purple flowers as they curled around the crumbling brick; and something touching about the woman with her brood of children, swilling out her garbage pail and throwing the swish of water over the vegetable patch. She had been young once; that heavy, soiled dress hid a body that was a girl's once, that looked in a mirror and smiled – not grimly as now, comparing herself to the young girls strutting the streets – but softly, as young women smile, knowing they are lovely.

My shine was fading. The years were passing and I simply stood still, treading water, making my life seem full and important through an intellectual snobbishness which I could share with no one. I began to dislike the streams of young girls in the school more. As each year old paintings of past beauties were taken off the walls and replaced by that year's marvels, I felt a bitterness growing and could find no outlet for it. Martha's visitors continued to come, and I watched their faces ripen into old cheese and their attitudes sour. Sometimes I would see the immaculate gentleman: I felt ashamed to see him, feeling that now I must stay for ever. He never spoke, but once he almost asked me something, but did not.

The patterns of our life shape our bodies, our faces, but as we grow older we shy away from the patterning, we want the process arrested. I found it hard to accept the littleness of my life, knowing that as time trickled away there could only be less. It was like that with you: but with you I could have begged, knelt at your feet and pleaded – because I loved you and that made it all right. I did not beg though, I threw myself instead into the cause to replace what I had lost of you. I learned to love it. You were like a soldier always on duty, having soldier's thoughts. You gave your time meanly, in little rations, so that everyone should have an equal share. There was a strange sweetness about those days. My hair was tied in tight braids; I had only two changes of clothing, and I washed many clothes beside my own and yours. We cooked in rough pots and had very little to eat. Whenever anyone came to join us, you insisted that they be fed too. Some brought a chicken or some vegetables, mainly they came empty-handed and hungry. There was so much to do, so little time. We kept moving from one stream to another. You would not stay longer than one night in a place, and explained it by saying that you could feel things happening at a distance: you heard conversations about you going on in Jerusalem, plots in the desert. Wherever we went I could hear, not far off, your voice: teaching, praying with a terrible urgency, and sometimes you would shout if you felt people were not listening – always so fast, your voice, as though you feared that the bushes would part and reveal enemies. In those days you never laughed. I wanted to stop you with a mouthful of kisses, stop your crazed hurtling and catch you, catch you ... but you were impatient of me.

Could I have been so strong, so full of ingenuity, had I simply led the life of a wife and mother? Could I have found roots and berries and mushrooms with such ease, and killed wild birds with that little sling you taught me to use, had these things not been expected of me? Walked for hours with broken sandals in the heat and the dust, with only the little food we would glean from people's generosity – which was sadly lacking unless you had healed someone, and then they were prepared to feed only you. I could have done, endured nothing, if I had not been forced to my capabilities. We become what is expected of us, if we can: it is a matter of strength: 'He asked for water and she gave him milk. She put her hand to the nail.'

Once, as a wife, I did not have that strength. I longed then only for peace, for the internal unrest to cease. I could not make it happen. It was as if each day brought only debris to be picked up; a child's tears to be caught – and all this with the foul taste of onion in the mouth – O where are the roses? I admire the women who scrub the floors and grit their teeth and somehow find a way to bring gladness into the endless tripping from one drudgery to the next. It is brave and beautiful to turn your tears from the children. And I understand and miss the sensuality of making a perfect dish for one man: laying out the colours on the plate, letting the sauce ripple on the blanched fish; putting the olives just so, the parsley that much, no more. It is an act of love, the gentlest way with hands. Will he see it, or just eat it? Often it is only a woman who will say, how beautiful that looks. But I admire them most of all, those women, who can find these things enough. I am not one of them, but somewhere I envy them.

What did I expect of myself in Tiberias? An order, a cleanliness? Certainly my mind was meticulous, shiny as a well-oiled boot. Calmly I sat reading philosophy, sometimes writing down my observations. I stopped eating meat or drinking wine, and I looked on God with even less favour. I took upon myself some of the management of the school, and began a large tapestry for the wall, which would do away with the need for paintings of young girls. I felt that all the fire in me was stilled, in repose. I found pleasure only in observing minute detail, as I do now. It must be a comforting thing. Because today, wearing that soft, most wistful of blouses, I watch how the cuff fits so neatly against my wrist; how fine the cloth letting the flesh blush through. I love the shapes made by the creases, and how the scarlet brooch burns at my shoulder.

Why do we really only have time to contemplate when someone or something dies? Once, I would have given so much to have a big wedge of a day all to myself – now I have it. In Tiberias I almost had it . . . and the years went by, barely tugging the grass.

It was autumn in Tiberias and the wealthy started to hurry back to their winter palaces on the lake. There was no winter in Tiberias: it rocked in a warm, temperate basin warmed by pink hills. The rains that year were heavy; then a plague broke out, boxes were packed and the rich departed. When the girls were singing and the music mistress scratched at her lyre, a strange, dreamy girl with a voice soft as powder began to cough. There was a cluck of impatience and the music began again. Lydia continued to cough; her skin became mottled and her eyes rolled. I got her some water and the silenced class watched as she sat on a stool, her hands at her throat, her chest heaving. She was taken home, and died of the plague two days later. The school was closed.

Elizabeth came to my room early one morning, pale and shivering, complaining of great pain in her throat. I went straight to Martha and told her that we would leave immediately. She thought it unnecessary for me to do more than retire into isolation and send Elizabeth to the Infirmary, where she would die. I packed a few things and Elizabeth and I went down to the poor quarter where I had no trouble getting a small house at the end of the street, facing a bit of wasteland where poppies were bursting joyfully among the rubble. The house agent did not bother to mention to me that half of the street's inhabitants had been wiped away by the plague, nor did I mention my plight. Later, Martha sent slaves with beds and blankets and I put Elizabeth to bed. She seemed strangely bright and cheerful and said that she did not feel unwell; she was not coughing. Her cheeks were rosy and her mouth was darker than usual – that's all. She kept saying, 'You cannot stay here, it's dreadful. Leave me, I will be all right.'

'Don't be silly, you're ill.'

'Someone else can look after me.'

'Who?'

'I don't know, someone.'

'But I want to.'

'It's awful here, all those people, so dirty and poor and ill too. It is no place for you.'

'We will only stay here until you're better.'

'I may die.' No flicker in her eye, no fear.

'Rubbish. You have only a touch of fever. A doctor is coming. Poor Martha, she was so relieved to see us go that now she feels guilty.'

'Will the doctor come?'

'O yes.'

Later, when she felt more feverish and her hands and feet were sweating profusely, she began to whimper, 'Will the doctor come?' And always immediately afterwards she would ask, 'Are you sure you are all right?'

I went to get the doctor, keeping my veil close to my nose, and I would not let him be until he had promised to return with me. I had met him at Martha's, but he was no longer charming. He was exhausted and angry, and when he saw where I was taking him he stopped in the middle of the street and shouted, 'Do you think I have stayed up all these nights tending to rich people just to end up among this trash, visiting a damn servant on her death-bed?' I gave him more money. He walked briskly through the trash and saw to Elizabeth, leaving a small bottle of medicine.

Thinking this I feel so full of her and I am made conscious of how much we have suffered together. Perhaps the strongest marriage I have had, since any marriage to me must be in the nature of a prop.

My face, it is unrecognisable now, as is hers. Mine, not because the skin has fallen, or lines pulled features out of place, but because life, with a dirty finger, has scored all down the surface. It is the same with her – but I must claim most of the wrinkles on that brow. There is an invisible scouring cloth that wipes off the sweetness and leaves . . . but why am I weeping like this, so heavily, heavily? I who do not weep, who have not wept these years. My hand against my mouth, thoughts blurring – Elizabeth, if you will come and hold my head . . .

It is cold in this room and dark. I cannot find my shawl and the petals are falling with small gasps. I can see the sun shining through the green outside and the voices of the servants calling to the chickens. There was noise outside that hovel of a house in Tiberias, there was wailing and the house next door was nailed shut at window and doors. I was afraid to go outside, and went only once to the shop at the end of the street. There they looked at me angrily; nearly everyone wore black – one woman her dress so old and greasy that the black had become green. Where is this leading me? My breath is only harsh gulps. When I came back, Elizabeth lay so quietly beneath the covers; she was pale, her blood was in the doctor's pan. When she woke she was not frightened, she looked at me bleakly and said, 'It is awful that you should take care of me, it is for me to look after you.' O yes, how many times; no one else has washed me in deep warm water, fed me, dressed me. She did not know how it pleased me to wipe her face and hands and cook up a weak broth of barley. Her hands shook, so I fed her with a little spoon, and all the time she protested, saying it was not necessary. She began coughing and grew so frightened then that I had to hold her hands tightly to calm her, because as she panicked she almost suffocated. After the coughing fits she seemed weaker. I kept forcing her to drink.

She lay under a pile of blankets, shivering, her eyes wild with fear, and it was not the fear of death, but a fear of this unknown affliction that was sucking her breath from her. When the shivering stopped she spoke softly, she kept telling me of my goodness and I didn't want her to speak but waited in terror at the times when she went silent, hoping her mouth would move again. Once, there were people outside our door and I went to ask them what they wanted. They asked if there was illness in the house and I lied.

One came inside and saw her lying stiffly; he took her to be dead. He said to me, 'In the morning, see that she is buried in the proper place, over there, and then this house will be burned.'

My mind raced as he walked to the door and I said, 'She will be buried tonight, and I will be gone by the morning.'

He nodded, and said, 'We will burn the house.'

Elizabeth was not conscious. I gathered our things together. When I had them neatly stacked, I waited. Finally, her eyes opened and she whispered through cracked lips, 'I feel better, are you all right?' I gave her water and explained that we must leave. I helped her up but she could barely walk, and collapsed at the back door. I left her there and took our blankets and food through to the boarded-up house, and when I had settled a place for her to lie down I went back and half-carried her into the house next door. A wisp of a memory came back to me: Father saying that a man had been cured of his fever by layer upon layer of warmth being piled on top of him at the pitch of the affliction. Elizabeth's skin was fiery and yet her bones shone whitely through the skin. Her eyes slanted upwards into slits so that she looked evil, intoxicated. I forced water down her throat and then doubled all the blankets and tucked them firmly in about her so no air could creep in. I pulled an old rug off the floor and placed this over her too. Her face looked as though it had caught fire. Every time that her tossing lifted the blankets, I pulled them tight, and as the sweat began to glisten on her face I began to wipe it away: there was no end to it. At one point she gave a cry, then collapsed, her head falling sideways. I thought she had died; my own breath faltered. Her mouth parted with a harsh panting sound, which slowly, slowly became rhythmical again. When the heat of the day was sliding downwards, I saw that she was sleeping naturally; calm, cool breathing.

My head aches, it is the ache that begins in the left side of my forehead and spreads to the base of my skull. I tell myself: relax, be calm; but why is it always worse on the left side? If I tie a tight band across my forehead like the slaves do, I might check the pain. No, I know this headache, it has come before. It will not go away because it is the beginning . . .

While Elizabeth slept, I slept. When I woke, she was still deeply sleeping. I began cautiously to approach the boarded-up window; through a crack I could see the dusty street. No one sat in their doorways; a few children played knuckle-bones on the pavement, but soon a call sent them hurrying in different directions. I walked into the next room where there was a little hearth with its ashes stamped out. I did not dare to make a fire to cook on, but found a pitcher of water in one corner and mixed some of this into ground barley for Elizabeth when she woke. It was dark and I bumped into a tall stool and stood terrified for some moments in case the sound had been heard. I crept back to my blanket beside Elizabeth and began studying the weaving of it to distract my nerves.

A sound in the street made me move back to the window. Some men were carrying two long covered shapes down the street; they were singing a tremulous dirge; their bodies swayed as though stuck together by grief. Then came a woman: I saw her rush headlong down the street after the procession, howling with a voice that made me wince. She was holding a bundle so small. I knew. I felt my insides leave my body and fly into her belly. She thrust her bundle at a man who took it and put it between the two shapes and walked on. The woman began to spin in the road, her hands up to her head, tearing her hair. I began to beat my head against the wall, dust falling into my eyes. Then sat and rocked, rocked. Little head wilting like a daisy in the sun, then perking upright. When he was a baby, fresh from heaven, he was so quiet, pensive, pondering with such patience the saucepan's connection to its lid. Hands beautifully formed, eyes, huge, wistful . . . The dark tides began to swell, filling me, and no one to help me to that small rope of strength – belief – whatever it is that makes it possible to hold on. I looked at Elizabeth and saw that she was waxing as I waned. And suddenly, I knew *exactly* how she felt, where she ached, what she dreamed. I was extraordinary again because I was so certain. If I was so certain again I should be frightened.

I am becoming afflicted again. I feel it, a loss of balance, moths crowding into my head, big, grey moths with long feelers. I cannot stop it. And wondering why and how it should approach at this particular moment only seems to accelerate the pace. The reasons, O yes they will do, but equally, they will not do at all. Why was I content yesterday? It is a mystery for at this moment I feel I will never be happy again; never see anything save through black veils. If I walk, it will not help. If I could work, if there was some industry, some child, purpose. But I have done away with that, with all things. And they would not save me.

You have moved inside my brain. There is an absence. I cannot think, move – but I must. You have gone, there is a void as my brain opens. I cannot feel you. I lie alone. O where is your hand? The brush of your elbow? Loss, like the moon sliding into the sea, disappearing beneath waves. I cannot bear it when your presence forsakes me, when the air lightens, when thoughts wither. There is jasmin in the air, a thick clogging smell, I must get away . . . Will you go with me? you asked, will you be there? So I had to go. But I will not go again in my mind up that white road unshaded. The fig trees would not watch, they sheltered farther back, and the rough boys tumbling in the dust beneath them ran away. I should NOT have gone. Should not. How could you make me? You were so cruel and all those days so silent, giving me not one single word: the more you suffered, the more silent. Why did I go? How it cuts me. It is branded upon my heart and the iron is still pressed, red hot, burning into me. O God, that they should have done such a revolting thing. If I rock myself softly, softly, like a babe in arms, like a hushed lover, closing my eyes, breathing deeply, thinking only of breathing, it will pass – the whirling dust, the trampled grass, the grief-stricken faces. And now my face is neat and ironed, my agitating brain stilled. So often there is a saw in my head, moving back, forwards, back.

There was a noise; someone walking slowly towards me from the back: are they coming to burn the house? I hid in a corner, crouching down to my knees. The door creaked and a man stood there. He lit a taper and moved towards Elizabeth. He was a big man with pale clothes that glowed slightly in the light. He lifted the taper and his eyes began to circle the room; they alighted on me. I sunk deeper into the gloom; he walked, saying nothing. I heard his breath, then felt his breath. I fainted.

When I awoke, everything had changed: is it a dream? Or have I become someone else? I can hear birds sing, I can hear fishes plop in the water. My head is deep in a soft mossy place and there are flowers in great glass vases with slender green stems that rise and rise, supporting roses as I have never seen roses, and boughs of cherries; lilies large as doves. I cannot move my arms. They are tied above my head, but the thongs are silky. I could almost snap them. A little black-faced boy wearing a turban looks down at me; he screws up his nose and gives a white, shiny smile; my lips turn up a little. He touches me on the chin with one finger, then bounces backwards, laughing. When he goes I become frightened. It is difficult to lift my head; my feet are tied. I scream: no one comes. I listen; there is no noise. I scream again, calling for Elizabeth. She does not come. The room slowly fills with darkness. I hear footsteps and jerk my head in their direction. The door opens without a sound. I can only see the bottom of the door as my raised arms obscure the rest: there is the hem of a robe. The man that looks down at me: I recognise him. Boaz.

I can describe him perfectly now that his age is nearer to my own and he is no longer here to frighten me, except in dreams. I can be kinder to him also. Though he was old, weary of life, there was something beautiful, idealistic in him still. Age was not unbecoming to him because his eyes were bright as jewels; his hair was planted in neat rows, thick and wavy black. He wore a long white robe with streaks of silver at the ends of the sleeves and at the slit of the neck. There was no crease in his appearance. His mouth was long, it did not smile. Was it tender, or falsely so? His mouth did have a softness, but I did not trust it. His skin was finely textured and glossy as though oiled. It surprised me that his hands were broad and serviceable.

He walked to the base of the bed and looked at me, I averted my face. He turned to one of the servants who had just entered the room and snapped a question. The man walked close and whispered an explanation. Boaz, looking exactly as he had at the dinner that night – aloof, disinclined to speak, and rude almost – suddenly looked perplexed. He bent as though to unbind my feet, then straightened and motioned to a servant to untie them. While this happened, he watched, cold, almost disgusted. Then he walked up to the top of the bed, and when those cords had been loosened too, in just the same off-hand way as he had said, 'How long are you going to stay here?' he now said, 'There seems to have been a misunderstanding: you took fright and lashed out when you were brought here, so they resorted to the only solution that presents itself to simple people.'

'What am I doing here? Where is my maid?'

'If you weren't here, you'd probably be dead by now in a slum in Tiberias.' He sounded as if he didn't care, then smiled ruefully and added, 'Isn't it good enough for you?' My eyes followed the waving of his hand as it dismissed the sumptuous room with its crimson drapes and cream and gold couches.

'Where is my maid?' I repeated sulkily.

'She is well, recovering slowly.'

I did not like this contradiction and asked, 'Then I can see her?'

'She is not here.'

'She must be here.' I moaned like a child pleading for a lost toy.

'Later,' he said sharply, too sharply because I could feel my eye-brows lowering, they came so close to my eyes that I saw the darkness of them. Then it was upon me: my joints stiffened, I was full of rage – where can I put it? I want to hurt him, to hurt myself; rid myself of this sickness. A knife in my flesh would put the rage into a form I could understand. As it is I choke on it and it will not be digested. I jumped off the bed and went for him; he moved with great speed, pinioning my hands behind my back and forcing me down on to the bed. My anger evaporated and left in its place exhaustion; my voice sounded pitiful.

'You can't keep me a prisoner here. Please let me go.'

He stood back, lightly tossing my wrists away, 'No one is stopping you, of course you may leave. But I would not suggest you return to Tiberias – the streets are clogged with the dead.'

'But where is Elizabeth?'

Then he became gentle, treating me like a child who asks awkward questions. 'She is not far from here. When she is well enough to travel, you shall see her. You have been ill yourself and must stay calm.'

Ill? What did he mean? I put my hand to my head, utterly defeated. He left and the room emptied of servants. I looked around it in perplexity, not knowing how the fury had surfaced; unable to remember anything more than a taper being lit, a man's frame in the darkness.

*

There is a cold stone in my stomach. I want to take it out, look at it, push it with my finger, but I must get it out – it weighs down my stomach and sits on my breath so it comes out in gasps, rising, falling like waves. I fall through the trees, through spiky top branches and land on my face in the slime. The leaves will fall in a blanket and smother me, curling their fingers around me. But I will lie again with you. You promised. We have all been promised and now I believe the promise that once I was too clever to believe, and the abnormal green of the trees no longer frightens me.

It always begins with the breathing, but if I think, I can stop it. What happens? The breathing becomes fast and painful and my stomach pounds and hurts in the hard places. The joints in my limbs become rigid. Fingers, jaws and eyes grow, then set. My body begins to shudder with the tension: knives, no breath now. Up at the top of a high cliff, pursued, and the screams stick to the roof of my mouth. No way back, the edge smiling and the black dream eating me, eating – full of sickness, full of it. My little boy turns in his sleep, snuffles – my senses return. This white room, white walls, keep me here, keep me safe – not out there with the faces. A bee buzzes; leaves subside in my head. I stare, stare. Impossible now, like a tide filling too fast for me to run back.

Elizabeth, her hands bending my body, moving my knees up to my throat, pulling my arms round to my knees: 'Now hold, hold tight.' I am so small, a tiny seed quivering into being, opening like two shells of a poppy pod. They fall, fall, revealing my red/black face emerging through a silky mass. Trying, pulsing to grow as the emptiness swells and leaps to swallow my one eye. Is it breaking up? Will I be left unnourished? So small. Is it a fish or a finger? A mist rises around me, growing into me as I into it. I open, I fill. I am a mouth in a black place. I am made of water, of blood, warm, full, lapped by a calm tide. No – no, I am a mouth crying. All I will ever be.

What is it like to sleep? I cannot remember. But I am not tired and I do not understand why she keeps handing me this food. A little bread cut into small pieces, a grape with no pip – it would be enough. I have no anger now, it has returned to the moon. I know if I thought, I could stop it. But I won't. I love my pain, I hold it jealously to me. But Elizabeth looks so tired. I will take care of her, I need no sleep, she must sleep.

'I know what you are thinking, Elizabeth, but you are wrong. I am quite calm, Elizabeth, quite calm. It is you who are frightened. But you must not be because I understand these things. I can tell you exactly what I am thinking and then you will see that my mind is not muddy: Boaz was an epicurean, but tired of it – that was my thought. He gave the air of a jaded scholar too much handled by books, no longer finding the same magic in them. He had a brisk, busy mind, beginning to slacken a little with boredom. He was a man who loved deep, round cushions, pears with graceful necks, glasses with gold lips, silk sheets with no ripples. He liked to dally with his eyes on some small thing that might jolt him out of his apathy – I fell into that category.

'I ran out into the gardens, thinking I would leave, but knowing when I walked to the gate I would find it locked. He wanted me for a prisoner; he had stolen me from you and would not let me go. But the gate was not locked. There were slaves patrolling the borders of the garden, they always kept me in sight, but when I turned the latch, they did not move to stop me. But still I was a captive. You see, don't you? I could not go. I had nothing; I was empty – I had to go back so I was his prisoner. You see? I am tired. My head has this life of its own; it is so far ahead of me, it is full of pictures, the most beautiful pictures you can imagine. I will lie down. Yes, draw the curtains.' Lie flat, press down the spine; I have no stomach.

It was like a palace; there were tall black pillars and spires with stone eagles on them. There were no flowers in the garden, only long green grass shaking in the wind and peacocks among the cabbages. The grounds were hemmed in by a square of trees, all cypresses and very old; the leaves were black against a sky entirely blue. I walked back to the gold door; it opened as I got to it and Boaz stood there. At his feet lounged a dog with an aristocratic face.

Boaz stepped aside to let me pass; then following me as though I were an important guest, he said, 'Let me show you to your rooms.' We walked down long cool halls with ferns in brass vases. The floors had intricate mosaic designs in bold colours and the walls were the colour of wheat. He opened a door and stood aside, saying, 'These are your rooms.' The first was a room with a ceiling as high as the Temple. It was so beautiful that my mouth flew open. The floor was carpeted with green wool inlaid with tiny white daisies; a gold cage of white doves rocked from the ceiling; urns of blood-red roses and baskets of grapes were placed on low tables; there were white silk couches and a little fountain that bubbled in one corner. When I began to walk towards the centre of the room, a cloud of yellow butterflies flew up into the air, then came to settle on the roses. The door closed behind me. I flew at it and wrenched the handle; it was open, and I was abashed. Boaz turned and looked at me; almost wistfully he said, 'Anything you want you may have. There is a cord by the door.' Was there something a little mocking in his smile?

Through an open door I walked into another room where there was a high bed with white drapes and a fur covering. There were silver mirrors all around the walls and arrangements of lilies in four vases. Beyond this room was the room of books. I had never seen so many; all the walls were lined with beautifully bound manuscripts in Hebrew, Greek and Latin. The room was empty apart from an oak desk and a small plum-coloured couch. The ceiling of the room was rounded into a dome and a delicate carved staircase led up one wall to the ceiling where an oval glass window dimpled with light. When I climbed to the top there was a square platform and a little sandal-wood stool. Sitting on it I could see out across the waving grass, beyond the cypresses to a stretch of water I knew to be the Sea of Galilee. There was a little notebook with a fine piece of charcoal tied to it, and on the outside of the book, printed in gold, was my name. It alarmed me so that I dropped it and began hurriedly to descend the stairs, clutching at the rope support, my breath hot and ungainly.

I walked back into the Temple-room and this time the scent of the roses intoxicated me. I sat on a couch and gaped; my mind whirled and could settle on none of the beauties with concentration. But I fell asleep, and when I awoke he was there, watching me. I started up in anger, but he quickly said, 'I have just come. I am told you have slept for twelve hours.' But there was no one in the room to have told him that. I had nothing to say to him and sat there rubbing my mouth in agitation.

'You have been ill,' he said, 'you will get better here and thrive on all this beauty.'

'What do you want?' I almost snarled.

'I want nothing. I am simply an observer of life, not a participator.'

'You must have a motive.'

'No. And it is certainly not pleasure if that's what bothers you. I take pleasure in nothing.'

'But those books . . .'

'Are mine. I give them to you. There was a pleasure once in reading words placed as they should be, phrases well-made, holding little flashes of truth. Not now. Even good wine dulls the palate taken in large quantities.' I began to walk up and down anxiously. I approached the roses and stared at them, not knowing what to do with them.

'You must rest,' his voice said as he moved towards the door; there was a trace of concern in it.

A fish in a golden bowl; swimming, swimming. There are meadows at the bottom of the water and the ferns are studded with pearls. I used to sit on the little stool, looking through glass transparent as water, and dream. I never walked in the grounds, but paced up and down the rooms. Sometimes I would open the door to the corridor and look out quickly as though to catch someone listening, prying – but the corridor was always empty. Once I walked to the end of it, dragging my hand along the wall, and found myself in a courtyard, and all around the courtyard were rooms and rooms, and perhaps beyond them more wheat-coloured walls. I did not want to find out.

Every day Boaz came to see me in the morning and he would ask me first if there was anything that I wanted. I only shook my head. He would try to make me talk to him about Hesiod, Plato, the Psalms – anything, but I was only fiddling with the books; the world in my own head had endless possibilities and they could not be seen by him. I did not like to be with him, but there was something lacking when he left. Servants came with delicious food arranged on polished trays and laid it out with the greatest care. I pushed my fork listlessly into thin slices of meat and white fish garnished with nuts. I liked to look at the fruit and polished the grapes and plums with the soft napkin, then put them back on the dish.

Once Boaz came into the room with an Oriental woman; she had draped over her arm a white linen dress smothered with the most exquisite embroidery. She laid it out carefully on the floor and showed me the birds, the violets and cornflowers; the stems of the anemones twirling up from the hem and branching off into blooms at the bodice. Boaz said, 'It is yours. Put it on. This woman began to stitch it when she was a child of six and has just finished it; do you see the little pomegranates sewn in crimson around the neck and falling down the sleeves?'

The dress filled me with exhilaration. I took off my silk dress and lifted my arms to let the other tumble down my body. Running into the bedroom, I looked at myself in the mirror, lifting the loose waves of linen and turning till my face swam. Then I saw him watching me and the ecstasy died. He left, taking a sad frown with him. I swirled again: O I was happy, happy, full of new wine that's how it felt, a light happiness far from tears. Not the happiness I felt sometimes with Samuel, not that kind: it trembled in your throat and belly and caught at your eyes, making you fear the loss of it. This was fearless happiness, forgetful. I became the dress and it was beautiful ... I leap, spin, glide, billow. I gleam and cascade; I am more golden than the butterflies. I am a waterfall, a flower with its petals unfurled. Now I am seductive, cruel, bending my body into a grimace, up into an arch. I am the harlot, the one with the veiled face; flower behind my ear, laughter spilling from my thighs: greedy laughter, knowing, wanting and getting, getting.

What were you doing in the trees? Why did you shout that one word – 'Go.' I did not go. You lay on the floor of the garden, you banged your head on the stones, you cried, how you cried. And those fools what were they doing? Sleeping. You rolled on your back and bayed at the moon, cursing it. Your face so worn, drawn into a flat oval, steep and austere and then it became colourless. I ran to you, gathered you to me. You lay still, then began to pound with tears – your need so desperate, so devouring – to fly your terror at my breast and be rid of it. It slipped, I could not catch it. Too heavy, it reached the hard earth and spread like thick oil. I would have gladly lain at your feet, uncovered them and asked you to take me beneath the hem of your skirt. But you were sleeping. Old lover, new child, let me protect and nourish you if it is all I can do. I could not contain you. I too let you down, was not noble enough to tie you to the earth. They slept, you slept. A chant began in the early hours, a call to prayer. It was taken up in each corner of the city. Jerusalem, you were built on prayers, and they so fragile that a child can blow them away.

I am confused again. I want to be quiet without these dark guilts; these tears hot and hopeless. I have no strength to alter the course of things. I try to be strong, or cold – making a hard face which nothing can crack. I must cling to indifference because there is nothing else. O I wish it were later. Over, not approaching.

'Elizabeth, what is that noise in the garden?'

'It's the swallows.'

'What are they doing?'

'Come, stand by the window, I will draw the drapes.'

The swallows are maddened by the light, they lurch through the air and look as though they would crash into the trees.

'Elizabeth, a hawk has taken a baby chicken.' Lord, how the air whisks him up into the belly of a cloud – gone.

'I am tired, Elizabeth, and the light hurts my eyes, take it away.'

Why is she fussing with the cord so long? But I know, she is trying to hide her face from me because the impatience in my voice has cut her and she would like to cry. I will tell her a story instead, not a sad one. 'I was telling you, Elizabeth, come and sit down. I was telling you about Boaz. You must take that wrinkle out of your forehead. I am not excited, it will not make me too tired. I want to tell you this, it is important. I could see the earth from my position on the moon. It was like looking through milk. It may also be the vision a fish has looking up through water. From up there I could see water, sticky green, and people were throwing all their garbage in the water. Then the moon turned and I looked down on an island surrounded by cypress trees and the branches were laden down with white owls. The moon, and often I hate her, she tipped again and I fell. When I awoke Boaz was looking at me. You don't believe this? Well he talked and he talked and everything he said lacked enthusiasm. He would not tell me what he wanted. And that was all I was waiting for.'

He used to ask me to come to the banquet-room and dine with him. Once I actually went and he was so quiet that I went again. He knew that I hated him for watching me; for his endless old man's gazing. That night the air had the texture of thick cream; the candles flickered on the goblets, the food was coming and going and his eyes feasted only on my face as I sat looking up, looking down. Then I threw the glass and it shattered with drops of glittering purple on the wall.

'What is it? What is it? Why are you keeping me here?' I screamed, standing up and stabbing the table with a knife. His voice was like steady breathing. 'You can go whenever you wish,' rubbing his finger across his eyebrow.

'Where can I go? What can I do?'

He shrugged.

'No, you are trying to confuse me. You want me here for a purpose. If you did not, I wouldn't be here.'

'Perhaps.'

'Have you no wife, no friends? Why do you spend all your time with me?'

'O I have wives, but they have lost their varnish. Society bores me.'

'What do you like?'

'I like things I cannot have. I like to observe what I cannot have. I know how quickly the plum withers to a prune. I seek no pleasure, I seek the denial of pleasure.'

'Then that is a pleasure.'

'Of course.'

And of course it was wicked of me to blame him for the injustice of my life; no amount of wealth could fill in the holes, and I know it is the worst thing for a woman to expect a man to remove the dissatisfactions of her existence, and blame him if he can't. But we all do it. We women, particularly our race, have been treated too gently, been led to expect that all things will come our way if we but smile and stir our loins occasionally. Nothing will come to us unless we reach out for it with our own two hands. That much I do know. You helped me to understand it by deserting me: there came a time when you preferred to find yourself in the reverential pool of Peter's eyes rather than the piercing shaft of mine. But I had almost forgotten. There was that lovely evening when you seemed to change back again. We were at the house in Bethany. The room was so warm and feminine, unmistakably a woman's – intimate as if a petticoat lay in a corner.

We had finished eating. I took the things away, pouring the last drop of wine into your mother's glass. Her little face wrinkled up with a giggle as she said, 'I have drunk more than usual. It's always the way if I don't count the glasses I am poured.' You smiled at her indulgently and she took courage to complain lightly, 'I don't understand why he should stop taking wine, it's not poison. And him so thin . . .' looking at me as women look at one another when asking a question about a man. I smiled, knowing as you did that there was no need to explain. She seemed to be thinking hard and stopped brushing the little crumbs into her hand. She said, 'When he was young, O eleven I suppose, he was convinced he was a genius. He told me. He also told me that when I had given birth to him I had planted a little mark which was the beginning to his death. I never understood that, it made me feel like a murderer. But he was not concerned. He said it was his duty to make that little mark grow. There was no mark on him. He was a perfect child. I used to tell him, you are perfect, perfect. I never thought that about the other children. He was special to me.'

You were looking a little embarrassed, so I said quickly, 'When I was a child I thought that my heart was a flower and that I would live as long and no longer than a bloom.' She laughed and you looked at me so tenderly that I knew you wanted to hold me. Such a long time since, how sad it made me. It was part of your sadness too, though you would not say so. Did you think you were protecting me by withholding your tenderness? Did you see the tree unbranching? I often think how sad it was that you belonged neither to the earth, nor the sky. You longed for heaven as though it were a place you had left and missed all your life on earth. There were times though when I am sure you were afraid to return in case you might miss the world you seemed always to despise. Is that why you wanted it destroyed? Didn't you know that both are prisons?

I am calm now. If I hold my hand out – see, it hardly trembles. Could I go outside I wonder? Elizabeth would not approve. The grass is yellow and dry and it is all flattened in one direction. Today I am better. But my thoughts will keep jumping and repeating. There is a headache starting again, somewhere I can hear it humming. I would like to unpick my life instant by instant, and peer at each stitch before it is unwound for ever. All I will see is chaos, and out of that what is there? God took chaos and made a world of it. Isn't that what we all do?

Boaz – he will not be gone. I can see him sitting opposite me, so spruce with a small eddy of lavender rising from his robes. In my presence he was always restless, moving from one couch to another, toying with the plants. And staring. I think, and do not forget I can be more lucid than anyone – I think that though he had scooped me up out of my ragged life and placed me in his luxurious one, yet still he looked at me as though the same light shone on me. I retained the aura of dishevelment and distress even though he had removed it. His first impression coloured his perception of me for ever. I had not changed though my linen was costly, my dresses gorgeous, my nails long and manicured and I was never hungry. Part of my appeal for him was my original destitution; even without it I retained it.

I bullied him into letting me see Elizabeth. I caused such scenes that he grew frightened for my sanity, but I knew what I was doing then: I had learned how to use my hysteria. And Elizabeth came. O how thin she was. He would not let her stay; it was as if her comfort to me threatened him. It took me a long time to wheedle her back, but when she did come she was not allowed to stay in my room at night and he only gave me a little time with her each day. He was jealous of our intimacy; of the fact that I would chatter and reminisce with her and that she had the capacity to make me content. She thought that he was evil and hated him. I had begun to lose my fear of him, but I still shuddered when his cheeks stiffened if he saw Elizabeth and me sitting on a couch together whispering. He could not ask what we whispered about, but for some reason it seemed to torment him.

Some nights he would look up and ask quietly if I would come and visit him later, when I had finished my sewing or reading? As I sat alone, I would think of him; the book would fall upon my lap and I would consider going to speak to him. I seldom went and he never referred to my absences. If I did go, I always wished, upon seeing his face lift, that I had not gone, and I would then leave quickly. And I knew, because his man-servant told Elizabeth, that he sat up all night waiting.

When we did speak – desperately, it seemed to me, he would try to discover things about my past. For hours he listened carefully as I told him stories of my life, some false, some true, yet at the end he looked puzzled and said that I remained an enigma. I, who had hitherto thought of myself as a shadow, a reflection in the glass of men's eyes, now knew that I had gone underground, to a deep level impossible to plumb. The sea had swallowed me – before I had merely been a leaf on its starry surface. He was part of that sea, the sleepy moonlit part that let me sink without drowning. I see now that it was an enigma that he wanted; he had created me and I played the cold moon woman that he loved, because she had always been there a little. With him, there was nothing to fear, no one to hate. Only emptiness vast as space, still as air. No pebble dented the water, no bird woke me from sleep. In dreams a small boy ran to me, threw himself at my feet and rolled like a puppy in his happiness. I held him to my cheek and hummed. A tall man in a leather apron with sunlight falling in coins from his hair: he made me tight as a closed fist, drawing him inwards with my clenching – leaving me utterly wasted with pleasure.

It has gone, the headache, quite evaporated. I will make Elizabeth walk with me by the lake; we will buy fish for dinner and I will cook it. A silver fish; nothing will stop me going out. I am sick of these people who know better than I do what is good for me. Does she think she is my mother? What has become of your poor mother? Well, I cannot go and see her: I was not your wife. They do not come here anymore – your brother, I mean, and those others. They used to come; in the beginning many people came to ask me to tell them . . . No. We will go now, this very instant. There is no need to stop for a wrap or basket. I will get Elizabeth and we will just go. It is dusk, they will be going out in the boats.

'You must not fuss so, Elizabeth. I want to walk, I can very well walk a few miles and I do not want to ride, so don't speak of it. I will sleep tonight better for it. Come, don't sulk so. You are tired, forgive me for dragging you off like this when you are tired. It is just that I never get tired anymore.'

She looks up at the sky; it is so black. 'I will get you a cloak.' I pull at her arm and run with her down the path. Here is the rain. O how lovely. I will catch it on my tongue.

'Don't tug me away. I said DON'T. Can't you see that the rain has come for me? You go to the trees if you like, I'm happy here.' Down the bridge of my nose, cooler than tears into my mouth, so sweet. Tilt my eyes to the sky: are you there? Can you see me?

I am going to the sea, it is not far. I want to be there beside the water. I want to lick the sand. The wind pulls my wet hair out of my eyes; my feet fly. I can run faster than all of you. I will lift these dripping clothes and tie them around my waist. How I want to be there. And there it is – a faint glimmer through the trees. The waves are huge; they roar in my ears. The wind comes straight across the water like a knife thrown from those cold, far mountains. The sea has my anger, the waves abound with hatred; we are both full of rage – the sea and I. With my bare hands I could rip them all to pieces, tear at their eyes and let the flies settle. I will rip at myself no more – now I want only to maul them for the harm they have done me. My teeth grit together, my lips split and the taste of blood . . .

I am cold. Do you hate me? My face sodden with all the waters of the earth. No one to pick me from the mud. It is all over me. What happened? I hardly know how I got here. I feel so small, my face has shrunk, it does not feel like my face. A storm entered me; the lightning ran in my blood. I could hear it. My vision altered; a white light all about, so all things looked clear, my skin glossy; radiant as Moses' when he spoke to God. Something ran over my foot – was it a mouse? Elizabeth is not here.

The sheets are warm; quite dark in here, quite beautiful. I would weep, but it would not be enough. Elizabeth's face is hooked: the torrent of my pain is destroying her. The storm discharged its humours into me and it was healed, but my flesh is still burning. All things use me, abuse me – but I, I am the greatest abuser. I know what they will say when I am better, because I *will* get better – Elizabeth will say with relief: 'You are yourself again.' Back to myself again I shall be, shall I? No. Never. For I am only an echo, a memory of myself.

This weariness, it is as close as I can creep to endless sleep. Do I breathe? Do I really breathe? Why did you leave me in this dark pit? 'I am poured out like water . . . my heart is like wax; it is melted in the midst of my bowels.' Should I have cast a spell of veils like the Eastern women, to trap your eyes, your lips, heart – to keep you?

'Yes, Elizabeth, I will not go out again. You are right. It was stupid. There was something in the air. I felt better. No, don't shake your head like that, I know I'm not. I said I *felt* I was – I'm sorry, I didn't mean to shout.'

'It's all right.' Ah, how wearily she said that.

'Are you angry with me, Elizabeth?'

'I just don't know what to do . . .'

'Don't worry. I shall stay here quietly, I promise. I shall not even read. I'll sleep, anything you say, but don't be angry.'

Her head falls forward and she catches it wearily. 'It is such a pain.'

'O Elizabeth, I'm sorry, forgive me. It will pass. I feel, it might be foolish, but I feel that this is the last time. I do understand, I know what is happening. You must not be so frightened.'

Why is she looking at me that way; why is her smile so thin?

'Come and sit by me. See, I am better. I know what you are thinking: how long will I be better? I don't know, don't know.'

'You must try not to think, thinking is bad for you.'

'Yes, I will stop.'

Her feet drag out and I can see my eyebrows again and the muscles in my neck are pounding. How dare she! I know about all this: talking to me as if I were a child or a lunatic. He was the same, that fool, Boaz. He sat talking to me for three hours, telling me that I should learn to balance myself; to stop veering between my emotions. Did he tell me how to do this; did he lay out the plan? O no. He gurgled on, impressed by his intelligent words and his mind without a speck on it. I sat, saying not one single word, watching the wrinkles around his eyes and the arrogant twist of his mouth: did he think he had become a mind-healer? He – who had reduced all the loveliness of the world into a yawn; who had mellowed so much that he had become opaque. People – they make me sick. They talk to me with that simper in their eyes and all the while they are thinking, 'Poor lunatic, it's up to us to take care of her now.' And my mind is racing over and clear above and below their nudging thoughts. I am years ahead of them, worlds away, but they do not hear my thoughts; they do not even see me. But if I move suddenly – how they jump – that almost makes me laugh. They think I have a knife in my skirt. They do not see it sticking out of my throat.

I am close, so close to heaven. No one can know how this searing sometimes fills me with the most lambent happiness. The flowers have a right to bloom, the stars to shine. I have the right to drag myself over the coals for a glimpse of heaven. I have you in the nook of my heart. Do not stir. I see your spilling eyes. Do not cry for me. I have a rod of steel in my body. It is only – worse than any pain is the waiting for pain. I have always believed those words – who said them? Some Greek.

I am ten years old and I'm looking through the woods for a particular butterfly. It is red with little yellow marks like blobs of butter. I find a cave, more like a hole between two big rocks, but long enough to crawl into. Behind the rocks is an open place and I can stand up in it. The darkness slowly begins to match my eyes and as it does I think to myself: I know she is here, I'm certain. In a moment she'll come walking towards me, but she won't have that constricted look in her forehead. She'll pick me up. . . I have chased too many shadows. I cannot always be a child crying in the dark.

Today, when I woke and looked out of the window, I could see the fields. All the corn is trampled down by the storm; it looks as though hundreds of angry boots have stamped on each ear and then turned their heels at the last moment. There is a thick trickle of muddy water running out from the path into the stumps of cabbages. To love these things is as real as loving a God.

I wish she would stop bringing me all these soups; they look so slippery and they will burn my mouth if I drink. I sometimes wonder if she makes the soup so hot to hurt me back. It worries me the way her eyes move quickly away from me. Have I become ugly? Or is it that she is ashamed of her thoughts; I know her thoughts about me, even the ones she does not know about.

You pulled at the grasses; the red of your scarf made a poppy where the dull colours needed one. You were talking, as usual, about God, and I said, laughing, 'God has not come looking for me – I think he may be too old for me.' You pushed me roughly, as a young boy pushes a mate, and I put my arm around your neck. O that was long, long ago. I said to you, 'You must think your God pitiless; you think him incapable of understanding that a man needs some soft skirt to rest his passions in.'

You agreed, 'Yes, he is without pity,' but you would not allow that therefore he must be cruel also. It is the quick flashes in people's faces that stay most brightly with me: the way you had of looking sideways, and once, when I was reading some poetry aloud, there was a phrase about love, and you flushed deeply. I did not read any more that day. O you made me so happy. Waking in the morning, sleepy and still exhausted, but knowing that you slept under the next tree and that soon I would see you; all day long be able to watch you.

Why did I stay so long with Boaz? That is the kind of question you would have asked, without the smallest trace of jealousy, had I told you the story. But of course I did not. But I will answer your question. I stayed because he radiated strength. He was a magic man who could produce anything; he understood everything without needing to mention it. Soon he seemed to whisper, I know all about you, though you tell me nothing. I have seen to the bones of you; you need not pretend. It is the grit in you, the grime that I admire. He stopped asking questions; it was as though each tiny movement, each indolent stretch I made, gave him all that he needed to know.

One day Boaz asked me to walk with him in the gardens. I was curious; he had never asked it before. I nearly refused because I was very tired: my mind the night before had been dizzy, frantic, like night trying to avoid morning. We walked through the tall grass to a high wall with a door set into it. He opened the door with a key and ushered me in. Inside, there was a large oval of mossy grass with a delicate fountain cut into the centre. At the far end was a little stone house with a gilded dome and arched windows. The rest was taken up with bushes of jasmin and wild roses and curling purple flowers shaped like trumpets. Two flamingoes stepped dispassionately across the grass. I looked at Boaz. I felt at ease with him among the heady scents and the utter stillness of the place.

He did not respond to my look, merely asked, 'Do you like it?' I nodded, walking away from him, past the fountain and into the little summer house. There was a small chair there, just one; nothing else. I sat down, spreading the scarlet skirts of my silk dress around me and feeling completely benign. He did not bother me and I sat there a long time, calmer and growing more so. When I walked outside, he was standing looking at the fountain and something so lorn and lost about him touched me. I needed to talk to him about himself, and the slightly repellent quality that he had for me disappeared.

When I had reached his side I said, 'Sometimes I have the feeling that this is all a dream, that I will wake up and find myself in a dark room.'

He smiled wanly and said, 'Of course it is a dream. And because it is so lush it must be the dream of a young man.'

'Which young man?'

'The young man I was once when I had the cynical idea to squander all my inheritance on a beautiful palace, and then fill it with priceless objects – all the things people strive and kill for. I wanted to leave the place empty, as a rebuke, a mockery I suppose, of the hollowness of wealth.'

'That is just a gross indulgence because you've never been poor. Anyway, you do live here, the house is not empty.'

'This is the first time I have ever lived here in my life. The house has been empty for over thirty years.'

'Why are you here now?' I was afraid, asking it, and moved a little away.

'You are part of the dream; the one about the unobtainable woman,' he sniffed scornfully, 'but your passion and fierceness is more than I had bargained for.'

'What do you want of me?'

'I want nothing more than to see what will become of you in the opulence that you deserve – and certainly crave.'

'I don't believe you.' I said it softly.

'That is because you have not lived as long as I have.'

'But I am not happy here.'

'You, like me, would not be happy anywhere. You don't have the capacity for it.'

He was enraging me by his complacency, so I thought I would push him to the limit of his so-called generosity. 'You would give me anything?'

'Anything money can buy.'

'And ask nothing in return?'

'Nothing, except your presence.'

'Well then, let me go back to Tiberias.'

'Why?'

'Because I hate it here, hate everything about it. I feel a captive, part of a game I don't understand.'

'So, all this is not enough for you?' He knew it all along.

'I want to be free,' I insisted stubbornly.

'But you are – you can go anywhere, do anything; you have jewels, dresses, no concerns about your future, or money. You can work or live idly – it's up to you. I give you endless possibilities . . . no woman could ask for more.'

'Take me back to Tiberias.'

'Yes, you are part of the dream; all you want is love, but you don't have the heart for it.' His face sagged slightly, his neat phrases had fizzled out and he looked at me wearily.

'Will you be happier in Tiberias?'

'Yes.'

'Tell me in what way.'

All I could stumble out was, 'All this glitter is choking me, driving me mad. I want to see people on streets, children. I want to walk by the lake and feel that I am not being watched. And most of all I want to feel something again . . .' Suddenly, being deprived of it, I was maddened by the desire for freedom, for some small joy, some streak of gold in a world that seemed entirely grey.

'We will see,' is all that he would say and he took me back to the house in silence. Looking at it from the outside with its glowering curves and shapely arches, I hated it fiercely.

In the next days, when I pestered him constantly about taking me away, he would not deign to say a word of his plans. I watched, seething inside against him, but fearful of doing the wrong thing – despising him for his power over me. I knew that I could not go unless he allowed it, in the same way as I understood without experiencing it the horror of poverty: that it was the greatest evil. At the same time I hated myself for my timidity, my lack of courage. Boaz, with his eyes unflickering, his well-manicured hands lazing in his lap, would suddenly turn on me a yearning look, and then I would want to pick up a glass and thrust it into his face. To force myself into a more calm state, I would slip into the cool waters of a dream: reliving days spent under pine trees in summer when the corn was deep orange and the paths in the forests purple; but I would always cull out the memories carefully.

One day I actually caught myself looking at Boaz and thinking: he would not be a good lover, of course not – because he does not like women, not real live flesh; even a cursory touch of his hand reveals that. I knew that his mouth would scratch; his weight would be crushing, ugly, he would leave me bruised and full of self-contempt. But even as I thought it, I knew it was immaterial. He would never attempt to woo me, except with the pitiful longing of his eyes; his aim was not to possess me. I had known that from the start: I should be chilly, unreachable. And I was surprised how easily this unobtainable face had slid over the wooden frame of my head.

But I had to escape him because with that stunning clarity with which we sometimes see the nastier sides of ourselves, I realised that my boredom, my frustration, was bringing destructive forces to the surface of my nature. I could see them in my face: my skin had a grey, warped look and my eyes were huge and black and they gleamed unnaturally. I became obsessed by the idea of getting away; all day I would wander up and down my corridor trying to formulate a plan. I was too afraid just to walk out, I could not march back to Tiberias and start again. I did not have the mental strength for it and as the days passed I became physically frail and could not keep any food down. I knew that Boaz was relying on my fear to keep me there, my lack of resources, and I hated him so deeply that I wanted to kill him: I was in the trap. My own inability to act or decide ate into what little reserves I had and I could no longer create scenes, or manufacture violent hysterics to manipulate him.

I grew thin, and the tight-fitting dresses that he liked me to wear hung limply on me; my hair was lank and it slipped out of the curls that he liked to see in profusion all over my head. Yet it was quite extraordinary how this affected him: he would tempt me to eat by bringing me my meals himself – only fish, I would not touch anything else. He brought dresses and shawls and beautiful fragile silk slippers which he laid out in front of me; sometimes he would almost seem to weep if I said I was too tired to try them on. But the amount of care he lavished on me only confused and frightened me. When I awoke in the morning my door was often open and I was told, through servants' gossip, that he made pilgrimages all through the night to my bedside and sat there, hour after hour, just watching. I grew emaciated on his care. Then for seven days I did not see him at all.

One morning he walked in looking haggard and defeated. He lowered himself into the small green chair by my bed and said, 'Today we are going back to Tiberias,' and added softly, as if to himself but really to me, 'Women will flinch at nothing to get what they want.' Then how sad he looked as though he had relinquished something precious; it passed through my mind: can he care for me? But I would not allow that.

Why were you always bullying me to pray, as though it were the remedy for each fluttering doubt? What kind of a prayer could I make? O Lord, help me, keep me, Lord, who does not exist. You were as good as God for me, until you left and then you became the same.

There is a blondness in the fields like a small boy's hair. It must be nearing the time of the harvest. All things happen at a distance. Sometimes I feel myself slipping into that sloth of resignation, when the mind droops and self-pity (woman's closest crutch) eases itself closer. It is like being in a very dark place and the walls cold to lean against. At other times it is as if I were in an unlit barn and the door gapes just enough to catch a streak of light: an angle of a roof or some moss on a stone – it is these little glimpses that keep me going.

I forced myself out of this dark room of tight shutters and went outside, looked up at the sky. I was stunned by the heat and felt at the same time that a great weight had lifted off me. I raised my arms in adulation to the sun. Elizabeth ran to me, afraid of the way my head tilted back perhaps – I know these things frighten people, and she lives, through me, on the ragged edges of life. I submitted to her humbly and let her lead me back inside. I did not want to hurt her. I am aware that my faults outnumber my misfortunes. I lay down quietly and watched her slow walk to the window; the shutters made a harsh sound, I thought.

It must be the morning, very early, because a milky blue light creeps through the slats. I must see the sky. Is that a man playing his pipe outside my window? A sound that the white and black goats will follow obediently. No, that must be somewhere else. There is no one outside. I see two curved red lines on the upper part of my arm and a faint trace of blood where my tooth cut through. I wonder when it happened? It was a few nights ago. No, before dawn when I woke reeling in the grey light, looking for someone, then fell back on the pillows drenched in tears. If I can return to the distance. . .

When the gates flew back and the draped carriage rolled through them, my breath shut off and I did not know if it would return. Boaz, sitting opposite me, tied back the heavy green cloth and looked fixedly out of the window. My eyes fell on to my lap and I saw a claw lying there: my hand blanched and thin as a twig. It revolted me and I put it behind my back. When I am ill I do not remember how things got the way that they are; time passes in such a way that there is no record of it; it goes with a sick velocity that is timeless. Had he given me something to drink before we left? There are drinks that make one forget. I did not wake until the horses drew up with a jerk and my head slipped on to a hard ledge of leather. I heard Boaz click with impatience; he hated to be jogged in any way. It was dark, he pulled his cloak about him and gave me a fur wrap. There was a welcome sound of laughter in the distance and music from far away. He helped me out but I resisted the arm that moved to support me.

It was one of the large winter residences owned by the rich on the edge of the lake. The sharp smell of stirred water came to me as I stood there, reeling a little in the strong wind. I was handed over to a middle-aged woman who led me to a large white room with thick goatskin rugs on the floor and small paintings in alcoves. She pulled back the covers on the bed and I fell into it, and just before I fell asleep I remembered that I had not slept for many, many nights.

I awoke with a great drought in my throat, feeling famished. I was brought bread, soft cheese and eggs, butter and milk, by the woman who had looked after me the night before. She had a long flat face with beautiful green eyes and a heavy veil hid all of her hair. She walked with small nervous hops like a bird and she stared very directly. When I had eaten most of what she had brought, I began rolling the bread into little pellets, and I asked her who she was. 'I am to take care of you.'

I shrugged, 'It won't be necessary, I have a maid.'

She looked fiercely at me and said in a sharp voice, 'I am not a maid. I used to be his wife.' I realised there was nothing to say to this. Then, 'Who are you?' she asked, turning away as if she did not want to know.

'Didn't he tell you?'

'He doesn't talk much.'

'I am a waif he picked out of the storm.' I laughed humourlessly.

'You speak too obscurely for me.'

'He found me. Ill, my maid ill – it was during the plague here. He took care of me, that's all.'

'Ah.' She seemed to understand.

'Why does he force you to wait on me?'

'He does not force me. I live here. He never usually comes here, but last night he brought you. You are my guest, that's all.'

'Don't you mind? If it's your house?'

'No house is mine. It is his, but he lets me stay here. A kindness . . .'

'So he never stays here.'

'Never.'

'Where does he stay? I met him in Tiberias, at a school I worked at . . .'

'I know the school – Martha's. She is dead. I don't know where he stays, it's not my business.' She spoke as animals seem to eat: not caring what is given. Yet her hands were long and expressive as she put the dishes and the torn bread back on the tray.

'You are so thin, you have been very ill. People of your constitution need lots of nourishing food. You will recover here.'

She walked to the door and as she turned the handle I said, 'My maid? Is she here?'

She looked crossly at me and said, 'I will see.'

No one came so I dressed in the same clothes, walked down the corridor to a long flight of stairs which ended in a bright open area with plants in urns, patterned mosaics and vines climbing the walls. Beyond this was a courtyard open to a sky which echoed to the stiff cries of gulls. Boaz was sitting under a palm tree, reading; he watched my approach with an apprehensive frown. I was cheerful, a bit false, and I said, 'I thought I would walk down to the lake. Where is Elizabeth?'

'She will be here in a few days.' He picked up his book languidly, aware of his power to irritate.

'Well, then, I will go on my own.'

'No. You can't go.'

I felt the angry stiffness returning to my knees as he quickly said, 'You must try to be patient, you are weak and should not get excited.' He tried to coax, 'Stay in the garden at the back, it leads down to the lake.'

'I want to go where the people are.'

'And so you shall; but not today. You must rest.'

I kicked at the earth and began to walk away. He said, 'You could go for a few moments I suppose . . .' I turned with pleasure, but he added, 'if I came with you.' But then I did not want to go.

I spent the next few days in the garden by the lake. It was full of white and blue butterflies which rested on bushes of wild strawberries which at that time were covered in lacy white blossoms. It was spring-time and I was beginning to thaw. I began to eat properly and my face opened. I walked happily up and down the garden, past the heavy green bushes and the syrupy smell of honeysuckle. The birds were busy with sticks and snatches of cloth making nests in the pear trees. On the edge of the garden, at a discreet distance, and always busy with some activity, was Boaz's wife. She had the same name as my mother, so I never called her anything. I resented her presence, but, in spite of myself, began to pity and wonder about her. I could not feel too angry with her as she was so obviously a victim – of her own devotion perhaps – I felt that she loved Boaz in some way.

I was impatient for Elizabeth to arrive. One afternoon she came walking down towards me and I began running up to meet her. Our movements disturbed the flock of butterflies; they rose up and swarmed around our heads. Elizabeth was frightened and began beating them off with her arms; I did not notice because my head was thrown back and I was watching the sea rise and ripple in their colours. I caught sight of her panicked face and pulled her away. We walked quickly down to the water, and the butterflies remained in the same place, as if caught in a vast blue and white net. From time to time Elizabeth shuddered violently, as if she still felt their wings on her. We sat down by the water and I saw how tired and tight her face was and did my best to reassure her.

'I will take care of you here, Elizabeth, we can go for walks by the lake and see the fishermen, and the children playing in the water.'

'Do you think he will let you out of here?' she asked, shaking her head slightly.

'Why not? He says I can do as I please, as long as I don't go out alone.' She looked uncertain, so I touched her arm and said, 'It will be all right. I am strong now, I can arrange things. If it doesn't turn out properly, we will go away.' Her eyebrows flashed upwards in scorn, then settled into resigned arcs. For the rest of the day I knew she was thinking of the butterflies and seeing them as a bad omen.

The next day he could not keep me from going out. What bliss to walk out of that front door into a fresh breeze and warm sun. It was what I wanted, what I needed more than anything. I felt glorious and began to run as soon as we reached the corner and could not be seen from the house. We walked down to the forum and had grape juice in long cups and went down to the shore where the children chased each other through the water and clung to pieces of wood, catching the surge of the waves to carry them back to shore. There was a great hubbub, and a Roman, angrily shouting, kicked over the stall of a trader. The smell of the spicy meat on sticks oozed up from the sand where they had fallen; the spices made a pattern like ants on the sand. The poor trader looked up into the eyes of the Roman whose boot stamped the ground arrogantly. His head fell in a deep shame which over-flushed his anger and all of my body took up swords on his behalf and I trembled with the desire to stick them into that well-fed foreign flesh. The trader picked up the debris of his stall and moved off. The incident was over, the sherbet sellers who had been silent began again their unintelligible squawking, swinging their trays to avoid the heads of children. If these things made me too ebullient, Elizabeth would look closely, nervously at me, so I had to hide my elation; and eventually I was persuaded to a quiet place among the willows. Elizabeth, with a flushed urgency which I had never seen in her before, began to press me to get in touch with Joshua and ask him for money so that we could go to the cottage outside Magdala, or anywhere away from Boaz. But I was full of confidence then, and I thought it better that things move in their own way. I felt I could handle Boaz and I certainly was not brave enough to contemplate the kind of change she was suggesting. I kept telling her, 'If you give me time, just a little longer, I can sort out what I want to do, how I could manage independently. Now I am just trying to recover from what has gone before.'

Pride has a way of disappearing when it's not wanted. But it shocked and angered me when she said, 'There is something about him that attracts you. If there wasn't you would not stay.' I nearly slapped her.

I told myself going home, in silence, Elizabeth lagging unhappily behind me, that there was no reason to feel apprehensive: Boaz allowed me every freedom, left money for my use without referring to it, had dressmakers and perfumers and two different shoemakers call – and barely troubled me with his presence in spite of all this generosity. I refused to take seriously Elizabeth's fears of his intentions and found it strange that she should place such a morbid insistence on her view that he radiated malice. The game interested me; I wanted to see its conclusion as much as he did.

Tiberias, because it floated on an opulent wave of luxury and vigour, brought back my own spirit and returned my emotions to a level where they did not undermine or threaten me. When I had had my fill of the pleasure gardens with their arbours of fuchsia and red lilies, I crept back to the humble back streets, where no flower but the humble poppy grew. I loved the women with their rough, energetic faces; their high foreheads and big mouths. Their clothes were dark-blue, dusty, and their arms were never empty: they carried bread or firewood, or a pitcher that caused one arm to fly wildly in the air; and always the children followed or sagged like a sack on their backs – hungry, tired, smiling. When I saw a little child with a feverish glaze in his eyes lying on a mat beneath a tree, it was at such moments that I knew my susceptibility.

Life is merely a repetition of old habits; and we always say, It was better in Egypt (having forgotten old perils by replacements, which being closer must be worse). So I found myself sneaking back with nostalgia to the street of the whores, which had so frightened me when I was last in Tiberias. Now they did not frighten me; now they were my sisters, but finer, wiser sisters than me; they made me ashamed. Look how she walks swilling her hips – O so brave she is. I look at them all with admiration, respect: they have not plumped for the soft cushion, the full plate; they struggle, they fight each day with a blow; they give and they get their pay. I, so pitiful, so cowardly, giving nothing, taking a silky road and excusing myself with these little comforters: I am not well, I have been reared on roses, not dirt; I would not have the strength to take on poverty; my attacks . . . Those whores, they could not be condemned, but I could. I thought, how touching is a woman fading, with her beauty diluted and the scars of life on her. Back in the fierce glare of the mirror, my little insomniac face swayed stupidly in front of me.

I became obsessed with the street and would drag Elizabeth unwillingly there at dusk. I would watch the whores' faces, guess their lives, long to speak to them; envying also the way one would lean her heavy breasts on the window ledge, shaking out a coarseness at a passing man. I laughed with her to see the little scurrying look, his guilty eyes sneaking between the open bodice, then hurrying along to a safer destination. One woman turned on me angrily, shouting, 'Get out of here, there is no work.' I was frightened by her violence and shook my head quickly, denying her accusation. She then took in the richness of my clothes and shrugged, but her eyes swooped down on the cobalt scarf at my throat and, what was it? envy, hatred, or both? Her face erupted and I unwound the blue silk and gave it to her. She looked at me suspiciously but I smiled and insisted that she have it. She took it and shrugged again before walking off.

Elizabeth lowered my happiness about this by saying, 'You think you have given her something that will help because it is beautiful. She sees in it only what she can get for it.'

I replied defensively that I did not care what she did with it as long as it helped. But it hurt me to remember that as she had walked away she had shouted again, 'Get out of here and don't come back.'

Walking home, past a little cottage garden, I saw a big woman in a muddy-yellow dress pulling onions, and beside her a delicate rose-tinted child sitting in the earth blowing the dust off them before dropping them in a basket. It caught at my heart: a feeling of lack.

When the doors of the grand house swung back on oiled hinges and the slaves ducked their heads, I felt smothered and sickened by the copiousness of my existence – ah, but people would say, most women would enjoy it and be grateful. As soon as I had entered the house, Boaz would appear, and endeavouring not to sound suspicious would cross-examine me about my activities of the day. Every casual reference to a market or public garden sounded like a lie when the words reached and registered in his eyes. He would throw in sly questions later, while we ate, like, 'Did you hear the music at the waterfront?'

Quickly I would say yes, without thinking that when I had been there, there had been no music; forgetting that it was so often a trick question. I could never answer calmly, I rushed into lies which concealed only innocence. The lies accumulated in his brain, so that he became feverish in the casualness with which he continued to ask them. His tactics began to infuriate me: I resented being questioned and I was afraid that he might find out how much time I spent with the whores. With practice, however, I became cunning; I rehearsed my answers and they fell smoothly from my lips. I could account for each second of the day, and by now of course I was lying.

Sometimes, I almost pitied him. I wondered what he imagined I might be doing with my hours. I knew that if he knew that I had made a few friends in the whores' street he would presume this to mean the worst. A jealous man is a disagreeable thing. When he saw how tidily I answered his barrage of questions, he retreated into a silence, and then announced viciously one evening that Elizabeth would not in future accompany me on what he referred to as my excursions, making the word seem like an iniquity. I responded with anger, and this brought out an infuriating calm in his manner. His hands, which of late had looked shaky and old, seemed to straighten visibly when he observed my disquiet and how little I could do to alter the situation.

'Are you trying to chain me up again?' I said, forcing my voice down.

'My dear,' O so repulsively serene, 'when have I ever chained you up? It sounds positively indecent.'

'Don't mock me. . .' My voice growled in my ears and he continued to peel a pear with great skill. I tried very hard not to lose control.

'Well let me at least know your plans,' I said, grinding my hands together under the table, 'Are you saying I may now go out unaccompanied?' At this his eyebrows raised and a segment of pear slid between his pale lips gracefully. 'Or are you saying I am not allowed out of this house at all?' This last ended on a high, strained note. He cut out the core of another segment of pear with a little mother of pearl knife, then threw his bright eyes straight at my face with an intimidating composure, and said, 'You may go out with Miriam instead.'

'Your wife you mean.'

'She is no longer my wife.'

'That is not what she says.'

'That is immaterial. She has agreed to accompany you wherever you wish to go.'

'And will of course report back to you.'

'And does that alarm you, my dear?' But I saw how much it alarmed him.

'And what if I refuse?'

'O but you cannot, how can you refuse?'

I stood up, shaking, so much so that the little table in front of me tumbled to the floor with the quick clatter of breaking crockery. I went and stood in front of him with my hands clenched and he looked at me, a long way ahead of me. My breathing began to slow down and as I turned to leave the room I saw that a moth of sadness, of despair, fluttered for an instant across his eyes.

What did he fear in me? A sensual inclination? A search for an alternative existence? Both existed. I saw that he was afflicted by a disease that seemed, in spite of his outer passiveness, to be heightened by my smallest outings, by any return home a little later than I had said, or by a light in my eye, caused not by a doubtful assignation, but by a colour in the sky or the lapping of the placid water over the children's toes. I decided to be utterly agreeable, to ask him to suggest where I should go – or perhaps he would like to accompany me? He never did, but my swift turn of humour undoubtedly disturbed him more than ever and I could see his tortured ponderings as to my motive; and his finding in his imagination the most alarming conclusions. I could not maintain this poise once it became clear to me that no amount of good behaviour would relieve me of Miriam's presence whenever I left the house. I would stride off briskly in some direction and feel her behind every curve in the road or in the midst of a crowd. She, poor woman, never bothered me with speech and kept always a tolerable distance, which dated from the time I had turned on her with some fury. As I walked, my eyes were distracted from the sights that gave me so much pleasure by my brooding on how each move I made was to be recorded back to Boaz; how he would slice up each hour of the day to see if I had had the opportunity to sneak off and make some arrangement. I had no pity for his sickness, though I should have known that the torture of the imagination is far worse than any pain in reality. His suffering was evident in the harsh way he would look up when I entered a room, as if he thought he might find some clue in the way my hair was dressed, or most particularly in the contours of my face. I determined always to be calm with him; to tell him my activities minutely.

There came a time when he never left the house at all, hardly even ventured into the courtyard. He stayed in his room and if I asked him about this over dinner, in mock concern, he would complain of fatigue or mention some work he was reading. Life was becoming daily more oppressive: no visitors entered the house; no male slaves were allowed to wait on me, and he grew more suspicious of Elizabeth, only allowing her to come to me for one hour a day. The only person he seemed to trust me to was his wife and he did not see that the poor woman was becoming increasingly distressed and worn by my rages. The very sight of her face carrying a tray for me, or waiting patiently while I adjusted my veil, was driving me to distraction. It is always the weak who are the easiest to turn on. I could not sleep at night thinking that Boaz might come sneaking into my room, which I was unable to lock; and I spent my days in fidgety anxiety, scratching my fingers and pacing the rooms. Elizabeth, and I'm sure Miriam also, pleaded with him to allow me more freedom, but he was inflexible. I began seldom to go out, there was so little pleasure in it. I noticed that my confinement to the house caused him considerable relief and something of his upright bearing and arrogance came back to him. But by then I was set on a course of destruction and it seemed that the nature of my existence could only be redeemed by the severance of his life or mine.

It was a day of stifling intensity; the heat flared through the shutters. Miriam walked through the door with a pitcher of cold water, which wordlessly she set down on a table where there was a collection of beautiful alabaster pots containing scents, oils and spices. I flew over to the table and hurled the pitcher to the floor, where it cracked cleanly in two. My hands flayed at the pretty pots and they landed on the floor where the oil made silver patterns in the water and the mingling of the scents was unbearable. Miriam fled. I caught sight of my wild red face in the hanging mirror against the wall and hurled my head at it, kicking and tearing at the beautiful silver, screaming, screaming...

It is at times like that, like today, here, now, that I feel such terror: madness or grief tugging at my elbow again, beckoning me on. If I was truly brave I would end it quickly, cleanly, releasing myself and those others – there are always others. Have I the strength to live through another attack? It requires so much to hold, to lean over the brink, to look down. And for one exultant moment I know, really I know. But that pure moment is not worth the terror, the anguish. Will they put me in a little cell? Will I ever come out? My eyes – how veiled, how sluggish they look. I am constantly searching in the mirror: it is there that things happen first. It is there that I see I am a woman of no account, a blade of grass frightened by the breeze. Must not think that – only that it gets better, it does. If I can but force myself to that resignation of my will, my dreams... I must be calm, quiet as a worm.

It happened so fast. Always that terrible speed. There is no time for the eyes to grow accustomed to the utter change of light and tone. Just that vicious plunge that can never be anticipated. It is like a blow in the temples; all things flooded by red, then a sticky blackness. If I can pre-empt it, if I can only force my mind to detail it, it may not come, I may avoid it just this once.

Boaz was standing looking down at me and the air was full of the sick-sweet smell of musk and lavender, jasmin and balsam. The hem of his robe had a dark line all around it and it made me laugh, how it made me laugh to see a line of dirt on him. His face contorted and I was afraid then, and backed away, thinking perhaps he might kick me for I was so near his feet. But he bends, see how gently he bends and lifts me from the floor, from the creeping odours, and leads me to my bed. He smoothes back the wet curls from my forehead; with a soft cloth he wipes the blood off my hands and the tears from my face. I look at him looking at me. I do not need a mirror to see how I look: I know my eyes, I see them from the outside: they are wide, staring and bright as polished jade. My mouth is so soft it would be crushed by the impact of another. My skin has set, has frozen.

He is talking to me soothingly; he is chaffing my chilled hands, he is saying – how sweet and young his voice is suddenly: 'We will go and take you to the waters, they will heal you, many have been healed. It is nerves, that is all.' His face, it crumples and his head falls on to my breast: my breast, my small white breast that I love, that I cherish. My hand snakes up from its docile position on the satin cover, it moves into his hair, it gently curls into the thick black waves and then – Ah, how swiftly it wrenches, ripping a twisted coil of hair until it leaves his head and plays with great sweetness around my white fingers. They stiffen and I snatch the hair off them, disgusted, shaking ... falling. And he, no sound, no yelp of pain. There was a sigh, a soft sigh. That was all.

There are times when you say: that is the end, there must be no more of this. But endurance has no limit; the heart can always move over just a little bit more to accommodate that new despair, which at one time there seemed no possible space for.

I seem to be steaming, embalmed in running salt, a haze rises off me. And in this room endlessly I hear one voice, a voice choked with tears. I do not think it is mine; I wish it were mine. I would like to have for but one instant the rhythm of my hips, the waves of my thighs, undulating, thrusting as once they did. There is no peace here, no sleep like a lover's dream. If I can remember – O I must – all the radiant hours, the inexpressible happiness that I spent with you. I have been lucky, happier than most women; my life has been ... what has it been? This morning when I woke, I felt that a thick blanket plugged my mouth. I cannot recover from that, but I am trying. Will no one help me? If only there were something I could take to diminish the intensity of my thoughts, or even some person to whom I could turn to help me bear the weight of the morning: it would seem to stretch to eternity like a clear sky with no cloud. Your weight, it was such a gentle, unforcing thing; the tender ripples of your muscles. You had no great strength. And yet, look what you made of your life: only a humble carpenter with not even the gift to become a master-carpenter. How far you climbed: could I too? So much gentleness in your hands, such beauty in your feet. If I could lay my head on your knees and embrace you; if I could feel again the strength that you had in the beginning, on those vivid days when you could do anything. I must keep this picture of you, keep it untarnished by the agony of those last weeks. At times, truly, I feel the most heartbreaking gentleness; I am not a violent woman.

. I wish I had not done that to Boaz. You see how clear, how explicit my thoughts are? I remember wrenching at his hair; how I feared him, and his head when it surrendered, how I hated it. His scalp was bleeding slightly and I was sorry for it. But you see, he should not have touched me; he should have known that I was brittle as cracked glass and must cut, cut for his coming too close, my white flesh. I was inviolable. A wise man would have known. But he did not, because he did not see that his twisted passion had made of him something that he was not — a lecherous old man.

That was the beginning. It is important for me to elucidate these things. I want the truth, or a closer shade of the truth I already know. Now if I sat Elizabeth down and said, as I have sometimes done, listen I will tell you this or that, it would be lies, partly. I cannot show any living soul all the dirt of these crevices. Again, I could write a testament, to you, to me — but it would equally be distorted. O they will write about you, already Peter has begun, or at least he has got someone else to write it down for him. But I will not write. My love letters are unwritten. Am I too fastidious to write? No, I simply do not want to. You enter my head through the words in my heart. That is all memory is. And after death there is only this. It is how you live on, through me, through anyone who holds a memory of you. No one who has not known you will ever be able to know what you were.

But in my memory of you, there is another memory — that of myself. And how can I wash her out of myself? Until she is gone, I cannot look at my present face: this scrubbed mask hung on a blank body. You too are still within me, with her, and until I can get rid of both of you there is no room for another, no space for a new life to grow.

Boaz was the beginning and he made me afraid of myself. I used to think, it will be best to lie quite still, to let them cover me, to take their food. I stopped speaking. Only once when the curtains were drawn I cried out in fright, thinking that in the dark cloud of the room a multitude of locusts were gathering. They assured me that I was wrong. They even put a candle and left it lit in the same place. When I say they, whom do I mean? For I did not see Miriam again. It was only Boaz and Elizabeth. And I did not trust her because she was talking to Boaz about me and she hated him, so should not have been talking to him. He was serene again and floated past me in his immaculate robes like a priest. I knew that he liked me to be prostrate. I used to speak to myself, as I am doing now, saying, ignore this, take no notice of that look that he is using to try to pry into your head. Never let them see your thoughts. All the time I was only aware of how my eyes lived their own life: a furtive, darting life – they were ahead of the rest of my body.

There is this terrible loud breathing, it snares my throat; then my throat begins to water as in nausea and the flesh is without bones but weighed down with rocks. When they bustle about me, I can contain it, but when they have gone, my rage ferments like wine that would burst its bottle. I fly from the bed and hammer against the door. It is locked: that is interesting and it stops me for a moment. I am confused and wonder when it was done. I am dejected by the lock for they should know I would do nothing dangerous; there is no need to lock the door. Elizabeth comes and looks at me lying still on the bed, 'I heard a noise, are you all right? Shall I bring you something?' I smile at her with sweetness. I would like to get my hands about her neck and tighten them. It is that look that I hate, that awful smile. She says, 'Shall I bring you some more flowers?'

I smile again, then growl, 'Why, if you know I will tear them up?' She is silent; are her lips pursed in annoyance? I yell, 'Am I annoying you, Elizabeth? Am I saying something you don't like?'

'O no,' she says, lying like the fool that she is. The nonsense of this behaviour is tearing my brains out by the roots. I need something to hold on to; not me, not my crazed leaps, but something unalterably simple: Elizabeth – but she is confounding me with her lies.

'You are frightened again, Elizabeth.' Was that my voice, that strange sing-song?

But O God, her face, like twisting leather it rumples, tears – and her hand clutches her brow; she shudders horribly; I can feel the scald of the tears on her cheeks.

'Elizabeth, Elizabeth, don't go, don't go. Please, I shall be sick, my stomach keels.' I must get to her, but when I run she retreats with a whimper. I am turned to stone.

Boaz – his hands stick into me. Where did he come from – so fast? He throws me down and straps me to the bed with tough linen. What is he doing? I am not fighting. I lie quite still, passive; I have stopped. I do not understand why he is treating me with such brutality. I am meek, silent. But look, another band fixes my legs so I cannot move them at all. I was not kicking. I am hardly breathing ... he stands up, why does he look so exhausted? Then, a cunning smile on my face, I say, 'You enjoy tying me up.' His face blisters with rage, he would like to strike me. Then I hear Elizabeth, her low sobs; they save me. I weep, I weep. He will not let her come to me.

It is winter here, my love: no sun, no flower, the birds are all northern, they do not sing. Only a dark like the bottom of the lake, and in the distance I swim on the water: a swan with a neck that aches, aches. Far in the distance I am, a speck, almost out of sight. The water might give me another birth, but it is so tired of moving with currents, of finding no rest – incessant motion. Why can we not be still, as you are?

And then there are always days when everything is utterly clear again. After weeks in a dark wood, I awoke and knew that I was no longer sick in the head. It seems to be very easy for other people to know this too. For Boaz came and sat by my bed – 'Ah, you are yourself again.' What have I been? Whom? Why do they never tell me? There was something about his bearing that reassured me: it was his remoteness. Then it shocked me when he said, almost tossing out the thought with impatience, 'I will marry you.' I stared. 'It is the only way I can help you; stop you moving closer to the precipice. I will also let you be free.' I was frightened. I thought, No, I cannot stop now. I need marry no one. There must be something. It will happen, if I wait, without hope, or even desire, it will happen if I wait patiently. I shook my head wildly at him, as if a noose encircled it. Instantly, he began to try and calm me, to say, 'Think about it another time, do not excite yourself. Everything will be as you want it.' He left me. I had said no word to him, but after he had gone, plans began to vibrate in my mind. . .

You kept on walking in your white robes with the sun blazing in your skull, with dust on your eyes – walking for them, for us, for me, walking. No, do not make me, force me down that road again. Separate me from it. Why must I take this last step? Must I? Tell me if I must, if I can, and I will try anything, do anything . . . I cannot proceed. I am stuck forever in the dry blood. The white road with dust on the stones and the grey of the olive trees flaring. Those boys who played on the ground did not know – they rolled over laughing, and ran to join the procession. I did not cover my face like your mother. I was looking down. There were little dark crescents of blood on the road; the sand moved and smoothed their edges. I did not weep with the women, for I was certain that you would not allow it, it could not happen, not to you. Why then did they weep? It was as if they did not know, had not believed one word that you had said. I remembered some words that I did not want to remember; I re-arranged them quickly and they lay down quietly in my mind. I noticed that the blood on the sand fell in larger splashes. It was not possible. The crowd jostled and re-formed and I caught a glimpse of you and felt extraordinary terror. Your back looked broken, it was running with blood. Your head hung unnaturally and your mouth gaped open as if gasping for air. A swirl of dust and someone's back hid you. I stood quite still. People pushed past me, clicking their tongues impatiently. But still I knew that they could not kill you, not repulsively, with such shame. They could not: the vileness of that tree, your body could never hang on it. I knew that you would die victoriously, on a battlefield, routing your enemies, crying out, 'For God, for Love.' The walls of the city would tumble down; the Romans would perish with a wave of your hand. They always said, if God was with you, no man could put you down. . .

My mouth is so dry; dust in my eyes. The hill comes nearer; there are shapes on its brow. We all move slowly, like people in a trance. No one is crying now. The soldiers shout because silence unnerves them. They simply want to be done with this and go home. I am waiting. See how the grasses wilt; the strange shapes that sandals make on the ground; a white flower stands stiffly between two trees. The rough boys have stopped kicking the stone between their legs; their heads hang and their faces are sullen. A voice, clear and pretty, begins to sing a psalm softly: the words trickle over our heads. It is not a lament: that comforts me. Someone, a tall man, I cannot see his face, has taken your mother's hand and her head lifts a little. The soldiers push everyone back and the crowd retreats in a ragged line. I begin to force my way frantically through them but they seem stuck together and will not move. Suddenly a child falls from someone's shoulders; the crowd splits in two and I run forward and reach your mother. She turns and looks curiously at my dry eyes. A soldier pushes me back roughly and I feel my anger stirring. Your mother says something to him and he lets me stay with her.

I see you, to one side, bent double, bleeding. Why don't you scream out, fight, protest? Where is your great anger, your flailing speeches? Are you mocking them with humility, or are you simply biding your time? I try to run to you, but a man pulls me back, his face ugly with some emotion too deep to penetrate. Who is he? I recognise him, but his name, it escapes me. O I could have done it, if they had let me. I had the strength to take it all.

It was so quick, so violent. All the time I was saying to myself, it is not true, not true. In a minute all this will be over, it is just a nightmare. . .

Far above me; my lips could brush your feet – shall I kiss them? How cruelly they are folded, spiked, so much blood, so much. I am afraid to lift my eyes. Your flesh, that body that I know, it has become singular, quite strange to me. It is as though you have entered a private domain, like a woman giving birth. Your torture fills me with awe – that you must suffer it alone. The muscles in your thin legs quiver purply through the skin; the hip bones butt out of the soft linen around your loins. How sunken your stomach and grotesque the harsh angle of your ribs and the scooped hollows of your arm-pits. Your head drips blood, no hand to wipe it away. You are suffocating – O I know it – your mouth opens, gasping for air, your ribs are distorted, heaving. I pull at the guard's tunic, 'Please, you must help him, please he cannot breathe – help him. . .' The guard's eyes are sad on me; he gives you opium juice on a reed: poppies, the petals of death – but you turn your head away. And then there is only this: I know what I must do . . . I will close my ears to the gulps of your breath, to the groans and the wild wet cries. I must turn back to you, lift my head and heart up to you. I must cover your eyes with mine, your mouth with mine, your body with my body. I will give you breath, strength – take it, all of it, all of me. Let me put my hands on the soft vulnerable parts of you, wipe your wounds with wet silk, pour on unctions and bind up your wounds. I will stop this dying, stop it with tenderness, stop it with love – end it, end it. Your body jerks, your head begins to lift. Your eyes focus on me and your eyes and mine – like two gulls, twin souls, we soar far above the lake. You are silent now like one who experiences no pain; there is no look of fear in you. Your face streams, not with that wildness, that glittering flame, but softly, as people who love look. And O, you are beside me now; your words in my eyes, 'Hold, hold, no one will hurt you again. I am with you always.'

You throw your head up, you raise it to heaven and scream with a huge and heart-rending rage at him – your God, your vile, bloody, miserable God. Your head topples like a stone, your eyes have died. My nails cut into my palms, deeper, deeper; my knuckles push in my teeth. You are dead. Now, now you are dead. My tears strangle me . . .

They are bringing you down – broken, heavy with death. I begin to retreat, forcing the cloth of my veil into my mouth. Your mother runs and falls at your feet; she draws your head to her and cushions it against her breast. Your body – blanched where the skin has drained and begins to set in dark pools – the glossy pallor of your twisted mouth – your eyes slightly parted as if you sleep. You are so beautiful. If I touch you, will you be warm? Your mother throws back her head and screams at the sky. And I, suddenly, shatteringly forlorn, know I cannot take those steps forward and gather you into my arms, kiss your face just once more. Not wife, not mother, not sister. But I have to, have to touch you, feel your skin, know its chill. I must do these things to save myself. I need to howl, howl. I cannot. I stand quite still as the sky darkens and your mother's cries pierce it; on the edge, on the rim of your death, being only a strange woman – who should not be here at all. . .

It is light; there is a blueness in the air. My mouth is so big, my eyes small. It is returning, I can feel it – this sudden rush of terror, ecstasy, extraordinary peace. O what is it? What is it? It is you, it is you.

Now I am with you, so much part of you that I have become you. I am full, full to tearing. I am racked by grief, spilling with tears, howling, howling. The room spins, descends into pitch.

Five

Elizabeth told me today that it is five weeks since I have been in the open air. I know how the time has been for her, it is all there, written plainly in her eyes. I would say that Elizabeth is dangerously thin and she looks old now. I feel at these times that I have been absent from her, far away. I cannot remember how it was for me. And there is something that I must ask her, though I am frightened of her answer.

'Elizabeth?' She looks up; does her face reproach me, or is it just worn? 'I want to ask you something; you will tell me the truth, won't you?'

'Yes.' She begins to fold my clothes neatly to put them away; I can smell the wind and the trees in them. She looks up from this reluctantly. 'When I was ill, did I, did I hurt you? I mean, did I attack you?' My breathing is suspended and she says nothing. Then, 'No, it was different. You were not angry. You were full of grief – tears, only tears. You did not hurt me.'

I smile at her. Now I can breathe like other people. 'Will you take me outside for a little walk?'

'Just for a little.'

Now I know where I am. It is her tone, her manner with me that tells me, returns me to the correct surface. She takes me out into the garden and I stand in sunlight, swallowing air, like a fish surfacing. Air has never tasted so beautiful, nor any day looked as clear as this – like a strip of sunlight pushing its way through a dark sheet. But then – O my head is too heavy, I am lost and sad, and tears tumble silently down my cheeks. Elizabeth glances quickly at me – it's the look one wears when a snake slithers across the path. She takes my arm and leads me firmly back to the door. I am very calm, I do not need this administering. I say quietly, 'Though I am weeping, I'm happy.'

I remember how sadly you said it – the wail of a small boy in a man's mouth. 'You'll never know, no one does unless they have lived it, how terrible it is to be a bastard, to grow up without a father. I always wanted so much to be a son.' How well you filled that gap. Poor child, sad child; you must have known that grief was attached to you like a crease in your leg. It is this that made me weep.

It has taken me so long to understand your death, but still I do not understand what it means – except that you are no longer with me, your feet are stilled and my fear is heavy, as it always was. They used to come and ask me in Jerusalem to tell them, again and again, about the empty tomb. This buoyed them up, it was their salvation, and they began to delve into the Scriptures for verification. I remember the morning so early, so white the sky, and the leaves shivering slightly in the cold wind. I wanted only to rest my head against the stone, to be near the serenity of your body. I wanted your peace to trickle back to me, because all night long the madness had tried to creep up, hoping to find a niche where it could enter me.

The stone – gone. I felt as though it had been hurled against my stomach as you and my mother joined hands – stolen from me – not even the touch of a silent face, or a hand white and cold. I stood there wanting to scream; my body shuddering, my blood hot in my face.

You were there, beside me, and smiled, then moved away – ah, how like you. Slowly you walked backwards and I knew: not a vision, not a spirit – you: small, ungolden, so thin, so thin. Small teeth in a wide, hurt mouth; wrists caked with dark blood, circles big under your eyes, purple and pained and no exultation left. You did not have to tell me your God had deserted you, your heaven had fallen – I knew. And I was certain that I would never see you again.

I did not tell them this. I told them only that you stood there and spoke. I lied about what you had said because you only said, Mary, closing your eyes.

How calmly I can think it. They did not believe me. Peter sniffed scornfully and said, 'She's hysterical, ignore her.' Later, though, he chose not to ignore what I had said; he put it to good effect. But it was not real. Of course not. I can say that now, because I also see how that beautiful vision sustained me through those last bleak years when I could no more have faced your desertion than once my mother's death. I will never see you again. Because now you are truly dead: I have watched you die again. Can I accept that no one will ever be as perfect? You were so beautiful – because I loved you so.

And now, what shall I do with myself? I will wait for Elizabeth, because it is her, not me, who decides how the days shall turn. It was her, not me, who emerged from Tiberias an altered person. All those years dutiful, hidden in her shyness; a perfect docility to my will; a caring and sheltering that no other person, certainly no man, could have maintained. A man would have thrown me off and received the sympathy of his friends. But she remained. Then suddenly, miraculously, seeing the extent of my deterioration in Tiberias, her kindness hardened into a purpose; her strength carried us out of that walled house with its lush flowers and violent dreams – and out, out into the country. With money she had begged or stolen from Boaz, she found a little cottage on the northern end of the lake. She nursed me there through a violence that I seem sometimes to remember, but she never mentions; it was doused finally only when I met you.

Each morning she would don a large apron and scrub the house from top to bottom. She would tolerate no other servant in the house. She fed me only on fish, bread and fruit and ate the same herself; never tolerating any meat in the house. In the late afternoons when it was cool, she would see that my hair and clothes were neat and then lead me down to the sea and we would walk by the water and watch the fishermen. Each day I was allowed to stay out a little longer, until I was truly better. When our money ran out, she sent a message to Joshua and organised through a copper-smith in the village for regular sums to be sent to her. She would not permit me to concern myself with money, or with my clothes, she saw to everything.

Children always played on the sea-shore in the afternoons and I used to watch them. One day, when Elizabeth had gone down to the boats, I walked up to them and joined in their game. We all held hands in a circle and ran round and round; when one child called halt, we had to stop immediately and anyone who did not had to leave the game. I was very good at it. The children were all laughing when Elizabeth came back and whispered hoarsely to me to come away. I was not angry, just hurt that she should think badly of what I was doing. I went with her because I was embarrassed by the children's eyes and the way their feet scraped at the stones as I left. After that, Elizabeth let me be near the children, but she would not let me speak to them. I would sit further back in the sand and pick up handfuls of it, letting it trickle through my fingers. Sometimes I used to do this over her skirt because it irritated her.

I am sitting with a book on my knees, poring over it, my hands cupping my face. Elizabeth comes in and with a gentle but determined movement takes the book from my hand.

'What are you doing, Elizabeth?'

'Your forehead was puckered, you looked unhappy.'

'I was not, I was thinking.'

'Well, you know how that last book – it upset you. . .'

'Elizabeth' (I am trying to be calm, I don't like this) 'I was crying because it was beautiful and sad, not for any other reason.'

'Well have a little rest.' She walks out of the room, but I see that she has taken *The Symposium* with her and I feel so frustrated that I begin to cry.

It is dark; I have just woken up and I see at the other end of the room, lit by the window, a white face – round, smooth-featured. It is Elizabeth's face, filled out by the moonlight. It is all I can see of her because her black dress folds into the dark.

'What on earth are you doing here, Elizabeth?'

'I was just making sure that you were sleeping properly.'

'Why should I not?'

Her voice is patient, superior, 'Come now, you know you have terrible nightmares. . .'

She is walking slowly so as not to disturb me, but I feel the roughness of her soles walking on my face. She is marching in a direction and she plans to take me with her. There is no nervousness in her now. She feels more content each time I shriek feeling that birds are attacking my hair. She is trying to help me drown in my own blood, so that her hand can pull me back and have a right then to decide how I shall live. I do not need this new person she has become, this encroaching mother. Always she is telling me that I am not strong; I must not excite myself; then she pushes me back into a bored state where I just dream, or cry. I cry very often, most of the time. She tries to stop me. She does not know how I need to cry, and that even if I cried for the rest of my life it would not be sufficient. Do you hear my cries from your pinnacle of heaven?

My formation has been so slow, as if little by little I were trying to purify myself. My heart beats slowly, has always beaten slowly, having learned early to control its more frantic movements. But touch, I cannot forget touch. What else is as real as a child's body in your arms, or a hand on your breast? Your kisses, when they stopped, became as deadly as poison − but more deadly were those long stretched hours waiting for one little kiss to drop from your lips. Elizabeth has not known these things. She is angry when I try to talk of you, will not allow it. Just as she would not let me teach the children their letters by the sea.

I am going up into the woods. The earth has a petticoat of yellow daisies and how pretty it looks; the trees thick with leaves. I fill my skirt with daisies and put one behind my ear. I am so happy. I walk a long way, smiling. Out of the trees I see Elizabeth running towards me, her veil flapping back. There is something that frightens me as she swims into focus, something angry and vicious about her face, like those women who burned the house . . .

'What has happened, Elizabeth, what on earth is the matter?'

'What are you doing out here on your own?' Such scrubbed words that I laugh, and see her frown.

'Why should I not be out here?'

'You cannot expect me to look after you if you are going to do what you like.'

'I haven't gone far.' She sees the daisy in my hair and snatches at it. Ah, that hurts me and I begin to cry. She is satisfied and leads me down, her hand nipping into my arm; her black dress swish-swishing.

She has closed the shutters tight and the door makes a click. There is no light in here. I curl my body into a circle and cry until my face is no longer familiar. I feel like a small child left, shut up alone in a room and everyone else has gone. For something I am being punished. I have been reproached again, deserted. As you were. You did not believe that He would leave you to die. I know. You said there would be suffering, but not death. You believed He would come and bear you in His arms, lift you high into the heavens. You would lean upon His breast and He would call you His firstborn, His dearly beloved One, His Son.

O why would you not listen when I said, 'I am a wall, and my breasts like towers.'

I am getting better. I know it when I am able to feel sorry for Elizabeth, although I resent her playing Adam. I am not content without a husband. She knows this and it rankles. I cannot be warm to her now, take her hand or hug her, because she has enlarged, become too big for me. She cannot show me any affection, thinking it will be misconstrued. I am cold here. I am shivering. My passion is no longer perpetual; it comes, it goes; but when it goes it is not because I am forcing it back by bringing other things forward, but because it is simply receding into the past as I move into a present which I cannot yet see. Then I become alarmed. I do not want you in the past. I want you here with me. I am still not robust enough to go on alone.

My face is drooping with unhappiness. I am stuck on that wheel again; it spins on the same axis of memories: your desertion, your cool tossing away of my passion. To save myself I make a long list of your failings. But at the end of it, like a mother, soothing, never mind, never mind, my dearest – I would forgive you anything.

Sometimes my death is so imminent that I feel it will appear suddenly like the edge of a cliff overlooking dark water. Easy to plunge sapphic into the stream and be borne off wildly laughing, until my mouth is plugged with flowering foam. God will not be waiting. Will you? At this moment it is very clear: my life must either end or begin now. I am not yet forty. It is time. Alcestis was willing to die for her husband; Orpheus did not have that heroism – he entered hell alive and was punished. I have survived hell. I am alive. And I do not have the nobility of Alcestis. Only you did.

Today they have harvested the fields and the colours are all softened: the stubble a yellow, almost luminous; the pale greens strangely more ephemeral than the sky. In contrast, the air seems solid, as if you could lift it and carry it away. Often I dream of the pines, but the wind in them was plaintive and the birds' wings restless.

Is it easier for other women? The ones who know, who believe their mothers when they are told: this is how it will be; this is how you will be. When they are grown and married, they settle happily into a pattern and the pattern does not alter or aggravate. I have always been like water, sometimes flowing, often in flood, or as now - stagnant, waiting for some pull to fling me into motion again. So here I am, and what shall I say, what decide? I have thrown all my frenzy at you, knowing that you can comprehend it having lived on the same whetted edge. Now I am depleted. Shall I be brisk and know that something is over, irrevocably gone? Shall I move on? I know that there are some things that people do not recover from; like a broken vase that you stoop to recover the pieces and find that you are bleeding and cannot arrest the blood. Will I ever be good to anyone again? Or even to myself? For in these last months I have been crueller to myself than to anyone: pushing my face back into the murk, forcing my eyes to open in it. It has been the hardest thing, remembering myself. I would far rather have forgotten. Now that must happen if I am to proceed.

What is Elizabeth doing? Look she is taking my precious little pile of books out of the room.

'What are you doing with those, Elizabeth?'

'I think you have been reading too much, you look strained and tired.'

'And what business is that of yours?'

'It is my business.'

I am silenced. 'Elizabeth, are you going to burn them?'

'Really, what a thing to say!' Out she goes, bearing off the books. This cannot continue. She is so harsh to me; the impatient way she pushes food at me, her bullying tone. I feel she has deserted me like those others. I have been quiet, gentle. Did I pull her hair when she took the books away, or pound on the door? She cannot accuse me of being inflammable. I am almost sweet. Perhaps it is this that threatens her? If I am recovering, she will not be needed. Is it possible that she would rather I be sick for ever? Am I letting her – who settled for something sterile years ago – lead me into an old maid's world where she holds the wool? No! My kinship is still with men, one man, all those men. My love, my loyalty is for them. Without them I may not ignite, but I would rather that than be quenched.

I told her to give me back the books. She looked at me in a way half-mocking, half-threatening, but faced by my composure, she could not refuse. I went into the garden to read. I could see her shadow hovering about the open door; there was a thwarted anger in her, and I pitied her.

Now I understand it another way. I have been reading Plato and when Sophocles is described, I see you, you who were also incomparable, as he was. Your lying beside and not touching, it is all there – expressed as a perfect, a controlled and heavenly love, which makes all other love ludicrous. You sought an absolute Beauty, absolute Love – unique, eternal. When your eyes fixed on that you were happy; when your vision wavered from this true goodness, you plunged into despair and felt yourself no longer immortal.

I am swept away by these ideas, but later they sag horribly. I can't accept the body as 'beauty tainted by human flesh and colour and a mass of perishable rubbish'. But perhaps you could – without reading one word of Plato. Poor you, sad you, sad Sophocles. I am not sad. My breasts are not tainted; they are rosy and there is laughter in my hips. I can move on. I cannot care for all that philosophy, religion, politics. In the night what I care about is whether there will ever be another head to rest against my breast, another body to fill all the cold spaces in me.

I have been lying here like a stone, now the stone yawns and stretches. I think I am getting better.

I close my door and push a chair against it. I can hear Elizabeth busying herself outside, not daring to come in. I open the shutters wide and breathe in the air. I reach from the top of the cupboard the little oak box. Slowly, reverently I open it, touching the little wooden leaves that you carved for me. I am reading what you wrote. O you should have been a poet because nothing I have read is so purely and simply beautiful – 'Ah, the day dies like a cinder.' And suddenly, how clear it is – without an autobiography, they will have to invent you!

Without these words of yours that I alone have, you will remain an enigma always. That is how it should be. I am dissatisfied with languages, they're too slippery, too flimsy for emotion and experience. Often I have felt that I would like to spread the words that I use more thickly, in globs and lumps, as a painter can – but again that would be putting them down and I won't do that.

How happy I am. I put the papers away and know that I will read them again and again. I only put them back on top of the cupboard because I do not want Elizabeth looking through them. I will go up to the woods now and see what the daisies are doing.

Today, today I am certain. I have returned to the calm sea. The anemones are rocking their babies; the shells are opening with love and I am full of these things. It is the end of mud; the beginning of cool, clear water. I have so much love that I can give it to everyone, there would be enough. Now I hold the essence of everything that has been before: the birth from the bag of blood; the diamond from the seam of death. I am glutted with content because I am alive; because there are trees still to make leaves and mothers to smile. All the things that have comforted me, let me comfort them now: the bruised apple that the child throws; the dead rose under the foot, the baby with its belly swollen with hunger. I will lavish them with love because I float on it, it carries me to heaven, because all that heaven is is to be at peace. Look, the little cracks in the skin are spreading and my eyes will always be puffed by too many tears – but love, my dove, I could be sixty and you would still love me. And O how I love you. I am coming to you. No, I will not snatch out my breath; I will hold it evenly over the years, the sweet, sure years living as close to you as I was once, by keeping this peace, this absolute peace that you are. After the catching fire, after the fever, there is this: this moment when each cell is refilled with hope, each nerve with love.

Do not tell me, do not insist that this intoxication will pass away. Because I know. I am waiting. But wherever I go, your face will shine in my heart, not with that terrible ache, but with the peace that comes after death and grief: an acceptance of life.

What happens when you are left in a dark, cold room – alone, alone? I will tell you what happens. You begin to study each corner, each curve in the wall; each ray of light through a keyhole – and when that is done, you begin on yourself – pore by pore, hair by hair. When that is over, truly over, you are strong, STRONG – so that no man, no dream, no death can overwhelm you again. And so I have succeeded. O it is a triumph – a bloody triumph.